And In The Beginning

Armageddon's Blade: Book One

Manna Clarke

THE FERNWEH ARCHIVES

Published by The Fernweh Archives

Cover design by Covers and Cupcakes, LLC

Edited by Tory Hunter

Formatted by Angelique Anderson and Manna Clarke

eBook ISBN: 978-0-9756313-0-0

Paperback ISBN: 978-0-9756313-1-7

The Fernweh Archives

Australia.

www.thefernweharchives.com

Contents

Acknowledgements

The seeds of this book were sown on a rickety chair at a makeshift desk squeezed into the corner of a tiny apartment in St Kilda. Without that refuge and my friend Tiana, it never would have manifested into the story it is today. Thank you for the original sneaky beers, and I'm sorry for the 3am clatter of my keyboard.

To the Hinwoods, who welcomed me on their vacation and then extended it so I could visit Griffith Observatory... and *then* sat patiently while I stood in awe of The Big Picture, thank you. Those days meant so much to me. I think I left my heart behind.

Kaddy. Dear Kaddy, I don't think I would have gotten through all the late nights and anxious days if not for you, your talent and ability to distract me with a coop night on Far Cry 5.

And my family – specifically my children, my sister, and the WPCC. Your support is invaluable, and I don't have the right words to express how grateful I am for everything that you do. I'm awkward, and sometimes I'm silent but I love you dearly.

There are so, so many others, and I know I will miss somebody. So please know if you have helped me at *anytime* over the last four years, for whatever reason, I thank you.

Foreword

In regards to trigger warnings, this trilogy will contain some of the following themes: action violence, mentions of blood/gore, romantic suspense, abandonment, genocide, biblical references, depression, anxiety, sexual manipulation, mental, emotional and physical trauma. In later books, the spice level will increase.

Dedication

This book is dedicated to my boys. I'm not sorry for embarrassing you whenever the opportunity presents itself.

Like *now*.

I'm proud of the men you have become. Don't ever stop growing. The world is waiting for you.

And to Datchi, who is likely to cross the rainbow bridge before the year is out... thank you for sitting with me through all the long nights, for listening to me rant about my characters, and for interrupting my live streams to showcase your meowy talent.
My heart is already broken.
To everyone's lost furry friend.

Part One

Somewhere behind Orion

The Tadpole Galaxy

Somewhere in deep space.

The quiet blinking of the monitors was distracting enough for Nasaru to look up from his latest briefing. It was entirely unexpected, and even though it caught his eye a few moments before, the navigator ignored it while he finished reading the dispatch. However, the slow fading in and out of the red light continued its quiet insistence. It burrowed into the edges of Nasaru's concentration like a Silph-worm invading a shell, and with a resigned sigh, he switched off his hand-held device and activated the viewscreen with curious eyes.

"Odd..." He mouthed the word in near silence to avoid distracting any of his colleagues. "That isn't supposed to be there."

With deft fingers, he sent an alert to the ship's captain and waited for further instruction. When none came, he stood up, detaching himself from the network as the on-board computer system took over. In the odd event that anything went wrong, he would be notified instantly anyway, so leaving his post wasn't really a big deal while they were so far out of the regular space traffic. His tall, muscular body stretched as he unfolded from his seat and stood to his full height of a little over six feet. Nasaru felt his spine crack with a satisfying crunch when he reached for the ceiling with both hands. He groaned aloud, complaining good-naturedly under his breath as he stepped away from his console and left the control bridge, heading out into the corridor to seek out the whereabouts of his captain.

It didn't take a specialist to notice that several key members of the command crew were also missing from their posts and, despite his training, the brief frown that marred Nasaru's otherwise genial features betrayed his concern. On the upside, that same training allowed him to school his expression back to neutral before anyone noticed anything out of the ordinary.

Something was up. Something he wasn't privy to.

That realization alone was cause for concern, but this time, the navigator was more successful in keeping his expression neutral. He continued his stride through the dull grey corridor to the captain's strategy room with a cheerful whistle, raised his hand and rapped out an unconcerned knock against the solid metal door. His bio-scan and security clearance granted him entry, but the respect Nasaru felt for the captain made him knock, regardless. All conversation halted as the automated doors activated and disappeared into the walls with a barely perceptible *swish*. It was painfully obvious why they had stopped talking and therefore, Nasaru couldn't help but grin into the silence when half a dozen heads swiveled in his direction.

"Captain. There's something that needs your attention in sector six."

The captain's expression was predominantly bored when he turned his attention to the door. In contrast, however, the raised brow warned Nasaru to proceed with caution. He was one of the Anunnaki elite, rising through the ranks to a Command General faster than *anyone* in their long history, but despite his exalted rank, he had chosen to operate as a fleet captain and serve his people in space.

Members of the Anunnaki Space Force bartered years of wages for the opportunity to serve under him, and Nasaru was no exception. Though right now, the navigator was beginning to wish he was anywhere but on *that* ship. The captain's steely glare was nothing to be trifled with... and Nasaru had just been pinned with it.

"What's so urgent that you just *had* to come and tell me yourself, *navigator*?"

"Comet." Nasaru shrugged like it wasn't a big deal, but he knew that General Alalu had been scouring their territories and beyond for an oddity like this for some time. Rumors whispered he even jumped through time in his desperate search for the key to their ultimate victory over their ancient enemies. It was nonsense, of course, but that was just a glimpse into the almost legendary status held by the ship's captain. "It's just emerged from the space between galaxies into ours at the junction of sectors six and seven. I've got a scan running now but—"

His mouth snapped shut when Alalu held up his hand for silence, his expression no longer bored. In fact, it now reminded Nasaru of a Tilden-beast that finally cornered its prey and was waiting for the moment to strike, a memory only enhanced by the faint olive-green hue rippling over his skin.

Nasaru ignored it, which was probably for the best. Nasaru learned the hard way to ignore a lot of things that were *supposed* to be normal but were in fact, not.

"Run scans." The captain's voice was curt, but his interest was poorly concealed. "Tell no-one. Bring your data here."

"Sir." Nasaru nodded and politely dipped his head, withdrawing to do exactly that. Once back at his console, he tapped into his system using his personal code instead of the general ship access and pulled up the scans he was running on the errant comet that entered their system. He didn't like what he was seeing one bit, but orders were orders, and *his* were to make a full report. Mumbling quietly to himself, ran a hand up through his unruly dark hair and started pressing buttons, eternally grateful that once upon a time he had a scientific background.

Eight hours later, it was with slightly less enthusiasm that the navigator knocked on the strategy room door again, this time with a small black device held in the palm of his right hand. Everything their systems could find on the comet in such a brief time existed *only* in his hand. Everything else had been encrypted, as was expected.

"Captain. I have the information you requested." Nasaru held out his right hand, opening it to reveal the small black disc that was about to change everything. When the captain nodded, he slid the disc into a thin opening on the side of the table the command crew were seated around and activated the contents.

All eyes shifted instantly to the three-dimensional display that appeared in the center of the room. It hovered above the conference table like a miniature version of the emptiness that existed in all its terrifying glory outside of the relatively thin walls of their spaceship. Only it wasn't empty. Instead of a few dying stars, the space bordering sectors six and seven was filled with the image of a comet, one of those rogue phenomena that could not be explained with simple interplanetary science. It had an unusually long dust tail, longer than any they previously seen inside their galaxy, easily spanning several million kilometers. The ion tail was even more spectacular, glowing a soft blue that stretched an even longer distance across the black void of space. Before anyone managed to speak, data flashed in below the three-dimensional image. Row after row of information appeared, displaying carefully calculated data estimates about the comet's mineral content, density, speed, and anything else their computer system detected without using a probe to collect proper samples.

"Trajectory?" The squeak of a swiveling chair alerted Nasaru to the fact that the captain stood to read the mineral report. The intent in his tone was a little out of place, given the captain usually only cared about tactical advantage, but the navigator pressed on without comment.

Nasaru flicked his way through the display, scrolling it sideways to zoom out of their galaxy and into a larger image of known space, both explored and unexplored by their people. "It will miss everything important in our system. But it's had an interesting history. Look here..." He pressed a couple of buttons before, once again, the image zoomed in. It crossed the dark space between galaxies, moving almost faster than their eyes could follow as it tracked the comet back through the path it carved through the known universe. A spiral galaxy appeared, and with the flick of his wrist, the image changed yet again, zooming in on the disruption caused by the comet's passing that, centuries later, was still evident in the outer whirls. "...It seems to have bounced out of *this* one." He shrugged, emphasizing to the captain that he wasn't one hundred percent certain yet. Even their technology could only do so much in a few brief hours. "It's possibly the remains of a planet that got spun out of one of the solar systems. It's a young one. Look at all these stars. Not a supernova in sight."

Alalu all but pushed Nasaru out of the way in his haste to get to the control panel. He leapt backwards, his eyes never leaving the captain, whose eyes narrowed to thin slits while he took over the command prompts. General Alalu entered his own codes, pushing their computer system further than Nasaru *ever* could. More data erupted onto the display, and from the collective gasp that erupted around the table, the navigator could only guess their ship scanners stumbled onto something important.

Now he *really* wanted to be anywhere but where he was.

"Ahh. *Perfect.* Ready the drive and set a course." Alalu flicked one strangely elongated finger at the three-dimensional display. "We're jumping."

"But sir, the rendezvous." The ship's second in command finally spoke up. Nasaru glanced over at the commander. Naturally, he was curious about the rendezvous, but he remained silent. "You're needed at high command."

"I'll handle it. This is more important." Alalu waved the same hand at his second, his piercing gaze shifting to the tall, rangy woman sitting on his left for a split second. His attention then shifted back to Nasaru, who moved to retrieve the disc from the console. "Leave that. We need to get closer to that—"

His eyes went back to the display again, his finger singling out one particular star out of many. "...system. From this distance... Bah. Let me know when we're ready to jump."

Nasaru took the dismissal for what it was, saluted his superiors, and left the strategy room to prepare for the jump. He had his orders and was obligated to comply. But despite his acceptance, Nasaru couldn't help the uneasy feeling that he was missing something important.

Something he was *not* supposed to miss.

Sumer

One hundred and seventy-three rotations of the sun.

That's how long the War with the Anunnaki had been raging, with neither side getting the upper hand for long enough to claim victory. Both sides tried to avoid direct conflict for the first century or so, choosing subterfuge instead of violence to gain victory, but eventually all attempts proved futile, and the real, physical hostilities began to take place. Nobody really knew *why* either side shied away from using weapons of mass destruction. Well... nobody but the leaders and *their* inner circles, and Luma was *definitely* not either of those. No, she was just a student of the *Way*, a woman devoted to her Ascension and therefore the Ascension of all her people. The only problem was that Luma was *far* too easily distracted by the War and everything about it to devote her *entire* self to her studies, and as a consequence, remained a student for way, way too long.

She was almost as old as the War itself. But that was not unusual for her people. By some accidental grace of the Universe, the Sumerians were a long-lived race, and often lived for seven or eight hundred of their planet's solar cycles. Their extended lifespan had been a point of contention between Sumer and Anunn for untold centuries, as longevity was something the Anunnaki could achieve only by artificially replicating a specific mineral that naturally occurred on Sumer.

No, the unusual part was *not* that the simmering envy of the Anunnaki resulted in a full-scale war that encompassed an entire solar system. Or that Luma and others her age or younger lived their entire lives anticipating an attack. The *unusual* part was that Luma *knew* she should be almost ready to Ascend, but so far spent all her waking hours in avoidance of *exactly* that. In her eyes, there was more she could do on the ground than from her next phase of existence. An existence where she would be expected to stay out of mortal affairs, no matter the cost. Or so she told herself. Her biggest problem *there* was the fact that as a devoted student of the Way, Luma lived a passive life, swearing by a creed that was older than time to 'first, do no harm.' Damu's code was one of the first oaths taken when a child was identified from their peers to prepare to Ascend, and Luma was no different. In fact, it had come in handy countless times when captives from the War arrived at her compound for healing while they waited for either word that they would be transported to the Neutral Zone for a trade or moved to a high security holding area for *safekeeping*.

On the surface, it was all very humane. At least on their side. Returned citizens were also sent to Luma's compound to recuperate, however in direct contrast to their Anunnaki guests, the Sumerian's eyes were dark, and forever haunted. Those tormented memories they would share with nobody until their minds had recovered to a more stable state.

More often than not, Sumerian military intelligence would disturb the peace of the compound before any real healing could begin, and at that point, Luma and her fellow Initiates were politely but firmly asked to leave.

It was one such day at the compound when a transport loaded with survivors of a raid on the outskirts of the southernmost capital arrived. Luma had been dutifully following her morning routine when the loaded shuttle arrived, her daily path to *mudutu*, to knowledge, interrupted by the chimes that signaled for all Initiates to be ready.

On a whim, she ignored it, and in a rare selfish moment, turned her attention back to the dilemma in her lap. Although she was outwardly calm, Luma bristled with excitement. She was on the verge of understanding something that eluded her for *months*. Stopping now would mean losing her train of thought, and for someone as easily distracted as Luma, that would be disastrous.

Another chime sounded, not ten minutes later.

And then *another*, though this one resonated *only* inside the library where she was sitting with her legs curled underneath her in an out of-the-way spot on a window ledge. Luma glared through her long, dark hair in the direction of the chime, but turned her attention back to the musty parchment laying across her thighs before her thoughts could scatter.

"Luma."

The voice that came through the discreet intercom system was soft, yet determined. There was no mistaking that it belonged to the head of the compound, Master Gula herself.

Luma jumped and squeaked simultaneously, her hands immediately rolling the parchment back into a scroll as she leapt to her feet and rushed to drop it on the nearest table. One did *not* keep Gula waiting, especially since she had *already* Ascended and come back to guide those who were yet to take those last, final steps. Which happened to be most of the population, though their numbers had fallen significantly since the beginning of the War.

Two steps. That was as far as Luma got before the large double wooden doors marking the entryway swung inward, with Gula striding through the opening as soon as there was enough space for her to fit. On her right was a man Luma had never met before, but she immediately decided that *he* was far more intimidating than Gula would ever be. That piercing stare seemed to look *straight* through her.

"Of *all* the days you could ignore the call, child, you chose today. *Why* is that?" Gula's tone sounded mildly amused, though Luma wasn't fooled. She knew Gula would not have come unless it was important.

The newcomer at her side cleared his throat and arched an expectant brow, as though whatever Luma said in her defense would never be enough. *Mul*, one dismissive glance from him already made her feel like *she* wasn't enough.

Luma withered. Intimidating wasn't the right way to describe *him* at all.

She twisted her torso, looking back at the parchment she carelessly dropped onto the table.

"I'm..." Words failed Luma in that instant. How could she explain she ignored the chimes that requested her *help* for her own selfish gain? When she turned back to face the two elder Sumerian, her pale green eyes were troubled. "The Vortex Theory."

"I see." Gula's response was far less dramatic than Luma expected. The man at her side, however, turned the full force of his stare on her again, and although his light brown eyes were alight with curiosity, he remained silent. However, that d id *nothing* to reassure her *at all*, and instead of falling silent herself, the Initiate all but vomited more words out of her cursed mouth.

"It's been evading me for *months*, but the last few days I've *almost* understood it." They fell out of her before she could stop them, her selfish act coming to light no matter how much she wanted to hide her shame. "I just need *time*. I would have come... eventually."

"I hope the irony of this situation doesn't escape you." Gula shifted her gaze to the discarded parchment and sighed. It was not the first time she had caught Luma studying something she simply wasn't ready for, nor would it be the last. "Your curiosity will be your undoing, Luma. Do not be so impatient, child. Your turn will come. It has been Foretold."

Her grey eyes took on the odd glow that occurred when Sumerians connected with the *Kuan*, the gateway to their power source, and the same place their Prophecies came from. "But 'ware your choices, for your path is forked."

Luma knew better than to interrupt when an Ascended one connected with An-Ki, so she held her tongue and bowed her head to examine her feet while she waited for Gula's newest Prophecy to end. The fact that it concerned *her* was secondary. Sometimes Prophecies came through and were simply a warning to study harder, or to stay off the landing pads when transport ships came in. They very rarely meant anything dire anymore. Not in any circle Luma moved in... which may have partially explained why she felt so comfortable ignoring the chimes. Initiates being told to study harder through a Prophecy was no different to a parent chastising their child, and Luma was not the first student to ignore a warning.

It just did not make sense to her. All of those Ascended ones that could touch An-Ki, and not a useful Prophet among them. To Luma and the other Initiates, and even some of the citizens, it was no wonder there were rumbles about them losing the War. But these words of discontent and ill-ease were whispered only in the recesses of Luma's mind. She loved her people, she *really* did, but sometimes they were just... too slow to act. Too passive. Or maybe too arrogant. And *because* of that, the Anunnaki caught them by surprise when they attacked without warning one winter morning when the sun was too weak to stay above the horizon for more than a few hours at a time. They arrived under the cover of darkness, knocking out the power supplies and sabotaging the heating units that held solar power, stored since the summer before.

Chaotic memories kept coming. The body of a friend that suffered a horrific death on a simple mission to the space-station. A discarded escape pod stained with green-tinted blood buried in the forest. Sumerians that died screaming from mental trauma instead of being healed. One after the other the memories invaded Luma's already troubled mind with images of anything it could conjure. She became so caught up between the memories and the sheer humiliation of being chastised by Gula and her mysterious visitor, that she almost missed her mentor's next words.

"Your brother is here."

For the second time that day, Luma squeaked, her mind instantly going to the brother she was never supposed to think about instead of her twin Lumasi, who Ascended before his fortieth revolution of the sun. She stared at Gula for a long moment, her mouth dropping open as for once, words failed h er.

Then it hit her.

The transport ship carried the injured.

"I must get to him." Luma sidestepped the Masters so fast that neither could react before she raced through the doors behind them. She sprinted left, but skidded to a halt as her training kicked in and she reversed her steps to bow politely to both Gula and her guest. "With your permission, Gula. Master."

In that moment, Luma could have sworn the strange man's mouth curled ever so slightly upwards, but when she flicked her eyes from his lips to his face, all she saw was the same dark, piercing expression he had been giving her from the moment he entered the library.

An unfamiliar sensation blossomed to life in her stomach, something different to the nervous intimidation that had already taken root. Something warm and inviting. Luma's breath trembled as the strange heat curled its tendrils outward and feathered along her spine.

"Go." Gula's voice broke through the spell, and Luma didn't hesitate to turn and run when she shooed her away. She *wanted* to see her brother, sure. But she *needed* to get away from that all-knowing stare.

Gula waited until Luma's footsteps faded into silence before she let out an exasperated exhale.

"Fiery." The tall man at her side finally spoke, his voice strangely soft for someone who had *clearly* intimidated the younger woman so much. "Reminds me of the stories my father told of *you* when you were both Initiates."

"Never me." Gula smiled then, though she shook her head before giving her old friend a sidelong glance. "That one is more distracted than I could *ever* be. Somewhat more-so now. What did you do to her?"

"Me?" His amusement was clear, as was his apparent confusion. "I was just standing there."

The Healing Chambers

When Luma scurried out of the library, she ran as fast as her feet could take her to the opposite side of the compound. It had been *decades* since her brother returned to their home planet. He departed mere hours after Ascending, telling his tearful sister that he would return for the celebration when it was *her* time.

"Not unless I come to you first." Words spoken through brave tears that were both happy that his soul found enough peace to Ascend, and miserable that her time with Lumasi in his mortal life was over.

He had faded before her eyes as his body and soul became one with An-Ki. With that connection in place, he could begin the final stages of his training and learn to fully understand the gift that the Universe bestowed upon him.

That day was over one hundred cycles ago... and Luma had not seen him since.

She dodged other Initiates, narrowly avoiding both patients and prisoners alike as she rounded corners and sped through hallways in her frantic search for her wandering brother.

*He's Ascended. What could **possibly** be wrong with him?*

In the brief time it actually took her to cross the compound and burst through the door to the infirmary, Luma's treacherous mind once again betrayed her and invented all kinds of illnesses or injuries that her twin brother could be ailing from.

"Well *finally.*"

At first Luma didn't see him. Her eyes were too busy searching the beds of the injured and checking the visual screens for notes and names to pay attention. She darted from one bed to the next, her heart racing like a chained animal fighting to escape its tethers.

"I don't understand..."

And suddenly, he stood directly in front of her, his tall, well-toned body casting a shadow on her shorter one when he blocked her frantic search of the ward.

"Sister, it has been too long."

"Lumasi!" Her feet were moving again, those long years of her passive self-defense training becoming useful enough to guide her movements. Luma threw herself at him, all her fears disbanded by the obviously healthy man standing near the Healer's workstation. "I thought you were injured!" Her voice became muffled as she made contact with his body and wrapped her slender arms around his chest.

"Luma..." If Luma was truly paying attention, she would have heard the shock in Lumasi's voice even though he only spoke one word. If she had been paying attention, Luma would have *seen* the tightness around his eyes and the shadows that lurked there. But all she saw was her brother, and all she felt was the memory of his hug and the comfort she used to take in his presence. "I told you I would be back, silly girl. But Luma, I *have* to ask...*why are you still here?*"

His words were *just* harsh enough for Luma to drop her arms and pull away from him. A small, confused frown appeared in response to his tone, and when she found her voice again, it was tainted with a sullen defense.

"I have unfinished business here, Lumasi. You out of *everyone* should –"

"*No!*"

To Luma's surprise, he closed the distance between them and gripped her by the shoulders. His face wore a mask of worry, and something else Luma could not place. She opened her mouth to speak, but her words were cut off again by the rippling of the room around her as Lumasi connected with An-Ki and transported them somewhere that wasn't the infirmary. Probably so he could yell at her in private. Their passage through the Aethers was so swift that Luma had no time to appreciate it. Nor did her curious mind have a chance to examine any part of the grey nothingness that surrounded them for the briefest of seconds.

"Lumasi, *what are you doing?*" Wrenching her shoulders backwards, Luma tried to break free of his iron-strong grip, but it was no use. Lumasi had always been stronger than her, and since he Ascended nothing had changed. In fact, it appeared his physical strength increased along with his mental, and Luma could tell he was nowhere near using his complete strength on her.

With a low growl of frustration, Lumasi let her go and stalked away. Luma watched him pace back and forth like a cornered beast, wondering what she did to make him so upset with her. Or didn't do.

"I'm sorry." His apology took her by surprise. Luma nodded but had no idea what else to say. For the second time that day, the sting of shame flooded through her, only this time she did not know why. "I reacted harshly Luma... Of course, this is *your* life and Ascension is your choice to make, not *mine*. This is your journey. *Your* path."

His voice faded into silence, and this time Luma caught the shadow that flickered across his eyes.

There was something else there, something else he was *not* saying. Regret filled Luma and battled with the shame. First, she let down Gula, and now her own brother. She could not believe his first words to her in over a hundred cycles were filled with such bitter disappointment.

"No, I'm the one who is sorry Lumasi." For the first time since he teleported them, Luma took note of their surroundings and recognized her own chambers. She motioned for her brother to sit where he liked and flopped down into an overstuffed chair. "I have left *you* waiting, and it isn't fair. I just... wish I knew what was ahead of me."

Fear gnawed at her insides, but Luma pushed it down and told herself that the rumbling was just her stomach reminding her she missed the morning meal. Again.

Lumasi remained standing for a long moment, but eventually folded himself into a low chair underneath the window. He squirmed around a little before pulling a book out from beneath his thigh to examine the cover. "Interesting read. But no. Listen, Luma... I thought..."

"I know. And *I know* you cannot tell me why, but I just... need more time." Luma *was* ready to leave her mortal life. She had no ties to keep her on Sumer, no lover to hold her back... and even if she *did*, Ascension was no barrier. Not really. Truthfully, she was just terrified of what lay ahead. Occasionally, when she entered a meditative state, Luma saw the flashes of what Gula called *possibility*. A world burning, a winged female crying, her tears falling onto the blank, staring face of a man who barely breathed. A man hidden in shadows, laughing. A solar eclipse, a room filled with blood, and a man with two faces. An archive and a dead woman. The list went on, and Luma did not know what any of it meant.

The *complete* irony was that Luma would never know what it meant if she could not ready herself and take that ultimate step.

"Time is relative, sister. I suppose I just miss your wit." Lumasi's voice interrupted her thoughts, and Luma pulled her attention back to the conversation. He leaned forward in his seat and regarded her with a stare not unlike the piercing gaze of the stranger she met earlier. "We don't have a lot of time before I have to leave again... are you hungry? I could really go for some Nasa cake."

The Space Between

The Anunnaki ship erupted from the darkness of space in a blaze of light, its extremities shining brighter than any beacon should anyone be looking for them. Only, nobody was. Nobody *could* be, out here in the vast nothingness that existed between galaxies. Before the ship completely stopped, the bridge crew went to work, scanning the emptiness for anything that might pose a threat to their existence. Out here there was no back-up, nobody to call for help should trouble arise. In fact, *should* trouble arise they would easily be outnumbered, especially since Captain Alalu had dropped most of the crew off for shore leave while his hand-picked team completed the mission only he and his second in command were *truly* aware of.

Sure, Nasaru knew *where* they were going, but not *why*, and no matter how hard he tried to insert himself into the inner circle, the captain still held him at arm's length.

Such was life. He was *only* the navigator after all, commissioned to follow his captain's orders, no matter what.

Once he had the navigation controls under his full command again, he shut down all outward facing lighting and dimmed the thickened quartz windows, so they were sitting in total darkness. From the outside their ship ceased to exist. Unless they got scanned, but Nasaru didn't think there would be anyone out there with them. Whatever they were doing, they were doing it alone.

As instructed before the jump, he pointed their own scanners at the galaxy in question, dutifully following his captain's orders to obtain as much information as possible from their hidden vantage point. It would take a while, despite their advanced technology. One could only make a signal move so fast, so Nasaru knew he had several hours before the data stream returned, and he could begin sorting the information. And it would be at least double that before he could report anything back to his superior.

Once he was certain everything was in order, he made his way to the galley to brew himself a hot *nag,* the kind his people loved to enjoy in a quiet moment. Intent on doing exactly that, Nasaru settled into a chair by the darkened windows and stared out into the emptiness beyond.

What are we doing out here?

"Good question."

Hot liquid spilled onto Nasaru's wrist when the voice of the ship's science officer sounded in his ear. He winced, forming a fist in response to the burning sting that settled into his skin. "...didn't realize I had spoken out loud."

Kumarbi grinned his apology and leaned against the window with his arms folded across his chest. "I have asked myself the same question. But usually where nobody can hear me."

"Aside from that planet..."

"I know. But the Captain knows best."

Nasaru sipped the *nag* without comment. Of course, he trusted his Captain. It was his job to trust he would lead the crew with the best interests of the Anunnaki in mind. But that didn't mean he couldn't be curious, or want to question the reasons why.

"You're right, Kumarbi, he does. And I will give him my best efforts, as –."

A low vibration on his wrist interrupted the navigator. He glanced down at the small display and quirked his brow when he read that the data stream was already sending back packets of information for him to process. "Speaking of..."

His pensive mood evaporated between one heartbeat and the next. Without taking his eyes off the display on his wrist, Nasaru waved his goodbye to the science officer and headed swiftly back to his station.

...only to discover that Captain Alalu beat him to it and was seated comfortably in his chair reading from the larger screen with eager eyes.

"Anything interesting yet, Sir?" Nasaru set his cup down in the receptacle made for it and patiently waited for his superior to respond. When no answer came, he repeated himself, but was silenced by a finger. The captain didn't even bother to look at him. Nasaru clenched his jaw at the insult, but held his silence.

Alalu read for what seemed like hours, but in reality, was about half of one. Nasaru remained silent and attentive behind him the entire time, though his eyes scanned through every minute detail that crossed the screen. Eventually the captain stood, reaching his full height in front of the navigator. In the cramped space between them, the two inches seemed a lot taller. He took a step backwards to make way for his superior, faltering slightly when the captain turned, and his expression became visible to Nasaru. It could only be described as *calculating*, and even though trepidation curled deep in his stomach, it only fueled Nasaru's curiosity further.

"Encrypt these files, Navigator. Encrypt *all* of them as they come in. Send them to my personal workstation." For a moment it looked as though Alalu was going to elaborate, but instead, he brushed past Nasaru on his way to the bridge exit. At the threshold he paused, and glanced back, his expression even more intense than before. "I'll have some additional data for you and the Scientist in a few hours. See that I'm not disturbed until then."

Nasaru didn't have time to react before the captain was gone. A heavy sigh escaped him as he slumped down into his chair, and despite the data he saw with his own eyes, the navigator still had absolutely no idea what was going on.

This was bad. This was very, very bad.

Precisely three hours later, Nasaru found himself summoned to the captain's strategy room with the equally clueless Kumarbi by his side. They spent the last few hours poring over what information they managed to compile, but none of it was enough for either officer to paint a picture about what the captain might be after. In the end, they had just thrown their hands in the air and decided that speculation was above their rank, and they didn't *need to know.*

The Anunnaki military was like that.

It was a shame for Nasaru on several levels, the first being his own curiosity. Second, his scientific background coupled with his navigator training ensured that he was always seeking new and interesting worlds for their people to explore...and perhaps even conquer...if the conditions were right.

Sometimes even if they weren't.

Like the War with the Sumerians. There was nothing on their planet that the Anunnaki *needed,* not since they celebrated a measure of success and learned to replicate what they *wanted.* There was just a deep-seated hatred of their light loving planetary neighbors, who, in their eyes, had everything the Anunnaki did not. That, to the Anunnaki ruling council, was worth waging War for.

The sliding of the automated doors drew Nasaru abruptly from his thoughts. He suppressed them, pushing them down into the deepest corner of his mind as he stepped into the strategy room after the Scientist. What he found there drove a chill down his spine.

The captain, holding what looked like odd green vegetation in one hand and a strange rock in the other. Nasaru's mind considered several possibilities at once, curious about how the captain obtained the objects in his hand in such a short time period. The on-board laboratory had been cleaned of all experiments before they departed their last port, and he knew the hydroponics bay cultivated nothing *that* green.

He absolutely refused to entertain the most obvious answer.

It could not be possible. But possible or not, the foliage wasn't the weirdest part. No, the weirdest part was the strange glow in his captain's eyes.

A glow he had only seen in entertainment pods and heard in Anunnaki horror stories.

A glow that only happened to a Sumerian when they passed into their accursed immortal realm.

"Sir." Nasaru said that word entirely too many times for his liking lately. But lately everything seemed to be going awry. He let Kumarbi get excited about the obvious signs of life Alalu mysteriously obtained and stood just inside the door, waiting for further instruction. At this point, Nasaru wasn't sure why he was even there.

"Ahh, Navigator, how *nice* of you to join us. I have a task for you." The glow in Alalu's eyes subsided, but not before he trapped Nasaru with the full weight of his stare, causing the navigator to question every single decision he had *ever* made in his entire existence. With the lessening of the glow, the overtly intimidating aura in the room also faded, and it took every ounce of skill within Nasaru to remain still as a wave of utter relief washed through him from head to toe.

Instead, Nasaru merely nodded his acceptance and braced himself for whatever task Alalu ordered next. "It will be my honor, sir. Tell me what you need."

"I *need* someone to find the path of the comet through here." The captain's mouth thinned to a fine line and for a split second Nasaru swore he saw his artificially tanned skin rippling with green hues. It was clear that the captain was trying to either find fault with Nasaru, or he was irritated that whatever caused his eyes to glow had apparently faded. "Think you can manage that from where we are now?"

It was meant to be an insult to his abilities as a navigator, but Nasaru simply raised an eyebrow in the most outward gesture of defiance he would dare to make. "It's already done, sir. I sent the information to that terminal while you were... unavailable." His hand flicked to the captain's terminal off to one side of the room, and to offset the fact that he'd just made the captain look like a fool, Nasaru pushed on. "I can make adjustments from here if the report wasn't to your liking."

Alalu glared at Nasaru, his sudden discontent shining through for all that were present to see. Nobody commented, though it did not take a genius to observe that all were confused. Until this moment, Nasaru had been the next one touted to join the inner circle, but with the captain now singling him out for reasons he knew none of them could fathom, that now seemed unlikely. "Show me."

"Yes, captain," As directed, Nasaru moved, though he kept his head down and his thoughts clear. Within seconds, his report brightened the screen, and he flicked the data to the computerized three-dimensional display above the table in the middle of the room. After a deep inhale to calm his frayed nerves, the Anunnaki navigator began to deliver his report. "As you can see, the comet passed through here some time back. By these estimates it was millions of rotations ago. I can't tell from here if any of the planets in the nearest galaxy were impacted by tail debris, but..."

Nasaru's eyes flicked to the vegetation in the captain's hands before returning to the display. "...from the, ahh, scans..., I'm theorizing it was either long enough ago for the ecosystems to recover, or it didn't hit that one at all."

"No, you're right. The one I ... probed ... had no sign of recent meteor activity. Just one Kur-cursed population of giant lizards and a few bipeds that were too stupid to speak a civilized tongue." The captain's tone was dismissive of the potential life on the planet he mysteriously probed. It was a typical reaction, one commonly seen in regard to anything that didn't involve the absolute success of the Anunnaki race.

The ruling council that started the War would have been proud. If there were any left alive.

"Giant lizards, captain? Any...?" The science officer finally spoke but was cut off by a quick shake of the captain's head. His shoulders sagged in acceptance, and he fell silent again. Obviously, whatever he was searching for, Alalu hadn't found it. Or didn't care enough to look.

Nasaru figured it was the latter. He turned his attention back to the captain, who was speaking again.

"... about that planet that needs more investigating."

"I'll ready the probes again, sir. If you'll just tell me what to configure them for."

"*Everything*. Get as much detail as you can. Report back as soon as they return." The captain's wave of dismissal was final, and with a nod of acknowledgement Nasaru hit the panel to one side of the door and turned to leave. As the door slid closed behind him, he could have sworn he heard a faint rushing sound, but when he twisted his neck to glance back it was too late. The doors were sealed shut.

Hours passed, and the probes had not returned. At that stage, Nasaru wasn't concerned. Getting a quick scan was one thing, but probes took longer. Despite the advanced technology owned by the Anunnaki, probe speed was limited to their engine capacity. The rate at which it could gather and analyze local data once it arrived at its destination was dependent on how thorough the order configuration was. And even though Alalu *ordered* him to be thorough, Nasaru cast a nervous glance toward the entryway of the bridge now and then. His self-preservation was on high alert, as was the need to constantly reassure himself that the captain did not appear to impatiently demand what Nasaru was unable to offer. It was a point of deep concern for the navigator. *Everything* about this mission felt wrong. Sure, he was all for getting new information. And collecting intelligence for the War. But this mission seemed... personal. To Alalu anyway.

And the way he looked at Nasaru when the officers entered the strategy room earlier that day made the navigator wonder what the captain had seen. Or thought he had seen. It nagged at him like a festering sore, but there wasn't a great deal Nasaru could do about it aside from mentioning it in his own report to central command. That, and hope that whatever the problem *was,* it would soon be forgotten.

A day passed, and then another. By the end of the fifth, Nasaru had collected all the information he was going to get from the planet without stepping foot on it himself, which was *completely* out of the question. Even if he had the means, it would be too problematic for him to even *mention* it, so before the idea could take hold, he shelved it and focused on collating the data. After a cursory examination, he separated the hemispheres and then divided the planet into groups that separated land and water. An easy enough task, considering the giant continental mass that currently dominated the surface of the planet. It stretched from pole to pole and wrapped around at least half of the center. For a long moment, Nasaru could only stare at the screen with a far-off look in his eyes. Icy white poles, vast blue oceans and just about every single shade of green he could imagine filled his vision. The explorer inside him yearned to step foot on the surface with nothing but a data recorder and the clothing on his back for company. He wanted to inhale the fresh, damp soil and stand barefoot on its ocean shore with a breeze at his back and the frothy blue waves licking at his ankles.

It isn't fair.

The thought surprised Nasaru, effectively pulling him out of his reverie and back into the present. He glanced around the room, shoulders sagging in undisguised relief when he saw that nobody was paying attention to his lapse in concentration. Another reprimand was something he could ill afford, and it was with careful keystrokes, that Nasaru refocused on his analysis of the data. Only this time, he didn't allow himself to get distracted.

One by one his reports piled up. After he completed the first five with no sign of the captain, Nasaru left his post and headed to the strategy room to deliver them personally. Or he would have, if the second in command hadn't stalled him at the door and abruptly informed him that the captain was to remain undisturbed until further notice.

As curious as he was, Nasaru shrugged his acceptance and gone back to work on the data. Between that, his own outstanding reports, and the unexplored galaxy beyond the safety of the ship, his time was well occupied.

No distractions. No snapped orders. The ship was quiet. Peaceful, even, and Nasaru could not remember the last time the ambience felt so...pure. But pure was not normal on an Anunnaki vessel, and while the rest of the officers made the most of their sudden downtime, Nasaru could not bring himself to relax.

The closed fist banging on the door to his quarters was the first sign that the captain was ready to receive him. Next was the second in command's muffled voice demanding Nasaru present himself in the strategy room *immediately.* He leapt off his bed and pulled on his boots, and before the commander could knock again, Nasaru opened the automated door with his uniform shirt clutched in his right hand. His bare torso rippled with goosebumps in the cooler corridor air, but Nasaru ignored the chill, nodded to his superior and headed down toward the service lift that would take him to the captain.

It was about time. Fourteen days had passed since the captain locked himself away and the navigator's nerves were stretched tighter than a primitive bowstring.

"Nasaru!" Alalu's voice boomed at him as he strode into the room and saluted, as was proper. "Are you *with me*, navigator?"

The question was an odd one. Nasaru blinked his surprise at the captain before responding. "Of *course*, Captain. I serve at the pleasure of the ruling council for the good of the Anunnaki."

And the detriment of all others. Although he had heard it uttered many times before, Nasaru was far too clever to voice that last part aloud.

"The ruling council are idiots. Narrow minded fools who can't see the bigger picture."

Nasaru stiffened and, for the second time since he entered, experienced the uncomfortable surprise that the captain threw at him. He raised a brow and waited. Maybe the captain forgave him for whatever he had done wrong, after all.

"But I can. *I can see it all.* And I need to know... are you with *me*?"

Nasaru couldn't miss the gleam in the captain's eye, nor the same strange glow he had witnessed just two weeks prior. Only this time it was brighter, as though whatever caused it was stronger than before. Staring at him was daunting. Intimidating, even for an officer with Nasaru's rank and experience, and something deep inside the navigator told him that his very life might depend on whatever he said next.

He nodded curtly to his captain and saluted him again. "To the end, captain."

It was enough, or at least seemed to be. Alalu glared at him for a moment longer before his aggressive stance shifted, and he slapped a much-relieved Nasaru on the back with a firm hand. "Good answer. Now I want you to *prove* it. I wanted to make another jump, but I don't have the power to make it happen. So,"

He waved Nasaru over to the table and activated the display, directing it to the data the navigator sent to him while he was secluded away. "The comet we tracked here gave me the idea. It doesn't have what we need, it's too late. But *this* one..."

Nasaru squinted as he followed Alalu's movements. Or tried to. He understood the technical side of what Alalu was saying of course, but the *why* of it all escaped him. *Jump? Power?* He had spent more than his fair share of time over the last fourteen days trying to anticipate what they were doing in this unexplored sector of space with no back-up, but it was to no avail. *None* of this made sense. And with the captain's reappearance, Nasaru had more questions than ever. Voices intruded his spiraling train of thought, and the navigator realized that his growing unease caused him to lose track of the conversation.

"...minerals that *our* race needs to thrive. I'm proof of that. But we need to do it with no interference. What I need you to do is give part of *that* comet a nudge."

Alalu glanced at his navigator and not a single soul in the room could deny the resolute determination in his eyes.

Nasaru examined the data on display, his dark eyes tracking the path of the comet through the system in question. Nothing seemed out of the ordinary at first. But then, the display changed. Nasaru gripped the edges of the table to support himself as his face drained of all color.

"I'm not sure I'm following what you're asking, Sir." He knew. Oh, Nasaru knew what Alalu was asking him to do. He knew what was coming, and *every* fiber of his being screamed against it... but Nasaru had sworn an oath. And an oath *must* be kept, no matter the price.

Alalu snorted his derision and zoomed in on the comet on the display. It wasn't large as far as comets went, but its' tail was impressive, filled with chunks of space debris and rocks. Fragments of planets that hadn't formed properly spun wildly across the image, caught in the gravitational field generated by the rogue space rock that was making its way through the galaxy to unknown destinations.

"Find a piece of the tail and deflect it to *this* planet in *this* solar system, Nasaru." The captain spoke to Nasaru in a tone usually reserved for dense children. The attempt at humiliation made Nasaru's skin crawl, but he said nothing as yet another image blossomed to life on the display. A solar system, young in comparison to the one they called home. A small yellow star blazed brightly in the center, orbited by nine main planetary bodies and what looked like the remains of a broken one sitting between the fourth and fifth.

The expression on Alalu's face was nothing but triumphant when all attention focused solely on the third planet. Like the star sitting happily in the middle, the planet was small in comparison to its neighbors, a pretty blue and green marble collared with white that hung like a decorative bauble in the black emptiness of space.

"When the dust settles, *this* planet will have what the Anunnaki need to thrive. *This* planet will win the War."

"But Sir, there's life on the third –" For the record, Nasaru objected. He would have it known that he did what he was about to do under duress. He didn't get any further than a shake of his head before Alalu was standing over him, his eyes glowing with that strange ethereal light and his claw-like hand raised in a tight grip around Nasaru's neck.

"Kill the lizards, *navigator*. We've got work to do."

The Inner Circle of Sumer

In the long rotations since Lumasi's visit and subsequent departure *everything* had changed. The War with the Anunnaki altered tempo one day when reports started to filter in of ships going missing. Rumors floated that they were vanishing in a spray of light with nothing left to salvage. Not one single survivor. Not one single body found drifting in space. No debris field. Nothing. It was as though the ships and everyone on them ceased to exist. The rumors were denied, but the lack of injured Sumerians being admitted to the hospitals and the small handful of witness reports only fueled them further.

Even those Ascended ones who returned to help despite their code weren't safe. Horror stories filtered through the people, whispers of Ascended ones fading from existence, their immortal lives snuffed out like a single flame on a windswept night.

To the Sumerians and their blessed existence, it brought a new kind of horror.

For Luma and the other Initiates, it meant their whole lives were disrupted. Her entire compound had been moved, Initiates and Masters were relocated to the Capital, *Ur Nuru*, where they could be better protected. Nobody said anything, but the Initiates were gently encouraged to study harder. Two increased their *shi* so effectively they had touched the edges of Bab-ili and departed, and another was showing signs that soon he too would be offered the rite of *Ankida*.

But not Luma. She studied as hard as the rest, harder than ever since her discussion with Lumasi. But unfortunately for Luma, she remained stuck, her *shi* rising *just* enough to keep her counted among the Initiate and not left behind to join her fate with the rest of the compound. It wasn't for lack of trying. Luma tried so very hard to be worthy of Ascension, but there was always *something* that distracted her. If that wasn't enough, in addition to the increasing frustration that bubbled inside of Luma, most of the time the distraction came from her *own* mind and the pressure to join her brother in whatever it was that he needed her for.

Even now, as she sat cross-legged under the moonlight in her meditative state, there were parts of Luma that were *unable* to just let go. Images and voices swarmed in her subconscious mind, and the harder she tried to avoid them, the louder and more insistent they became. She tried to chase them away, to banish them into the depths of her mind, where she could barricade everything behind a locked door. And for a day or so she succeeded, but the next time Luma crept beneath her covers they were back, urging her without explanation to do things she didn't understand *or* know how to process.

Tonight was *no* different. So far there was no escape from the torment, no inner peace to be found, and soon enough Luma's frustration bubbled over and threatened to steal her focus. She shifted from side to side on her buttocks and huffed all the air out of her lungs in an attempt to regain control, centering her mind's eye on the single figure of a tree that had become her favorite focus point.

It wasn't any tree that she recognized. Nothing on Sumer reached so high or commanded such presence. It was just a tree, manufactured by her mind when she was a child, but for Luma it had become the essence of comfort. And comfort was definitely in short supply right now. Luma approached the tree with her usual reverence and tilted her head upwards to stare into its branches, painting each one with sharpened clarity as she absorbed what small measure of peace she could.

A moment was all she got, but that moment was enough.

Luma knew that perhaps if she approached Gula with her dilemma that the Ascended Master might offer her some insight, but Luma *also* knew that these little lessons from the universe were *meant* to be solved by the person they were sent to. She dismissed the idea with a snort, and the image of her tree wobbled. If she or one of the other Initiates ran to a Master with *every* little problem they stumbled across, the Sumerians would have failed their journey to enlightenment before the first steps had been taken, two millennia ago.

What Luma could *not* have known was that if she *had* gone to Gula, she would have found herself immediately surrounded by other Masters all *demanding* to know what it was she was seeing. She would have found herself supported and encouraged to explain with as much detail as possible every single image that entered her mind. But between the War, her duties as an Initiate and the pressure of her studies, her mind and body were exhausted. Luma trudged through her days on autopilot, unable to think straight enough to even consider seeking out the Master healer for a sleeping draught that would help her shut down for at least four hours and not the single hour of sleep she was stealing here and there when time permitted.

There was simply too much to do, and not enough time.

That, she didn't need a premonition for. It pulled at Luma hourly, an urgency she couldn't place and didn't have a moment to examine. In her more lucid moments, she wondered if it would always be so. In that, Luma wasn't alone. Those closest to her grew concerned, suggesting in quiet corners that the distracted Initiate was losing control of her path to *mudutu*. She witnessed their hushed conversations, betrayed by worried glances as she passed by. They frightened Luma, those whispered rumors questioning if she would become one of the Lost, stuck between Ascension and a mortal life.

What if I'm just not good enough?

The tree pulsed, expanding and contracting briefly before it shattered into thousands of fragments in Luma's mind.

So much for *that*.

Luma opened her eyes and cast an irritated glance at the moon that hovered in the night sky outside her window. This time her exhale was one of despair as she gave up trying to find serenity this night. She had been trying since sunset, and so far, her only achievement was a numb backside instead of the lasting inner peace she was striving for. With a groan that could have been heard in the hallway outside, Luma unfolded herself from the floor and rose to her feet. She wandered over to the window, arms raised in a languid stretch as she moved to get a better view of the night sky. Maybe the moon would offer her some comfort where her mind could not.

"I don't know about you, *Nanna*, but I just…"

That was as far as Luma got before something dark flashed across the bright lavender colored moon. It was followed quickly by another, and another, and yet again, until she counted at least ten of whatever it was. She considered dismissing, but at the same time Luma considered sending a message to her superiors, however, her weary mind could not piece together what had just happened, right in front of her.

"It must be a military exer–"

The night exploded.

Chaos blossomed on the horizon, moving closer with each mushroom of fire and debris as every single dark streak that Luma had counted destroyed its target in a single, terrifying strike. She froze at the window, unable to do anything but witness the rain of red and orange horror that marched a path of destruction toward the city.

Sirens wailed, and in an instant, the sleeping city below where Luma stood paralyzed in shock erupted into a fiery nightmare.

Nasaru and his squad crept through the burning city, slipping in and out of the shadows on silent feet like only an Anunnaki could. The way they blended into the darkness came naturally to them, and the team used it now to their advantage as they skulked their way to their ultimate destination hidden in the hillside ahead.

The tall, stately building dominated the skyline above them. It was where the Sumerian rulers, such as they were known, presided over their people, and even now, bathed in the ruddy orange glow of the fires devouring the rest of the city, it looked nothing less than majestic. Two Anunnaki soldiers cursed the sight of it and spat on the ground, but a sharp rebuke from their squad leader stalled further comment. Their orders were clear. Get in, plant the device Captain Alalu and *his* superiors invented and get out again. *Without* being seen. Not one member of the infiltration team knew what the device would do, but after witnessing what had befallen the unfortunate planet on the other side of the universe, Nasaru was filled with apprehension. The navigator had not been told *why* he was sent along with the strike team, but there he was, sneaking alongside the other seven Anunnaki through the increasingly smoke-filled city. It threatened to choke them, combining with the hot, fiery ash that settled over the city like a dirty blanket that muffled all sound.

...All sounds *except* for the screams of the dead and dying Sumerians. *Those* Nasaru could hear as clearly as if they were tearing through his soul.

Luck was on their side. They approached their breach point to the building without raising an alarm. As they got closer, Nasaru noted that what they assumed was one single building was in fact, a cluster of them intricately connected via subtle arches and corridors. Any other civilization would call the structure a palace. But not the Sumerians, they just referred to it as 'The Leaders' house' and ignored the prestige that went with living in the most secure, yet most utterly beautiful building in the solar system. He rolled his eyes at the thought, grateful that nobody could see his expression through the camouflage masks they all wore.

Their luck held out, and as they made their entry into the palace undetected and moved swiftly into the depths of the vast complex, Nasaru's mind was free to remember just how they reached this point in the first place.

There would be a heavy price to pay for his sins.

Nasaru watched in horror as his calculations came to life. The fragment of the comet's tail was first harnessed, and then blasted into a collision course with the third planet of the solar system that Alalu introduced them to just under three rotations ago. Within seconds of its impact near the equator, most of the life on the surface had been eliminated. Those that weren't immediately incinerated were slowly buried in ash, choking to death on the hot air that altered instantly from a breathable oxygen mix to something toxic and deadly. Nasaru could barely contain his grief as he watched the beginnings of a nuclear winter spread across the globe. The few species that survived the blast wave and resulting acidic ash cloud would either find refuge in dark caves or the deepest recesses of the oceans and it would be decades before the atmosphere was habitable again.

His anguish knew no bounds. It made no difference which way he tried to tell himself it was okay. His soul *knew* that the destruction of the primitive life on this planet was on *his* hands, no matter who delivered the order.

But that wasn't the worst of it. Oh, no. *That* came much later, when Alalu revealed to the rest of his carefully selected crew the small container of minerals he mysteriously harvested from the planet they just destroyed.

"This is all I could find, but after the dust settles there will be more."

"How…"

"Science my boy. *And* your comet." The condescending clap on the back happened too fast for Nasaru to react.

The second in command became as jubilant as Alalu at that point, requesting that the captain let them return to their own territory so that they could put his bounty to use. For once, their leader had not disagreed, and soon enough Nasaru pointed their ship towards the relative safety of Anunnaki space. Once there, Alalu, his second, and a team of scientists from the Ruling Council's research division sequestered themselves away on their home planet to work on whatever idea was churning around in the captain's devious mind.

Nasaru immediately took leave as soon as the captain disappeared, citing that he needed time to catch up on reports of the War, and check on his family. The family part was true. But what he *really* needed was time to come to terms with his actions, and the part he played in the Anunnaki War Effort. He even sought absolution from the highest of Priests in the sacred temple, and although it was readily granted, it did little to appease the gnawing guilt that tore at the insides of the Anunnaki navigator.

It wasn't supposed to be like this.

Time passed, and although Nasaru was offered another, more lucrative post, he politely declined, preferring to stay where he was just in case Alalu required his assistance again. He didn't have to wait long before the captain made contact, but nobody could have been more surprised than Nasaru when he learned what Alalu required of him *this* time.

A new mission, *right* into the heart of the Sumerian capital. A mission that would either win them the War... or force the surrender of the entire Anunnaki confederate.

So, there they were, an eight-member strike team inside the heart of the enemy camp.

Nasaru's dark reminiscence was interrupted by the sound of a quiet struggle taking place just ahead, and he peered around the Anunnaki in front just in time to see the squad leader overpower a Sumerian male. The unfortunate man was quickly silenced with a quick twist of strong hands that delivered a relatively painless death. The sound of his separating vertebrae made more noise than the struggle had, a sickening crunch in the silence of the night. Nasaru scanned the darkness ahead as the squad leader half lifted, half dragged the deceased into a side chamber and dumped him behind the door.

If the body was found anytime in the next hour, the mission would be a bust. But if they didn't complete the mission within the next two hours, it would all be over regardless. It truly was all or nothing, and the weight of their task was enough to make Nasaru's steps falter.

He took point after the first death, slipping through the dark corridors slightly ahead of the rest. Twice more Nasaru intercepted lone inhabitants of the city, and twice again he was forced to silence those attempting to flee as they headed for the dubious safety of the tunnels beneath the main hall. Those bodies he took care of himself before the others could intervene, and when the squad leader questioned his actions, Nasaru simply shrugged and returned to the scouting position in front.

It was almost too easy.

Almost.

With hushed whispers and subtle hand signals, the Anunnaki team slid into the chamber where their goal lay and split immediately into two groups of four. The first had orders to guard the second while they got to work on the true purpose of their infiltration. The four guards positioned themselves facing outward from the center of the room. Each had their weapon drawn and held at the ready, while on the floor behind them the others began to sort their equipment.

For at least five minutes everything went smoothly.

For at least five minutes, Nasaru breathed calmly, if not easily. He stood inside the circle of guards while the other three worked, his dark eyes looking everywhere. Quick hands carefully unpacked a sphere from one of the packs and set it down in the center beside a slender grey pedestal. It rose from the floor as though it grew from the stone itself, and when Nasaru traced his eyes from the base to the top, he could not deny that the graceful arc was seamless. Nor did he deny the awe that filled him when he stepped into the circle of soft blue light that emanated from the stone itself.

Legends stated that the blue glow was the source of the Sumerians' power, and part of the reason they led blessed, light filled lives while the Anunnaki festered in darkness.

The imbalance. It was the *entire* reason for the War, with the Anunnaki wanting to deny the Sumerians what they couldn't have for themselves. Nasaru grimaced behind his mask and shifted his weight from one foot to the other.

Six minutes. Seven.

Ten. It wouldn't be long now.

Maybe everything will be okay. Maybe -

Before he could finish the thought, the wall directly ahead of him rippled as a curtain was pushed quietly to one side. It shifted in the dim light to reveal an unmarked passageway that a group of perhaps fifteen Sumerians entered through. They were led by what Nasaru identified as members of their military into the supposed safety of the large room, but what he and the Anunnaki *couldn't* have known, was that the same room they based the success of their mission on was the mustering point for residents of the palace that couldn't be evacuated via ship. Once there, the Sumerians would use the tunnels carved below the city for their egress from the battlefield.

It was all rather comical, really.

Half of the Anunnaki team stared at the Sumerians, easily picking the soldiers from the civilians. Immobile, they remained like statues, hands tightening slowly as they readied their weapons. The Sumerians, for their part blinked back at the dark-clad intruders surrounding their pedestal. To the last person, their expressions were identical mirrors of disbelief. Like they were unable to believe that someone had infiltrated so far into the palace, right under their noses.

Without a doubt it was the longest ten seconds of Nasaru's life. Seconds he used to scan the doorway the Sumerians entered through, *and* the one they were undoubtedly heading for. His mind absently categorized each of the terrified faces as one by one they realized the danger. Faces, young and old filled his vision. Some were as tall as he, others shorter, some dark haired and some light. It was almost a sampled representation of the entire race. He started to turn his head to see what his team was doing and, just when he thought there had been enough shocks for one lifetime, Nasaru's ears picked out a soft feminine gasp in the eerily quiet room. Deep brown eyes zeroed in on a scared female standing to one side of the first soldier that walked through the door.

Oh. Naga beleti.

And then finally, abruptly, the terrible silence was broken.

"Scatter! Redum! Get those civilians out of here."

After the paralyzing confusion of the initial blast, Luma's training kicked in. To a point. She stepped away from the window, uselessly closing it against the noise as she searched desperately for a pair of shoes. Anyone else would have them lined up neatly under their bed or at the bottom of their closet, but not Luma.

She hated wearing them, and as such hers inevitably wound up shoved to the back of her closet or stuffed under things and covered in dust, and as she got on her hands and knees searching with frantic fingers in the darkness, Luma cursed herself.

If only I was more like the others.

Precious seconds flew by, seconds in which the muffled screams and explosions grew louder. Closer.

She cursed again, reaching further under her bed, and swearing by *anything* that was listening that she would do better. Her heartbeat increased as her panic rose. Frustrated tears rolled down her cheeks when her fingers caught nothing but air and whirls of dust, and just when she thought she would have to give up and go barefoot, her left hand closed over a boot heel. The Initiate didn't waste any time, she yanked on the heel, pulling it closer to her body while praying its pair was close by.

This time she was in luck. Luma pulled them onto her feet without bothering to look for socks, tying the laces quickly so she could join the commotion in the hallway.

She never got the chance.

Before Luma even got to her feet, her door flew open, and a soldier filled the space instead. She scrabbled backwards on her rear, only halting her retreat when she recognized the uniform that identified him as a Captain in the Sumerian Guard.

"*Sinnis*, you need to move." He strode forward and grabbed her arm in a rough grip before pulling her to her feet in one swift movement. "There's a large force of Anunnaki ships in orbit."

Luma let herself be manhandled, though she reclaimed her arm as she gained her feet, rubbing at the spot where he had grabbed her. "What do you mean, in orbit? The city..."

He snorted his disbelief at her naivete and directed her attention to the window. "They're *firing* on us from orbit, girl. A ground force is only a matter of time. You need to head for the tunnels, *now*. The Ascended Masters will evacuate those that make it to the extraction zone."

Why the Ascended couldn't just help their people before they fled was a question Luma would never get an answer for, nor would she voice. Not until she was one of them herself.

If she ever got to that point.

With a meek nod, Luma allowed the captain to lead her out of her room, where she joined another pair of soldiers and several initiates, including Neperdu, the one who was nearly ready to Ascend. The smile on his face when he saw her wasn't false, nor was the twinkle in his ice blue eyes, and Luma found herself relieved that he was safe. At least for now.

"Luma. Thank Enki you're safe." Neperdu tried to say more, but he was cut off by a simple hand signal from the soldier who found Luma.

"Quiet. Follow me."

Neperdu blinked his surprise at being spoken to so abruptly but remained silent as ordered. Luma could feel his lingering glance on her back as the small group began to follow their would-be rescuer through the palace, though she dared not turn around for fear of being yelled at. Again. Neperdu confused her.

They had only spoken a few times, but one of those times lasted from the evening meal to the soft chimes that signaled the sun would soon crest the horizon. An entire night of intense study, mindless banter and the odd, coy glance that left a smile and a flutter in its wake.

And the next time after that, when Neperdu caught Luma in the moonlight as she was heading to bed and offered to escort her the rest of the way... He left her standing in the doorway with tingling lips and a rising heat in her lower stomach that was as unfamiliar as it was welcome.

Well, at least she thought it was.

For the entire span of her life so far, Luma had ignored the physical desires that some of her fellow Initiates embraced so freely. It did not interest her at all, and in one hundred and seventy years, not a single soul had gotten close enough to spark fire in her blood the way Neperdu did.

None that she would admit to, anyway.

Luma knew she could not afford the distraction, especially now, and so she resolutely kept her eyes forward and her mind clear as she fell in line with the rest of the Sumerians gathered by the captain.

"I forgot something!" Luma winced at how loud her voice was as it echoed and bounced off the walls in the hallway. With an apologetic shrug to the captain, she turned on her heel and dashed back to her room, ignoring his cries for her to return to the group as she flew through her doorway and slid on her knees to the chest at the foot of her bed. *This* time, Luma knew exactly what she was looking for, *and* where it was. She wrestled with the clasp and shoved the lid back to rest on its hinges so she could use both hands to dig around inside the box. It was silly of her to be so attached, but the silver-colored ceremonial dagger nestled into a leather holster was the only physical thing that remained of her mother. Tiamat left the mortal realm not long after Luma's twentieth year. It had been whispered that the great leader departed with a broken heart, but Luma always had the feeling it was more than that. What, she didn't know, but as the dagger slid free, Luma took a second to quash the longing in her bones for the one who birthed her. She swallowed back her grief and climbed to her feet, tucking the precious dagger into her boot before straightening and, without wasting any more time broke into a run to rejoin the rest of the group. They hadn't waited for her, but Luma wasn't surprised. What *did* surprise her was the silent reprimand she received from Neperdu when she caught up to them at the far end of the hallway. It was just a glance, but the shadow in his usually bright eyes told her louder than words that he was disappointed.

Who wasn't, at this point?

After another ten minutes of all but running through the building, Luma was never more grateful for the shoes on her feet. Or for the soldiers that accompanied their mad dash to safety. The protection they offered was probably unnecessary this deep in the compound, but they proved their worth more than once by keeping their ever-growing group of scared Sumerians moving. A handy skill, considering the curious nature that drove one or more to the windows each time they passed close enough. Even Luma strayed, drawn by the screams of her fellow citizens as they lay dying in the streets below. Each wail, each cry of torment and agony tore through Luma, burrowing into her soul where it took root and weighed her down so heavily her feet started to drag.

Powerless. That's what she was. Impotent and unable to do more than cower in a basement with the children and wait for the end to come.

It filled her with despair, but Luma was also honest enough with herself to admit that anger fueled her fear.

Etutu damn the rules, if I was Ascended, I'd -

Luma knew *precisely* what she would do... which was probably the reason she wasn't ready.

"The entrance to the tunnels is in the Kussum Emuq. We need to cut through here." The soldiers' voice was so quiet that Luma, who hovered right behind him again could barely hear a word he said. She sidestepped around him as he pulled on a door that blended so well with the hallway, she would never have seen it unless she knew what she was looking for. At his direction, Luma moved past him and into a stairwell, where she waited several steps up to make room for the others. In short order, and without a single complaint, everyone they collected was through. They kept moving, climbing one staircase and descending another before they reached what looked like another dead end.

Once again, she slipped through the door on the heels of the soldier and stood by his side. It could not be said that Luma wasn't paying attention to her surroundings, but she was so focused now, so intent on getting free of the palace so she could help her people that she walked into the soldier's back when he stopped in front of her. His back had gone as stiff as a board, his entire body rigid and unmoving as he stared at something only he could see in the center of the room.

"What is –" The question froze forever on Luma's tongue when, a split second later, her eyes picked out several strange black clad figures hunched over a small object beside the *Pillar of Emuq* that sat at the epicenter of Sumerian culture. She stared in growing confusion at the shady figures, her mind unable to process the information before her hand flew to her mouth in an attempt to stifle the gasp that filled her lungs.

Fear clawed its way into her heart when she spotted two more on the other side of the room, and it blossomed into a near panic when yet another pair moved to the edges of the light carried by the Sumerian soldier. If just one of them reached out... Luma shrank backwards, but the press of people behind her stalled all thoughts of escape.

"Scatter! Redum! Get those civilians out of here!"

All hell broke loose. Literally.

There were precisely two places in the room where someone could hide and Luma was near neither of them. She stared in abject horror as a masked figure suddenly towered over her with his weapon drawn. Her dagger, so far away in the side of her boot was no use, and in this moment her wits seemed to have escaped her. A weapon discharged and from somewhere to her right there was a painful shriek... and then nothing.

"What on Sumer was that?" A voice in the throng, high-pitched and unsure.

"I don't know. *She just vanished*!" The first voice got a response in the milling confusion, but it didn't seem to be an answer that anyone wanted to hear. Bodies began to fall on both sides. Luma felt rough hands grab her at the same time a large body collided with her back, and she flew sideways, tumbling to the floor a couple of meters away. Her head bounced off the stone and her vision swam. She tried to regain her bearings, but the ringing pain inside her skull left her stunned and gasping for air.

Time slowed to a painful crawl. Luma turned and all at once saw Neperdu wrestling with the masked figure that tried to grab her while a few Sumerians escaped through the opposite doorway into the tunnels. Their terrified wails echoed back into the chamber, fading out as they fled toward the gathering point. She cried out when the Sumerian Captain who pulled her from her room fell bleeding to one of the intruders, but that shock was *nothing* compared to the horror that wove through her when the pedestal in the center of the room flickered.

"*No...!*"

The pale blue light that was the ultimate source of comfort for the Sumerian people wavered as though a battle waged within, and Luma could do nothing but stare as she watched all colour drain into a sickly grey that painted the room with dis-ease.

It had to be the Anunnaki.

One of the figures on the floor turned his head and glanced between the pedestal and the object on the floor before nodding once at his companions. He reached out and flicked his gloved fingers along the side of it, activating whatever it was to full power.

Beat.

The pedestal pulsed again, and this time Luma felt it underneath her as it reverberated through the floor. The Anunnaki near the pedestal then turned their attention to the remaining Sumerians, though by now several others had heard the alert and entered the chamber to join the fight. Luma scrabbled backwards, trying to remain unnoticed as she climbed to her feet with renewed determination. She was terrified, shaking with the effort it took to remain in the room and not flee after the others who had already vanished into the tunnels. But her feet held firm, and with the dagger of Tiamat held tightly in her left hand, Luma swore that if *this* was the time and place where she was to die, she would not go down without a fight.

Even if it was a short one.

Beat.

This time it was stronger. One of the Anunnaki soldiers called in their harsh language out for the others to hurry.

Luma ran to help Neperdu, who was still wrestling with the first Anunnaki. They were evenly matched, with similar size and strength, though Luma could see the enemy soldier tiring as her fellow Initiate toyed with him a little. She reversed her grip on the dagger and raised it, she intending to plunge it into the Anunnaki's back, but he stumbled forward in a missed swing when Neperdu faltered and fell sideways, his face paling in shock as he was hit from behind by a different kind of projectile.

"Luma..."

This time, Luma saw *precisely* what happened.

It could only be described as *complete* disintegration. Neperdu took a step forward and raised his hand to Luma, who rushed toward him without thought. He stopped after two steps and shrieked when pieces of his body began to ebb and fade. It was horrifying. The very atoms that made up her friend were coming apart, and from the agony in his cries, Luma knew that Neperdu could feel every single nerve ending and molecule as they detached and faded. His pain seemed to go on forever, but eventually it was over, and the last thing Luma saw of Neperdu was the unending shock in his icy blue eyes as they disappeared into absolutely nothing.

Neperdu was gone. Her soldier was gone, and Luma was almost completely alone.

Oh, stars. This must be their new weapon!

Now, more than ever, Luma was determined to escape. The Elders needed to know exactly what she had seen. Her eyes scanned the room, seeking a path to safety, but as they connected with the Anunnaki who held the weapon that stole her friend's life, all rational thought departed. With a frustrated cry Luma ran forward again, not caring that he now aimed his weapon at *her*. If she could just get closer...

Beat.

Overhead, the lights flickered, and from somewhere deep beneath her feet Luma felt something crack.

Another shadowy figure approached the first. Luma threw herself at him with her dagger held low, trying to gut him before his friend could stop her. She sliced at his stomach, but as deadly as it was, her blade only cut cloth, and before she could swing again the air was knocked out of her lungs for the second time when his bunched fist slammed into her ribcage. Something snapped beneath her skin, sending a sharp, stabbing pain deep into her stomach. Luma grunted and sucked the air back in through clenched teeth. It was idiotic at best, charging him the way she did. But Luma had no time to regret her action, the Anunnaki yanked her forward, deftly disarmed her and took the prized dagger for himself.

Beat.

The walls vibrated this time, and the sickly grey light pulsed again. Another deep snap echoed up through the chamber and for a second, all eyes shifted to the walls. For a second, nobody moved as they witnessed a large crack snake along the stonework, rippling under the pressure of the vibrations below.

By the time the crack reached the ceiling far above, Luma had resumed her struggle. Her captor was strong, so much stronger than she, but she struggled anyway, only stilling when the razor-sharp tip of her mother's dagger pierced the soft skin on her neck. A copper scent wafted past her nose, a sensation swiftly followed by a warm, sticky trail that slid beneath her shirt and trickled down between her breasts. It was the only weapon she had ever owned. And now she was going to die by it. Luma looked into the eyes of the Anunnaki soldier, and what she saw reflected in them made her shake. They were cold. Emotionless. Except for the utter contempt she could see in there. Her mind raced, green eyes darting in every direction, even though her body remained frozen in place.

There was simply nothing left for her to do.

So much for all those lessons. Stupid, stupid brain.

Nothing but...

Luma lifted her right foot, bent her leg at the knee and rammed it upwards into the Anunnaki's groin. His responding grunt of pain was satisfying, but not enough for him to let go. Or even loosen his grip a little.

Beat.

Then, suddenly, Luma could see something *else* in her attacker's eyes something she wasn't expecting. Surprise, as two arms seized him from behind, forcing him to release his captive. Luma stumbled back a few steps, immediately raising her right hand to cover her wound, but her eyes remained on the struggle in front of her.

Two Anunnaki. Fighting with *each other* instead of the remaining Sumerians.

She could not believe what she was seeing.

The first was at a disadvantage to the newcomer's taller height, but to balance that he was burlier, broader across the chest than her dubious savior. It didn't take an expert in hand-to-hand combat to notice how quickly the first Anunnaki gained ground, sending his opponent backwards with a flying kick swiftly followed by several well-placed punches. The taller Anunnaki tried to dodge the next one, but it landed badly and skimmed off the side of his head, dislodging the mask he wore. With a muffled curse, he sidestepped the next attack entirely and twisted his torso to follow the movements of his fellow soldier. And then, without warning he struck, using the soldier's own hand to twist his arm and deliver a death blow via the dagger he had stolen from Luma.

Green-tinted blood spurted out of the Anunnaki's throat when the victor pulled the dagger free. He shoved the dying soldier away from him, watching impassively as he fell to the floor gasping for air while blood flooded into his ruined windpipe. Luma stared in fascinated horror as the dying man bled out. His features rippled and his body undulated as he took his last struggling breath and died. She had heard the stories, of course, but never witnessed it for herself. Curious as ever in the middle of battle, Luma pushed aside all fear and bent down to pull the dead man's mask off.

So it was true. Dead eyes stared blankly at the Initiate, but they were not the eyes of a human. His yellow pupils were widened slits surrounded by a black iris with whitened edges set into an otherwise human face. If not for the reddish-green blood that made him look more monstrous than he actually was, Luma would never have known the difference.

But now she did, and her voice erupted in a low hiss. " *Shapeshifters...*"

Beat.

Another crack appeared. This one laced across the floor, and the snapping rumble from deep within the ground sounded like it was coming closer.

Ripping his mask off entirely, the taller soldier turned to face the pedestal in the center of the room with an unreadable expression in his eyes. Without taking his gaze off the pedestal, he flexed his left hand and a ball of light appeared, glowing with that same sickly grey that struggled to light the room. He sighed almost regretfully as he raised the same hand and the ball of light shot forward, streaking toward another Anunnaki soldier, striking him down where he stood. It moved on, darting to the next, and then the next, from soldier to soldier until he was the only Anunnaki left standing. The ball of light returned to his outstretched hand and disappeared back into the nothingness from which it had come. And he did it all without looking at anything but the Sumerian pedestal.

As if somehow, it could help him.

And then, finally he spoke into the now silent room, his shoulders slumped in defeat.

"Ana harrani sa alaktasa la tarat. Eli baltuti ima"idu mituti."

"Road whose course does not turn back; the dead will be more numerous than the living..." Luma repeated the Anunnaki's words verbatim. Cold tendrils of dread crept down her spine, and she was only dimly aware of the surviving Sumerians making their way into the tunnels. She knew she should follow them and make her escape, but instead Luma stayed put. Her wound was forgotten, the pain replaced by an abject awe as she stared at the dimly lit profile of the soldier who attacked his *own* people to save her. And then, like a blast from the ceremonial fires of Apsu it hit her. Luma swept aside all thoughts of the dead Anunnaki as she scrambled to her feet to face the one who had spoken. A lot had happened this night, and much of it would traumatize her for years to come. But his words were the biggest shock for Luma by far.

He had spoken in Sumerian.

"Well. At least you pay attention when it matters, Initiate."

That voice.

Beat.

It was laced with sadness and heavy with exhaustion, but Luma knew it. She heard it once before, several rotations ago when her brother Lumasi visited.

And worse... she made a *complete* fool of herself in front of him.

The End of Everything

It was chaos.

Utter, utter chaos. When he eliminated the leader of the infiltration team, Nasaru had exposed himself as a Sumerian sympathizer and condemned himself to a slow, painful death. But when he used his powers and called upon An-ki to strike down the remaining Anunnaki and save the girl, Nasaru exposed himself as something *else* entirely.

Beat.

There was no going back. There never was. With his eyes locked steadily on the grey light, Nasaru ran a hand through his unruly dark hair. It wasn't fair, but in this moment, fairness didn't matter, and all he could do was tilt his head back to accept what was *then*, what was *now*, and what *had yet to be*. And with that acceptance, his mind finally began to settle, and that bolstered Nasaru just enough to face Luma properly. But when he turned, his eyes flicked to the tunnels and back again in alarm.

She hadn't moved an inch.

She just stood there, her mouth moving with hushed words that he couldn't quite hear, and he didn't need the lights to burn brighter to recognize the unhinged terror in her muted green eyes.

Beat.

This time, the ceiling cracked. Nasaru and Luma could now clearly hear the loud booming sound that echoed up through the floor. It was hard to miss something as deafening as a mountain falling to pieces from the inside out. The entire compound rattled like a child's toy, shaking from its deepest foundations to the highest tower climbing several hundred meters above where they now stood. Screams rang into the night, joining the chaos, and with each passing second, more Sumerians dashed through the room that Luma and Nasaru stood immobilized in. Oddly, not one of them seemed to notice either the Ascended Master or the frightened Initiate.

It was better that way.

With his hands raised in front of him, Nasaru crept closer to Luma much like he would approach a wild animal. Slowly, he reached for her, but it was no use. For every step forward he took, she took one backwards, her lips still moving with words he couldn't hear.

He didn't blame her, really. Not after what she had just seen... and what she was undoubtedly thinking about him.

Traitor was about the nicest word Nasaru himself could find, and he could bet the rarest gold on his *entire* existence that whatever Luma thought was worse.

"Luma." Nasaru needed her to understand what happened, but there was no time to explain. As much as he'd hoped this

path would not be put in front of him, that Luma would flee down the tunnel to safety and he could report to Lumasi that she was safe...and *still* unable to help, Nasaru also knew that *because* she *chose* to stay and face him, he had one more thing to do before he could move on and seek out his absolution.

"What have you *done* to our people? You...*You betrayed us.*" Finally, Luma found her words again, her entire body shaking in anger -and a fair amount of terror- when she realized that whatever she *thought* she knew, it was nowhere near all of it.

"No!" His response was quick, and betrayed the hidden pain he carried in his soul. "Everything I have done has been *orders*. You need to under —"

Beat.

"*Stars.* There isn't time. I need you to listen."

"What is that ...?"

"The planet is breaking up. Sumer is *gone*, Luma. *Lost.* Eridu is elsewhere for you now." Thousands of years of civilization, destroyed in a single night by one race obsessively determined on taking what they couldn't have for themselves, and Nasaru now knew that even with this easy victory, Alalu and his people wouldn't stop with the destruction of Sumer. No, they already had their sights set elsewhere... and it was *there* that the last stand of the Sumerians would take place.

But first, they needed *time*.

"You did this! You *murdered* our people." There was no polite way to say it. And even if there was, after everything that happened, Luma wasn't feeling very calm. In fact, she was the direct opposite as she stalked towards him with one palm held firmly against her bleeding neck.

The words hit him like a stone anvil. Nasaru clenched his jaw and held his silence, absorbing the truth of her words as the punishment they were intended to be. He reversed his grip on the dagger in his hand and offered it back to Luma. Even if she chose to drive it through his heart and twist the blade until he begged for mercy, the worst she could do was make him bleed.

Immortality had its perks.

The offered dagger slowed her down. Nasaru saw skepticism register in her eyes as she took it from him, examined it and sheathed it in her boot all without letting him out of her sight. He didn't have to read her mind to know that she considered attacking him at least once.

Beat.

The chamber shook so violently that Luma lost her balance and lurched towards Nasaru, not resisting when he swept in and halted her fall. She looked up at him, her dusty green eyes confused and angry in silent accusation, and in that moment, he could have sworn she saw *everything* he had done. And then, from far off down the tunnels, Nasaru felt the last of the Masters leave with those that made it safely to the extraction zone and he nodded. *So be it.*

Just the two of them remained, and he could get Luma out on his own.

Those were his orders. He *had* to get her out, no matter the cost. It was Foreseen.

"...why?" This time, her voice was softer, and though Luma would never admit it, she was grateful that he'd caught her fall.

"There isn't time! I need to get you out of here."

"I'm not going anywhere with you until you tell me, *traitor*!" Against her will, her mind already decided she was going to let him continue to save her, but Luma pushed herself away from the man who *helped* the Anunnaki destroy her people anyway. She tried to stalk away, but the chamber was shaking so violently that she didn't even take two steps before his arm was under hers again, holding her upright.

"Luma. You have *no* choice anymore. You're needed –"

"*I don't care!*"

"As stubborn as your brother." Nasaru took hold of her arms and wrenched her back to him, holding her close. He had risked *too* much for it to all fail now because one stubborn girl refused to take the final steps to answer her Fate. "But at least *he's* where he's supposed to be. Imagine how much you *could* have helped if you'd just..."

Bah. Anger stirred deep inside Nasaru, and he shook her arms to try and make her see reason.

That swept a little of the wind out of Luma's sails, and she twisted in his hold to stare at him, her own anger shining like a beacon in her eyes. Using her brother's name like that, as if he *knew* him. *How dare he?* Surely he'd just heard of him that day when he visited Gula. *Surely.* But right now, in this moment, that day seemed like an aeon ago, and it came to Luma's attention that whoever this Ascended man *was*, he still hadn't told her his name. Nobody had *ever* mentioned his name. Or the fact that he visited her old compound at all.

Odd.

"You..."

Nasaru watched her face contort with confusion and fear as she made another futile effort to wrench herself free from his grasp again. He hadn't been wrong when he told Gula she was feisty. But her feisty attitude wasn't what he needed right *now*.

"Yes, I know Lumasi. He is Isimud." He paused, but not long enough for Luma to react. "We both are."

Isimud.

Whatever snippy retort Luma had brewing froze forever on her lips as the word sank in. The Isimud were the elite hand of Enki, the supreme ruler of her people. If he could be called that. Some legends stated that Enki was an Ascended Sumerian that had refused to leave, instead choosing to remain with his people to ensure they were guided correctly.

Another joked that he was overly fond of the cheese that could only be made from the goats in the blue highlands behind Ur Nuru. Luma didn't know which part was true, her experience with their leader was limited to watching him from afar during ceremonies, but she *had* heard all of the childhood stories about the Isimud and the things *they* allegedly did for Sumer and her people. Most of those she dismissed as flights of fancy, tales told to children to enhance their sense of adventure during play time. And to make them behave.

"You're..."

Only now... this man in front of her was... It was true. And her own *brother* joined their ranks. *Worse*, he hadn't told her about it. To Luma that rated higher on the scale than whatever this man had done.

"The hand of Enki. Yes." Nasaru's iron-tight grip on Luma softened just enough to let her blood flow freely again, and he ran both hands along her arms to ease the shock replacing the anger in her eyes. If it were even possible. It wasn't every day she would learn her brother was a spy, from a man she thought was a traitor and would probably hate by the time his mission was done. "*Everything* we do is for our people... including letting Sumer fall to the Anunnaki."

Luma whispered again, her mind delving into the memory of a vision she had been *blessed* with a few rotations' past. Image after image flashed through her mind on repeat, but this time one stood out from the rest. And this time, Luma could see his face.

She looked up at him, her eyes widening as she realized that maybe he was right.

Ina lu itti sina pana.

"The man with two faces..."

"Most people just call me Nasaru." His tone was dry, but a hint of humor flashed briefly through the melancholy in his brown eyes. Before she could stop herself, one side of her mouth curled, but Luma quickly shoved any sympathy she felt for him away. Her anger at what he'd done, her confusion about the entire situation and the guilt that echoed for what he'd said about her were too vast for her to process anything else.

"I have seen you before..." Luma reached up and tapped the side of her head, her wide green eyes even more perplexed. "In here, before... even before that day with Gula. Only now you have a face."

Or two.

"...why do you think everyone has been telling you it was Time?" If he wanted to, Nasaru could have seen what Luma was thinking from the moment he first recognized her in the chamber. He could have seen everything, but it was the most impolite thing an Ascended Sumerian could do. Now, however, he reached out make that connection, curious about what she was seeing... and how it involved *him*. It had been so long since a proper Seer was borne among them that he brushed his manners aside and went searching for what only Luma could see. His hands, still holding her arms tightened again as he saw *himself* shifting from Anunnaki to Sumerian and back again. From Sumerian to something else again entirely.

He knew his Fate, and had known his dreadful reward since the day he took the first isolating step as an Isimud... but to see it in someone else's mind? The reality of it sped toward him like the comet he helped Alalu sling toward that unfortunate planet, and Nasaru knew there was no escaping it, and there never had been.

Beat.

Everything shook constantly. In reality just a few moments passed, but to the pair standing alone in the chamber with the pedestal and the device that effectively ended the Sumerian race, time still appeared to creep at a quarter of its speed. The entrance to the tunnels collapsed, huge sections of it falling in a cascading ripple of tile and stone. A dust cloud billowed out of the rubble, whipping around the pair in the chamber unnoticed as their odd conversation continued.

Luma would have fallen *again* if not for the grip on her arms, and she watched in complete fascination as Nasaru's eyes lost focus while he concentrated on something else, his mind clearly going somewhere she could not follow. But as she observed, the light, feathery touch of another consciousness connected with hers, probing into her thoughts, and she swallowed hard as yet another vision rose in her mind. An embrace, much like he held her in now, only much *much* more intimate.

Stupid, stupid brain.

Unbidden, her cheeks flushed with a heat Luma didn't recognize. At least not at first. She swallowed again, wishing for that particular image to be *anywhere* but in her mind. Not while she was connected to a Master, and not when it involved *his* hands decorating her naked body and *his* mouth putting that same flush on her cheeks again.

The spark Neperdu alighted could *never* compete with the furnace Nasaru created in her soul.

For his part, Nasaru's hadn't fully detached from Luma's mind when he caught what she saw next, and his face paled in shock, eyes widening as he recognized what he yearned for all these long centuries.

No, no please. Not that.

He wrenched his mind away and refocused on her again, absolutely crestfallen about what he now needed to do. Before he entered her mind, Nasaru had been hesitant, but now? Now the Ascended one was *devastated*, and the aching in his chest had nothing to do with the battle they just fought.

It's Her.

Tilting his head back to stare at the ruined ceiling in dismay, Nasaru swore, closed his eyes, and surrendered his life to the will of the Universe. As he always had.

The Ascended one needed to move quickly. If he hesitated for even half a second, Nasaru knew that one glance would be enough for him to throw *everything* to the wind, and if he did that, it would all be over.

"I'm *so* sorry Luma. One day I hope you will understand."

Faster than her eyes or mind could follow, Nasaru reached inside himself for his doorway to An-ki It funneled into him like a shining, celestial conduit that then flooded through to the stunned woman he still held upright. She cried out, stiffening in his grip as it infused her body, and he dropped his head to reveal brilliant amber eyes that glowed with the raw power of the Universe.

Beat.

The chamber shook in its death throes, and without hesitation Nasaru wrenched more of it into himself and wrapped it around both of them like a protective cloak.

He was just in time.

Not even a second later, Sumer exploded in a multi-colored flash and set off a cascade that would also destroy both of its moons with a light display so intense that it could still be seen millions of years later.

The Ascension of Luma

There was silence in the chaos.

All around them the world had quite *literally* fallen apart, however, wrapped as she was in a cocoon of pure power, Luma heard nothing but the roaring in her own ears and the quiet, lamented words Nasaru whispered into her hair. It was strange. *So* strange. At times Luma swore she could hear him in her mind, his rueful apologies seeping into her thoughts like gentle summer rain. They burrowed in with words like *forgive me* and others that she couldn't grasp the meaning of before they too settled into her subconscious mind destined to no doubt resurface at some inconvenient moment in the future.

There was silence in the chaos, but Luma could *hear* her tears as they tracked down her cheek, carving a path over pale skin and through the fine hairs that grew there. She could hear her heart, beating in time with Nasaru's as his tone changed from regret to resolute determination, and he began to speak the Rites that would grant Luma permission to take the ultimate step into Ascension... whether she wanted it yet or not.

"Stop..." It was the barest of thoughts, drifting faintly from her mind into his, and driven entirely by fear. *"I'm not ready."*

"Oh, my dear Luma..." Nasaru didn't stop the Rites, instead channeling his consciousness back at hers while his mouth did the talking for him. For all his remorse, and for all his tenacity, Nasaru's mind pressed against hers was like a warm, comforting blanket that enveloped Luma and calmed her more thoroughly than his power ever could. *"You were ready long ago. Don't be scared, my Irnini. The Universe is waiting."*

Somehow, having Nasaru's mind fused with hers allowed Luma to remain in that calm state, even though there was part of her that wanted to scream her fears into the cosmos. And then maybe yell at *him* a little, too. When she pushed back with her consciousness to delve into his, he met her presence with surprise, and the image of a door that he swung gently closed. But the swing wasn't fast enough to stop Luma from dipping her mind into the doorway before it sealed, and she was closed off from whatever Nasaru was attempting to hide. Images swam through her curious mind, one confusing picture after the other... and she sensed at least one of them involved her.

"One day Ilati. One day you will see." It was a mild rebuke from the Master, but a rebuke just the same, but all Luma could do was nod and wonder. At least, that's what she thought she did.

"This isn't how it's supposed to be."

As much as he tried to reassure Luma while he guided her through what *must* be done, Nasaru could still feel her resistance. It didn't help that outside of the cocoon of raw power that enveloped both of them, an inferno raged that could rival the brightest supernova. Given more time, Nasaru would have transported Luma safely to another location, but she just *had* to argue with him until they reached the point of no return, at which point *everything* was thrown into the realm of chance. It was infuriating for Nasaru. *Frustrating* beyond belief that the simplest choice could alter events so dramatically...but then he was living proof of that anyway and would be for eternity...and so therefore Nasaru held his frustrations in check. *"I know. But this is how it is now. Flow with the river, Luma. I will be with you for the duration."*

To prove his words were true, Nasaru drew Luma closer and wrapped his arms around her so that she could feel something tangible, something warm, while her mind and soul were being introduced to An-Ki. It needed to create a connection with Luma's entire body right down to the subatomic level and beyond, where the Universe would fuse with her soul and change her life forever. Under normal circumstances, Sumerian culture honored Initiates with a ceremony at the main temple and their Ascension was celebrated for three full days and nights while the twin moons were full in the night sky. But these were not normal circumstances, and the twin moons of Sumer existed only as fire and debris. All Luma had time for now, and all she had left, were the Rites, and even then, they were pushing their lu ck.

After that... Nasaru only knew his path, not hers.

"I. I feel..." Luma tried to enunciate what she was feeling physically and emotionally, but her mind was overloaded, and she couldn't put words in her mouth. As afraid as she was of Ascending, the touch of An-Ki inside her soul was far more intimate than she could have anticipated. She felt her head loll backwards and her body sagged, trembling against Nasaru's warm chest as his mind whispered words of comfort to her terrified soul. Even if Luma wanted to try to escape like she did before, her struggles would have proven just as futile. She was stuck, held securely against him while her resistance to her own Fate, the one she unwittingly chose for herself, eroded away one gently seductive murmur at a time.

"M-Master." Luma's thoughts betrayed her fear, but she no longer cared if he saw. There was nowhere to go but forward, she knew that... but still Luma resisted. *"Nasaru. I... I can't —OH."*

Without warning, Luma's back arched and she stiffened from head to toe, her breath coming in short, ragged gasps as she stared directly into the heart of the shining amber hued irises that belonged to the Master who forced her Ascension. Her own eyes reflected in the glow, and they widened even further when she saw the faded green colour illuminated to an emerald shine as An-Ki completed its assimilation within her body. With her connection now complete, the initial surge of power ebbed away, and with it, her body gradually melted against Nasaru's comforting presence. Her breathing slowed, but Luma still trembled, only now it was due to the raw, *awesome* power that the Universe gifted her.

It was *everything* and *nothing* all at once. It was the simultaneous birth of the universe and the death of everything at its end. It was feeling complete where she didn't know emptiness existed. It was An-Ki, the power-core of the Universe and it had accepted *her* as one of its' own. Through her connection, Luma could see it all. She could *feel* it all. The lives of her people from the time the first one gained sentience to now, the lifeless raging inferno that used to be Sumer. Her own life from birth. She saw Tiamat and Lumasi, Gula and her childhood friends. A vortex in space and a new planet and people there, humans, like the Sumerians were, and now *their* world was burning too, and Luma *knew* without knowing how, that this beautiful planet was her destination.

It went on, more visions, new faces, and through it all Luma could still hear the gentle voice of Nasaru, now devoid of all negative emotion as his mind circled around hers, embracing her physically and mentally as he welcomed her to the ranks of the Ascended.

He was watching, of course. He kept one eye on the navigator ever since the moment they first discovered that planet in the new galaxy and sent the asteroid hurtling towards the surface. Sure, at first Alalu remained thoroughly convinced that his navigator was exactly what he seemed... but when he'd come back from his little jaunt to the surface of that same strange planet infused with a power beyond anything an Anunnaki had been able to absorb before, *he knew.*

Nasaru was anything *but* what he seemed. *Exactly* what, the captain hadn't been able to find out, his disguise had been *that* good... right up until the moment footage started streaming in from the covert recording devices installed on the equipment taken to Sumer by his strike team. Claw-like fingers curled into the armrests on his seat, scratching into the smooth surface as he reviewed what occurred in the precious seconds before the home of his enemies blasted into nothing but a bitter memory. Back and forth the images flew, first one way then the next as he tried to decipher what they were saying.

An argument, between Nasaru and a Sumerian female, a flash of power and then... nothing.

"I wonder..."

After several hours of unsuccessful staring, Alalu had a flash of inspiration and abruptly stood up, marching over to a different console to change the readings the ship recorded with its sensors. If he could just isolate what was *meant* to be there from what *wasn't*, surely there would be answers.

"*Got you*, you *spineless* excuse for a God." Alalu sped back to his chair and activated the weapons control panel on his console. Leaning forward in his seat, he entered a new set of coordinates for the system to target and grinned maliciously when the ship accepted them all without fail. Seconds later, the proposed trajectory from the ship to an anomaly deep within the unfolding chaos that used to be Sumer and her moons flashed on the screen.

His fingers caressed the controls for a moment as he relished the absolutely *perfect* way he was going to use up the last of the minerals found on that new planet. Oh, how he wished he could see the look on his navigator's face right at the end, but alas, it just wasn't meant to be.

And, he had an appointment with his *own* destiny to get to.

Indulging his malicious glee with his finger hovering over the controls for just a second longer, Alalu finally relented and pressed the switch that would end that meddling infiltrator's life. He watched in complete satisfaction as every single weapon in his ship's arsenal launched to detonate at the precise coordinates where Nasaru was hiding with his unfortunate female companion. Collateral damage amongst a planet of collateral fatalities. Alalu was completely unaffected by some irrelevant female's fate. Especially a Sumerian one.

The death of his navigator could prove a little tricky to explain. To get around it, his loss would be recorded as that of a traitorous sympathizer in the Anunnaki ship's log. No mention of his real identity would appear, or Alalu himself would face an intense tribunal, and those rarely ended well for anyone involved. Besides, if he was being *completely* honest with himself, Alalu wasn't strictly following orders anyway.

The first weapon detonated with exquisite accuracy. Then the second, and the third, and so on until Alalu was absolutely certain there was *nothing* left of Nasaru. He locked the ship's sensors on the precise location the Sumerian cowered in, and by the time the last missile contributed to the inferno, the readings that betrayed his position faded to nothing.

"He was good for one thing, at least." Alalu's jubilant voice rang clearly through the empty bridge, echoing off the walls and consoles. It circled back to him as he entered new commands into the ship's navigation system, and he chuckled manically to himself as each order was accepted. The ship responded immediately to his commands, and the captain pondered his next course of action as he leaned back in his seat to consider his options. He had a couple of stops to make first, but it really was time to go.

"At least he got rid of the lizards for me."

Part Two

Somewhere in Time

The Prophecy – 1983

When the night burns like day, watch the skies.
Be ready.
When the Earth burns like Hellfire, watch the horizon.
Be vigilant.
When the Son burns for the End of Time, watch yourselves.
Be true.
...and when the Truth brings you Despair,
Be strong.

The Night Burns

She tumbled. Twisted and turned. She was battered by fragments of her own planet, the tiny little pieces of Sumer that hacked and shredded her skin into horrific rags of loose flesh that streaked her lifeblood in a sickening imitation of an ion tail dragging through space behind her.

Luma lost track of time. In fact, she lost track of everything *except* the mindless agony that tore through her soul and dominated her consciousness. But after an eternity even that shifted backward into the depths of her mind along with everything else.

Most of the time.

It was never ending, and yet it passed in the blink of an eye. Her body was pulled and pushed, broken, incinerated, and healed, and no matter how hard she begged for the end to come, death eluded her.

Sometimes, in her more lucid moments, Luma screamed for Gula or Lumasi to help.

They didn't answer. They never did. No help came. And so Luma continued to tumble and spin out of control through the rift in time and space resulting from the series of secondary explosions that struck the protective shield surrounding her and Nasaru amidst the raging celestial inferno that was once their home.

For Luma, it was bittersweet. Her Ascension into immortality still pulsed in her veins when the first blast hit, and Nasaru still whispering in her mind. She could already sense the haste in his instructions, but that quickly turned into alarm when the shield wavered, and flames licked their skin. He held on, struggling to maintain their connection through the subsequent barrage, but in the end, his efforts were in vain, and the last thing Luma remembered was the resigned horror on Nasaru's face when his shield failed, and she was torn out of his arms. It severed their connection instantly, spinning her in one direction and Nasaru another before a final blast obscured him from her sight.

So, there she was, spending eternity spinning naked through space. It wasn't how Luma pictured her life would play out, and not a single one of her uninterpreted insights had *ever* hinted at anything like this.

If she'd been more lucid, Luma might have realized it meant that this part of her life was temporary.

But she wasn't, and she burned.

21st December 1983 The Solstice

Luma snapped back into full consciousness with a ragged, unintelligible moan. She tried to breathe, but all she could manage was a mucus-filled gargle tainted with the coppery flavour of her own blood. Air. She *needed* air. It was all around her, but not a single gram of it made it into her ruined lungs. Despite her desire to take a breath again, her cursed immortal body survived without air, but what it could *not* deal with, was the *excruciating* pain that sprang into existence alongside her awareness.

It was worse. Far, *far* worse than *anything* else she felt tumbling for an eternity through time and space.

Her body was broken. Shattered and bleeding out onto un-forgiving ground that still rumbled with the aftershocks of her impact. The terminal velocity should have killed her, but thanks to Nasaru that couldn't happen. Not one bone, not one muscle or even the tiniest vein had escaped damage when she ploughed into the hard packed earth. Even her skull was in pieces, held together by matted hair and skin that miraculously resisted burning up in the atmosphere. She felt rather than heard herself trying to speak, but all that came out was another garbled, wet moan that trailed off when it only made everything hurt *more*.

Help me.

Her silent plea went unanswered, cast out to nobody, because Luma knew by now that nobody was listening. Nobody would come. So, all she could do was lay there, staring at unfamiliar skies she couldn't even see because one of her eyeballs burst and the other had been severed from the optical nerve. Her heart's blood continued to ooze into the ground, but Luma knew by now that wouldn't matter either. Death was no longer an option, even though she wished with all her being that she perished with her people.

Slowly, grotesquely, Luma felt her body shifting in the hole she inadvertently created upon impact, The same way it had during her chaotic tumble through space, her new-found immortality kicked in, and the broken parts of Luma mercifully started to merge back into place.

Bedi...

It was agonizing in the worst way. Bit by bit, piece by piece, Luma could only lay prone, helpless in the twisted heap she landed in while vein, muscle and bone knitted back together. Her spine was crushed in so many places it bent at an impossible angle; one leg tangled below her torso while the other...Luma didn't know where it was. Only that it hurt. Her right arm lay slung across the lower part of her face, molded against her jaw, and over the top of it, she could make out vague patches of light in the darkness as her eyeball regained its shape.

She was powerless to help herself, rendered impotent without the knowledge she needed to access her new powers. Nasaru tried before their link abruptly severed, but ultimately, his instruction failed, and now all Luma could do was lay and lament as her torn skin closed over and her blood stopped pouring. Even the emotional relief of crying was gone, stolen because her tear ducts were still separating from the mush inside her skull. She couldn't even move to a more comfortable position as her crushed bones knitted themselves back together and became whole again. It was pure pain, just more of what Luma already suffered on her time-skewed journey through space. Hours passed. Or maybe more aeons. Luma had no way of knowing. The only thing she knew was the pain.

And then... miraculously it started to fade, and other things started to creep into her awareness.

Eventually Luma found she could form coherent thoughts. Not long after that, the stars twinkling in the sky far above shifted into focus. The constellations were as unfamiliar as the cold, tangy air now filtering into her lungs, but the warm tears that welled and ran down past her temples were a welcome relief.

Is it...is it over?

With timid movements, Luma tested first one leg and then the other before unfolding herself from the uncomfortable knot she landed in. The effort cost her, and she lay flat on her back, breathing hard for many long minutes before trying to move again. She tried again, leaning on her elbows to try to get a better view, but her impact carved a hole far too deep to see out of, so

Luma rolled onto her stomach and climbed to her hands and knees.

One hand in front of the other. That's all.

She crawled across the bottom of the hole, moaning in pain as she clawed her way to the crumbling edges of her would-be grave. The night air licked at her freshly healed body. It was cold. Unforgiving, but after the burning through space and the smoldering ground beneath her, it was a welcome change.

"*Aaahhh.*" As Luma climbed over the edge, her newly healed ribs cracked again, and her head dropped onto the still steaming earth while she waited for them to heal. New tears fell, this time in frustration at herself. "This is what I get for... *mmm...*"

Reaching back down, Luma lifted her left leg and hauled it the rest of the way out of the hole. She lost her balance and rolled away from the edge, sucking in deep breaths of freezing air and began to take in her surroundings.

Where in the Universe was she?

"Good show."

A deep voice pierced the silence to Luma's right. Her eyes shot open, and she twisted her head sideways to seek out its owner.

"I thought I was going to have to get in there myself and toss you out." The voice sounded masculine, and incredibly happy about something, but Luma was too confused, and too exhausted to give the tone any thought when she couldn't understand the words to begin with.

What is... Maybe he's just happy I survived?

A bright light blinded her newly refurbished eyes. Luma raised a hand to block it and tried to squint past the glare to see who was speaking, but all she could make out was a shadow against the night.

She rolled again, rising to her knees as she tried to stand. Her whole body wobbled and shook, but she forced herself upright and ignored the inner protest at being made to move so frequently after such an intense healing. The lingering pain faded as Luma straightened before the strange being who had spoken to her. Chilled air feathered over her skin as the breeze caressed her body, and only then Luma realized she was as naked as the day she was born. But her nudity didn't bother her anywhere *near* as much as finding out where she was and how much time had passed. Besides, after what she just endured, how could *anything* possibly be worse?

"Asar basu ni?"

"So it *is* you. Come along then."

Luma raised her hand to shield her eyes again but made no other movement. The chill that swept through her had nothing to do with the freezing temperature and everything to do with the tendrils of dread creeping down her spine. Even though she had quite literally just been sewn back together, her senses were aware enough to know that something about this felt wrong. The way the being held the light, and the amusement in his tone...it seemed deliberate. Almost malicious. She took a step back, her body half turning as she prepared to run, but a hand wrapped around her forearm and yanked her backwards.

"Uh-uh. Na adannu na su'ati." The overly cheerful voice hissed in her ear. Luma felt something sharp pierce her neck, and a second later her vision clouded over. Her body lost all resistance and collapsed backwards into the being who seized her, and as darkness claimed her, Luma could have sworn she heard him laughing.

Worse, she understood *every* word.

"The navigator sends his regards."

21st December 1983 The Collision

It was a clear, moonless night.

Recent increases in atmospheric gases resulted in the Auroras at both poles putting on a spectacular show that danced across the sky in a brilliant display of colour that reached the mid-latitudes. This, in turn led to millions of people from all over Earth heading outside in the middle of the night to witness such a rare phenomenon. Scientists gathered data; photographers took the best shots of their lives. Citizens smiled and pointed, simply happy to just experience the never-before-seen event with their own eyes.

The strangest part was that NASA had not released a statement explaining the phenomenon, instead the organization remained silent while their own scientists worked to figure out *why* there were so many strange particles in the Earth's atmosphere. And where they came from. The Hubble telescope was still in development, and more than one official at NASA cursed the fact that its launch had been delayed just a couple of weeks prior. If they just had it in place... but instead their new, modern technology was grounded by red tape, and therefore the only option was to work with ground telescopes that gave them nothing but pretty images of the brilliant phenomenon. What few satellites Earth *did* have, were redirected outward to scan for any signs of trouble. New, untested prototype probes hurriedly launched in secret gathered more detailed information on the particles. The Hubble astronauts, trained and ready to deploy on their scrapped mission immediately volunteered to take the shuttle anyway, and in a few short hours blasted into the thermosphere loaded up with Earth's most advanced cameras and testing equipment.

But they learned nothing.

They saw, *nothing*.

As far as any of their tech was concerned, the particles were normal, and it was just another beautiful moonless night. *Perfect* for stargazing.

That is, until one of the stars in Draco started to get brighter.

The star was dim at first, pulsing and twinkling along with the others in the night sky. However, as the night wore on, its illumination changed one by one those in the Northern Hemisphere turned their eyes to Draco. They pointed and whispered amongst themselves, frozen in place as the star slowly dominated the darkness around it. The more thoughtful of them raced to phone booths or hurried back inside their houses to make anxious calls to observatories and colleagues. Others pulled out tripods and cameras, frantically setting up lenses to capture images and record video to preserve the gradual brightening of a previously undetected star in the northern sky. It was almost surreal, and the residents of Earth that were lucky enough to be outside that night lapsed into silence as they watched.

And witnessed.

The sky flared brighter as the rogue star burnt away the blackness of the night until it was as radiant as the midday sun. *Bigger.* The light grew until eventually those standing under it could not see without sheltering their eyes. Sunglasses, hurriedly fetched from bags and cars were rendered ineffective. Many found themselves attempting to point their cameras in the direction of what *had* been the night sky in the hopes that later they could see. From there it only got worse, with many flooding emergency rooms seeking treatment for blistered sunburns and overexposed pupils.

More particles, larger than before, entered the outer reaches of the exosphere. For those that could still see through the burning supernova that suddenly erupted in the night sky, fear took hold.

Whatever was coming from Draco was on a collision course with Earth.

Satellites and cameras tracked the mysterious space flotsam as it approached the Earth and pierced through the upper thermosphere in a blaze of trailing light. Around tables and countless screens, NASA held its collective breath, only releasing it when many burned off on their way through the mesosphere. The smartest of them worked fast, and within minutes they calculated that most were on a trajectory that would scatter them across the Canadian tundra and further east into Hudson Bay.

More burned away, their speed and trajectory too much for their composition, and most pieces fell to Earth as harmless lumps of a planet nobody knew had ever existed.

The biggest piece was an anomaly that would confuse scientists for decades. It fell at the same speed as the others yet lost no noticeable mass as it carved a path through every layer of the Earth's atmosphere. It alone continued undamaged, racing to its predicted point of impact without slowing or altering course.

One lonely meteor.

Falling.

It struck *precisely* where the models predicted, exactly seven minutes after entering the atmosphere and circling nearly half the globe. Earth rattled upon impact, and from all over the North American continent, measurements from the Richter scale poured in. The meteorite landed hard, blasting a crater approximately half a mile wide in the frozen tundra. The impact drove thousands of kilograms of dust and rock into the air, but it soon cleared, blown away by a surprise Arctic wind that howled down from the north.

An hour after impact, the US and Canadian military arrived on sight in full force with excited NASA scientists in their midst, eager to collect samples and take observations while their colleagues analyzed the satellite data. But what they found there would shock them all. What they found was quite literally impossible.

The crater was empty.

Raphael stood at the edge of the meteorite crater and observed the commotion below. People ran back and forth in the settling dirt, shouting orders at each other but it was apparent that despite the number of bodies present, nobody was listening. She was all but invisible from the vantage point she had chosen, and even if someone *did* look in her direction, their eyes would have been encouraged to slide past her without registering what was right in front of them.

It was one of her gifts, and extremely useful when she wanted to remain unnoticed... which was basically all the time.

Like so many others, Raphael tilted her face to the skies to watch the aurora but hadn't given it much thought beyond the sheer beauty of the cascading light as it rippled and danced across the night. It was awesome and rare, even for someone like her, and Raphael felt an even more rare moment of happiness as the light bathed her in its ephemeral wonder. But then her attention had been diverted by the phenomenon unfolding in the night sky to the north of the lonely strip of beach she lay on. It took a little time, but Raphael managed to maneuver herself into a better position to see what had fallen to Earth.

And apparently, it was nothing.

They scurried about in their lab coats and military garb, poking and prodding the ground with all kinds of bulky equipment. There were machines set up to read air composition and measure quality next to dumpy levels on tripods that would measure the angle of the crater walls. Containers and vials of all sizes held nothing but grey dirt, flakes of ash, smoldering rocks, and dried winter grass. It all seemed fairly normal for a scientific research location...if she discounted the military. Confusion reigned in the crater, but above all Raphael could sense their concern.

There was nothing there.

Even centuries old craters elsewhere in the world still held traces of impact, but this one... it was as though something just dug a giant hole in the ground and left again. To Raphael, that alone was worth investigating. And so, with graceful steps she descended into the crater, aware that at any moment someone might take notice of her presence and demand to see her clearance. Several times on the way down Raphael had to correct her balance when loose dirt slid out from beneath her feet. She paused about two thirds of the way down the steep slope to pull her long dark hair into a loose ponytail. Equally dark eyes set in a youthful face scanned the crater on constant alert, and as Raphael's feet touched the unnaturally smooth bottom, she sighed her relief into the cool night air.

She missed nothing during her observations, for despite her careful investigation, there was nothing to see. According to the mumbles of the scientists and the military, and the voices that drifted to Raphael during her descent, whatever created the hole in that they all currently stood in had vanished. In fact, the *only* anomaly that Raphael detected were the minute particles that hovered unseen in the air. They tickled at the edges of her awareness, familiar and yet somehow alien at the same time.

Be ready.

Father's voice surfaced in her mind, words spoken long ago to his seven children, and the charge he had lain upon Raphael and her twin brother. Ready for *what*, Raphael never figured out... but the night *had* certainly burned as bright as day. She stood amid the scientists perched on the edge of a shallow trench within the crater, comparing his words with the events of the night. However, one occurrence wasn't enough for her to cry wolf, and so with an exhale that betrayed a long-held frustration, Raphael turned to leave. As she stepped around a man scooping a sample into a small vial, Raphael caught something out of the corner of her eye. Something the scientists missed. She returned to the edge, pushing past the man on the ground before dropping into the trench.

There!

"Ma'am?"

Moving quickly, she reached out with her left hand and focused, aware that one of the military captains had called and was approaching with one hand hovering cautiously over his weapon. The ground in front of her quivered, and without further warning a small object shot out of the packed grey earth and into Raphael's waiting hand. Without even looking at it, she closed her hand into a fist around it, and tucked it into her jacket as she gracefully twisted back to face the captain. Whatever it was, Raphael would examine it later.

"Is there a problem, Captain?" Her voice was calm. Authoritative and focused.

"Ma'am, this place is for authorized personnel only..." the captain swallowed nervously, his Adam's apple bobbing noticeably. He didn't quite believe what he had just seen. "I'm going to have to ask you to report to the command tent with me for clearance."

In truth, he didn't know if she outranked him or not. Half the commanding officers present were out of uniform, and he had cleared four already. The sheer presence of this woman was *almost* enough to make him leave her be... But orders were orders, and even though she was intimidating enough to make him leave her be, he had no choice but to ask.

Raphael smiled at his nervousness. It was expected. The smile itself was a rare occurrence for her, but necessary for the position she put herself in. However, there was little trace of humor in her mahogany eyes. "Lead the way, Captain. I have what I came for."

The young captain nodded and turned away, gesturing to a dusty spot near the rim of the crater. A white gazebo had been hastily erected at the foot of a steel staircase that was dropped into place and a couple of official looking men were observing the frantic scurrying of the people in front of them. "It's just this way—"

An odd sound whispered in the breeze. The captain turned, seeking out the source of the cascading bells that interrupted his sentence. But he forgot all about the bells when alarm replaced the curious expression on his stoic face.

Raphael and whatever she found on the crater floor, had vanished.

Unbeknown to both Raphael *and* the military, a third party watched the commotion in the newly formed meteorite crater, and he was smiling. Behind him lay the meteor, stuffed into a box designed *especially* for something of its kind. It was unguarded, as was the Watcher. He learned to hide himself from Raphael and her kind long ago... and as for the humans, well...

He'd been with them since the beginning, and *not one* of them had figured him out yet.

Sometimes, the Watcher wished that his opponents were smarter. It would be so much more *fun* if they were smarter.

"See?" His gravelly voice was genial as he addressed the box, not really caring that it wouldn't answer. He wore the confidence of one who knew there was no real opposition to deal with. No competition at all. "*Stupid*, all of them. If they just reconfigured their sensors... *Bah!*"

Turning his back on the crater and the scurrying military, the Watcher bent at the knee and crouched to touch the box with two elongated fingers. He tapped out a staccato rhythm on its lid, humming tunelessly to himself. The smile turned vindictive. Vindictive, and satisfied.

"... but they haven't, and *you're all mine*. Would it be too cliche of me to laugh like the genius I am right now?"

The Watcher reached for his belt with his free hand, still laughing at his own joke as he pressed down on a metal band wrapped around the carefully crafted Italian leather. The air wavered in a shimmer that enveloped both the Watcher and the prize that everyone was searching for, and, with his manic laughter echoing across the tundra, he too disappeared.

Ruminations in a Memory

What if I told you that the legends were kind of true?

That monsters existed? That the twisted tales we teach our young to keep them in line all have an element of truth?

That the Devil exists, and he walks among humanity leaving a massive path of destruction in his wake? That he'd been doing it for hundreds, if not thousands of years, right under our noses?

But what if I told you he wasn't what you think?

What if I told you that if he exists, then logically so must the Angels, Heaven, and God?

You'd tell me I was crazy, right? But if I'm the one that's crazy... then why is the world still burning?

.... You cannot answer, can you?

What if I asked you to listen?

Part Three

Somewhere on Earth

Thirty-Seven Years Later

She breezed through the crowd milling around on the footpath at Venice Beach, easily dodging pedestrians who meandered like cows wandering in a paddock. Children darted away from their parents to run gleefully onto the sand that lined the boardwalk, eager to splash in the un-seasonally warm waters of the Eastern Pacific Ocean. Skating was easy for her now, though the first time she'd put inline skates on her feet and tried to roll, Raphael had fallen flat on her ass.

Of course, that was nearly thirty-five years ago, and Raphael could clearly remember the *last* time she fell, exactly five months and twenty days after she first let go of the railing. The toddler in the pram was thankfully uninjured, but Raphael needed to think fast to hide how quickly her fractured patella healed after the collision.

With her sweater hiding the break, Raphael smiled through the pain and reassured the gathered crowd that her knee was merely twisted, and she just needed a moment to recover. The parents of the child, however, seemed unconcerned that their pram rolled across the boardwalk and put not only their child, but others at risk too. As much as she wanted to casually mention that they be more careful, it was not *her* task to chastise neglectful parents, and so Raphael held her tongue and departed before her irritation made her speak out of turn.

From that day on, Raphael used her *other* senses to avoid collisions of any kind and had not taken a fall since.

She skated north along the footpath, twisting and turning between pedestrians without a care. Whenever a space opened, Raphael spun in circles until she was dizzy before continuing her trek. Sure, Raphael liked to dodge, but the open spaces beyond the crowds were what *really* helped her to gather her thoughts. When it thinned out as she left the main part of town behind, the only thing Raphael had for company was the ocean and the odd seagull. And that suited her just fine. Ever a solitary creature, Raphael initially balked at the command that sent her to Earth to watch over humanity. She even dared to argue with her Father about it, but after several hundred or so years walking among them, Raphael adapted.

Some days, Raphael even felt like she was at home, and *that* was something she had not felt for far too long.

Not since her Father sent Raphael and her twin brother, Azrael away.

"Watch over them. Guide them. But you must *remain in the shadows until the time is right, no matter what."*

"But Father—"

"No matter what, Raphael."

Even an Archangel had to follow orders sometimes. But only when they came from God.

From the first day of their exile, Raphael hid in plain sight within human society, using the skills her Father taught to their best advantage. She rarely saw Azrael anymore. They might be twins; but time passed, and the siblings no longer viewed the world with similar eyes.

It was understandable, really. Or so she told herself. Raphael was the Archangel of *Healing*. Azrael was the Archangel of *Death*. Both held strong opinions on how to guide humanity and butted heads more than a few times over their differing opinions. It grated at Raphael's pride that most of the time *she* was the one to acquiesce to her brother and the immaculate schedule *he* followed. Just *once* she tried to convince him to allow a human to live beyond their allotted time... and it ended in a disaster so heartbreaking that Raphael swore she would *never* repeat it.

Ugh.

Even after a century the memory of such a wrenching loss caused her to falter. She tried to concentrate on the way sunlight reflected off a lighthouse on the bluff ahead of her instead. But as always, once the memory reminded her of its bleak presence, Raphael found it almost impossible to think of anything else.

One hundred years. Even if she *had* convinced Azrael to deviate from his schedule, the passing century meant any human would have died from old age by now. It also meant Raphael would be in mourning regardless. It was both sobering and melancholy, and so distracting that as Raphael rolled around a bend and took the left fork, she narrowly missed body slamming into a man running in the opposite direction.

"Dammit! *Fuck*."

He muttered a few more choice words under his breath, leaping to his right at the same time Raphael swerved and ran into a timber railing instead.

So much for not running into anyone again.

It was a sign. One for Raphael to stop fooling around on her skates and return home. The last thing she needed was attention, even something as small as this.

"Watch where you're going."

Raphael braced herself on the fence and turned her head to respond to the man she had nearly mown down. Both hands rested low on his hips as he caught his breath and when he straightened, she needed to tilt her head to see his face. Eyes the colour of whiskey glared from beneath a shaggy mop of hair so dark it was almost black, and high cheekbones drew her eyes down to the unpleasant turn on his lips.

"My ...apologies." She twisted around and leaned against the railing to face him properly. In a single glance, Raphael saw everything. How deep his breath filled his lungs, the sweat coating his body in a layer so dense it seeped into his clothing... and the faint smell that caused her nose to wrinkle ever so slightly in response. "I wasn't paying attention."

He opened his mouth to retaliate but her apology brought him up short. At this time of day, frustrations often ran high along the jogging trail as people wound down from their days, and Raphael could tell that her regret had thrown his irritation into something else.

He raised his hand to shield his eyes from the late afternoon sun, his expression now curious. "Whatever. Me either. Listen, uh…"

Raphael's head tilted to one side as the now flustered, sweating man ran a hand through his dark hair. Strands of it immediately fell back down over his forehead and he shook them away again. The action was almost absent, as though he did it so often he no longer noticed when it happened.

"It's gonna be dark soon, don't go too far that way." He lifted his hand and pointed with his thumb back over his shoulder. The lighthouse loomed behind him, shining a pale orange in the setting sun. "Folks around here say it's haunted or something. Weird things happen up there. So I'm told."

One side of Raphael's mouth curled into the barest hint of a grin as she turned her head to examine the building in question. Human superstitions were amusing at the best of times, but when they involved her directly? *That* was just plain hilarious.

Such was her odd sense of humor. Raphael let it show and gave the man a more genuine smile. He *did* try to help her, after all. "I'll be careful."

She kicked off the railing and rolled backwards, away from the jogger. Now that the initial surprise had passed, there was something familiar about him, but Raphael was certain she had never met him before. Unless…

Hmmm.

Dilemmas like that made her nervous and increased her desire to leave. "And again, I apologize. Good night."

He shrugged as she turned away and picked up speed again, heading *precisely* where he warned her *not* to go.

Earth was her home now and Raphael adapted accordingly. She had to, or else she would be disobeying the last orders her Father ever gave her. Hidden in plain sight. Living in the shadows. After many years of wandering, Raphael found a small measure of solace in the strangest place and had lived there for nearly eighty years cultivating the very urban legends that the human warned her against.

The lighthouse was hers. The *one* place on Earth she made her own, and although on the outside it looked like it would fall apart in the slightest breeze, it was as sturdy as the day it was built. Inside it was a completely different story. Over the years Raphael had collected various oddities from around the world, and as a result the interior of the lighthouse resembled something like an unorganized museum. Bookshelves were sprinkled with seashells and uncut gemstones, and several walls were adorned with paintings, one of them unironically depicting her as a stern male wearing flowing robes while holding a scepter. Never mind the hideous haircut, Raphael had *never* held a scepter in her *entire* life. The furniture was sturdy and comfortable. Many of the pieces were blue, with other colours scattered in between. Her style was eclectic for certain, but her home was warmly lit with candles and fairy lights dotted around. The odd lamp sat here and there next to a cozy looking chair with a half-read book or device lying on it. She even had a bedroom with an indulgently soft bed, though Raphael didn't need to sleep as much as a human. But that didn't matter, it was *hers*, and when she needed it, it was there.

What mattered was her mission, and her mission dictated that she remain in the shadows. To do that, Raphael needed to appear human, and so she lived as one, though as she walked through the doorway into the large living room that overlooked the ocean, the archangel felt something she hadn't felt for years.

Dread.

At first, she scanned the room using only her eyes, but when nothing seemed out of the ordinary, Raphael opened herself up to the power source bestowed upon her by God. She turned in a circle with all her senses on high alert before strolling casually over to watch the last of the sunset as it dipped into the ocean in a final blaze of glory. One hand rested on the floor-to-ceiling window as she probed outward with her mind to test the wards that guarded her sanctuary. Raphael exhaled slowly and closed her eyes as power flowed through her and into the world. There were no words to describe how it made her feel.

Whole. Complete. Loved.

Those came close but fell woefully short at the same time.

Her mind traveled through the lighthouse and beyond, assessing each warding individually before moving onto the next when it bounced back to her without taint.

It was so subtle she almost missed it. *There!* On the runes she carved into the cliff face that dropped two hundred feet into the ocean the air was warped, a slightly twisted shimmer the only evidence that *something* had slipped through. Something that she couldn't ignore or brush off as a curious human, and for the second time that day the voice of God echoed in her mind.

"Use this rune with the others. It is designed to detect one species only."

"I do not understand, Father? Who do we need to fear?"

"Trust me my precious child, it is better that you do not know. Pray to the Universe that you never find out. If he comes, then so does Armageddon."

Someone even her Father, *the creator of all life* feared... and it appeared that whoever it was, had found Raphael.

She fixed the ward, struggling hard to conceal any outward sign of the anxiety that crept into her bones and put fear in her soul. She opened her eyes and turned her back on the window, moving hesitantly to the hallway. Above her head, a floorboard creaked in the now eerie silence as the old lighthouse shifted in the evening air and the sound made Raphael squeak.

"You idiot..." She berated only herself, her voice singing quietly into the otherwise empty room. "There's nothing there."

While that might have been true, it didn't stop the archangel from exploring the house one room at a time with one of her favorite weapons held low against her thigh. Naturally, she found nothing. Not even when she pulled a little harder on the power flowing into her and searched again.

She was completely alone in the lighthouse, but it still didn't feel right.

Still moving with caution, Raphael headed downstairs again and into the kitchen, intending to pour herself a much-needed shot of single malt. Her heart had not raced so hard in fearful anticipation since the Battle of Babylon thousands of years prior, and Raphael had to force herself to pause and take a moment to regain control of her fears.

Inhale. Exhale. You know the steps. Everything is fine.

After a few deep breaths and a whole lot of internal nagging, Raphael clenched her jaw and continued her way to the liquor cabinet.

It was then that she saw it. Her favorite whiskey, sitting innocuously on the benchtop *nowhere near* the liquor cabinet where she left it. A glass sat on the counter next to the bottle, pinning a sheet of paper beneath it.

The very room *reeked* of anticipation. And a dry, dusty odor that she couldn't place. Raphael stalked over to the bench, picked up the glass in trembling fingers and stared at the paper beneath it in horror.

There was *one* word on it.

One word, scrawled in a neat hand.

Boo.

The Dunmharfoir

"*Wait.* Don't I know you?"

Rian Murphy stopped dead in his tracks as he jogged down the steps of St Timothy's Catholic Church in Los Angeles. He was bone tired after the long-haul flight he'd just flown in on, but the need for absolution would not wait.

Seriously? Nobody knows I'm here.

Flashing a smile that didn't reach the eyes hidden behind expensive sunglasses, the Irishman shook his head and flashed the stranger a convincing smile around the red-wrapped candy hanging out of his mouth. "Yeah, nah mate..."

The accent he responded with wasn't even close to his native one. Instead, a near-perfect imitation of an Australian drawl sounded quietly in the space between them. Rian removed the sweetly sour candy from his mouth and used it to point back at the thick double doors that had swung closed behind him. "I just got 'ere 'ay. Just stopped in t' ask for directions."

He shrugged a set of broad shoulders and shifted his feet on the stairs. Just another lost tourist looking for the beach. "Not a bad church though, if yer into it."

It happened now and then, people thinking they knew him. Sometimes they were even right. But not this time. Rian was quite sure he would remember meeting what looked like some kind of cop heading in the other direction.

He *always* remembered the cops.

"No, no I'm *sure* I—" The man scratched at the stubble on his cheek, confusion clouding his features before his face returned to a more relaxed expression. He had been so certain. "My mistake, man. I guess you just have that kind of face. Have a great day."

Rian's smile remained intact as the other man waved a nonchalant goodbye and continued his way up the stairs, but he held onto his sigh of relief until he was swallowed by the darkness beyond the church doors.

Getting recognized was the *last* thing he needed. *Especially* when he had somewhere to be.

A small slip of paper no bigger than a post-it note was tucked into Rian's front pocket. It was the same slip of paper he retrieved from under the confessional seat inside the church after the priest had granted him a small amount of peace. He hadn't even looked at it. He didn't need to; he already knew there was a code typed in small lettering on the underside.

There always was.

Several years prior, Rian's employer somehow found out about his semi-regular visits to church, and after making a cryptic comment about irony, started delivering instructions to the Irishman via whatever Catholic church was convenient. And just like the rest of Rian's instructions, this one would be written in a code that could only be deciphered using the Bible.

A code that would lead him to his next project.

Rian Murphy had a new target.

Rian sat at ease in the courtyard of a café on a tree-lined street and observed his target from behind dark sunglasses. She was in the parkland leading away from the cafe, playing with a tan and white dog so small it would fit into his backpack with room to spare.

Begrudgingly, Rian admitted to himself that despite his preference for larger dogs, the tiny animal was ridiculously cute. But it was also *very* distracting, and with no small amount of effort, he ignored its antics and kept his eyes focused firmly on the target instead. Well... enough to glean at least *some* of the information he needed without rousing suspicion.

"Thanks." He flashed a genuine smile at his waitress when she placed his order on the table and picked up a spoon to stir his coffee before turning his attention back to the grass. And his target.

In truth, there was not much to see beyond the physical, and he wasn't there to notice how the photograph in his new file didn't do her justice. And he *definitely* wasn't close enough to see that the only sign of life in her emotionless eyes occurred when she looked at her dog. So Rian sat comfortably at his table, drank two cappuccinos, indulged in a blueberry muffin, and observed. When she moved on, he threw a few bills on the table and followed at a discreet distance for a couple of blocks.

He veered off before she reached the winding street that led to her house, satisfied that she was simply returning to the elaborate home tucked against a hillside in Los Angeles. With his reconnaissance complete, Rian returned to his new base to make his own preparations. He paid cash for a month, which gave him a comfortable window to operate in, but Rian didn't think he would need it. He rarely did. And even if the task took longer than anticipated, Rian's employer knew better than to rush him.

Well... he did *after* sending an 'consultant' to 'help'.

Rian grumbled at the memory as he examined his reflection in the bathroom mirror. A pair of black dress pants covered his hips but the crisp white shirt and deep green vest he needed for the night still decorated the hook on the wall behind him.

"Dumbass."

What a fool the man had been, interrupting Rian at a border crossing unofficially run by a drug cartel in South America. He traced the ghostly white streak below his ribs. Over the years it had faded, but it remained an unwelcome souvenir of the bullet that shredded his stomach during his struggle to escape.

The consultant was not so lucky, taking a slug to the temple a split second before Rian broke free. The loss was regrettable, but Rian had been left to operate alone after that.

It wasn't his only regret. But it *was* the only one that had Rian dancing so intimately with death. So far.

His eyes fell on another scar on the opposite side, higher on his chest. *That* one still ached now and then but Rian refused to entertain it, instead turning his head from one side to the other while he decided how much to enhance his beard. It was an almost perfect covering for his face if he let it grow out of control, which also made it easier for him to be identified, and so in the end he used a few tricks to make it appear just slightly fuller than it actually was. Once satisfied, Rian attempted to tame his hair. At first, he just combed it down, however the stubborn dark curls he inherited from his mother refused to cooperate.

"Ahh, *bollocks.*"

After fifteen minutes and a fair amount of product, Rian won the battle and wandered back out to the living room to double check his notes. He flopped down onto the couch and sat the file on his lap, his eyes already scanning the document.

Subject lives in the Hills.

No obvious source of income.

Sugar daddy? Inheritance?

Social. Is rarely home. Neighbour said she travels a lot.

No bodyguards.

As with the park, there wasn't a great deal there. However, Rian had worked with less, so he wasn't concerned. Even if he *was,* her face was on his list, and that was all they paid him to worry about.

He tossed the file onto the cushion and when he glanced at his watch, his lips pursed.

"Huh...*showtime.*"

As with most nights of the week, *she* was dining out, but tonight would be the first real opportunity for the assassin to get up close and personal. And with just a bit of luck, tonight would be the only one he needed. He already had his escape routes planned, and flights booked from several different airports just in case. As much as he loved the thrill that hiding in a city after completing a job, Rian tried to leave the lights in his rearview mirror as quickly as possible.

Only an amateur hung around to admire his work.

He finished dressing and called an Uber to take him to the high-end restaurant that matched his clothes. The eatery had been identified as one his target frequented regularly, and after a lunchtime trial shift, the manager offered Rian not only the waiter position he applied for, but the supervisor's role too. It amused him, but since his only *real* hospitality experience consisted of pulling beers at the pub in his village when he was barely seventeen, Rian declined.

Only now, two hours after arriving, Rian moved around his section with the ease of someone who worked restaurant tables their whole life. He balanced a freshly opened bottle of 1990 Krug champagne on one arm as he weaved through the tables in his care. Like a good waiter, Rian paid equal attention to all of them, however there was just one that he considered important.

"Ma'am, can I offer you a refill?"

She didn't respond to Rian directly, instead lifting her champagne glass in silence for him to refill. He topped it off with an elegant flourish and after a brief pause, also refilled her companion's glass before she dismissed him with a bored flick of her wrist.

Good.

Rian's lip curled in satisfaction as he turned away and returned the bottle to the ice caddy at the waiter's station. She hadn't even registered his presence.

For all intents and purposes, Rian was invisible.

The Sin

Envy watched her dining companion shovel food into his mouth with utter revulsion. It wasn't enough that he ordered his steak *well done*, he *also* ordered a bowl of clam chowder to dip his side of chunky fries into. Worse, she *had* to sit there and smile her way through him slurping up the odd smelling crustaceans one second and chewing as though his mouth was a swinging barn door the next. It was disgusting. Her stomach churned so violently Envy thought she might throw up the baked spinach ravioli she ordered. All over him.

But as entertaining as that would be, it was not an option. At least not until he agreed to walk down the merry path to corruption. That was *her* job. Corrupting the moral code of humanity, and it had been that way since she crawled out of a laboratory and into awareness centuries ago. Fierce and incredibly loyal to her creator, Envy was *everything* humanity made her out to be. Vain. Glorious, dissatisfied, and deadly. Beautiful.

She was also *bored*. At first it was simple enough, but ever since the industrial revolution Envy found it all too easy to lead them astray. Every kind of human fell to her charms. From kings and queens to politicians, from artists to engineers, it was a rare soul that could resist Envy. Much of the time all the Sin needed to do was lure them into her bed and at that moment of victory all resistance crumbled. On the odd occasion Envy had to follow through with the promises she made before the inevitable fall took place. But one thing was for certain.

They *all* fell, and when they did, Envy rejoiced.

Now, with her fingers betraying her impatience as they tapped out a slow staccato on the tablecloth, Envy gave the would-be-politician a sultry smile. He grinned around his ruined steak, once again giving her the unwanted front seat view of his mastication. His watery eyes appraised her constantly, but all Envy gave him in return was the same smile. She knew that look. Envy knew that in his mind she was already on her knees, or bent over his desk, or any other scenario his overactive imagination could produce.

None of it was off the table...but Envy decided to make him work for the honor.

While he gorged, she indulged in the champagne their discreet waiter kept at an acceptable level, and with the taste of the sweet vintage coating her tongue, Envy was able to change the staccato to a sensual back and forth that played into his desire.

"Tell me, counselor." Envy leaned forward when his plate was almost empty, granting him a delectable view of her neckline and cleavage. Sometimes her physical attributes did all the work for her, and Envy put in a lot of effort to ensure it remained that way. "What will you do if you can't get your proposal over the line?"

It was a very real question, and Envy smirked behind her champagne flute when he visibly blustered.

"Do you doubt me? Where's the *faith*?" His retort was quick. The counselor's body might have been sluggish and obese, but his mind was quick, and that lightning-fast ability to think on his feet was *exactly* what Envy was looking for.

She sneered at the mention of faith and absently held her glass out for a refill. As always, their waiter was there in a heartbeat and gone again before the liquid had settled. She made a mental note to increase his tip. "Faith is for losers who blame their failures on a God that doesn't exist. It's *results* we're after, counselor, not *empty promises*."

Her date swallowed the last of his food, picked up his own glass of Krug and drained it in one go. He belched noisily, giving Envy yet another full view of nicotine-stained teeth that had bits of food stuck in obvious cavities. "The reserve is gone, Maysa'. Those stupid tree-huggers just don't know it yet."

"Hmmm..." Once again, Envy resisted the urge to vomit. And stab him in the throat with her fork. She stood as if to leave but glided smoothly around the small table to stand beside the counselor instead. One of her hands trailed over his shoulder and she leaned down, threading her fingers through his dirty blonde hair. Soft and intimate, just like a lover might. "See that it is, counselor."

Her pink stained lips hovered dangerously close to his ear. Envy heard him swallow before a shaky breath passed through his lips. The familiar rush of victory blossomed inside her. This man would do *whatever* she wanted whether he saw her naked or not.

"See that it is, and you can have *anything* you want."

And with the counselor's fall all but confirmed, the delighted Sin straightened, turned on her heel and sauntered out of the restaurant. Her languid stride drew every eye to her curves, and she was still congratulating herself as she handed a card to the waiting valet, not caring that she abandoned her dining companion and left him with the sizeable bill. Moments later, she was along Wilshire Boulevard with the top down. Once she navigated out of the traffic, Envy made a call, her slender, manicured fingers navigating to a number few living creatures had access to.

"Envy, my girl. Is it done?"

The smooth, masculine voice filtered through the speakers loud and clear. Envy smiled; confident that as always, she had done well. "Yes *Sir.*"

Pagan, they called him.

Heathen.

Primitive.

He was only ever spoken of in hushed tones. The fear humanity regarded him with was a well-earned badge of honor that started wars and ended civilizations. He had many, *many* names...but Envy knew him best as *Father.*

While not technically correct, he offered a sympathetic ear when the rest of her family had abandoned her, and therefore Envy's respect for him ran deep. "I expect the land in question will be yours by the end of the week."

"Excellent. You know what to do if it isn't."

"Naturally."

The line went dead. Unfortunately for Envy, so did her engine.

"Fuck." The same manicured hand now came down hard on the steering wheel, and Envy muttered several other impolite words under her breath. She was just warming up to a few more when she noticed inky black smoke rising from the vents on the other side of her window. With a disgruntled sigh, she climbed out of the car and after fumbling with the latch for long enough to start cursing again, popped the hood. Smoke was pouring out of so many parts of the engine that even *her* lack of knowledge could tell there was something seriously wrong. She threw her hands in the air and rounded the car, heading back for her phone. Her fingers had just closed over it when she heard the crunch of gravel somewhere behind her.

"Need some help?"

Her body jerked backwards out of the car, and Envy spun, finding herself face to face with a man standing about six feet from her trunk. He was vaguely familiar. That unshaven face and smooth dark hair was *definitely* nice enough for her to take a second look, but with her annoyance at the car clouding her mind, she couldn't place him. Or the lilt in his European accent.

It didn't matter, if he wanted to be some kind of knight in shining armor, who was she to stop him?

"This *stupid* car. I swear I'm sending it back." Waving her irritation at the hood, Envy played her part well. She stamped her foot and marched back over to shoo away the smoke that was still oozing from various places within her engine. "*Look* at this! I've barely had it a month."

"Ahhh, no problem, Miss. Why don't you call for a tow? I'll see if I can help in the meantime."

Without thinking, Envy did as he asked. Her call connected immediately, and a truck was promised to arrive within the hour. She hung up the phone and turned to her would-be-savior, sparing a moment to admire the way his dark blue denim hugged his ass as he inspected her engine.

Interest sparked in her eyes. After the meal she had just endured, something a little more palatable would be sure to sweeten her night.

"Do you think you can fix it?" Envy sidled over to where he stood and wrapped her fingers lightly around his forearm. As she suspected, it was firm. Pleasantly so, and that only increased her hunger.

"That's why *I'm* here. To fix a problem."

Envy registered a quiet click, but her mind was too deeply focused on her imminent conquest to register it as anything but another noise coming from her engine... and so it took her by *complete* surprise when four bullets entered her chest in rapid succession.

Rian bundled the still bleeding body into his trunk, taking extra care to ensure it remained on the plastic lining. It was only a rental, but even the smallest drop would give him no choice but to destroy it...and that was something he preferred to avoid wherever possible. Just twice in the past Rian had to use fire as a forensic countermeasure, which was two times too many as far as he was concerned.

Not that he didn't love a good fire.

This time he didn't think he'd need it. He drove to her house and parked his car inside the circular driveway at the foot of a staircase leading to an ornately decorated entryway. The double doors were immaculately white, set inside pale-yellow sandstone with intricately matched stained-glass panels on either side. The blood red roses stood out in stark contrast to the white, much like the blood pooling on the lining in his trunk. It was pretty to look at, but Rian had no time to admire how well her glazier completed his work.

He checked his watch. 11:13pm.

Plenty of time.

The late hour meant that there should be less people around, but Rian didn't take any chances. He scooped his target out of the trunk, his gloved hands cradling her like a sleeping lover and not the lifeless corpse that had been ordered. A quick glance down at the plastic made Rian frown. There wasn't as much blood as he expected for four bullets and a fresh body.

"Huh..."

Maybe she lost more blood on the road than he thought. Or suffered a medical condition that caused clotting. Either way, Rian made a mental note to go back and check as he walked up the stairs, keyed in her entry code like he belonged there and made his way to the living room.

Laying his burden down on the white couch, Rian finally took the time to *really* look at her. Her light tawny skin was flawless and her face beautiful, even in death. She looked peaceful, without the air of dissatisfaction that hung around her like a cloak when she was alive.

Something stirred within the assassin. A sealed door deep inside him cracked open, and before he could react a denied emotion slipped through. He crouched down next to her, exhaling through the wave even as he fought to contain what he hadn't allowed himself to feel for a long, long time. Not since his entire unit was lost during a simple reconnaissance mission in the coastal waters off the Republic of Côte d'Ivoire.

Regret.

"*Ach*. What a waste of life. But you pissed off the wrong person, love. I'm sorry. It's nothin' personal." He stood out of the crouch and jogged back to his car to get her bag and the phone that had fallen out of her limp fingers and landed with a crack on the bitumen. Deflecting the investigation onto the tow truck driver was a little too sloppy for his liking, but Rian figured the charges would not stick once the time of death was established and the forensic examination completed.

What it *did* was give Rian the time *he* needed to disappear.

He slipped back inside and locked the door behind him before heading back down the hallway to add a few finishing touches to the scene.

Only when Rian walked back into the living room, he was completely alone.

"What the fu—"

With his nerves suddenly on high alert, Rian pulled out his gun and moved closer to the couch, but he didn't get very far. Something solid crashed into him from behind with all the finesse of a charging bull. The weight forced him to the ground, knocking the air out of his lungs and before Rian could react further a pained voice hissed in his ear.

"*Who did I piss off?*"

Ice crawled through his veins.

What the fuck?

She had been dead. So dead that her body had gone limp, and her blood stopped pumping. So dead that when he checked, her pulse was non-existent. *So dead that —*

A hand slapped down on his shoulder, breaking through the momentary panic that threatened to overwhelm him.

"...answer me."

He didn't. He *couldn't*. So Rian did the only thing he could. He bucked his whole body off the floor, dislodging his *living* target and rolling to his back so he could scuttle backwards out of her reach. But he underestimated how quickly she could move, and, in an instant, she was straddling his hips with her hands locked in a vice-like grip around his neck.

"*Who?*"

The words came through gritted teeth. Despite the anger that infused her, Rian could see the pain in her eyes. Three bullets hurt, but apparently not enough to kill.

Even if he wanted to, Rian still couldn't answer. Her grip was surprisingly tight. Or not, considering she was still alive. He felt his tendons straining under the pressure, and his Adam's apple popped painfully under the heel of her palm. Rian kicked his legs, but this time she was ready and somehow, her slender body suddenly held the weight of an anvil.

"I..."

Darkness clouded the edges of his vision as he choked out a single word. He opened his mouth again but this time all he could manage was a few indecipherable grunts. Desperate fingers tapped the floor, seeking his gun but it was nowhere he could reach it. Her lips curled into a cruel grin, sending another shot of ice through Rian's veins. If he didn't get out from underneath her soon, it would all be over.

He'd have failed, on *so* many levels.

"Who??"

"*...can't.*"

He clawed at her hands, but she didn't budge, and so, with the last of his strength Rian slammed both fists into the inside of her elbows. The impact knocked her grip loose, and he used the sudden leverage to launch himself upright. His forehead smashed into her nose and with a cry she rolled sideways, giving Rian the opening he was looking for. Moving the other way, he scrambled to his feet and put a little distance between them.

"I put *four bullets* in you!"

His target sneered at him from behind her hand as she tried to stem the flow of fresh blood from her nose. She wavered unsteadily on her feet, But Rian didn't drop his guard again. Not even when winced in pain and lowered her hand to press against her stomach. Not even when his own head spun from the lack of air in his lungs.

Maybe *never* again.

"You can't kill *me*, you *idiot*."

What the fuck? What the fuck...

"Someone seems to think the opposite." With all his years of experience and everything he had seen, Rian had trouble keeping his cool. In fact, it was *only* that experience and training that gave him the ability to ignore his instincts and get the hell out of there.

She darted forward faster than he could blink, striking him in the stomach so hard he doubled over. Without missing a beat, she drove her knee into his groin for good measure.

"Good Christ..." Rian wheezed as untold agony exploded through his groin and radiated outward from his crotch to engulf his entire body. Anywhere else, and he would have shaken it off, but Rian was as sensitive as any other man and barely managed to remain on his feet. To his left, he saw the muzzle of his gun sticking out from under the couch and he stumbled sideways, sucking air deep into his lungs to cover his intent.

"...and you're not going *anywhere* until you tell me who it was."

It was impossible, but Rian couldn't deny what was very obvious and very real in front of him. People did not get up and walk away from four bullets to the chest. But not only did she manage that, she appeared to be getting *stronger* as the moments passed by.

His instincts screamed a little louder, and this time Rian felt obliged to obey the need to run. The only problem was that the job was unfinished and leaving it that way would ruin his professional reputation. Without warning, he dropped low, retrieved his gun from under the couch, and trained it on her.

"How about I just shoot you again and be on my way?" He fired a single shot into her left leg below the knee and took a step backwards. "A smart girl like you should be able to figure it out."

"*Ouch.*" She looked at her leg in disgust as more blood began to ooze out of her body. "If that leaves a scar, I'll fucking kill you."

Rian could *not* believe his eyes. *Five* bullets. And the first four were kill shots. His gun dipped briefly, and he took another step backwards. It was well past time for him to get out of there and cut his losses. To regroup before he took another shot at fulfilling the contract. His eyes flicked to the doorway behind her, then to the one on the side that led to the entrance. There was another, wider opening behind him, but Rian didn't need the kitchen.

He *needed* to get out.

"You should be —"

"*Dead?* Tell that to the others who tried."

Rian flinched ever so slightly and watched in confusion as she raised her hand and opened her palm. At him. The air wavered around her in a kind of shimmer and a split second later an unseen force blasted him backwards. Rian went sailing through the air, crashing into the sandstone wall with a bone clattering crack. His skull bounced off the immovable surface and he hit the ground in a tangled heap. The last thing the assassin saw before darkness claimed him was his target's face hovering over him.

...and the strangest thing to his mind was that she didn't look angry.

If anything, she looked *terrified*.

The Hopeless One

Levi walked down the corridor toward his office lost in thought. A deep blue reusable coffee cup warmed his hand, but as yet the agent hadn't taken a single sip from the smooth, full-bodied brew. He already knew it would be lukewarm by the time he got to drink it, which was more than he could say for the freshly baked raspberry muffin tucked into the satchel slung over his shoulder.

The case he was working on just ended in yet *another* dead end, and the defeat tasted sour on his tongue. He had been so *certain* that *this* time, the lead would pan out and crack his case wide open. Unfortunately, Levi *also* convinced himself that he would *finally* find a tangible link between this case and the twenty-seven other unsolved murders on his desk and *that* was where the bitterness lay.

Different case files, different bodies. Hell, forensics even determined that eleven of them indicated different murderers. But serial or copycat, they all had *one* thing in common.

Angels.

Or rather, a voice whispering in the head of the killer, a voice connecting the six who were already convicted. A voice that *always* said the same thing:

The Angels made me do it.

Witnesses at four of the crime scenes Levi visited mentioned similar words in their statements. Worse than that, a grand total of *twenty* of the unfortunate victims, *including Levi's pregnant fiancé* had died with the words carved into their skin like a sick, taunting memo that could never be erased.

The FBI didn't like it.

Similar murders meant crossed jurisdictions, and crossed jurisdictions got messy, *especially* with cold cases and local law enforcement that did not want to cooperate.

Levi's superiors did not *want* to see the connection, because then they would have no option but to devote resources that didn't exist to a taskforce they had no manpower for. But even they couldn't ignore the evidence forever. When Levi stumbled across the second case, the file got dismissed as a conflict of interest. The mild reprimand in the return email bluntly reminded the agent that he had actual cases to work on and further distractions not tolerated.

He didn't listen.

If anything, Levi smelled a rat. And so, he found himself sneaking around chasing evidence late into the night until a collection of folders stacked three feet deep decorated the floor behind his desk. At first, there were only the two yellow folders, but by the time Levi compiled the evidence he needed, fifteen other case files had joined the stack.

He found his evidence... and in the process uncovered a series of murders so horrific Levi knew he would *never* let it go. It was evidence that nobody, not even the Director himself, could ignore. But it was still an uphill battle for Levi to be heard, given the differences in each case. He wasn't stupid, he knew damn well his personal interest compromised his ability to be impartial *and* that it cost him a promotion to Supervisory Special Agent the year before.

A wiser man would have let it go. Several ordered him to. But Levi *couldn't* even though he tried. There was just...*something* about the case that had nothing to do with his own connection to it. Something he could not explain beyond the knowledge that he was *right*.

And if he was right, *that* meant there was a nationwide conspiracy of murders that he had barely scratched the surface of.

So, in Levi's mind, there was no question. *He had to be*, or *none* of what he'd been working on over the last ten years would be worth it. Ever since that fateful day when the call alerted dispatch and he responded to an emergency at a church fete, Levi Malach had been focused on this, and *only* this case.

Sure, he solved others in-between, but it was impossible to stay away from this one. Hard to stay away from a case that ruined his life before he'd even known it was possible.

That was the reason he gave himself, anyway.

"Agent Malach. Got a minute?"

A deep baritone voice somewhere to the left pulled Levi out of his reverie and back into the moment. His head turned in response, one eyebrow already raised in question. "SAC Wilson. Thought you were due in tomorrow?"

Without breaking his stride, Levi altered direction to greet his indirect superior. Special Agent-in-Charge Thomas Wilson was a sober looking man who, by all accounts had refused a promotion to the Washington field office so he could remain in California and stay near his family. So far however, aside from the odd coffee, Levi's interactions with the senior agent remained strictly professional and he had not given Wilson's personal life much thought.

"Ah, yeah. But something came up and Head Office dumped it in my lap. So lucky you, I'm spreadin' the love."

Levi nodded his understanding, though kept his expression neutral as he inwardly sighed. A higher *official* workload meant less time he could devote to his other investigation, but he would *never* let it be said that Levi Malach wasn't a team player. When he needed to be. Or had no choice. "Got it... so meeting room in thirty? I've got some paperwork to file, so—"

"Levi..."

It was rare for Wilson to use anyone's given name. Hearing it brought Levi up short. He shifted from one foot to the other, his brow furrowing as it dawned on him that the SAC might have another reason for stopping him in the hallway. His eyes flicked to the tablet device in Wilson's left hand then back to his face, but neither gave Levi any kind of answer.

"Sir?"

Wilson glanced in both directions before lifting the device to glance at the screen. "Quantico wants to know where you're at with Angel case."

It was everything Levi wanted to hear, but at the same time hearing those words sent a chill down his spine. Realistically, Levi knew he should feel elated that someone at headquarters was asking about a case only he seemed to care about... but instead all that surfaced was dread. "I linked some more circumstantial evidence to three of the cases but... nothing we can act on. Whoever is doing this is *good*. Better than good."

He shrugged and waved his free hand helplessly to emphasize his frustration. "And you already know I only work on it after hours, so progress is... slow."

Usually, Wilson preferred to let Levi's actual boss run his team without interference, so while the questions were welcome, Levi also maintained his guard.

"I see."

Wilson's response was abrupt, but to Levi it also sounded a little disappointed. He paused and broke eye contact, glancing back down at his tablet, and it was *then* that the investigator in Levi knew that Wilson was holding something back. Something that involved him. He opened his mouth to probe further, but his superior beat him to it.

"So... I take it you haven't heard?"

"... *what?*" In an instant, Levi shifted from idle wariness to full alert. His fingers tightened on the forgotten coffee in his hand, and he subconsciously stood taller before taking a step forward. "Where? *When?* Does this mean—"

Wilson raised both hands to slow Levi down, his mouth opening and closing several times before he could get a word in. "Hey... don't shoot the messenger, Malach. I came to find *you* as soon as I heard."

Levi didn't buy it, but he nodded curtly for Wilson to continue.

"... *where?*"

"Griffith Observatory. The vic was still alive when paramedics arrived on scene about half an hour ago. LAPD and forensics are waiting for you on site. Take Addison with you."

Levi turned on his heel and strode toward the elevators before Wilson finished speaking, but the SAC's next words brought him up short.

"Find the link that binds them, Agent Malach. This has gone too far."

The unexpected trip to Griffith Observatory took far too long for a twenty-four-mile drive and Levi grew increasingly agitated with every passing moment.

What are we going to find?

Is this the one?

He tapped his finger on the steering wheel and gnawed on his bottom lip while every single file he ever read scrolled across his mind. It *had* to be this one. He could *feel* it. *Taste* it. Something big was about to happen, and the wait was driving him wild. It rendered him silent, much to the dismay of Claire Addison, an agent fresh out of the academy that had not been permanently assigned to a specific team or unit within their field office. Her enthusiasm, while a breath of fresh air in the often too serious office, was not something Levi was in the mood for right now. Nor was the incessant line of endless questions that fell out of her mouth. Most of her running commentary was irrelevant to the case, and *that* meant Levi's responses were monosyllabic at best. He was certainly not in the correct frame of mind for personal interests.

"Addison..."

There was simply too much pain in personal interests.

"Sir?"

Levi killed the engine of the black Suburban they borrowed from the carpool, his keen eyes already scanning the sight that lay before them. Here and there people stood around, gathering in small groups guarded by uniformed officers.

"I want you to take some witness statements."

But it wasn't the people that held his eye.

A wide expanse of lush green grass rolled away from them and met with the pristine white stone that made up the observatory. It was an imposing building, perched at the top of the range overlooking the city, and consisted of several levels, some of which were hidden beneath ground level. Behind the dome sheltering the telescope, Griffith Park itself fell away from the peak, cascading down a collection of sprawling hillsides covered in scraggy brush and hiking trails that wound past the outer edges of the park and into metropolitan Los Angeles.

Overall, it was a beautiful place, visited by thousands of locals and tourists every year. A place for family gatherings, scientific observation, education, and wonder. An icon on the Californian skyline... an icon now tainted with the stench of murder.

"Talk to the police, find out where they've stashed anyone that might have seen something. I—"

"—what are you going to do?"

Levi flicked his fingers irritably at the windshield, indicating the scene beyond. "I'll cycle round to the site itself and talk to forensics."

"We're supposed to stick together. The handbook states that—"

"I *know* what the handbook *says*, Addison." His tone was curt, cutting through her obsession with the rule book. Levi *liked* the rules. And most of the time, he liked the comfort they gave him... but for *this* case he was willing to throw the rulebook out of the window. Along with anyone that shoved it in his face. "Just find out where any witnesses are, *then* find me at the crime scene."

The door release clicked as his fingers wrapped around the handle. Levi shoved the door open but stopped just shy of climbing out. He squeezed the steering wheel a little tighter with his other hand, forcing himself to take several deep breaths as he moderated his own rudeness. He wasn't being fair to Addison, and he knew it.

"...Two birds, one stone for the beginning, okay?" He glanced over at her, wincing slightly at the hurt he could see reflected in her eyes. "Look, I get it. You're excited, this could be a big case for you..."

Over the years Levi learned it was best to remain private, but the controversy surrounding him had an insufferably long memory, and he was positive Addison knew all about it by now.

"...but I'm sure you already know what it means to me. So... please."

"Okay..." Addison dropped her gaze and studied the glove compartment in front of her. "Sorry, sir. I'll talk to the witness-es."

He sighed into the awkward silence, nodding once to accept her apology even though he knew damn well it was he who owed one to *her* and not the other way around. "There's no need to apologize Addison."

The words were friendly enough, though Levi made sure he kept it professional. "Let's just see if we can't catch this asshole."

Walking away from her was easier after that. While Addison was right, he was also not wrong. They were not exactly breaking protocol because they were both at the same scene, and since it was already secured by the LAPD, they were safe to walk around without smothering each other.

Levi crossed the lawn, ducked under the yellow crime scene tape, and headed straight for two men wearing uniforms that identified them as employees of the coroner's office. An empty body bag lay crumpled on the ground behind them, the black-colored plastic a stark contrast to the vivid green grass it was resting on. Their trolley was nowhere in sight.

"What've we got?" He flashed his badge and introduced himself to the pair, emphasizing his question by nodding at the body bag on the ground. "Thought there was a body?"

"There is, Agent Malach. We're ahhh... not needed yet."

The pair shared an awkward glance, which made Levi spread both hands in confusion. "...huh?"

"Paramedics are still trying to save her life. I guess the victim got lucky... apparently the one who found her is a doctor."

"No shit?" That surprised him. Nobody *ever* got that lucky. "So where am I headed?"

"Uhhh. The Gunther Depths of Space Hall." The coroner's assistant flicked his thumb toward the van they arrived in, and the ambulance parked next to it. "As far as we know they're still down there."

Hope versus despair.

"Thanks guys, with a bit of luck you're not gonna need that bag... but if this is what I think it is..." Levi's voice trailed off as he turned his head to peer through the open doorway and beyond, into the depths of the observatory. Part of him wanted to race in, to not waste more precious seconds that could be the difference between speaking with a live witness or pulling clues from the body of a dead one. But alongside the eagerness that prodded him to act, there was a large part of the agent that stared through those doors with trepidation... and maybe even a little fear of what he would find when his feet finally remembered how to move.

This was the first time a victim was located so quickly, though not the first in Los Angeles. As far as he knew that morbid honor went to a man found in his penthouse apartment the year before Levi received his assignment to the local field office.

The moment dragged on, and the longer he stared, the more Levi convinced himself that despite the momentary elation he initially felt, the less he *actually* wanted to see the crime scene. A break in his case meant that someone else had lost their life. Someone *else's* family had been ruined... and as much as he wanted things to progress, *nothing* was worth that soul-crushing heartache or the question that so far, had not been answered.

Why?

However, standing in the morning sun with a tortured expression on his face and a wrenching in his heart would not get the case solved. Or get him continued support for the declaration he needed to pursue it openly. And so, after taking a deep breath to bolster himself, Levi headed for the entrance on heavy feet.

"Dammit."

He crossed the threshold, passing out of the heat and into the cool, refreshing air circulating inside the observatory. Walking was the easiest thing in the world, a natural two-step process that put one foot in front of the other and something he had been doing successfully since he was only a year old... but *this*? This felt different. A strange feeling of darkness hovered at the edge of Levi's consciousness as he followed the signs leading him to the crime scene. An awareness he could barely perceive guided his steps, urging him forward when he wanted to pause. Apprehension churned his stomach and clawed into his bones, and as he approached the entrance to the Hall, Levi acknowledged that somehow, today, his life was about to change forever.

Again.

"—can move her now."

"Yes ma'am. Thank the Lord you were here, or we'd have lost her."

"I will admit He *does* work in mysterious ways. She is lucky."

Who... I've heard that voice before.

"Hold up." Levi held out his right hand to stop the paramedics that were leaving the Hall. There was a standard emergency stretcher between them, and they guided it with careful haste toward the elevator that would take them back up to the ground floor. Behind the first paramedic, Levi could see blood seeping through, staining the blanket that covered the patient. His mouth formed a tight line at the sight, but he quickly returned his attention to the woman guiding the stretcher. "This our victim?"

"Yes sir." They wheeled the victim around Levi, but slowed their steps so he could keep pace. The lead paramedic pressed the button to open the elevator doors before turning back to face Levi. "But we *really* need to get her to the hospital. Doc said she won't make it without proper medical care."

"...she awake?" One glance at the stretcher told Levi all he needed to know about the unconscious woman lying on it. He moved to the side to examine her but could see little past the oxygen mask covering the lower half of her face. He wouldn't be getting anything out of her yet. If he ever could at all. "What are her injuries?"

"Three stab wounds to the chest. Collapsed lung. Multiple lacerations and..." The male paramedic swallowed his revulsion, but before he could continue the elevator pinged and they maneuvered the stretcher inside. "...words. Carved into her stomach. Sir, we really need to get moving. The doctor down there can fill you in."

Levi stepped out of their way and waved them off. He could catch up to them later to get their statements, and if he didn't, their police reports would be made available for his case file. The first priority *had* to be allowing them to do everything they could to save the victim, so he concentrated on where they directed him instead.

For a crime scene, it was remarkably neat, though that was at least partially attributed to the pristine location that the victim had been left in. Levi had visited the observatory less than a handful of times, despite living in the area for the past eight years. The Hall was exactly how he remembered it, and he eyed the hanging planets with regret as he started down the stairs into the main area. A bright flash caught his attention when he was halfway down, drawing his eyes to the crime scene technicians and the evidence bags that lay in a neat row along the wall at the bottom of the staircase. He nodded a greeting, but first and foremost in Levi's mind was the witness, and so therefore he put his focus completely on her.

For now.

She stood alone with her back to him, and from the bottom of the stairs all he could see was long, mahogany hair tied in a loose, messy bun on top of her head. It was odd that he noticed it, but nowhere near as odd as the feeling that she had thrown it up there to get it out of the way and promptly forgotten about it. She was shorter than he was, which wasn't hard, given his own stature leveled out at around six foot two... but for some reason Levi immediately noticed *exactly* where the top of her head was in relation to his own height. He cleared his throat as he drew closer, his identification already held loosely in his left hand.

"Ma'am?"

Silence.

The muffled sounds of the crime scene technicians behind him were the only things he heard.

"Ma'am?"

Still, she said nothing, but for some strange reason Levi didn't think he was being deliberately ignored. He frowned and moved to her other side, taking care to tread carefully around the smeared puddle of blood that stained the floor at their feet.

When she *still* didn't acknowledge his presence, Levi followed her line of sight in an effort to make sense of what she was so focused on, but all he could see was the wall. He stared at her for a long, confused second before his gaze shifted back to the wall, his eyes roaming with increasing agitation... but whatever the doctor saw remained a mystery.

A bloody, yet delicate hand rose into Levi's peripheral vision, and without speaking, she pointed a single, slender finger at a small rectangle about halfway up the wall. It was drawn over the top of a cluster of stars, and it was only *then* that Levi registered what he was *really* looking at. His head swiveled from left to right as he reacquainted himself with the image of the galaxy printed along the entire wall.

And then, like a whisper drifting in the wind, he *finally* heard it. But her voice was so quiet he almost missed it.

"Sorry... I didn't—"

"The Big Picture. It's amazing that no matter how much we *think* we can see... it's only ever part of it. I tend to forget that."

Was she rambling? A little unsettled by what she'd just seen?

If so, Levi completely understood, and he would do his best to empathize with her while she gave her statement. He cleared his throat again, his stance a little awkward as he held his badge up level with her eyes, so she had no choice but to see it.

"My name is Levi Malach. I'm with the FBI." Levi folded his badge back into his jacket pocket and waved his hand at the blood on the floor. "If you don't mind, I'd like to ask you a few questions about what happened here."

The silence dragged on for another beat before her voice rose quietly in the Hall.

"I know who you are, Mr Malach. The paramedics asked me to wait for you, but I really should have gone with the patient."

To his investigator's ears, the doctor sounded distant. Perhaps even a little resigned to the other woman's fate even though it was undecided. It was odd, but Levi would swear he heard the slight echo of dismissal in her tone, as though the events of the morning had caused her an inconvenience. However, at the same time Levi was forced to admit there was also sorrow hovering along the edge of her words.

Who are you?

It annoyed Levi to no end that she refused to face him.

Her voice sounded *so* familiar, but for the life of him, Levi could not place where he had heard it before. So gentle, musical, and light... yet delivered with the strength of a hurricane. Levi found himself leaning closer, following a subconscious yearning that blossomed somewhere deep within his soul... somewhere so deep he didn't care to acknowledge it existed. Their shoulders brushed together, and he pulled back with a start, rubbing absently at his jacket as he settled back into his own space again.

What the hell was that?

"Let's start at the beginning, Miss...?"

God, if she would just *turn around,* he *knew* he could place her. It had absolutely no bearing on the case, but it gnawed at Levi just the same. He watched intently as her blood-stained hand dropped against her side and her shoulders rose and fell in a deep sigh. For some reason it gave Levi the impression the doctor was fighting her own battle… and unwilling to face it at the same time. But as much as the agent could, and did, empathize with that feeling, unfortunately Levi didn't have time for it. Nor did the poor woman breathing through a ventilator on her way to whichever emergency room was closest. He opened his mouth to ask *again*, but the words died on his tongue when the enigmatic woman at his side *finally* turned to face him.

The world fell away. Their eyes met under the banner of galaxies and as Levi stared into brilliant amber depths that threatened to swallow him whole, he swore he could hear waves crashing against the granite he had built around his soul.

A flash of late afternoon sunlight reflecting off dark hair. The smell of his own sweat… and a near miss by the ocean rose unbidden in his mind.

I know you.

"You can call me Raphael."

A Fragment

Of all the names Levi thought she might say, *Raphael* was *not* on the list. It would have *never* made the list. Not in a million years. Tennis players were named Raphael. Painters were named Raphael. Hell, even *Ninja Turtles* were named Raphael. Dainty women that rode around on roller-skates and turned up at crime scenes covered in blood were *definitely not* named Raphael. He wanted to ask if what he'd heard was correct, but instead all Levi could manage was a slow blink while his mouth worked silently in an echo of his surprise.

"That's usually the reaction I get..."

He almost missed the faint curve on her lips as she tilted her head and nodded her answer to his silent question. "Sorry. I was just... surprised."

"There is no need to apologize." Her... *Raphael's* smile faded along with the light in her eyes. She wiped at the blood on her hands but gave it up as futile when it all it did was smear red stains across her skin. "My Father was an historian *and* expecting a son."

"I see." He didn't. "You're the woman from the foreshore that ran into me."

"*Almost.* I almost ran into you, Agent Levi Malach... there's a big difference."

"Maybe so..." There it was again. Quick as a flash. For some reason, Levi felt honored, as though what he had just witnessed *twice* was as rare as a benitoite gem and equally as precious. "Do you need us to call anyone to come get you, Miss—uh... *Raphael?*"

To Levi's surprise her name rolled off his tongue and took residence with the same kind of comfort he received when he crawled under his blankets after an exhausting day. But only on the days when it wasn't a reminder of the cold and lonely existence his life had become. He brushed it aside without a thought and slipped his identification back into his pocket, switching sides briefly to retrieve his notepad and an ever-present pen.

"You can use my phone if you..." He glanced at the blood on her hands and shifted gears mid-sentence, willing to help her out, but even more willing to continue with his questions. "...well, I'll hold it so you can talk."

"No..." Raphael's brow creased as though the request sounded odd to her ears. "But thank you Agent Malach, I am fine. What do you want to know?"

"Oh. Okay. Well, let me know if you change your mind. What time did you get here?"

"About 8:30."

Levi made a note before glancing back at her with a raised eyebrow. "It's my understanding the observatory isn't open to the public today... how did *you* get in?"

"I was supposed to be meeting a ...friend." Raphael averted her eyes and examined the statue of Albert Einstein behind them with a little too much interest. "Security let me in."

Security?

"*Friend?* As in, 'sneaking around in an observatory after hours' romantic friend?" Levi felt his left eye twitch. Something about it bothered him. Hell, everything about seeing her *here* bothered him so much he could barely maintain the impassive expression he needed to keep her talking. It left a sour taste in his mouth... and he had no idea why.

"*What?* No! Distant cousin." The rapid denial was satisfying. It came at him laced with fury... and a little disgust, but before Levi could apologize for overstepping, Raphael continued. "I guess she works here, sometimes? I'm sorry to say I'm not sure, Agent Malach."

She paused and tugged at her shirt before looking back at him with troubled eyes. Levi folded his arms across his chest and motioned for her to continue.

"It's much easier to say *friend* than it is to explain the relationship." Raphael shrugged it off as unimportant and moved on without letting him comment. "Her message said she wanted to show me something. But when I got here, I found..."

She raised both hands, palm up and stared at the blood on them like she had never seen it, or even her own fingers before this moment. "...*her* instead."

It was a ridiculous thought. Unless she was in shock. But Levi didn't know that. He didn't know anything... and he got the infuriating impression that was how Raphael wanted it to stay.

"So... you made the 911 call?" Levi made another note to follow up on that, and the lax in security later. With any luck, hearing the emergency call for himself would shed a little light on Raphael's state of mind at the time. From there, he could compare it to the almost unnerving calm she was, for the most part, projecting at him.

"I did. I dialed, put the call on speaker and tried to stop the bleeding."

"Right, right." Levi knew his questions were leading her, but he wanted to hear more than what she said with only her mouth. "And you're a doctor?"

A slow nod was all she gave him. Levi ignored the tightness in his stomach and exhaled as he made yet another note.

"That's right. At UCLA Medical. You're welcome to check."

"I will. And I'll be checking on your *friend*."

A friend that was *just a cousin* that may or may not work at the Observatory and who had arranged to meet someone that just *happened* to be a doctor, who security just *happened* to let in during a murder dump.

Sure.

"Now tell me about the victim."

Raphael grimaced at the resentment in his tone, though she kept all other outward emotions suppressed. Finding the victim bleeding out on the floor had been a gruesome sight, though not the worst she had seen.

Not by a long shot.

"I walked through the main hall…" Agent Malach's questions were exasperating, but the Archangel knew this was part of the human process, part of the tedious steps one had to take when explaining things to beings that meandered through their short lives blinded to the reality of the universe. In truth, she could blow his mind with one simple sentence, but the end result would be counterproductive. And the opposite of blending in. So instead, Raphael played along as duty demanded. "…through the same door you did."

Playing the game was much nicer than thinking he was stupid. However, it was a shame she was about to make things worse for *herself* in the process. And that irritated Raphael enough to make her toes curl. "This is probably all on camera, Agent Malach. Surely you can—"

"I want to hear it from you first." He cut her off with a wave of his hand, then shuffled his feet and relaxed into a less aggressive pose. "The cameras will help, Raphael, but I need your point of view. For the record."

From one end of his sentence to the other, Agent Malach's tone shifted from resentment to something softer. Something more contrite. Raphael took the unspoken apology for what it was and used it to calm her own mind.

"I came down the stairs and... I thought I saw someone kind of half sitting... right here." She spread her fingers at the blood-stained floor at their feet. "...And I thought...I thought it was my cousin. I called out to her, but the lights flicked out and when..."

Raphael trailed off as the memory started replaying in her mind.

Without warning, every single display light blinked out, drowning her in total darkness. Her stomach dropped, her steps becoming hesitant as a quiet shuffling whispered in her ears. One step. Two. And before she could take the third, the lights blazed to life again as if nothing had happened.

But something had.

"When they came back on, she was laying there with... completely naked."

For a heartbeat, her guard dropped, and her voice rang like soft music in his ears. It didn't last long, but those short seconds gave Levi an insight into his witness. Had he not been watching for a break in her story or a chink in her armor, it would have slipped by him completely.

"Tell me about the words." He didn't have to ask what they were. The deepest part of Levi's soul *knew* the horror that was carved into the victim. And it also knew how.

"Such precise cuts." Her brow furrowed at the intensity Agent Malach radiated, but Raphael was comfortable in the healing space, and could give him the clinical responses he required. "Whoever did this needed to keep her completely still. Maybe even unconscious. Unless…"

Another, more shocking thought crossed her mind. "Unless they used a sedative. But who does that to someone?"

Levi felt the blood draining from his face as her meaning clarified in his mind. In a shocking instant his thoughts raced, circling so rapidly he grew dizzy.

What if she had been awake but unable to move? What if…'Belle.

With a determined set to his jaw, Levi wrestled his thoughts back on the present before he spiraled into the past. "Unfortunately, Raphael, this isn't the first time we've seen a case like this."

The heavy weight in Raphael's stomach returned and she rubbed at her forehead to dispel the sudden onset of foreboding that spun through her body from head to toe. "There are *others* like her?"

"I can't say much but… there's an open case."

An open case.

She dropped her hand and took half a step closer before realizing. "How many? Where? Is that why *you're* questioning me and not the LAPD?"

"I'm not at liberty to discuss it." Once again, Levi's suspicions sparked into existence, and he dismissed her questions with a shake of his head. "I'm sorry… you understand."

"Unfortunately, I do." More than he would ever know, Raphael understood the need for secrecy. She plucked at the front of her shirt again and wrinkled her nose in distaste. "Is there anything else you need, Agent Malach? I'd like to go home now."

It would take more than a hot shower to wash the scars of this day from her skin.

"No, I think that's all I need for now, Raphael. Thanks for your time." In a strange way, he meant it, and in a move that was completely out of character for him. Levi slipped a card out of his coat pocket, scribbled on the back of it and held it out for Raphael to take. "Uh... Give me a call if you think of anything else... I put *my* number on the back."

Raphael took the card between two sticky, crimson fingers and tucked it into the back pocket of her jeans without looking at it. It was unlikely that she would volunteer any more information to the agent. Not that there was anything she *could* tell him. As things stood, Raphael was as confused as the human... and that was a bad sign.

"Thank you." Her voice was pensive as she shoved her hands into her pockets to hide them from curious eyes. Giving him one last glance, Raphael turned to leave, but was stalled by a hand tugging on her sleeve. Levi's fingers were gentle, but firm. They filled her sight, curling around her bicep with an unmovable force that had little to do with his physical strength. Bemused at the intrusion, Raphael's eyes wandered, drifting from where his long fingers warmed her skin to his well-shaped arm and higher, where she finally settled on his face. She stared at him in a daze as the heat from his connection to her spread outward and flushed through her body. The sensation was so unfamiliar it removed her ability to speak, and so all Raphael could do was raise an eyebrow to convey her query instead.

"Did your cousin show up?"

"... no." Raphael jerked backwards, pulling her arm free from Agent Malach's gentle grip. She avoided his eyes, her breath shaking as she turned her head back to examine the stunning galactic display lining the wall. With the trance broken, Raphael's mind cleared, though it took her a minute to get the rest of herself under control. It was past time for her to leave, but as her eyes danced from star to star, Raphael decided to give the agent one last nudge.

"That image..."

He deserved that, at least.

"It's only a fragment of the universe. Take care of yourself, Agent Malach."

"What—"

His reaction came too late. Raphael was gone, and Levi could only stare in disbelief at the empty space left behind after she ducked around him, dashed up the stairs and disappeared from sight.

What the hell did that mean?

Five hours later, Levi and Addison waited on uncomfortable chairs in the emergency department while the doctors continued to try and save the victim. They scoured the crime scene, exhausting all avenues in the hopes that *something* would lead to a break in the case. But eventually Levi interrupted the forensic technicians one too many times, and with a mumbled apology collected Addison and headed to the hospital instead.

"I'm going to get a coffee, sir... can I get you one?"

Addison's voice cut through Levi's concentration. He lifted his eyes from the notebook in his hand to nod an enthusiastic yes to her offer. Coffee wouldn't solve *all* his problems, but it would be a good start. "Please. Here."

With deft fingers, Levi plucked a note out of his wallet and handed it to her, idly wondering if he would get to drink this one. And where his reusable cup was. Unfortunately, for Levi, his coffee was doomed to be nothing more than a passing thought, because the moment Addison reached the exit, the double doors to his left swung open and the same surgeon who had asked them to wait several hours prior walked through. Levi didn't miss the blood on his scrubs, or the tired slump to his shoulders. He stood, preparing for the worst, but as the surgeon tugged on his mask and turned to address him, the agent felt a small sliver of hope.

"Agent Malach. Agent Addison."

"Addison!" Levi winced when his voice bounced off the linoleum. It got her attention, but also drew the eye of every other person present. He ignored the disapproving glares and turned back to the surgeon. "Doctor... what news?"

He glanced from Levi to Addison, including her in his response. "If nothing goes wrong, I think she'll make it. We've got a plastic surgeon consulting about the cuts on her abdomen and she's getting a quart of blood now... but she's out of immediate danger."

"Thank God." Levi heaved a sigh of utter relief. *Finally.* They had a live witness. Maybe now, the case would move forward and get the consideration it deserved.

The surgeon snorted. "You can thank the doctor on scene for saving her life. If *she* hadn't been there, you'd be questioning a corpse instead."

"I'm sure she'd be happy to hear it..." Or not. Levi had not quite decided what to think about his witness. "We haven't been able to identify the victim yet. Any idea when she'll wake up?"

The doctor removed his mask completely and balled it in his fist. "We're keeping her sedated for now. It'll probably be morning before she's in any shape to talk. Could be later. I'll call you directly if anything changes."

"Sure... I'm going to set a guard, but do you mind if we take her fingerprints? Might help speed up the identification process."

After a hesitant beat, he nodded. "Yeah, yeah, no problem. Nothing invasive though, okay? Just fingerprints. Her clothing and anything else we found is already on the way to your forensic lab."

"Not my first rodeo, doc. We'll be careful, I promise."

The doctor retreated through the doors, but before they could swing shut, Levi grabbed one and held it open for Addison to pass through. He accepted his money back when she offered it, crumpling it into his pocket with a resigned sigh.

They walked in relative silence, with Levi focusing more on the mild headache behind his eyes and his notepad than the agent he had been partnered with. The entire day bothered him. From the moment Wilson waylaid him in the corridor to now, and *everything* in between. Even his witness seemed a little... off. A little suspicious. But for the life of him Levi could not put his finger on why. She answered his questions easily enough. And with detail... once she'd started talking. But there was no escaping the suspicion that no matter how forthcoming Raphael *had* been, she was holding something back.

And if Raphael was holding something back... then that could mean she was more than *just* a witness.

Lost in a Memory

With a sigh that bordered on melancholy, Levi slumped down into the chair at his desk and ran tired fingers through his dark hair. He needed to configure his latest report, but so far, the right words eluded him. Upon their return to the office, he'd submitted both the victim's fingerprints and photographs for analysis and settled in to wait for the FBI database to find a match. Waiting was nothing unusual. Searches like that often took hours, if not days, depending on the search area, and given they had nothing but basic information about the woman lying in intensive care, the search parameters remained wide. Nobody matched her description in the local missing persons database, so the only option left was to wait.

So far, the only satisfying thing about *that* was that Levi had *finally* gotten his coffee fix. And a little to eat besides. Crumbs from his muffin lay scattered on his desk. It had been delicious, if a little stale, but was nowhere near enough to sate the rumbling in his stomach. However, it filled a gap and would suffice until he was finished for the day. Then maybe he could head home to dig through his fridge for the leftovers he'd forgotten to bring in yet *again*.

An hour passed. Levi stopped typing and leaned back in his chair, tilting it just enough to stare at the ceiling. His tie was askew, loosened a while back when the frustration at the details he was missing floated to the surface.

What am I missing? Why can't I see it?

Part of him knew he was too close to the investigation to see things clearly. But Levi couldn't let it go. He just could not get the image of the woman in hospital out of his head, or the similarities he *instantly* noticed between her and Annabelle. Same hair. Same eye colour. Hell, they even had the same *build*. It was uncanny, and though he fought hard against it, nothing could stop the path that his mind chose to wander down. He chewed on his lip, closed his eyes, and started counting off the usual tools he developed for times like this when he started to sink. As always, Levi held out the hope that maybe *just this once* he could avoid the inevitable. But as always, it was an exercise in futility. Memories of Annabelle were *especially* close today, and on the days when she hovered like a ghost there was little Levi could do to escape his own mind. Not when it was actively working against him.

Being alone with them was the hardest part, though he preferred it to any alternative. The nights were long, even when he buried himself in his work. Or occasionally, the bottom of a bottle. Relentless to the point of torture, the memories that flashed through Levi's mind did nothing to ease the pain of her passing... or the guilt about how *useless* he'd been that day. How *slow*.

His chest tightened, squeezing around his hammering heart while the fingernails on one hand dug trenches into his palm. Levi inhaled, his breath accelerating despite his efforts to slow it. This one would be bad.

If only he had moved faster.

According to the coroner's report, Annabelle died at *least* thirty minutes before she was found, and the call came in... but Levi still shouldered the despair.

What if there was a doctor present, like today's victim had? What if...

What if...

It started out the same as any other day in the medium-sized town Levi grew up in. Normal, except that it was the day of the annual church fete, an event always held, ironically, on the spring equinox. It was one of the town's signature events, with months of planning and effort going into every year. They had bands playing, carnival rides, food trucks showcasing local produce, a dance hall, a baby animal farm, pony rides... If the town could think of it, and fit the idea in, it became part of the festival.

Provided it was God-fearing, of course.

Levi was never really as devoted as the rest of his family. Sure, he believed in God and Heaven and everything else. With a father who led the biggest congregation in town, how could he not? He believed; he just didn't think God needed to know about every detail of his life. He was a good, obedient son and grew into a good, obedient man.

What did it matter to anyone if he had a physical romantic relationship with his girlfriend? He did the right thing and proposed when she announced was pregnant, like any good man would.

But for some residents in town, that was not enough.

For the most part, Levi ignored them, focusing on what really mattered instead, his growing family and ability to provide for them. Two months prior to the fete, Levi applied to the FBI academy with confidence that he aced the entrance questions, but since turnaround time for acceptance or rejection was up to three months, he had some time up his sleeve.

Time he spent studying as many FBI cases as he could access, and ensuring he was physically fit. That part wasn't too strenuous. Levi ran on the track team at high school and during college, and as a result, sported a lean muscular frame that was well suited to his six-foot-two body. He kept himself in shape with regular five-mile runs through the woods outside of town and supplemented that with a weight set Annabelle surprised him with for his last birthday.

He used it that morning before heading into the police station, eager to start his day. In that town, an early day meant he could wrap up early and join his family at the fete for some grilled corn and fireworks.

"Levi..." Someone called his name, but Levi didn't hear it in the present. He couldn't. The memories were far too vivid, and he was trapped.

The call came in at quarter to three, right before his shift was due to end. Levi heard the dispatch coming weakly through the speaker in the other room. The volume was low, and he had to pause his own typing and tilt his head to hear the thin, tinny voice as the call repeated.

"...deceased female at the fairground. Behind the animal farm. All available units respond."

Levi never remembered getting to the fairground. Later, when he went to search for his car, he wouldn't find it. All he could remember was shoving his way through the gathered crowd with fear circling a pit in his stomach. This was his hometown... murders weren't common and usually happened by accident. People were nice here. But this... He noticed a few people giving him startled glances, and not a few stepped back with terror in their eyes, as though they weren't sure what he was doing there.

And then, his father was there with his strong hand gripping down on his shoulder, his distressed voice telling him to leave it for the other detectives.

That only goaded him further, and in somewhat of a daze, Levi kept forcing his way through, shaking off his dad's hand as he pressed forward.

He remembered screaming when he saw her lying there with her skirt askew and her favorite shirt sliced cleanly down the middle. Long, caramel hair fell over her face as though she were sleeping... but her eyes. Her eyes told him otherwise. They were wide with the horror of her death. Sightless. The cornflower blue irises locked forever in an accusing stare at the clouds above.

At the Heavens she so fervently believed in.

"Levi!" Again, the voice came, but there was no way out for Levi. There never was. Not until he had seen it right to the very end. Even if he *wanted* to respond, he was trapped. Paralyzed against even opening his eyes to tell whoever it was to go away.

"Belle? No... Nononono!" Levi looked around, screaming a useless summons for paramedics as he dropped to his knees to check her pulse. But it was too late. He was too late. Belle was gone, and with his heart shattering into thousands of pieces, Levi placed his hand over her face and closed her beautiful eyes. Locked in his grief, he shouted for the other officers to clear the crowd away, demanding a last drop of privacy for his dead fiancé. Her entire torso was on display, though her small breasts remained hidden by her bra. The gentle swell of her stomach was obvious in the shadows cast by the afternoon sun, her rounded abdomen hinting how far along in the pregnancy she was. Resting his hands on her expanding stomach to speak to their child was his favorite thing to d o.

And now, that action was forever out of reach.

Now, her body was forever marred. Mutilated with ugly, bloody red slashes that cut her from rib cage to pubis. The words, when he could bear to read them, would remain permanently etched into his mind and turn him away from the very religion that he once found comfort in.

The Angels made me do it.

Out of the corner of his eye, Levi saw something curled in her fingers, which were half tucked under her stiffening body. Being careful not to disturb any evidence, he leaned closer and saw her phone clutched in lifeless fingers. His whole body started to shake. He knew what he would find... and sure enough, there it was. Two unanswered calls to his phone, dialed around the time of her death... when he was rushing through his paperwork with his phone on silent.

It was perhaps ironic that when Levi eventually returned to his now-lonely apartment that his acceptance letter from the FBI sat propped up on the coffee table with one of Annabelle's smiley faces drawn on the envelope in bright green ink.

He was still furious. He clearly remembered multiple screaming matches with his father, the town's faith leader, whose useless words of consolation did *nothing* to bring her back. Furious with his family *and* hers for taking the coward's way out and suggesting it was God's will because Annabelle fell pregnant out of wedlock. In the end, it was his family's attitude that drove Levi to the academy, and even now, ten years later, he returned only once. His mother begged, and against his better judgement, Levi relented... but Christmas ended in much the same way Annabelle's funeral had. With Levi sitting alone in his misery, waiting for the end.

Yes, he was angry. But for the most part, Levi directed his simmering fury at God himself, *and* his Angels... if he *existed* then he didn't care about his creations. And if he didn't care, then he could go straight to his own Hell. *Fuck him.*

A few years after her death, Levi tried dating again, but one disastrous date after another left him wrung out and teetering on a mental knife edge he didn't want to dance on. No matter what, he could not escape what happened to Annabelle, and couldn't stop thinking about her whenever he looked at somebody new.

So, he stopped looking.

Well-meaning colleagues tried, but Levi refused all offers to be set up. Letting go of Annabelle was one thing. But getting past her gruesome death and the intangible evidence that linked her with other unsolved cases that kept her at the front of his mind was quite another... and Levi had done neither.

No, Levi was still far too damaged, still blaming himself for her death too much to wish an end to his lonely existence by sharing his never-ending misery on another person.

By the time Levi's anxiety faded enough for him to regain control, the surrounding offices were dark and one glance out of the window to his right let him know the sun had long since set. He rocked his chair forward and stood, groaning when exhaustion rolled through him with the force of a tsunami. Ignoring the fatigue as best he could, Levi raised his hands in a stretch, but it ended in a drawn-out yawn, regardless. The hour was too late for his usual run along the foreshore, even though it would clear his mind and loosen the tightness in his body. His treadmill would have to suffice. It was a good investment but didn't replace the people he met. He rarely stopped to engage in conversation, but knowing they existed made all the difference.

Lamenting his run brought Levi's mind to the strange woman who *had* run into him on her roller skates a few days before. And how she ended up at his crime scene just in time to save the life of a woman left for dead.

Suspicious.

He remembered her before that of course. But there was something about her that had given him pause, making her stand out in his mind for reasons he just could not fathom. Something about the sadness in her eyes. Something about... *her.*

It was late, but nevertheless Levi checked his report and the status of the identification inquiry before he shut down his computer. He grunted sourly when no added information appeared and picked up the jacket he didn't remember removing. Levi shuffled out of his office on tired feet, emotionally drained and ready for the oblivion of sleep.

On his way to the elevator, he noticed a dim light coming from beyond the meeting room door and stuck his head through the opening to check for occupants. Staying late was not uncommon, but the room was empty. Paper lay strewn across the table, remnants of a meeting he missed. A vague memory of someone calling his name surfaced, and with a curious tilt of his head, Levi approached the table and scanned the papers. An updated version of Interpol's most wanted list sat on top, but it wasn't the list itself that had Levi's brows furrowing together in concern.

Right there, at number four were several images of a man who looked awfully familiar to the exhausted agent, and Levi felt his insides clench when recognition dawned.

"Oh no..."

He talked to him the day before. There was no mistaking that build, the dark hair or the distinct, inch long scar on his right cheek. He mouthed his name silently, however the curse that erupted was anything but.

Rian Murphy.

"Son of a bitch."

Revelations

Rian regained consciousness with a start, jerking into wakefulness with the energy of a man who just had a bucket of ice thrown over him. He gasped, twisting his body so he could sit up from where his body was dumped like a sack of potatoes. At first, all he could see was darkness, but a sliver of light filtered down from a window set high on the opposite side of wherever he was and created enough shadow for him to make a quick assessment. His eyes scanned left and right, picking out the vague shape of a staircase rising out of the floor along one wall.

"Don't bother trying to escape."

A voice drifted out of the darkness. Feminine. Determined. But to Rian's trained ears it was also tinted with agitation. The assassin turned his head in her direction, trying to pick her exact location out of the darkness as he rolled his shoulders in an unconcerned shrug. "Probably pretty pointless at this stage, wouldn't you say?"

"You're smarter than you look."

Rian detected a lilt of curiosity in her tone. He huffed out a breath, shifting into sarcasm while he assessed his situation. "I get that a lot."

A heavy pause followed, after which he heard a shuffling sound, like something was being pushed out of the way. Like furniture. Or a fridge. It could even be another body for all he knew.

Damn it, boss. Sending me on a mission like this. What the fuck were you thinking?

"I have a job for you, assassin. If you say no, I'll kill you."

Light flooded the room. Rian flung up a hand to shield his eyes, blinking the bright spots away while they adjusted to the sudden change.

"But I *might* kill you anyway... you deserve it."

Rian took in everything at once. He was in a basement, presumably *hers*, and she had secured his left leg to a support post in the middle of the room. At a glance he could tell it was a simple knot a boy scout could undo, but even though his head still swam from the impact, Rian wasn't stupid. It was *definitely* part of her trap.

"I've heard that before too." He was right in the assumption that a staircase lined the far wall, and about the window... but what astounded Rian was how *nice* the room was, in general. Not a speck of dust existed on the large pale grey tiles covering the floor. The walls were an ethereal white, reflecting the floors in the cool light. There was a comfortable looking couch facing a television that hung above a fireplace. A deep red rug drew his eye to a counter that looked suspiciously like a bar with a doorway beyond. It was stylish, and it was perfect.

"You're not wrong. But not for the reasons you think." Perfection aside, Rian suspected that if he looked closer, the price tags would still be attached to everything. He *also* suspected that the absent dust didn't dare go against whoever this... un-killable woman was.

"I don't care, *assassin*. All I care about—"

He tugged on the rope for effect, ignoring how the knot slipped with almost no effort, then turned his head to look at her.

"It's Rian."

"What?"

"My name, darlin'. If I'm to be doing a job for *you*, I'd prefer you used my name." The lie rolled off his tongue with ease. In truth, Rian was unsettled by the growing need to comply with her wishes. Not once in his morally grey career had he *ever* given a target his real name. But right now, despite his reluctance, the one his mother gave him slipped through loose lips.

He smirked as a frustrated grunt sounded low in her throat, but it quickly disappeared when she moved in close and yanked him to his feet with another burst of that hidden strength he would never get used to. If he lived long enough to even try. "It's only polite, love. Care to tell me yours?"

Anger washed over her face. Rian recognized the pure fury in her icy blue eyes. He had seen something similar in the mirror.

"You mean to tell me..." she chewed the words through gritted teeth, her entire body quivering with barely suppressed rage. "That you took a contract to kill me, and *you don't even know who I am?*"

"Not a clue. I just go where I'm pointed." As much as Rian tried to pretend none of this was bothering him, the nonchalant front was slipping. He was still shaken, still coming to terms with how this woman had gotten up and *attacked* him *after* he loaded her with bullets. "That's not how this works. I just do the job."

"Useless *idiot*." She hissed and pushed him away, clutching at her stomach instead when fresh blood seeped through her blouse.

"Now, miss—"

"*Envy*."

"...what?" The façade dropped. Rian pulled backwards out of her reach and reached up to massage his temple.

She swayed, body wavering as her hand slapped down on the support beam holding her would-be assassin captive. Being alive was one thing. Recovering was quite another, and even someone like Envy needed time. "It's *my* name, you simpleton."

"Envy... like a Sin." Ice crept into Rian's veins, and he snorted in disbelief. "Uh-huh, *sure* you are."

"The *one* and only. I'd bow, but" the fingers covering her stomach flexed, drawing his eye. "...y'know."

With visible effort, Envy took a few steps back to where she left Rian's gun and trained it on him. "And that's exactly what you're going to help me with. Turn around."

He complied but kept her in his line of sight when he looked where she directed. The bench he spotted earlier was easier to see from a standpoint, but what interested Rian was the sheet folded neatly on top and the small tray decorated with surgical tools.

Great.

"*This* is the job you want me to do? A little counterproductive, don't you think, love?" Rian ambled over to the table like it was his choice to be there, testing the rope around his ankle with every step. Even after reaching the counter, he had plenty of room to move, proving in his mind that it was more symbolic than anything else.

A test.

Like the bomb she dropped on him about her alleged identity.

Not a chance he was going to entertain that possibility. It just wasn't possible.

Envy? She must be insane.

Of course, insanity on *her* part did not explain why she wasn't a corpse. And *that* left him with limited options. Rian rubbed his temple again and ground his teeth when his fingers brushed at the tender spot above his ear. The bump on the head knocked his senses loose and now he was ready to be committed. Unless he was dreaming. Yeah, that made more sense than a walking, talking Sin. But since she was the one holding the gun, and had already bested him once, Rian thought it prudent to play his part.

"Are you always this annoying?" Envy dug the muzzle into his spine and shoved him out of the way. Her hands trembled as she spread the sheet out, but there was no hiding the grimace of agony when she hauled herself onto the countertop. Self-healing came naturally to her. Usually. The bullets currently implanted in her stomach and chest were impeding her body's processes though, and for that she needed the idiotic human to help.

It was him, or one of those holier-than-thou Archangels. Envy would rather die than ask for one of those fools for help.

By an odd twist of Fate, Envy could touch the same power source the Archangels could. But where they described it as sliding into a gentle current or a warm embrace, for her it was like swimming against rapids during a raging flood. While wrestling a shark.

It resisted her. It resisted her *every single time* she used it, and the aftermath left her weaker than a newborn kitten. When she coupled drawing on such power with five bullet wounds and a pint or two of missing blood, Envy was in no mood to deal with a human *or* his smart mouth. She cocked the gun at Rian from her makeshift operating table and bared her teeth.

"And stop calling me *love* or I'll shoot you for my own entertainment."

"Of course, love. Whatever you want, this is your rodeo." Rian was smart enough to keep his smile hidden, though turned his face out of her line of sight, just in case. He busied himself moving the surgical tools out of her way and had just lifted the scalpel to inspect the edge when he felt cold steel digging into his neck. "Sorry. Bad joke."

"Just get the fucking bullets out so I can heal, *Rian*." Envy leaned back on her elbows, her face contorting as one of the bullets shifted in her abdomen. She pushed Rian feebly as he moved without warning and slipped his right arm beneath her back to ease her descent to the counter.

Go.

Now would be the best time to incapacitate her and make his escape. He could be out the door and gone before she had the energy to raise herself back off the bench again. But with the mention of her name, Envy opened a door that Rian could not close, and therefore he surprised them both when he picked up a small pair of scissors and wiped them with disinfectant.

What are you?

"Bold of you to assume I know how to remove a bullet, *Miss Envy*." His eyes flicked to the staircase, then back to Envy. Anticipation dripped from her like the blood that leaked from her wounds. She was waiting for him to make his move. And that made Rian even more cautious.

Why would someone want to kill you?

He was a fool to stay. A large part of Rian wanted to put this entire fiasco in his rear-view mirror and be done with it. But if he did that the answers would *never* come, and his questions left hanging forever.

Who would want to kill you?

Is this relevant to...

So many of them lingered... including the most important one: *why send him?* Did they know who she was? Or *what?* Did his employer?

"You're an *assassin*, Rian. Or at least I'm assuming you are." When gave her a tight nod, Envy continued. "Whatever you were *before* this, you at least learned enough to keep yourself out of hospitals *now.*"

Rian remained silent, but all that did was confirm Envy was right.

"Armed forces or intelligence?"

Don't answer. She's a nutter.

"Army." Rian fought hard, but that same strange compulsion to speak eventually overrode his resistance. "Irish special forces. We call it the ARW... and you're right. I was actually a field medic. Among other things."

He sliced her blouse right down the middle with precise snips before gently parting the fabric from where it adhered to her stomach. Blood still seeped out of the bullet holes he made earlier. Rian couldn't help but admire his handiwork. Four precise shots. All deadly.

And yet...

"Quit staring at my tits and get on with it."

"I wasn't—"

Envy jammed the gun into his side again, but this time her only reward was a scowl from Rian as he took hold of her wrist in surprisingly gentle fingers and placed it by her side.

"You're a woman that likes to be admired, Miss Envy... and for the most part, I'm just a man."

"*Just a man* who put four bullets in my heart."

She tried to lift it again, but Rian held it firmly against the counter, his eyes flashing in momentary anger.

"You want me to do this? Keep still. That means no poking me with that fecking gun until I'm done, understand?" Rian picked up a small dish and set it down on the taut skin below her navel. The situation was weird, and he understood why she was so prickly, but he had no interest in getting shot to satisfy one of her whims. "I know my handiwork, Miss Envy. I *know* where I put those bullets. Moving around is only going to make it worse."

With another warning glare, Rian picked up the forceps and lifted them into her line of sight. "You want something to bite down on before I start?"

"I don't trust you, assassin." Much to her dismay, Envy's voice shook. Laying exposed like this made her feel way too vulnerable. And this smart mouthed assassin was not helping. Nor was he very... compliant. His mental blocks impressed her... but she would never admit *that* either. "Just get on with it."

"Yeahhh love, the feeling is mutual. But here we are." With her final approval Rian's hesitation evaporated, and he dug the forceps into the first wound. To her credit, Envy remained silent as he probed her insides. At one point her back arched off the table, but Rian's firm hand on her shoulder kept her in place.

"Feck. *Got it.*" Rian stared at the second hole and the fresh blood that obscured it. Dropping the bullet in the dish, he scrambled for the cloth lining the tray holding the surgical tools and held it against her stomach. "You're bleeding too much. I need to—"

"Keep going." The hand furthest from Rian reached blindly, seeking anything it could hold. Envy breathed hard, her teeth clenching through the black hole of pain that radiated out from her stomach. Her vision swam, and she clawed her way through closing darkness, only barely registering when Rian leaned into her line of sight and tapped her on the cheek.

"Stay awake Miss Envy. Here."

She blinked, immobilized as he disappeared again and the warmth from his hands left her body. Footsteps sounded on the tiles, and something clattered behind her, but before Envy could find her voice Rian was back again with a small towel held in his hand.

"This is all I can find. Bite it."

"*Nnnngg.*"

Asshole. He didn't even give her a chance to reply before he shoved the cloth between her teeth and resumed the task she forced him into. Envy grunted around it as the forceps probed her insides again, but just as soon as she resigned herself to the pain, he was hovering above her again. A warm weight leaned on her arm, soft, yet unyielding and Envy tried to focus on that instead of the searing agony in her stomach.

"You said you'd heal, right? Just nod." With her confirmation, Rian chewed his lip and drew his eyebrows together before vanishing yet again.

"I wish you had a clamp. It would be easier." Against his better judgment, Rian began to ramble. "Despite what you think, I don't actually *like* killing. Not that it matters. *Feck.*"

The forceps slipped off a bullet, sending a fresh pulse of blood onto Envy's stomach. Rian dropped a cotton pad onto her skin with another muttered curse and refocused on the rogue lump of metal. "A job is a job, y'know? The army made us kill people too. *Apparently,* that's different."

The longer he spoke, the more pronounced his accent became. Rian noticed the slide, but his interest in keeping Envy awake overrode any desire to hide his origins.

Or so he thought.

He glanced at her face and was surprised to see her alert and watching him as intently as ever. Rian realized his mistake, but there was little he could do to backtrack. In fact, Rian had the strangest desire to say more. "My ma would say you drank way too much of the black stuff Miss Envy. But I won't tell her if you won't."

Another bullet rattled into the dish, followed quickly by the rest. Envy exhaled heavily through the towel when Rian swapped the forceps for a needle and thread.

"Just gonna stitch these up, then I'll get the bonus one out of your leg."

She tried to spit out the towel, but the jerk jammed it in tight, so Envy simply nodded instead. For someone who was effectively her prisoner, threatened at gunpoint and forced to undo the damage he had done... the assassin sure was cheerful enough. It made little sense. But then, Envy rarely thought about anything except getting her own way. And once again, she had.

But it came at a cost... and she didn't know what price there would be to pay for his help.

Sewing up the damage took less time than removing the bullets, and when Envy heard the one in her leg hit the bowl, she raised the gun with one hand and removed the towel with the other. "Thank you... Now—"

Rian raised an eyebrow, nodded his acceptance, and backed one step away from the counter with both hands raised. He wasn't ready to die. Not when so many *questions* still clouded his mind, but if today was the day he met the reaper, so be it.

He had tried.

"In the head if you please Miss Envy. Don't drag it out."

Envy toyed with him and raised the gun level with his chin. The muzzle brushed against skin, but rather than press harder, she dragged the point slowly up to his ear and back down again. Oh, she wanted to pull that trigger and give him a taste of his own medicine. But like Rian, Envy had her own inner voice telling her to hold back. Usually she ignored the pesky, *do-gooding* nag that bothered her thoughts, but today it tugged on her with more force than normal, and so today, much to her annoyance, Envy decided to listen.

She spun the gun and offered it back to him with an impatient roll of her eyes. "Don't be so dramatic. Help me up. I'm thirsty."

Rian blinked at Envy and dropped his hands, taking the gun from her in the process. His schooled his features in an effort to hide his surprise. And his relief. Maybe he would live to see another day. "You should lay still for a while. Don't pull the stitches. I'll get you a drink."

What was happening?

Despite the countertop, there was no sink where he could see it. "Back in a sec." Rian kicked out with his tied leg and knocked the rope free. With a smirk hovering on his lips, he took another step back before turning away. He jogged to the stairs and took them two at a time, pausing at the top to gather his bearings. If memory served him correctly, he had surfaced near the back of Envy's house and the kitchen lay directly opposite. He passed through the archway and headed to the fridge, snatching a bottle of chilled water from an immaculately organized interior before the overwhelming urge to run could dominate his thoughts.

"So. You didn't run." Envy was still struggling to sit up despite his request. Or in spite of. As if she was going to let a human that had tried to *murder* her tell her what to do. Idiot.

Who does he think he is?

"I'm impressed."

Rian snorted sarcastically and held out the water bottle the same way he presented her wine before the night had fallen to pieces. "I'm sure you can imagine I have questions."

Envy froze, her gaze locked on the bottle in his hand as several things about her would-be-assassin clicked into place in quick succession. Pale blue eyes flew to Rian's face as recognition finally dawned. "You're the *fucking waiter*."

"I was wondering when you'd figure that out." Rian set the water bottle down with a rueful grin and moved to the end of the counter. He was still suspicious, still not convinced Envy wasn't a little insane. Or that she wouldn't shoot him out of spite. Given what he knew of Sins from the bible... Rian would not be surprised.

"You're *so* lucky I'm still in pain Rian or I'd..." Envy gave up on trying to sit and flopped back down on the counter with a disgruntled moan. She slapped her hand down on the water bottle, curling her fingers around the plastic.

How could this happen?

It had been years since anyone made an attempt on her life. *Centuries* since anyone got as close as Rian did... so why would she need to be more alert than she already was? "You're a fucking asshole."

"That's well established. Do you need me for anything else or should I just go sit in the corner?"

He was so *infuriating*.

"Leave me alone, *assassin*." Envy covered her face with her right arm, effectively dismissing him from her presence. It was bad enough Rian witnessed her weakened state, even if he *was* the one responsible for it. He didn't need to see anything else.

She didn't want him to.

"Get the fuck out of my house."

Silence followed. And then Envy heard an exasperated sigh followed by footsteps that gradually receded as Rian, the assassin she had set free *finally* complied with her subtle compulsion without his mysterious, maddening resistance.

Good riddance.

The only problem that remained was figuring out who sent him after her in the first place... and why.

The Dagger

So much for finishing the job by midnight.

By the time Rian left Envy's house in his rear-view mirror to slink back to base the sun was slipping below the horizon. He could clearly remember the last time he looked at a clock... and at that time, the sun was shining down on the *opposite* side of the planet.

In short, Rian lost almost an entire day in that strange house with the strange woman who was somehow immune to his bullets... and he *still* didn't know why. Well, he *did*. Envy *had* given him an explanation. Rian just did *not* want to admit it was possible.

The only thing Rian *had* known as certain as he sped down the freeway, squinting at his reflection with quick, agitated glances for signs of pursuit, was that his employer was waiting for an update. That one-word confirmation the job was complete, and Rian successfully fulfilled yet another contract. It was a straightforward process; one he navigated his way through more times than he cared to remember.

... though the end result was an ever-changing number Rian could *never* forget.

It was easier for him to deal with numbers. Numbers were just that. *Numbers* didn't stare back at him or bring him grief. Numbers didn't shake his resolve. Numbers would never take away the reasons why Rian set his feet on *this* path and not one of the others that branched out in front of him years earlier when his commanding officer handed him final discharge papers from the *Sciathán Fianóglach an Airm*.

But perhaps most importantly, *numbers* didn't ask him *why*.

Well... until now. And it was *this* number that Rian could not reconcile. Or move on from until he delivered his report.

Almost a week later Rian still struggled to come to terms with it. *Nobody* got up from that many bullets at point blank range. *Especially* when he was the one firing the shot.

Four bullets. Five, if he counted the petty leg shot. The sight of her standing there drenched in her own blood with an outstretched hand while she casually tossed him into a wall never left Rian's mind.

It was the strangest thing he had ever seen. —*Second strangest.*

Never mind that in her anger, Envy revealed the possibility of *others*, which, in turn, sent Rian's mind spiraling down a black hole of mind-numbing possibility that ended with the horrific realization that maybe *something*, somewhere also counted his numbers.

The implication of failure also loomed heavily over Rian, effectively immobilizing him from taking any further action. How could he report 'mission failed' when his success was determined before it even started?

How could he do that, and not end up at the wrong end of a deal made with the next person in line to take his place?

A knock at the door made Rian flinch, pulling him abruptly from his meandering thoughts. He made it abundantly clear to the hotel staff he was not to be disturbed... so whoever stood on the other side was either an employee... or something else. And in Rian's line of work, *something else* usually meant a bullet.

"Mister Duncan?"

Rian's shoulders dropped in relief when he heard his alias called through the closed door. It washed through him like water from a burst pipe but didn't stop him from creeping to where his Heckler & Koch lay on the bed. He checked the safety and approached the door, sidestepping the frame to lean against the wall beside it. Only a novice would look through the peephole, and Rian left that status behind long ago. The gun brushed against his denim-clad thigh, but Rian raised it in a heartbeat when he heard the lock disengage from the opposite side.

"Room service!"

Nope.

A cheerful masculine voice accompanied the cautious widening of the door as it slowly opened. Rian remained hidden from sight, only stepping forward to reveal himself after the attendant fully entered the room.

Click.

The sound of the safety releasing echoed like a thunderclap in the silence. Rian dug the muzzle into the back of the shorter man's head, prodding him to move forward and then kicked the door shut behind him.

"I didn't order room service."

To his credit, or perhaps his foolishness, the man at the wrong end of Rian's gun didn't flinch.

"It's on the house." Still, he didn't move. Not even when Rian shoved hard enough to leave a mark. He didn't even raise his hands. Or seem startled.

A thousand cold spiders ran carefree over Rian's body. From head to toe, his skin crawled, and the warning that began as a murmur roared to life. "Whatever it is I don't want it."

"Come on, Mister *Duncan*, you *really* shouldn't look a gift horse in the mouth."

It was surreal hearing the man's tone switch from the almost bored employee to somewhat amused. Rian ground his teeth together as he fought to control the spiders, but they raced over his skin regardless. The gun jerked slightly in his hand, but he covered it up with a dismissive snort and tried to ignore the chill that swept through his soul. "... Never really into horses."

"Now now... I *know* that's a lie."

"You don't know anything about me."

"I know that village you were born in is *enchanting* this time of year. In Mayo, the county, wasn't it?"

All at once the lingering boredom in the fake attendant's tone shifted pure delight. There was no way Rian could miss the threat when it all but smacked him over the head.

What the fuck?

Rian froze. His stomach clenched, and the ice invaded him entirely. Only the faint hope that the other man was bluffing kept him from acting without thought. He jabbed at his head without mercy, his lips curling into a sneer.

"You've got about five seconds to start talking. Who the *fuck* are you?"

Rian could not believe it when, instead of begging for his life, the strange man started *laughing*.

"Put your gun away and *I'll* let *you* explain why you're hiding in this room instead of completing your mission. A mission you're being *well paid* for, if I do say so myself."

...And just like that, *everything* changed. Rian's vision narrowed, and nothing existed except for the chuckling man standing *way* too comfortably in front of him. Every sense that Rian had *screamed* at him to run, but the words echoed in his mind, sprouting roots from his feet where there were none. He was immobilized. Stuck. Well and truly outmaneuvered. But Rian was nothing if not resourceful, and with one final, *petty* jab, he lowered his gun and stalked around the intruder.

"Jim..." Unbelievable.

He smiled like a proud father at Rian and inclined his head. "So they say."

A large part of Rian wondered why he wasn't already a dead man. He didn't relax at the friendly tone Jim offered, nor did he believe he was anywhere *near* safe. In fact, now that he knew who the man was, Rian was not sure he would ever feel safe again. He leaned back slightly, jerking his chin forward in an abrupt nod.

"Y'know, you should have led with that."

"And ruin your fun? Mister Murphy, you need to lighten up. Now..."

Rian could only watch with disbelieving eyes as the one known as Jim invited himself over to the small kitchen area where a bottle of Irish whiskey sat by the kettle. Without bothering to look to Rian for permission, he poured himself two fingers and strolled over to the armchair by the window. He lowered himself into it and crossed one ankle over his knee, motioning for Rian to come closer.

"Boy... *why* isn't your assignment complete? It isn't like you to keep me waiting."

"Ahh..." He was well into adult years, but Rian let the *boy* part slide. Although he refused to admit it, Rian was more than a little perturbed, and way too shaken to argue the point. He had *never* heard of Jim getting personally involved with one of his hired hands. Hell, until a few moments ago, Rian had no idea what he looked like. *Nor did he care.* All he wanted was autonomy, and with it, the ability to work on his personal agenda by tapping into the contacts he made while on assignment... and so far, things had gone smoothly. Maybe a little *too* smoothly.

Rian tucked the gun into the back of his jeans while he considered his response.

"...not gonna lie to you, sir. I put four bullets in her, point blank. Then she got up and threw me across the room like I'd shot her with a fecking pellet gun filled with thoughts and prayers. So I shot her *again*. And she got up. *Again*. Can't say I've ever had *that* happen before... so."

"So, what you're saying is..." Jim leaned forward, his eyes strangely intent as they pinned Rian in place. "...you missed."

Rian noted the lack of surprise shown by his employer. Another warning whispered in his mind, but Rian was too offended by the suggestion that he *missed* to pay attention to it.

"No, I'm *saying* you sent me after some kind of..." Rian waved his empty hand in the air in front of him. He hadn't moved far, even before the glare stalled him. Just enough to keep Jim in his line of sight. "I keep thinking, maybe she was high. That could explain it. Adrenalin kept her going... I've seen soldiers survive worse."

Only Rian knew it was a lie. He witnessed with his own eyes what Miss Envy had done... and how quickly she turned the tables on him.

What he truly needed was time. Time to get the answers she refused to give him, and time to figure out what the Hell was going on. To achieve that, Rian needed to stall. Again. But *that* was not possible with Jim himself hovering in his base of operations.

"Job's not over, sir. Not until she's dead." He finally found his feet again, and this time Rian managed to cross the room to better plead his case. "I'm just gonna have to be a little more... *inventive*, that's all. Besides, the longer I stay away, the more relaxed she'll become. Remember Antwerp?"

For the longest moment Rian was convinced he messed up. Asking for more time was risky, but not unheard of. An unmonitored target could do anything from warning the authorities to hiring a counterstrike. Not to mention it was unprofessional. Rian knew how this part of the underground sector of society operated. Second chances were rare.

"I remember." To Rian's surprise, Jim nodded in agreement. "Not to worry, son. I've got what you need. Here."

At some unspoken signal, Rian's door opened again, and a man nearly a foot taller and twice as wide as Rian stalked in holding a small black leather suitcase in his right hand. He set the case down by Jim's feet then stood silently to one side, waiting for his next order.

An order like... *Squash Rian like a bug.*

Rian watched impassively and leaned against the wall with his arms folded across his chest. Jim might have made himself comfortable, but Rian certainly wasn't. It was a long shot, but if he needed to run, the door was still his best option. If he made it to the hallway, there were three different escape routes already in place, and plenty of hidden corners of the city to disappear into. The only problem with *that* was Jim found him *here*. So therefore, Rian had to believe that his employer knew about the other locations too.

"What's in the case?"

"Something I've been wanting to assess for some time." Jim reached for the leather case and settled it on his lap without taking his eyes off Rian. "It's a prototype of sorts. Very rare. You might even say it's one of a kind."

The sly grin that hovered at the edges of his mouth was unsettling, but again Rian stayed cool. He had not gotten this far by having a lousy poker face and although he'd come close, Rian would not lose his nerve now just because his boss unexpectedly turned up.

"A gun?"

With a weapon that just happened to be the answer to his problems.

"Not exactly..."

Interesting.

Jim unlocked the case and lifted the lid. After a lingering glare at Rian, he dropped his gaze and stared at the mysterious object with an unreadable expression before spinning it around to show Rian.

This time Rian could not keep his surprise hidden. His mouth dropped open, and he swore his heart skipped several life-giving beats before he could snap it shut again.

"Holy Mother of -"

Jim's eyes flashed with triumph. "Impressive, isn't it?"

Impressive was nowhere near close. In his line of work Rian had seen hundreds of daggers. Most were utilitarian. Ugly steel made for an ugly purpose, and those that were not, were little more than butter knives, with no purpose except to be admired, like a peacock showing his feathers. But this one?

He had never seen *anything* like it. Not even in the Mediterranean or the oldest museums in Europe. From the top of the hilt to the point, Rian estimated it was about the length of his arm, give or take an inch... and he didn't have to touch it to know the oddly colored metal forming the blade was devastatingly sharp.

It was beautiful. It was deadly. And Rian could not take his eyes off it.

"You want me to stick my target with a fancy knife?" As much as he wanted to reach for it, Rian held himself in check. It was just a knife. "What makes it shine like that?"

Just a fancy knife that glowed like a reflection of sunlight streaming through the window. Only... when Rian turned his head to check the angle of the sun, the sky outside was overcast and gloomy.

Strange.

"I don't know."

To Rian's surprise, Jim's voice took on a nostalgic note. He hadn't really expected an answer, and hearing it sliced through Rian's own reverie.

"The metal came from the remains of a meteorite, and I have it on the *very* best authority that the region of space it fell from is…" As quickly as the nostalgia started, it disappeared, and Jim was suddenly on his feet with the new weapon held loosely in his left hand.

"Well, who cares what it is, as long as it works, am I right?"

The ever-present sly grin switched to outright laughter as he tossed the weapon carelessly onto the chair he invited himself to sit on. Rian could only watch in stunned silence as Jim motioned with a jerk of his head to the looming bodyguard that it was time to leave.

"Get up close. Make it nice and personal this time, Mister Murphy… I don't think you want to disappoint *me*." Jim tipped an imaginary hat toward Rian, then turned abruptly on his heel, and sauntered out of the room singing to himself.

It took Rian a full five minutes to realize he had been hearing the words to *Amhrán na bhFiann*… the Irish national anthem… and it was another five before he could come to terms with what it meant.

The Search Within

Finding Miss Envy again was easy when she made so much noise. After Rian relocated to a new hotel under yet *another* alias, he put himself to work again, and just like last time, it did not take long to get his hands on her schedule for the following weeks. Given what he already knew about her, it was no surprise to see Envy up and busy, or to note on his first surveillance run that she added a couple of burly security guards to her entourage.

They looked competent enough, but that wouldn't stop him. It never did. In fact, the *only* thing that bothered Rian about his current situation were the specific instructions he now *had* to follow. Because if he didn't, everything good left in his life would be compromised.

Find the target. Eliminate her. That's all there was to it.
Simple.

Rian spent several days watching her move around Los Angeles again, blending seamlessly into the crowd wherever he could. The hunt was his favorite part... and today, the hunt was good.

He tracked Envy to a large mall in Glendale, where he spent an hour listening to mundane talk about beauty products before the conversation turned into something worth risking his cover for. It was difficult to get closer, but the little surveillance microphone he brought along could only reach about ten meters on a good day.

"Sor— boss –u exp—n."

And today was not one of those days.

Rian cursed under his breath and, after three attempts, managed to slip himself into an alcove close enough to eavesdrop on the conversation without technology. It was too close for his liking, but the thought of home held Rian firmly in place.

"—Observatory was sloppy."

Hold up.

"We got interrupted during the dump."

Years of experience allowed Rian to keep his reaction to a minimum. His eyes widened just enough to make him turn his head, and he glanced down at his phone to cover his interest in the conversation.

Observatory? Dump?

It was impossible to get any closer without raising suspicion, but Rian needed to hear the rest of it. To his right was a small cluster of chairs, one of which had a single empty space left beside an elderly man. It was a risk, but after a quick check to see what his target was doing, Rian strolled over and slumped down in the seat with a dramatic sigh. He rolled his eyes at the older man and flicked his hand toward the store in front of him before beginning a mindless scroll on his phone. His eyes searched the screen, but they didn't see. Rian was wholly focused on Envy and every word that she said.

"Not my problem. What *is* my problem, is *my* name getting mentioned to the police."

Even with no line of sight, Rian could tell Envy was seething. There was no way to be sure, of course, but he was almost positive that whatever had annoyed her *this* time was at least on par with how she had reacted to being shot. And that only increased his desire to know more. He made a mental note to investigate whatever they were talking about later that night, then immediately returned his attention to the task at hand.

"...we cleaned that up Miss Envy. Boss took care of it personally. He wants your answer about the Gaia Ball tomorrow night."

"Why do you think I'm here, you *idiot*?"

"I'll tell him that's a yes. Good day, Miss Envy."

It was a resilient man that could remain unperturbed by the scathing notes Rian heard coming from his target. He couldn't help but feel the *tiniest* degree of respect for whoever she was talking to, but Rian also grimly accepted that he wouldn't hesitate to eliminate the other man from the equation if it became necessary. The option removed itself, however, as the man who approached Envy abruptly departed, and in the silence that followed, Rian could barely hear his own breath passing through his lips. Gratitude washed through the assassin along with the slow exhale, a rare treat in his line of work.

Today, at least, he wouldn't need to take a life.

He remained where he was for a few long moments, taking the offered time to sit quietly with his head bowed while he listened for any other sign of contact. When none came, Rian pretended to mutter his way through a text from his non-existent wife, rolled his eyes, and then sighed again for effect as he hauled himself to his feet.

Just another bored husband waiting for his wife at the mall.

Just another assignment.

Just another piece of the puzzle.

"Let's see what this Observatory thing is."

Later that afternoon, Rian lay slouched on the queen-sized bed in his new base with his laptop resting open on his thighs. In all honesty, the assassin didn't think whatever it was would be *that* important or even relevant to his mission. But it could prove fatal to leave a single stone unturned, so Rian wanted to be thorough... and in this instance, he was also more than a little curious about what could have gone so *wrong* that Miss Envy was risking herself even further by talking about it in public.

Once the system had booted up, it didn't take long before Rian was neck deep in news reports about a body found in the Gunther Depths of Space Hall. The reports themselves were wild, ranging from complete body mutilation and dismemberment to suicide. Each report was different, with no article mentioning anything close to a real, believable fact except for the one thing that they *all* had in common: The photograph of a lone FBI agent exiting the building with a slouch to his shoulders and a bleak expression on his unshaven face.

Rian zoomed in on the photograph, wondering if the agent had been bought by whoever Envy worked for, *and* if he was the one sent in to clean up the mysterious mess they discussed in the middle of a store. Although not as common as the media made it out to be, Rian knew from experience that it *did* happen. Hell, he paid his way through a near miss with a favor in London barely two years ago... and in Los Angeles, he expected no different. All it took was a word here, a note there, and Rian would find what he was looking for.

If he wanted to look for it.

As much as he wanted to speculate, Rian's thoughts developed no further than idle wonder. The photograph came into sharp focus, and Rian was hit with the sudden realization that he and this man had met once before.

The same day he arrived in town.

"Knew you were a fecking cop... *gotcha!"*

Rian grinned triumphantly and stuck his finger up at the screen, but his elation was short-lived. When he tabbed to the next article, the name of the disheveled agent in the photograph was right there for all to see... along with his current assignment.

FBI AGENT LEVI MALACH. CURRENTLY ASSIGNED TO THE INTERPOL TASK

FORCE TRACKING IRISH ASSASSIN RIAN MURPHY, TAKES BREATHER TO WORK ON LOCAL CASE.

The grin faded, replaced by a thin line of grim determination. "Well, *fuck* me. This just got interesting... what else are you hiding, *Agent Levi Malach*?"

Night had well and truly fallen before Rian surfaced again. During those long hours, he had only risen from the computer long enough to answer the door when his pizza arrived... and to swap out an empty beer bottle for a full one. Several times. And now, after what felt like a decade hunched over the small screen, Rian thought he was *finally* getting somewhere.

Beside him on the bed next to what remained of his six-pack were the results of his labors... and the reason for his aching back. Hours of research, and the only tangible information he could find on the agent were closed cases and the odd photograph. His social media was either non-existent or private, and there was nothing even *remotely* close to a scandal that Rian could find.

Yet.

Either he was squeaky clean... or Rian had not found the right hole to dig into.

The tightness in his back signaled that it was time for a break, so Rian swung his legs off the edge of the bed and stood to his full height with his arms stretched toward the ceiling.

"...God. *Ow.*" He heard his spine crack when he began to work the stiffness out. The snap of his own vertebrae sounded overly loud in the otherwise silent room, but the relief was instant. Rian groaned his relief as the knot of discomfort faded gradually into the background of his awareness. Despite his tiredness, he was too worked up to concentrate on a decent stretch, though when he bent over to touch the floor with his fingertips, he swore blindly to Heaven, Hell and everything in-between that in the morning he'd pay more attention to the myriad of aches that had surfaced over the past several months.

The last thing he needed was a failing body when there were still so many unanswered questions on his list.

After the count of ten, Rian took a deep breath straightened again. He stood still for a moment and held it while his mind passed absently over everything he learned that day. So much information, and yet the assassin *still* felt like he had learned nothing. Spots swum before his eyes, forcing Rian to let the breath go, and the deep exhale that followed was laced with frustration, which in turn, gave rise to the small knot of uncertainty that began to spin around and gain traction in his mind.

*There's something there. I can **feel** it.*

He kicked a stray ball of paper out from under his foot and made his way to the small fridge to grab another beer. Something about the agent *and* the story was nagging at him, lingering in his thoughts like a mosquito in summer. But try as he might, Rian could not put his finger on it. It was a buzzing he couldn't explain, an unheard voice in his mind that urged him to continue his search, even though he'd already wasted another day. There were more pressing issues at hand, that much was certain... but Rian was inexorably drawn back to the agent anyway.

Know your enemy.

"One more hour. That's all." The lie was loud on his lips, but Rian didn't really care anymore. He was committed. All in. And knew he would not stop until he'd uncovered *every* single aspect of Levi Malach's life.

Even if it took the rest of the night. Or the rest of the week.

Rian refreshed his search engine and started scanning back through results he had already examined with renewed determination. He sipped absently on the brew in his left hand, scrolling article after article without a clue about what drove the *absolute* certainty that there was still *something* left to find. Maybe he missed something. Maybe there was something so downright obvious he dismissed it. And maybe—

"Hold up. What's *this* then?" Rian's finger hovered over the mouse while his eyes scanned the writing on the screen. A trashy tabloid, nothing more. He grunted, ready to dismiss it as the clickbait it was all over again, but before he could close out, three words leapt from the article and caught his eye.

The FBI refused to comment on the case. However, sources close to the investigative team tell us that they have already made connections to the murderer this reporter has dubbed 'The Angel Maker'. At the time of publication, our own intrepid investigation identified several cases nationwide with similar circumstances. Are we witnessing the birth of a serial killer? Subscribe to this page and remember, you heard it here first!

Icy fingers crept down Rian's spine and branched outwards, filling him with dread. The same silent voice that urged him to continue searching fell silent, though somehow Rian could feel that a grim satisfaction replaced the urgency within. He stared at the screen without comprehension as the ramifications of the tabloid report gave fuel to a spike of apprehension so overwhelming Rian could do nothing but stare. He rubbed at his chest, struggling for breath as images flared into existence, memories he had slammed behind a heavy door and bolted shut.

They were the memories that drove him. Memories that gave Rian *no choice* but to push forward and move on. Haunting, terrible memories that called to him for justice even as his hands remembered what to do before his mind reconnected with reality. He moved like clockwork, white-knuckled fingers moving rapidly on the keys as he changed the parameters of his search.

Malach. Angel. Murder.

The ice flowing through Rian's veins pulsed in time with the rapid beating of his heart. He was *cold*. So, so cold that his hand trembled when he pressed his index finger onto the 'enter' key and confirmed the new search.

Within a second, the ice within Rian froze solid.

"What. The. *Hell*?"

His instincts were right.

He'd found it. He found the reason why he would *never* have been able to let this go. A reason so terrible it would change his life forever. It already had. Rian's whole body shivered as he zoomed in on the gruesome image filling the screen in front of him. Something churned in the pit of his stomach and curled around the ice, the rumbling knot of anxiety that Rian come to know as fear.

"Holy shit."

Rian Gets Stabby

The Gaia Environmental Summit was the *absolute* pinnacle of innovation. It was a prestigious showcase, a revolutionary think-tank where the greatest minds from the greatest companies gathered over a five-day period every year to demonstrate to the rest of the world how they were going to save the planet. Smiling faces made promises about clean energy, better fuel sources and safer operations. They pledged to improve fair trade, increase the quality of living in developing nations, and reduce the widespread destruction of the environment. Newsreels and celebrity dominated promotional videos highlighted ground-breaking technology designed to clean up existing environmental damage, ranging from the smallest scale mishap to the biggest disasters of them all. The best of the best, all focused in one place with one goal in mind: an end to climate change and the sustainability of the human race.

It was all very noble and glamorous. Celebrities and wannabes flocked, hoping to be seen at the various events held across the city. New scientists and inventors begged for an invitation, wanting nothing more than a single chance to prove that they could help save the small blue planet that humanity depended on for its survival. Donations were always very generous, and it was a rare year when the fundraising target were not met.

The ultimate event of the summit was the Gaia Environmental Ball, a party so important to the combined goals of the people of Earth that even the President sent a representative.

It was Noble.

It was Glamorous.

It was *Elite*.

Unfortunately, the Gaia Environmental Ball was also a farce.

Beneath the shine and glitter lay a seedy, often violent underbelly that *never* saw the light of day. The real deals happened behind closed doors and in quiet corners, decisions that were rarely made for the benefit of anyone but those making them. Invitees destroyed life-saving technology in hushed conversations for the sake of a dollar. Lives were bought and sold to the highest bidder without a care for the suffering involved. Land was earmarked for development and destruction. Rivers became dammed and redirected into valleys that would drown centuries of history and serve only a few. Animals were driven to extinction and entire ecosystems destroyed, and all for one purpose.

A purpose so secret, so *terrible* that nobody but the elite few knew, and anyone who stumbled onto the truth was quickly and efficiently silenced.

Rian moved through the sea of people that had already arrived at the ball, easily blending in with the designer chic guests fortunate enough to receive an invitation. In his left hand, he gripped a flute filled with Cristal, and every so often he tipped it in greeting toward a random stranger. The fruity aroma was a pleasant distraction from the heavy perfumes tainting the air, but Rian could barely taste the promised citrus when he allowed himself a sip of the pale gold bubbles.

One day.

Another promise, another item added to the list of things Rian would take the take time to savor when his personal mission was over.

If it didn't kill him first.

From time-to-time Rian interrupted his search to speak to another guest, but the distraction only lasted a few moments before he made his excuses and continued his deceptively random mingle through the crowd. He simply couldn't afford to miss the target Jim had sent him after. *Again.*

He was *positive* she would be there at some point. For what purpose, he could not fathom. When he consolidated all he knew about her so far, there was not one piece of information Rian had learned about Envy that would make him believe she gave a single fuck about the environment.

Yet there he was, tracking her at an event so hard to get into he had called in nearly all his favors just to get through the door.

***

"... and I thought this was a prestigious event."

The biting comment just over his right shoulder slowed Rian's step. Without missing a beat, he spun around with an amiable grin on his face. His eyes focused on the woman who had spoken in an instant. She wore her hair different, about half a colour wheel darker than when he last saw her, and piled on top of her head in a careless bun that he suspected was *very* deliberate. The elaborately deceptive hairstyle was not the only thing Rian observed in the quick seconds it took for him to glide closer. Experience kept his expression locked in the friendly smile, but Rian still knew how to appreciate a work of art when he saw one.

"Oh, don't be like *that*, Miss Envy. They say everyone is welcome here."

"Like what? *Pissed* at the man who *tried* to kill me?"

Her pale blue eyes flashed, betraying her irritation. Rian knew he had to tread carefully, or the situation would deteriorate faster than the bullets left the gun he shot her with. That did not stop the wink he gave her, or his glass from clinking against hers in the perfect imitation of a toast. In the immediate area surrounding them, the other attendees chattered and laughed, blissfully ignorant of the deadly conversation occurring in their midst.

"...like a snob, darlin'. But sure, you can run with that if it makes you feel better."

"Who did you kill to get in here?"

Rian didn't think he would ever meet anyone else who could do ice queen quite like the woman currently shooting daggers at him. It would be a bald-faced lie if he said his nerves were not affected, but Rian was a professional. As elite as the event he was attending. And the mask on his face proved it.

"Nobody... yet."

He caught it. The flash in Envy's eyes as it morphed into something else. Something like fear. Rian *also* caught the slight tightening of her fingers on the champagne flute when she tipped it to sip from.

"Dare I ask? Or is this one of those *I'd tell you, but then I'd have to kill you* scenarios?"

"... about that."

The glass paused halfway to Envy's plump lips, giving Rian a perfect view of the precise second understanding dawned in her eyes. The fear shifted into surprise before transforming into outrage. "You've got to be *fucking* kidding me."

"It's nothing personal, darlin'." God, he didn't want *this*. Missions were supposed to be in and out with little conversation, or better yet, completed from a distance with no personal contact at all. It was easy for others in his line of work to turn off their conscience and go numb to the truth of their situation, but Rian was different. The *job* he could do. The job he could *handle*... but being close enough to witness the betrayal in his target's eyes was an experience he preferred to avoid.

"You won't get away with this." Her chest heaved with a deep breath that for a split second drew Rian's eye. In that second he saw a smooth expanse of skin, and underneath that, the fluttering of her heart as she fought to remain calm.

"Probably not." The regret in Rian's tone was genuine. There was a very real chance the dead body on the floor tonight would be his. If it were, maybe Jim would leave his mother alone... but deep inside his soul Rian knew that if he failed here, he failed *everywhere*. He placed his glass on a passing tray and offered his hand for Envy to take.

So be it.

"Can I have this dance?"

"...you, *what?*"

Rian's dark eyes flicked to his empty hand and back again. He curled his fingers once and smiled through the awkwardness of the situation, his eyes pleading for her to not make a scene. "People are staring, Miss Envy. Say yes, and I promise I'll make it painless."

"Or *I* could kill *you* instead."

With more grace than he could have ever mustered, Envy placed her hand in his larger one. She felt tiny, almost fragile when he curled his fingers around her soft, warm palm, but Rian knew first-hand how wrong that assumption was. Envy put him on his ass with minimal effort once already, and despite his considerable abilities he had no doubt she could do it again. He nodded his thanks and led her to the dance floor, remaining silent until he held her lace-clad body lined against his with his hand resting lightly on her waist.

"You can try."

"I can... what? Oh. Shut up, *Rian*."

"Yes ma'am."

Neither Rian nor Envy spoke as he moved her around the floor, easily keeping time with the beat set by the jazz band tucked into one corner of the function room. While they danced, Rian examined the Gala decorations properly for the first time. Elaborate without being gaudy, the soft gold and green tones with a splash of royal blue set a perfectly deceptive scene for the misdirection that occurred there. Nobody would suspect a Gala founded with the purpose of saving humanity could be so treacherous... and in the same light, nobody would suspect Rian or his *own* nefarious purpose. He looked everywhere, and he looked at everyone. He analyzed his way around the room, only avoiding one thing.

"You move pretty well for an assassin."

Her words startled him out of his vigilance. Rian glanced down at Envy, finally acknowledging the one person he had not examined. Well, not with his eyes, anyway. Except for her cleavage. And her hair. But also, the fine lace that tickled his fingertips. In any other situation, Rian might admit to himself that Envy was not just a carefully constructed work of art, and that the word he was seeking was *breathtaking*. But this wasn't any other situation, and Rian was acutely aware that Envy's moves were at *least* as calculated as his own. His lips curled slightly in acknowledgment, his eyes lingering on her face for a moment before he returned to his examination of the ballroom.

"I'm good at my job, Miss Envy."

"I don't doubt *that*. I've heard... things. Who sent you?"

"I just take the contract and I don't ask questions. Are you really a Sin?"

Distract.

Himself, from the task ahead. Her, for precisely the same reason.

Her body tensed against him. Envy was poised to flee, but Rian's grip was like iron, and he held onto her sensual body with ease.

"That was a question."

Only a dead man would be immune to the soft curves that slid with him across the dance floor, and perhaps that was what he was. Because there was *no* way that Rian would allow himself to feel her warmth, or revel in the glide of lace and silk against his tuxedo if he were alive. He would not inhale her perfume like it was the air he needed to breathe or wonder if that faint honeyed scent lingered in the taste of her skin. "Does that mean... *the others* exist, too?"

"Also a question. But... yes."

"Damn. I guess I really *am* going to Hell then." The response felt automatic. Rian wasn't really listening anymore. Alarm bells started to swing in his head, along with a low murmuring chime that intensified by the minute.

This isn't right.

A silent voice, sounding so much like his own, whispered above the ringing of the bells. Rian blinked it away and refocused on the woman in his arms. She smiled up at him, the subtle curve of her lips filled with a sultry adoration. And those eyes. The pale blue that gazed at him through long black lashes no longer held the fear and outrage from before. They were warm, burning with a fire that melted the ice in his veins.

"I guess so. I'm thirsty, Rian."

"On it, Miss Envy." He led her to the edge of the dance floor before the music finished and placed his hand on the small of her back to guide her into the crowd. A drink was such a clever idea. It surprised Rian he hadn't thought of it first, but then Miss Envy was a lot smarter than he was, so it made sense.

Stop this. Now.

"For you, *mo chuisle*." Rian offered Envy a flute of Cristal, idly noting that a tremor rippled over his hand. He gave it a shake and wiped it on his pants before bringing his own glass to his lips. But before he could take more than a brief sip, something bumped him from behind. His body lurched forward, his feet stumbling back and forth as he corrected himself and straightened again. "What..."

He half turned, seeking the person responsible for knocking him, only to pause when an odd sensation of warmth radiated from his forearm to his chest. In an instant, Rian disregarded whatever tried to steal his attention, his gaze once again fixed on Envy. He beamed at her, eyes crinkling with unsurpassed joy when he saw how she leaned into him, her hand brushing back and forth along his arm. How could he have thought she was cold? This woman... he was *not* worthy of her time, but he had it anyway, even though he tried to kill her.

"Rian..." Long lashes blinked up at him as Envy trailed her hand up over his shoulder to rest on his collarbone. "You look so... *edible*... tonight."

A thousand images flew through his mind to accompany those suggestive undertones. Rian drew Envy closer, pulling her delightfully soft curves against his toned chest with a possessive hand that lingered unapologetically on her waist. "Is that so?"

Idiot. Get away!

Once again, Rian shushed the voice in his mind. He curled his fingers into silk as it faded away to nothingness, his thumb brushing a feathery arc on Envy's stomach. Remorse flooded through his soul and knotted his stomach when he recalled the exact moment he had pulled the trigger and marked her flawless skin. "I'm sorry I hurt you."

Her fingertips dug gently into his shoulder, but instead of a reprimand, Envy stood on her toes to whisper her sultry tones in his ear instead. "It's okay, Rian. I know a way you can make it up to me. Come."

With a silent nod and a spark of hope flaring in his heart, he followed Envy. She was right. Of course she was right. If he could make it up to her and find redemption, then everything would be okay. How fortunate for Rian that he bumped into Miss Envy tonight. And how *lucky* he was to be the one to follow her as she weaved through the milling guests to a side door leading onto a terrace *much* quieter than the ballroom.

From the railed edge, Rian had a clear view of the valley and further, to the ocean beyond. On the distant horizon, the last vestiges of the day faded from burnt orange into the pale purple that blended into night. To the right, his research informed him there was a staircase behind a wall of plants. Officially it was a fire escape, but the assassin had marked it as a potential escape route should the mission go awry. Not that it would now that Miss Envy graced him with her smile. Rian was *utterly* besotted with the way the twilight sparkled in her hair, and much to the dismay of the silenced voice in his mind, he didn't even glance in that direction. Envy led him to the left, away from the stairs, where the terraced balcony transformed into a wonderland bathed only by candlelight. Rian gazed in wonder at a wall of vines shining with artfully scattered fairy lights before his dazed smile turned to Envy. "Pretty. But not as—"

"Who sent you to find me today?"

Her hand was back on his arm. All thoughts scattered as Rian followed the path Envy's fingers danced along his sleeve until her palm lay flat on his chest. Surely it wouldn't hurt to give her a name? She deserved that much from him, at the very least.

"..."

Rian frowned when a rogue thought appeared in his mind, reminding him of the need for secrecy in *all* things.

The voice returned, as maddening as ever, and this time it fought Rian when he tried to dismiss it and give Miss Envy what she wanted. Her eyes held the promise of forgiveness, something Rian had not realized he craved until tonight. He waded in deeper, willing to drown for just a chance to earn delivery of that promise.

"I..."

Envy brushed her other hand along his jawline, her plump lips parted in anticipation as she closed the distance between them. "Tell me, and I'm yours tonight."

"Miss Envy..." Rian could do nothing when those soft lips pressed against his. Nothing but moan under his breath as his lips parted and he sank into the delectable gift that she offered. In an instant, Rian was swept away into a bliss he could *never* have imagined. A sweet citrus coated his tongue, the lingering taste of champagne he failed to detect earlier now forever associated with *her*. He curled his fingers into silk, making a loose fist in the small of her back as he crushed her body against his. Every nerve ending was a smoldering heat that ignited into flames wherever they connected. Rian wasted no time chasing more as he took the kiss to another, deeper level, filled with promises *he* intended to keep. It didn't matter that they weren't alone. All that mattered was the woman melting into him and the sweet, sweet taste of her mouth as he plundered it with his tongue. Rian's mind was already several steps ahead of his body. In it he roamed, seeking a more secluded hallway or closet where he could worship *every* flawless curve on Miss Envy's body without interruption.

"*Who was it?*" It came again, the persistent query that reached his ears only. A breathless whisper meant for Rian, and Rian alone. In a daze he pulled back from her lips and stared, mesmerized as her pale blue eyes slowly opened and begged him to answer. "That was just a taste..."

Rian's breath quickened when Envy traced her fingers over his pounding heart with one hand, and swallowed hard when he felt the other slip into his pocket in search of something *else*.

"I want *more* than just a taste, Miss Envy." He glanced down to where Envy was drawing her fingers in a lazy pattern, lips curling into a knowing smile when that same pattern began again inside his pocket. "... and I think you know I can deliver."

"My, my, Rian."

A low moan rumbled out of his chest when her cunning fingers wrapped around his hard length. How blessed he was. How lucky she had chosen him. Miss Envy wasn't a sin. She was an angel, sent to offer him absolution.

"If I'd known you were packing such a *formidable* weapon, I never would have let you out of my basement."

The raw hunger in Envy's eyes did not go unnoticed. She *wanted* him. She wanted what he *needed* to give her.

"I ...am the weapon."

"But do you know how to use it?"

The challenge made him seethe, and at the same time drove home the invitation and her promise. As much as he wanted to let her fingers keep working, the terrace was no place for what they both *really* wanted, and so Rian tugged Envy's hand out of his pocket and led her deeper into the candle-lit wonderland where the shadows were longer and the dark spaces easier to get lost in. There was no question now, Rian would give her what she asked for... and in exchange he would get the absolution he so desperately craved.

Rian's professional nature gave him the restraint he needed to get Miss Envy alone. Barely. Truth be told, if she had suggested he take her in the first dark corner he led her past, he would have complied without question. Only his training saved him from destroying her dignity, and only his need to *truly* possess her kept him on target.

"After you." Meaningless words. Rian was right behind Envy when she swept through the door he held open for her. Even more meaningless when he used her body to slam the door shut, giving her no time to speak before he took her mouth again with a ferocity that surprised even him. He lifted her higher, using his hips to pin her to the timber door while his hand wrapped a firm grip on her jaw.

"That's it... *good boy.*"

Rian groaned into Envy's neck at her approval. This was it. This was what he wanted, and he was mere seconds away from finding the divine reward on offer.

"Tell me what I want to hear,"

Fuck. That sultry voice in his ear, the grind of her hips and parted thighs against his. Rian bit down on her collarbone in frustration, sucking hard on her skin as his free hand slid down to knead her soft breast.

"... tell me and *then* you can fuck me, Rian."

"Tell you..." Rian breathed heavily against Envy's skin. Heat flared through him, spiking his arousal, but it wasn't the heat that confused Rian and had his mind reeling so fast the vertigo made him sway. Between the gentle, insistent pressure in Envy's voice and the ice that crept along the edges of *everything*, Rian could barely hold on. A war raged inside the assassin on three fronts, and until now the option he liked least was winning.

"Sure."

He slid his hand lower and dug his fingertips into her soft thigh as he hiked her a little higher against the door. The silk dress was the softest he had ever held in his hands, but it was still in the way, and so Rian moved his hand lower still, feathering his fingertips along the inside of Envy's thigh. "I'll tell you whatever you want to hear..."

"Mmm, yes. *Yes.*"

The same hand trembled in response to his internal struggle, and breathing hard, Rian pulled back from where he ravaged her skin. He was just in time to see Envy's lust-blown eyes widen even further when the tip of his dagger pierced her tender skin.

"Just as soon as you tell me what *you* have to do with Cote d'Ivoire."

"What are you talking about?"

"I think you know." Rian slid the dagger a little deeper, guiding it beneath her ribs. All traces of the heat were gone, replaced in defeat by the ice that now crawled through his veins. Rian didn't fight it like he had before. He didn't have the energy. Instead, he let it spread like a late autumn storm that brought a cleansing purification with the change. Wherever it touched him, the clearer things became, and before the dagger slipped another millimeter, Rian's mind was once again free. Mostly.

He *had* to do this. There were no choices left.

"You don't have to do this."

By now Rian could tell that the fear in Envy's eyes was real. It was possibly the first genuine emotion he had ever seen her display. But it wasn't enough to stay his hand. Nothing would be. "If this was a normal job, mo éad, I would find some other way, but..."

"But ...*what*?"

"I'm sorry, Miss Envy... I don't have a choice." *It's you or my mam.*

Despite her fear, Envy simmered with just enough anger to roll her eyes. "We've been down this road. You and I both know *I'm not going to die.*"

"I know." Rian nodded. If his bullets had not done the job, he doubted this shiny dagger would be any more effective. Guilt flared inside him, but he squashed it down without letting it settle. This was a job, and Envy was his target. Getting personal was a mistake, but Rian couldn't allow it to stop him. And he couldn't spare a moment to digest how things had flowed so far out of his control in the first place. His jaw clenched, and with a flick of his wrist, Rian drove the dagger home. "But I've just bought my mother some time."

"You lied..." Envy let out a gurgled moan when Rian yanked the dagger back out again. Red blossomed on Envy's stomach, and Rian felt a twinge of regret that the silk was ruined forever. Blood flowed and spread so rapidly Rian knew the wound *should* have been fatal. He cocked an eyebrow at her as he let go of her and stepped back to avoid getting stained. "...it hurts."

"..." It took Rian a moment to recall their earlier conversation. The beginning of the night felt like aeons, not hours.

"It's okay, Rian."

Rian watched impassively as Envy clutched desperately at her stomach in a futile attempt to stem the flow of blood. She tried to move away from him, but only managed a few meters before she collapsed with her back against the nearby wall instead.

Rian wrapped his hand around the door handle, watching for the hidden strength she had thrown at him last time. But her eyes weren't on him. Envy stared at the dagger in his other hand. Her expression remained the same, but Rian had seen enough to spot the surprise she tried to hide. He pointed the blood-stained tip at her, but the only reaction he got was a sneer.

"Tell your mother she's welcome." Envy waved her free hand at him, dismissing him from her presence. "But if I *ever* see you again..."

Just like she did in the basement.

Rian turned the handle and tugged the door open just enough to slip through. His head dropped, and he turned it to glance one more time at the woman who had turned his life upside down.

"You won't."

Raphael meets Envy

Raphael sat behind the wheel of her late model coupe, singing quietly to herself as the car wound its way through the lush, shaded street leading to her destination. Tall, spreading jacaranda trees lined the street, marching their pale lavender splendor along either side of her into the foothills. Raphael could remember when they were tiny, fragile saplings struggling for nutrients nearly five decades ago, but in contrast with the trees, the Archangel had not changed a bit. Although as the car passed beneath the fragrant shade, Raphael contemplated they had both been doing the same thing.

Watching.

At first, the temptation to confront the one residing in the exclusively decadent neighborhood surged stronger than Raphael cared to admit, but an unidentified instinct deep inside the Archangel urged her to bide her time.

In the end, her instinct won, and Raphael waited patiently. Until now.

Hiding in the shadows.

Even with everything that was happening around her, Raphael kept to herself... but after the events of the previous months, the Archangel knew it was time. Time for her to start seeking the truth. And today she finally convinced herself to stop procrastinating and get started. Today, Raphael was going to get some answers, whether her *friend* wanted to give them to her or not.

To that end, Raphael pulled into the curb about half a mile from the house she was about to visit. Around her, the trees swayed in a gentle breeze, but Raphael felt no comfort in their presence. All she could see was the road, and the task ahead. The distance itself was irrelevant. Raphael could pop in without warning, or disappear if she needed to, all without leaving a trace. At this time, however, a display of power was unnecessary, and Raphael felt no sense of urgency to reach her destination.

Or maybe, she just wanted to avoid it for as long as possible.

With a resigned sigh, she switched off the engine, and opened the door. The car itself, a low riding Audi R8 was part of her disguise, a heavily warded mobile unit that could get her close enough without detection... as close as she cared to be, anyway.

Without a backward glance, she left the car behind and walked the rest of the way to the broadly gated driveway closing off the house on foot. Raphael wasn't worried about theft or curious eyes. Not on this street. Besides, in a city full of the elite and privileged, nobody paid attention to yet another overpriced car. Or the woman driving it. Even if it *did* get stolen, Raphael could find it *and* the culprit without breaking a sweat.

She reached out with her power now and then, testing for the presence of another non-human. Or anything that might raise an alarm and alert the occupant of the house to *her* unscheduled visit. By all accounts, she was completely alone. Not a single otherworldly being in sight. And not many humans, either. It was odd. Very odd. As she approached the gates, Raphael slowed her steps.

Something wasn't right.

The elaborate metal entryway was wide open. She stopped mid-stride, her eyes narrowing in thought as she assessed what lay before her. The space between the metal bars was more than just an open invitation for anyone to walk in. It was a breach, a broken point in whatever defenses were in place... and the best way for Raphael to walk directly into a trap.

"Nice try, *cousin*... but you're going to have to do better than that." Raphael muttered under her breath, pulling gently on her power to investigate for herself. It was easy enough to render the gates and any trap infused into the metal useless. All she had to do was follow the ebb and flow of power, to let it guide her to anything out of the ordinary... not that there was anything ordinary about what *she* was doing. Well, not from a humans' perspective, anyway. Another moment passed before Raphael admitted she could not find anything suspicious, and with a small, yet satisfied grumble, she wove her own warding on the gates. One that would simply alert her to trespassers, giving her enough warning to escape before any kind of trap snapped shut.

One second wasn't much. But it was all she needed, and with her safety more or less assured, Raphael stepped through the gates and continued her casual stroll to the front door. Oddly, the garden lining the path was a little disheveled, which from Raphael's memories was not like the occupant at all. Small tufts of faded green encroached on the white flagstones, but aside from a cursory glance, Raphael gave it little thought. Nor did she care about the wilted flowers or the dry, lifeless fountain. If her cousin lost interest in gardening, it wasn't her concern... and in all reality, one less person wasting water in a desert for the sake of vanity was a welcome sight.

When she reached the top of the stairs, Raphael reached up, pushed her sunglasses back and smiled sweetly at the surveillance camera. Her other hand looped around the elaborate knocker and, still smiling, the Archangel banged it against the door three times. When no answer came, Raphael knocked again, and *this* time she let a concentrated surge of her power pulse through the property.

She would *not* be ignored. Especially by *her*.

"Envy. Sweetie I *know* you're in there."

From somewhere in the depths of the house, Raphael heard a muffled thump and a curse. The curse was followed swiftly by an apology, delivered by a voice she did not expect to hear in *this* house, of all places. *Or at all.* Half a minute later, footsteps scurried closer, and Raphael felt the deadbolts behind the door being thrown back. Soon after, the solid lump of timber block-ing her way shifted inward, and a wide-eyed face framed by long, black ringlets appeared in the newly created gap.

"She's not seeing anyone to—"

Raphael raised a single demanding eyebrow at the unusually attractive face that hesitantly greeted her while simultaneously trying to send her away. While she could not see much of the woman inside, Raphael knew that over the years there would have been little change. "I'm *not* asking. Open the door or I'll open it for you."

The crack widened a fraction as recognition dawned. Her mouth dropped open in an 'O', and her fragile grip on the door loosened as surprise replaced the hesitation clouding her face.

"Raphael is that you?"

"Kindness. What are *you* doing here?"

Raphael tried to keep her tone neutral, but the woman using the door as a protective shield wasn't the only one fighting to contain her surprise. She fisted her hand on her hip, covering her own reaction while her foot tapped impatiently for an answer.

Kindness is here? Does that mean...?

"I came to help." The answer was curt, yet polite. Excruciat-ingly so, and Raphael would be lying if she said it didn't bother her.

"What do you—" Raphael wanted to ask her *exactly* what that meant, to question her about... everything, but she was interrupted by the sound of *another* voice echoing unseen in the hallway behind Kindness.

"I said get *rid* of them, 'Ness."

Kindness turned away from Raphael to speak to the person still inside but leapt aside with an alarmed squeak when Raphael's open palm connected with the solid timber door. It flew backwards under the force of her power, only to swing wildly on its hinges after bouncing heavily off the wall. Timber creaked under the strain of an equal force that stopped it before it swung halfway back to the door frame Raphael stepped into.

The sunlight streaming through the doorway behind her was a *complete* coincidence.

"I didn't give her a choice. I'm not giving *you* one either."

"Raphael!" To the side, Kindness voiced her protest at Raphael's tone, but the Archangel silenced her with a glare before turning to face the reason she exposed herself to their presence in the first place.

Now that the door no longer blocked her way, Raphael could see her cousins perfectly. Kindness stood with her hands clasped in front of her, but Raphael could tell she was poised to run. Whether it was a dash to Envy's side or through the open door behind her was yet to be determined.

Cousins. A simplified term to describe one of the most complicated relationships in existence. The last time Raphael stood face to face with either of them was a time so *wretched* in her memories that even now she felt nothing but sadness... though she did her best not to temper it with blame.

This is not how I planned this to be.

Raphael sighed in exasperation and raised her hands to signal her desire for peace.

"Relax, Envy." Sure, she had come for answers, but starting another war when trouble already brewed on the horizon was the last thing she wanted. Hell, Raphael didn't even want the trouble that *was* coming... but she was already involved.

She just wished she knew how deep her involvement would go.

"...If I wanted to hurt you I'd have done it years ago."

"You mean–"

The tall, slender woman Raphael confronted was paler than she remembered. A cursory assessment told the Archangel that Envy's pallid complexion did not seem to result from a lack of sunlight. She favored her left side, and though she tried to hide it in a casual lean, Raphael did not miss the way Envy used the wall to support herself.

She nodded her confirmation and kept her eyes trained on Envy to gauge her reaction. "From the day you arrived."

"Well, *shit*." Envy threw her hands up as her usually well-groomed calm shook itself wide open and frustration took over. A heartbeat later, she pressed her palm against her stomach and scowled at her visitor. "*Mmm*. What do you *want*?"

Oh, something else *definitely* happened with the Sin, something that had little to do with her vitamin D deficiency. Raphael did not need powers to see that. But before she could respond, Kindness spoke first.

"Envy!" Black curls swung as the Virtue turned to scold Envy. "That's no way to talk to Raphael. She's *family*."

Envy snorted and cast a sour glance at Raphael. "Not mine."

"That was *your* choice, Envy, not Raphael's." Kindness placed her hands on her hips and her body tensed, but her tone remained polite. "Be nice."

"Whatever, 'Ness, don't you have some weird, good deed to do?"

"That's *enough*."

"You can't tell me what to do in my own house, *Kindness*."

Raphael listened to her cousins bickering back and forth without comment, though in truth she was a little rattled. Envy, she had seen many times in various locations around the planet over the years while pretending she hadn't.

But *Kindness*?

Kindness and the rest of her siblings disappeared several thousand years ago. Along with Envy's, for that matter... and Raphael did not want to think about what the return of one of the Virtues meant. Not now, and not ever.

Though it was beginning to appear she had little choice.

It was time to cut through the current argument and get to the point of her visit, so Raphael silenced them with a wave of her hand. "Did you *actually* try to make *me* a suspect in a human murder investigation, Envy? That's a little... *childish*, even for you, don't you think?"

"I don't know what you're talking about." Envy dragged her eyes from Kindness to Raphael, giving the Archangel a flat glare that had no doubt sent humans running. When Raphael merely returned the look with a raised eyebrow added in, the Sin shifted and pushed herself away from the wall. "Fine. Don't just stand there in the doorway being dramatic, Raphael. Either come in or get lost."

"Envy!"

Once again, Envy ignored Kindness. And this time, she wasn't the only one. Raphael and Envy were too busy glaring at each another to pay attention to the soft voice that pleaded between them. "You don't have the strength to argue with her. Please... she's here to help, too."

"I don't need *her* kind of help."

"Yes, as a matter of fact, *you do*."

Raphael watched with detached amusement as Kindness effectively bullied Envy into behaving herself so she could go sit down and rest whatever was ailing her. Curious, she let the door close and followed the bickering pair through to the living room, where several soft, white sofas surrounded the edges of a lush silver rug threaded with gold. A pair of Ming vases decorated a marble pedestal sitting proudly between a Monet and an equally priceless Picasso mounted on the wall. Such decadence could only suit a Sin... but the Archangel begrudgingly admitted to herself that it was stylish.

Maybe even tasteful.

"What's wrong with *you*?" It was second nature for Raphael to put her own needs aside, especially when confronted with something that needed healing. She had been doing it her whole life, and although she and Envy were not exactly the best friends Agent Malach now believed they were, Raphael would not start being selfish now. But he didn't need to know that. He didn't need to know *any* of it.

Envy sat gingerly on the edge of the couch, slowly easing herself back into the cushions. It was obvious to everyone that she was in immense pain, but she shook her head and pursed her lips. "Nothing. What do you want?"

"Don't lie to me, Envy." Raphael moderated her snippy tone, but her exasperation was clear. "I can see without even trying that there's something wrong with you."

Envy fidgeted in her seat, looking everywhere except Raphael. But when Kindness cleared her throat, she caved in and answered the question. "I got shot, *okay*."

"Five times!" After she corrected Envy, Kindness sat too, though her seat of choice was the plush silver rug that would put a sheep to shame. She made herself comfortable and looked from Raphael to Envy, waiting patiently for them to continue.

Raphael shrugged it off. Envy's injuries were not her problem. She knew darn well the Sin would heal on her own accord, much faster than any human. What the Archangel could *not* understand, was why they made a big deal out of nothing. She had seen Envy walk off a spear through the gut... a couple of errant bullets should not be a problem. "So? Why the drama? You'll heal."

"Then I got stabbed."

"... What?" This had to be some kind of weird joke she didn't know the punchline of. Raphael frowned at her injured cousin in confusion. "How is this—"

From her seat on the floor, Kindness held up a finger to stall them both. Her patience was almost as legendary as that borne by the Virtue himself, but Raphael could see that by now even hers was wearing thin. She flicked her hand at Kindness, indicating for her to continue.

"By the *same* person!"

Raphael did not see the relevance. "... okay. I guess... why?"

"See?" Envy leaned back a little, her face twisting with the effort it cost her. "She doesn't care. Why did you bring her here, 'Ness?"

"Me?" Kindness voiced her denial, black curls once again bouncing with her shaking head. "I didn't."

"I came because of the Observatory."

"I thought you said—*ugh*. You're not making any sense. What about it?"

"This." Raphael pulled a small card out of her pocket and tossed it onto the couch next to where Envy slumped. Her expression remained neutral as she watched her cousin examine the paper and the words handwritten in a small, neat script.

'We need to talk. Griffith Observatory. 8:30am. Don't be late.'

Envy dropped the paper and pushed it back toward Raphael, dismissing it and the message it contained. "Wasn't me. I haven't left the house for a month."

She waved the same hand over her stomach as though the reason should have been obvious to the Archangel.

Raphael's eyes grew wide at Envy's response and remained that way while she weighed up her options. *A month.* A month since she had left the house. If that was true, and Envy hadn't left the house, then there was no way she could know about anything that was happening outside the fence-line. Maybe even outside the front door.

In theory.

"I… believe you." That would at least explain the garden… but there was still something bothering Raphael… if Envy had been stabbed a month ago, she *should* have healed on her own by now. However, the Observatory incident happened before Envy's four-week convalescence had begun… so in truth, Raphael was torn.

Her involvement was still possible.

"She's not lying Raphael. I've been here nearly the whole time. The only human I've seen around is the one who stabbed Envy."

"What?" Archangel and Sin turned in unison to glare at Kindness, who had been sitting in silence. To her credit, she returned both stares without flinching, though her shoulders dropped a fraction under the weight of their scrutiny.

Envy found her tongue first. "What do you mean, you saw Rian Murphy here?"

The name meant nothing to Raphael, but Kindness shrugged off the accusation Envy sent her way. Raphael opened her mouth to ask why he remained significant... or even breathing but was cut off by her Kindness's quick response.

"What? Tall, good looking... for a human. Kind of broody?" She leaned back on her palms and tilted her head back as she recalled the memory. "I saw him outside the gate. He never told me his name... but I knew he was responsible when he asked how you were healing."

Envy tried to sit straighter but sank back with an irritated huff. "What did he say?"

"He said, and I quote, '*tell Miss Envy I had no choice.*'"

"Asshole."

"He called you *Miss Envy*. He seemed nice."

Kindness smiled serenely at Envy, who returned it with the crinkling of her nose.

"You think everyone is nice."

"Well... not *everyone*."

"And where is he *now*?" Raphael's voice made both Sin and Virtue jump. They were so caught up in their own exchange her presence had been forgotten... but she felt a certain amount of satisfaction when they both turned their attention back to her. "The man... Rian Murphy. Where is he now?"

"I'm not sure... I..." Kindness closed her eyes, and Raphael was surprised to feel a gentle surge of power coming from her. It was nowhere near the strength *she* could muster, but it was still strong. Stronger than she ever thought the Virtue was capable of. She waited patiently for Kindness to respond, and when she did, her voice breathless with the effort.

"It still feels like such a struggle... but it gets easier over time." Her eyes opened and she swayed on the spot, curling her finders into the rug to steady herself. "I can't see past the bottom of the hill anyway ...I don't know where he is."

"I do." Envy's tired voice rejoined the conversation, and her smile was smug. "What? You think I'm going to let him try and kill me *twice* and not want to know where he is at all times?"

Raphael crossed her arms over her chest. "Why didn't you just kill him? That's your usual style isn't it?"

"Ha. Haha. Very funny, Raphael. But not this time. I want *answers* from that fool, and he can't give them to me if he's dead."

The Archangel grunted at her cousin. "Fair point. I take back my comment. So?"

"So what?"

Raphael dropped her arms and clenched her fists by her sides before she could stop herself. "*Must* you be deliberately obtuse?"

"Yes... I really must. C'mon, Raph. Lighten up."

"*Don't* call me that."

Raphael healing Envy

"Are you going to let me help you?" Raphael's voice broke through the strained silence that lay between them. "I really don't mind Envy, I—"

"I said *no*, Raphael."

It was clearly a lie. Envy was turning grey with the effort it took her to remain upright, but she shooed Raphael away with an irritated hand. Out of the corner of her eye Raphael saw Kindness sit up, but Envy gave her no room to speak. "I'll be fine... go do a good deed somewhere else. You don't get to have *me* on your conscience."

Kindness pulled herself into a low crouch and shuffled toward Envy. "Envy, please... You *know* you're not healing. This isn't right. You're *almost* as bull-headed as Pride..."

Her voice rang with more determination than Raphael could have ever imagined her to project. *Stubborn* was probably closer to the correct word, but Raphael knew that a Virtue would never be so... forthcoming. Once more she opened her mouth to interject but closed it yet again when Kindness' next words steamrolled right over the top of her.

"... But at least *Pride* knows when to stop the knife before his nose gets cut off. *He* knew when to call it a day and—"

"Wow. Listen to *you*, *Kindness*. You're starting to sound just like me... you're all grown up."

The situation was *completely* out of hand. Envy's incessant need to counter everything with snark and Kindness's grating polite tones led to constant bickering that picked at Raphael's nerves and eroded away what little patience *she* had left.

"I don't have *time* for this. You're not telling me anything I don't already know, and this..." Raphael jabbed her finger first at Envy, then swung it at Kindness. "... little argument you have going on between you is *not* my concern. Good luck with your convalescence, *Envy*."

She ran her eyes over her cousin's greying face, dismissing her with a wave of her hand. "From the looks of things, you're going to need it."

With her jaw set, Raphael turned on her heel and stalked out of the room. She hadn't taken two steps before she grabbed hold of her power with such force the impact sent a blast of wind barreling through the house.

"Wait! Raph, please."

Raphael grit her teeth at the name. So much tension rippled along her jaw she swore she felt a tooth crack. But Envy's plea succeeded, and the Archangel stopped dead in her tracks. In her mind's eye, Raphael saw a time thousands of years in the past when things had been different. Before war raged and they stood on different sides. Before, when Raphael and her six siblings battled to free Envy and her kin from an existence so vile even her Father hadn't been able to maintain his zero-interference policy. Before, when Raphael still knew the love of her Mother, and the idea of having new additions to their family made her smile.

Now, when Raphael turned around all she saw were the reasons it was all gone. The reasons why she was alone on Earth in an exile she had not asked for and didn't deserve. Raphael saw Envy, the one who stayed and her Opposite, Kindness... the one who was *still* begging for her counterpart to change. She saw her own losses and more. The heartache and pain that had already been, and the sorrow that was yet to come. Her own life, intertwined with theirs and the equally sad, yet enigmatic face of her twin brother, who she had not seen for a century. Another face, so hauntingly familiar yet one she did not know. A man in a cage and a never-ending line of faces. The—

It just wasn't fair.

Raphael blinked away the images swimming in front of her eyes with a start and looked between her two cousins, her irritation clear.

"... What?"

Her glower could have stopped an iceberg. Raphael used it to her full advantage, pinning both Sin and Virtue equally while the wind whipped around her body, tearing through the room without a care for a single one of Envy's priceless possessions. Power radiated out of her with the suppressed fury of a hurricane, but Raphael wasn't even at half of her limit. Not even a *tenth* of the power she was granted, and for a long moment she just stood there, perfectly still... and forced them to remember who they were dealing with.

It was unlike her to put on such a display, but in this moment, the Archangel could not bring herself to care. Their existing rivalry meant *nothing* to the mission Raphael was on, or the answers she was looking for. All it did was get in her way and confound an issue already *so clouded* that Raphael was lost.

And lost was *not* where she wanted to be.

Kindness shrank away from Raphael first, her eyes widening in awe when she felt the raw power emanating from the same woman she argued in front of only a moment before. In contrast, Envy held her ground, her chin tilted upward in defiance, but Raphael could see the tinge of fear reflected in her eyes.

It took her a moment, but when she eventually spoke, her voice echoed the expression Raphael could see in her icy blue eyes. "I've. I've changed my mind... Raphael... *please?* It hurts."

In that instant, *everything* changed. As quickly as she had taken hold of it, Raphael abandoned her display of power, cutting herself off from the source in the blink of an eye. She dropped her head and examined the floor in shocked avoidance as the result of her actions filled her with a sudden chagrin that rocked her to the core. As an Archangel, she was *supposed* to be above such petty actions. Raphael had been taught better, by people *better* at this than she could *ever* hope to be. And this display only proved it. She was a woman alone in a world filled with turmoil, and her myriad of defenses were high… but that did not excuse her behavior.

"Of course." She glided back to Envy without hesitation, her expression contrite. "I was hoping you would."

Envy half stood during her plea for Raphael to stay, and now sat perched on the edge of the couch with her hand pressed to her stomach. When Raphael drew closer, she held her breath and forced herself to her feet, her eyes never leaving her cousin.

"May I?" Raphael reached for Envy's hand where it hovered over the mysterious injury that refused to heal but stopped shy of making contact.

The Sin was a lot of things, but stupid was not one of them. Raphael's little display put the fear of God in her, and while her eyes remained defiant, her hand shook when she moved it away from the cursed wound on her stomach.

Fortunately for her cousin, Raphael was above commenting, but she couldn't help the slight upturn of her lips as she nodded her thanks and focused her attention on the grotesque stains marring Envy's pale-yellow shirt. Both fresh and dried blood mixed with other watery fluids spread out in a wide radius from the darkened smear hovering over the wound itself. If that alone wasn't a bad enough sign, the putrid scent of infection certainly piqued Raphael's interest.

She nibbled on her bottom lip, betraying her concern. Sickly-sweet would have been better. But the stench wafting from Envy's stomach was way beyond a simple infection. Raphael flicked her eyes up to glance at Kindness, and with grace that only a queen could muster, she sank into a crouch. "Shot *and* stabbed, you say?"

"...*Yes*. C'mon, Raphael." Envy shifted her weight in discomfort, though she remained still. This was *so* awkward for her, and more than a little embarrassing. The fact that she had to resort to asking an *Archangel* for help was mortifying... but if begging got the job done and kept her in the game, then Envy would do whatever was needed.

Nothing would stop her from achieving her goal. Even if it made her skin crawl. "We both know you have more important places to be. You don't have to—"

"Rubbish. We might not see eye to eye, Envy, but Kindness was right... we *are* family. To me that still means something." The longer Raphael spoke, the more settled and detached her voice became. Her snark was gone, replaced by a curious tone as her inspection of Envy's shirt continued. "Except for right now, because you're my *patient* and that's *entirely* different."

Clinical. Impersonal. It was the same tone she used when dealing with human patients at the hospital when she found time to consult, a tool she had developed when her exile first started. One that kept her from going insane.

After all, she couldn't heal everyone. It was against the rules. Against the flow. And Raphael had discovered the hard way how badly things could get when she fought against the natural order.

"Okay..."

Raphael pulled her eyes away from Envy's stomach, looking up at her with expectation clear on her face. When the usual argument never materialized, she frowned, but Envy's only response was a tired sigh.

"*Father...* what the Hell happened to you?" To test her sudden compliance, Raphael plucked at the front of her shirt, pulling it away from the sticky wound beneath, but once again Envy just signaled her submission to the overzealous ministrations of her cousin.

Her pain... it must be...

"I already told you, I—"

She shook her head, dismissing the human's involvement. "No, I know but... can you lie down for me? I need to... *Envy. What* did this to you?"

Raphael scrabbled to one side as Envy hobbled back to the couch. Her mind spun rapid circles at the implication that Envy had not healed naturally on her own.

By all accounts, she should have... for her kind it was as natural as it was for Raphael.

"It was a... *ahhh.*"

Kindness moved closer and eased Envy into a comfortable position, fussing quietly over her as she fluffed a cushion and shoved it under her head. "Tell her what you told me, Envy. She might know..."

"A blade forged from an iron I've never seen, Raphael."

"What do you mean?"

"Not bronze or steel." Envy scowled at Kindness, but it seemed more out of habit than any need for spite. "Not even petrified wood or that rare metal found in the mines below the Congo."

"...Some new metal blend the humans have invented?" That didn't make any sense to Raphael. Human advancement had moved forward quickly in the last several hundred years, but a metal she had not heard of? Possible, but unlikely... though she would concede that Envy was closer to society than she was, and maybe she knew otherwise.

"Nothing I can find. And trust me, Raphael... I'd know."

Raphael listened intently to her cousin, but her mind and eyes were on the injury she had yet to see. With gentle hands, she took hold of the bottom of Envy's shirt and pulled it upwards to expose her stomach. When she finally laid eyes on what was troubling her so much, Raphael hissed between clenched teeth.

"What the..." Her hand trembled as she touched a finger to the angry red and blue lines radiating out from the barely healed wound above and to the left of Envy's navel.

"Oh, *that* sounds promising."

"Shush... let me work." Once again Raphael's voice grew detached as she brushed aside Envy's sarcasm and turned her complete focus to the weeping, inch-wide hole decorating her stomach. It was a tangled mess of tissue and infection, a strange blending of decay maiming the edges of new growth that would be eaten away as soon as it was produced. If Envy had not possessed the gift of accelerated healing, she would have been dead almost as soon as the injury occurred, and as it was now, with the decayed edges outnumbering the healed, it was only a matter of time before the rot completed its victory.

In short, Envy was dying. And without Raphael's help, it wouldn't be long before the first of the Sins was lost forever.

The only problem was... Raphael was not sure if she could help at all.

"Are you going to stare at my stomach *all* day?"

"Envy, she's got her thinking face on... leave her alone."

"She was thinking at the back of her eyelids a minute ago. I've been laying here for an hour already, Kindness. What could *possibly* be—"

"You're right." Raphael's voice startled them both. For the past hour, she had been silent, displaying no outward signs of activity at all, and she didn't blame Envy for growing impatient with her apparent lack of progress.

The only thing wrong with Envy's assumption... was that it was *wrong*.

Yes, Raphael had been sitting in silence. But it was with a connection to her power so delicate, so *frail*, that she needed the quiet to keep it aimed in exactly the right places. Now that she knew more about what she was looking at, Raphael was comfortable speaking again.

"... what was I right about?" Envy tried to sit up, but Kindness pushed her back down with a firm hand.

"The weapon that did this isn't anything a human made."

As one, Envy and Kindness turned incredulous eyes to Raphael. She spread her hands, highlighting her own confusion, and the surprise that rocked her when her mind detected minute traces of the alien metal deep inside the wound that speared up through her stomach.

One of Envy's eyebrows rose into her hairline, and she cast an almost sly, side-eyed glance at Kindness. "I don't remember saying *that*..."

Kindness shrugged as though Envy's smug smile didn't bother her, but the hint of amusement sparkled in her eyes. "Me either, but it was a smart thought, wasn't it?"

Clearly, their earlier argument was well and truly over, and although the mood in the room was still somber, the tension hanging heavily between the pair was no longer present.

It wasn't just Raphael who felt that relief.

"...an iron you had never seen. That's what you said. See here..." Raphael centered her palm over the top of the festering wound, sending a tiny pulse of power into Envy. She curled her fingers and lifted her hand in a pulling motion, smiling serenely when several minuscule, glowing particles detached from the mess in Envy's stomach. They rose obediently into Raphael's waiting hand and hovered there, waiting. In her other hand, Raphael conjured a small vial, and it was there that she redirect-

ed the tiny fragments for safekeeping so she could study them la
ter.

Something about them tickled at her awareness, but for the moment, the Archangel had other, more pressing issues to deal with... and therefore Raphael slid the vial beneath her shirt, tucking it securely into her bra for safe keeping.

Envy's sly grin broadened. "I didn't realize Archangels knew that trick."

"Me either." Kindness followed Raphael's movements with interest, but she blinked and turned back to Envy with a puzzled glance. "Wait, what trick?"

"Trust me, it's safe there, I can—"

"Of *course* it is... until your lover finds it later."

Raphael sat back from Envy with a shake of denial. "I... don't have a lover."

The Sin might have been down, but she was definitely not out. "Sure... that's what they all say."

"Do you mind?" Raphael fisted her hand and dug it into her own thigh. "I can always just leave, you know."

Kindness poked Envy in the arm and frowned her disappointment in silence. Envy's smile faltered and she rolled her eyes in defeat.

"I'm kidding, Raphael... Damn, how long has it been since you were able to take a joke?"

"Oh..." She didn't know where to look. Raphael could feel a knot of anxiety hovering. Envy didn't know. *How could she know?* "Sorry... I..."

Envy's expression softened for a minute, and in complete disregard for her own pain she reached over to place her hand over the top of Raphael's fist. "No, Raphael... I forget how hard it is for you. I shouldn't have teased you... not about *that.*"

So. She *did* know.

"It's fine... I'm fine. I *like* being on my own." Raphael could taste the lie, and it was foul. While it might have been true she preferred her solitude, that did not mean she wasn't lonely. But that was nothing her cousins needed to concern themselves with... and the topic was not open for discussion.

"...are you ready?" With visible effort, Raphael redirected the conversation back to the more critical issue. The one that she was actually there for. The one she *was* willing to discuss. For hours if she needed to. Anything to keep attention from her own life.

At Envy's nod, Raphael pushed her clothing a little further away from the weeping sore, exposing most of her stomach. Satisfied, the Archangel placed both hands over her focal point in a silent signal that she was also ready to begin.

A soft gold light appeared, glowing downward from Raphael's palm as she directed a thin stream of power through herself and into Envy. In this, she was nothing more than a conduit, a guide that would encourage the natural progression of what was already there... and oh, *Stars*, there was no feeling like it. In all of existence, *nothing* compared to the warmth that suffused her, the essence of *home*, of an acceptance she never felt *anywhere* else. It was surreal, it was pure love, and it was addictive. Raphael yearned even as she rejoiced when her soul connected with the center of existence, and through it, began to pull on the rivulets she needed in order to save Envy's life.

Progress was slow, and nothing like Raphael expected. In recent times, her true healing experiences were few and far between. The odd times when she intervened and assisted a human were simple tasks that generally required no more of her energy than picking up a book.

But this? *This?*

This is what I was made for.

She didn't speak, for words were not necessary. Nor was movement, but Raphael's fingers twitched in response to the silent commands she gave to the tainted flesh inside her cousin. Her mind probed the wound, joined in perfect harmony with the source of her power as she first gently bid the worst of the infection to fade, then commanded flesh to heal.

At first, nothing changed. But eventually the sinister red lines decorating Envy's skin faded to pink and slowly retreated from their sinuous crawl across her stomach. In a similar patter, their blue counterparts faded to nothing under Raphael's guidance.

But her work was not complete. Envy's infection ran deep, poisoning her bloodstream as thoroughly as it would if her system were human. Deeper she went, ignoring the gasps of pain from Envy as easily as she ignored the concerned questions from Kindness. She couldn't stop.

She wouldn't.

Not even if the fires of Armageddon were about to consume her.

Raphael had been told many, many times she was born to heal… and she didn't quite feel complete without it.

Finally, it was done. Raphael heaved out a deep breath and sat back on her heels, letting her hands fall into her lap. A quick glance at the window informed her that the sun had set, confirming that hours had passed since she left her car at the bottom of the hill.

"How are you feeling, Envy?"

From her place on the couch, Envy struggled to sit up, and this time Kindness helped her. Her face was drawn, but the grey tinge from earlier had transformed into a somewhat healthier pale. Raphael considered the alteration a win, particularly since her eyes reflected none of the pain that was present when the Archangel stormed through the door with righteous fury at her side.

"Like a two-day old kitten…" Envy traced her fingertips over her smooth, unmarked stomach and relieved burst of soft laughter escaped her before she could stop it. The Sin turned her head, her expression somewhere between troubled and grateful. "You did it, Raphael. Thank you."

"I'm not going to say I told you so." Kindness moved into the space Envy had made when she sat up, her own expression settled firmly into profound gratitude. "… that would be rude. So, I'll just say thank you too, Raphael. Thank you for coming when we needed you."

"Next time, just ask... There's no need for subterfuge." Raphael plucked at her jeans and mulled over the offer she made. Maybe if she made time... maybe if they all did, the path Raphael was treading on might not seem so daunting.

"And like *I* said, I'm here to help."

Kindness and her enigmatic offer to help was a question for another time. Raphael yawned and covered her mouth. *Father*, she was tired. "If you're feeling okay then I should go."

Both women protested, but Raphael waved them off with a smile. "I've got other work to do..."

There was no doubt in her mind that Envy's was more of a formality than any real desire to have an Archangel around. Climbing to her feet with a small, yet content groan, Raphael reached forward to touch both cousins on the shoulder in turn. She didn't even consider transporting herself away as she waved her goodbye. The healing had taken more energy out of Raphael than she cared to admit.

Besides, the walk back down the hill would do her good.

The Good Doctor Mason

The last several weeks were grueling for Levi. Ever since the day he recognized the picture of Rian Murphy sitting on the meeting room table, his life had become one misstep after the other. First, he had to mention the sighting to the task force. Then explain *why* it took him *so long* to report it... and why he was allegedly sleeping in his office instead of calling the alert. His only real stumbling point was that contrary to witness statements, he *hadn't* been sleeping at all. But admitting *that* was an even bigger problem, and Levi found it was easier to let his superiors believe he had simply stolen a moment for a much need power nap whilst waiting for lab results to come in.

For a while, that excuse worked. But then the observatory case went cold, and Levi's attention redirected to the Interpol task force instead.

Officially, anyway.

Levi accepted the reprimand on the chin. It had been a slip up, sure. But given Murphy avoided capture for at *least* a decade, one more miss in a growing pile of sightings could not be held against him for long.

Unfortunately for Levi, his little nap resulted in a performance review, and now the agent was forced to speak to an agency psychologist twice a week. Worse, the latest office gossip wagered on whether or not he was fit for duty anymore.

Of course, if he was completely honest with himself, Levi would be the first to admit that their concerns were valid, and that anyone who visibly blanked out like that while on the job was a considerable risk. But he wasn't, not by a long shot. So it was with a surly demeanor that the agent prepared himself for the *complete* emotional drain that accompanied a therapy session.

It was a feeling he was *well* acquainted with.

"Agent Malach."

Tap. Tap. Tap.

A foot to the floor. A pen scratching letters on a notebook. A blinking eye. Levi breathed deeply. *Slowly*. Listening only to the staccato he could pick out of the background and not the utter chaos in his mind.

"Agent Malach."

Doctor Eric Mason's voice cut through Levi's process. Tempered with an impatient note, his voice held a barely disguised frustration caused by Levi and the deliberate way he chose to ignore the doctor's last question.

"Not talking about *that* with you, Doctor Mason. It has no relevance here." Levi opened his eyes and smiled humorlessly at the short, balding man sitting in a low-slung chair opposite him.

That part of his life wasn't open to interpretation, and with a firm shake of his head, he brushed the question away.

"On the contrary, Mr Malach. An open case that you're *personally* connected to is *very* relevant. Why don't you tell me about it?"

It was a simple request. Innocuous enough, nevertheless Levi regarded the doctor with undisguised suspicion. He was *supposed* to trust this man, he knew that. But every question he asked led back to the same place. The same day.

The day he lost everything.

Levi's career hovered on a knife edge, and he was aware that by avoiding the issue he might doom himself to a life of mail rooms and low-grade assignments, however years later his loss still hurt. It still ached... and he wasn't going to go down without a fight.

"Nope. Everything about it is classified. Sorry." The apology was genuine, Levi's tone was heavy with the implication that he was *anything* but.

"Agent Malach," Mason's impatience became more obvious, but Levi still wasn't having it. "...aside from doctor-patient privilege, my clearance level is *higher* than your current one. I treat agents several levels above yours, so classified *isn't* an excuse you can use with me."

When Levi rolled his eyes, Mason sighed, but much to his chagrin the doctor did not back down. Instead, he surprised Levi and changed tactic.

"How about this? Don't tell me about your hometown. Forget about that for a second and just... tell me about the rest of it."

Levi had to respect his tenacity, even if he hated discussing the subject the doctor was prying into. "Sorry doc. I—"

From somewhere behind him, a soft buzzing filled the air, signaling the end of their session. Levi unfolded himself from the chair he slouched in and rose to his full height without missing a beat. "Looks like we're out of time. I'll see you Friday."

He strode to the door on determined feet, not looking back when he heard the shuffle indicating the psychologist also rose. He did stop, however, when he heard his name in an equally determined voice.

"Levi."

With one hand on the door handle, Levi turned his head to face Doctor Mason again, his stoic expression unable to conceal the raw emotion in his eyes. Too long in mourning, too long wasting his life chasing shadows... but it had been that way for so long Levi forgot how to be anything else. He learned a long time ago that sessions like this weren't going to help him at all.

In fact, they only made things worse.

"*What*? You've got everything else you need... that's not..."

"That's *exactly* why you need to talk about it." Mason's eyes were sympathetic behind his glasses where they were previously impatient.

Levi watched impassively as the doctor dropped his file on the table between the chairs and stepped around it.

"I *have* to report this Levi... You're a good man, and by all accounts a fantastic agent. I would hate to see you lose *another* promotion or your job because you couldn't open up. I just need—"

"—and if I do *open up* and you report that I'm unfit anyway? Yeah... I'm screwed either way. No thanks."

He slammed the bottom of his fist down on the door, betraying his frustration. "*Fuck.*"

There was no getting around it. The doctor was right. This cycle he was caught in had to end eventually, no matter what side of the pile Levi fell into. Maybe it would be better to just... get it over with. He yanked the door open and shuffled into the opening, but not before casting one last cautious glance behind him. "Stop by my office before you leave and I'll show you. It's easier if I just... *show you.*"

And without another moment lost, Levi was gone.

Later that afternoon Levi was not surprised when the knock on his office door revealed Doctor Mason. What *did* surprise him, however, was the pair of steaming coffee mugs he noticed in each of the psychologist's hands.

"Peace offering. I pushed you too hard and I did it deliberately." He held out one of the mugs to Levi, shrugging when the agent scowled at him through his half open door. "Would it make you feel any better if I said your reaction was favorable?"

"No." The temptation to slam the door in Mason's face was high. Levi barely restrained himself, the dilemma clear on his face for a long moment before he accepted the cup and turned away from the door, moving back into his workspace.

He *had* invited him, after all.

"...but I said I'd show you what I'm working on, and I will." Levi waved his coffee at something out of Mason's line of sight, indicating the doctor should see for himself. "Here it is."

Levi stood to one side as Mason entered and glanced around the office with a suitably curious expression. He tried not to fidget, but it was hard to remain still when his white whale was about to be exposed. For better or worse, Levi opened the door, and now he had to deal with the consequences.

Two full minutes ticked by before Mason reacted to the whiteboard pushed against one wall in Levi's office. At first he just stood there, staring at the black drop sheet covering the board with an unreadable expression on his face, but after an encouraging nod from Levi, he grabbed hold of it with his free hand and tossed it to one side.

His reaction was worth the anxiety clawing at Levi's stomach. Mason sucked in a low whistle between his teeth and ran his hand over his balding head.

"...I can see why you've got this covered up."

"Twenty-seven victims. *Twenty-eight* now. And those are just the ones I've *found*. My gut tells me there are more." Levi's focus was instant as he approached the board. He had one shot to convince Mason he wasn't either overly obsessed *or* unfit for duty... and this was it.

"But *maybes* and *mights* are not what I'm focusing on. It's the confirmed links I'm chasing. Out of the twenty-eight, I have just over half connected in some way. Four of the victims are distantly related." There was no elaboration from Levi, no glossing over anything that might make Mason decide in his favor. Just the cold, hard truth.

"Very distantly." He corrected himself after a short pause. "The rest... I don't know, doc, there's a link, I *know* there is. But establishing that it's more than a series of copycat murders or some kind of nationwide conspiracy is where I'm coming up short. It's all circumstantial and nobody is willing to commit."

Any one of those reasons should be enough. Hell, just the bodies should be enough. But somehow, it wasn't.

"Right. I see."

Mason's eyes never left the board. From Levi's perspective, the other man seemed troubled, like he had seen something he hadn't been prepared for. Or because Levi had finally convinced him that he tripped over the edge into insanity. His own eyes traced over each photograph, pinned line and data card, and he mentally linked the rest he suspected were connected as his gaze roamed the board.

"I'm no investigator, but... the words alone..."

"It's a lot to take in, I know." Levi pulled back and clamped down on his enthusiasm before it completely took over like it usually did when he was actively speaking about the case. Which was not often, but nonetheless, he was aware of his reputation. He took advantage of the brief lull in conversation to compose himself, sipping on the coffee Mason brought while he let him absorb in several minutes the horrific facts that were the driving point in Levi's life for years. "The chief knows I'm working on this between everything else. So does the ADA, but you know that. Look, this case... it crosses state lines but we're *still* being stonewalled. Nobody will invite us in... So, this is all we've got."

With a lingering glance at Annabelle's data card, Levi swallowed and turned his back on the board and sat at his desk. His foot tapped on the floor as a wave of apprehension flowed over him. He was focused on it. *Not obsessed*.

Or so he kept telling himself.

"I'm not the only agent working on multiple cases at once you know."

Even Levi knew that was probably the most ridiculous, petty sentence he could have spoken in his own defense.

He inwardly cringed and watched Mason with guarded eyes, wondering if this was the moment the psychologist decided he was a lost cause.

"No Agent Malach, but you're the only one in this office *personally* connected to one of them." The doctor held up his free hand to stall Levi's next comment before he could voice it and pushed on with his own observations instead, forcing the agent to listen. "You know what the protocol there is. And *you know* why they asked me to talk to you. It's not just about the lapse a couple of weeks back."

Levi kept his expression calm, though a storm raged inside him. Thunderclouds billowed with violent red lights flashing within. It wasn't anger at the doctor that suffused him. Mason was just doing his job. No, Levi's despair was borne on the deepening clarity that he was never, *ever* going to get the endorsement he needed to give these victims and their families a measure of peace. It wasn't fair. It wasn't right.

But there was also nothing he could do about it while his hands were tied.

"So make your recommendations, Doctor Mason. Have me ordered to drop it. Have me fired. You and I both know I won't stop."

When Mason only raised an eyebrow at Levi's honesty and sat down in silence on the other side of the desk, Levi wondered if perhaps his assumption that the doctor had already judged him was made in haste.

"...Like you said," Levi kept talking before Mason could interrupt. He *had* to make his justifications, and he had to make Mason see that he wasn't motivated by revenge. "There's a personal connection. But I'm telling you it was a *long* time ago. At first I was angry, now I just want justice."

He set the cup down carefully, refusing to give Mason the satisfaction of a reaction to what was obviously another deliberately baited comment. Leaning back in his chair, Levi tapped a few words on his keyboard, and brought up a new file to show Mason. He spun his monitor around and pointed at the list of names displayed in a bold black font. Each name had a number typed next it. Twenty-eight victims. Twenty-eight families.

"...But be sure to take a copy of this file with you so you can *personally* contact twenty-eight families and *tell them why* the only active investigation into the deaths of their loved ones has been canceled."

Rian vs Levi

Rian stepped out of the shadows cast by an awning and into the warm Californian sun. The same dark shades Levi had seen him wearing last time covered his eyes, but aside from the assassin being consistent with his wardrobe choices, it was hardly important. No, what was important *here* was the fact that after weeks of searching, weeks of false leads and dead ends, he had *finally* tracked down the man currently enjoying fourth place among Interpol's most wanted.

It was a fluke, in all honesty. A potential sighting by an off-duty police officer was called in, and after tracking the suspicious figure via traffic cameras for several blocks, Levi's team managed to locate him. Even better, they kept the surveillance in place without detection... which in turn, led to Levi joining the squad sent to apprehend him.

They followed Murphy's movements from a distance, tracking him into a department store, where several agents from the combined FBI and Interpol unit followed.

Two played the classic bickering couple, another was browsing through the sporting goods section, and yet one more watched the children's area just in case things went awry. Unfortunately for Levi, he pulled the short straw, and now picked his way somewhat awkwardly through the lingerie department, ostensibly seeking a gift for his girlfriend. According to the barely disguised humor in his earpiece, it was a better choice than a single adult male watching the playground.

It was awkward. *So fucking awkward*, but it had been so long since Levi had even *thought* about anyone in *any* kind of way, or the underwear she might be wearing that his disguise was perfect.

He had no idea what he was doing *or* what he was looking at, even the designs had changed since the last time Levi looked twice with any interest in satin and lace. So many styles. So many colors. So many... *everything*. Needless to say, it was confronting for the agent. The sting of loss still echoed in his chest, the bittersweet memory of a love long gone... and right there by its side stood the ever-apparent lonely hole of misery his life had become. Racks and rows of private, intimate clothing only reminded him of what he lacked, and Levi couldn't help but feel a growing petty resentment toward the team leader that grinned at his protest and sent him in anyway.

The tightness around Levi's dark eyes matched perfectly with his down-turned lips. One or the other Levi could have brushed off as concentration, but it was the combination that betrayed him.

Guilt. Sadness. *Anger.* A melancholy longing that would never be fulfilled. He felt it all. It churned in his soul, drawing a darkness over him that could only end one way. And the longer Levi was stuck in his own private hell, the more overwhelming it all became. He kept his head low, avoiding all eye contact as he browsed his way through endless displays of exquisite silk and delicate lace, but that didn't mean he was any less alert.

No, not for this.

Levi fought hard against the darkness lingering in his mind, forcing it to focus on the area he patrolled instead. He scanned it constantly, squinting back at his hands now and then when he held up a bra or pair of panties for closer inspection.

Just another confused man buying lingerie for his girlfriend.

That's a nice blue.

A series of images rose unbidden in Levi's mind.

Sensual curves hidden by the same blue lace. Miles of smooth, flawless skin he knew would be warm and supple under his hand. A candle in the darkness, the mournful sound of weeping, a hand, exploding out of a freshly dug grave and another, more certain feeling that if he could just -

As suddenly as the images appeared, Levi brushed them away, and with his scowl once again firmly in place, he shoved the expensive, flimsy piece back on the rack where it belonged.

Great.

Another vague moment was the last thing he needed. Especially on a stakeout. With troubled eyes, Levi scanned the area over the top of the lingerie rack wondering what he missed, but breathed a quiet sigh of relief when everything was still in place, still where it needed to be.

Elderly couple. Parent with pram. Clerk on her phone. Agent Foster flicking through a brochure.

Check.

Less than twenty seconds had passed between Levi picking up the hanger and returning it to the rack, but in the confusion it felt like an hour. An hour standing in front of a bra daydreaming about things that made *no fucking sense* and looking like a pervert.

Darkness hovered again, clawing at his sanity with renewed force.

I need to get out of here.

Levi took a hasty step back into the aisle, realizing too late that his fingers were still wrapped around the accursed hanger. He released it with a start, but not before he felt the cold steel muzzle of a gun prod firmly into his right side.

"Aww, I think your *little* lady friend will *love* it. You should buy it for her."

The oddly accented voice froze Levi on the spot. Years of training told the agent that with certain precise movements he could break free, but Levi was painfully aware how fast a bullet could move, *and* he knew damn well he would be dead before he could reach his own concealed weapon.

If he wasn't already.

Lady friend?

He kept his eyes facing forward, refusing to submit to the instinctive urge telling him to sneak a glance at the man grinding a gun into his ribcage. Twenty seconds of daydreaming. That was all it had taken for *everything* to fall apart. And *of course,* he was the one to ruin it. Levi clenched his teeth, trying to hide the frustration that was simmering inside him, but the bitter taste of disappointment caused it to spill over despite his efforts.

"I don't *have* a lady friend."

The muzzle dug in harder, driven so deeply into his side Levi felt his ribs complain under the pressure. One crack in the wrong direction and his lungs would fill with blood. Drowning in his own fluids was *definitely* not on his top ten list of ways to die.

"Sure you do. Kind of short. Pretty little thing. If she's *not* your girlfriend, why do you follow her around so much?"

That could only be...

"...the *fuck* do you want *Murphy*?" There was nothing... *nothing,* like the sudden, dreadful knowledge that no matter how careful Levi had been, no matter how skillfully the task-force tracked him, or how well they'd managed to conceal themselves... Rian Murphy was one step ahead of them, and he had been there the *entire fucking time.*

"A chat..."

Levi sensed the body behind him move in, and the hairs rose on the back of his neck as Murphy leaned in so close it was almost intimate.

"*With you,* Agent Malach."

"So?" That was a surprise. Levi didn't dare relax his stance, but he did release the breath he'd been holding. Slowly. "What's stopping you? Talk."

"Tell your friends to beat it."

Rian's voice was curt, betraying a little of the tension he no doubt masked beneath the calm exterior he projected. From everything he read about the assassin, Levi knew it would take a lot more than a few smart insults for him to lose control.

Or so he hoped.

He shook his head, letting out a wry huff. "Can't do that, Murphy... Y'know, I thought you were smarter than that. They'll let *me* die before they let *you* walk out of here."

"Bullshit."

It wasn't a lie. The desire to stop Rian Murphy put an end to the trail of bodies left in his wake far outweighed the loss of one agent.

"You think I'm gonna lie to you when I'm two inches from death?" It was closer to one inch, but in that moment Levi didn't care about precision. Death was death, and he would prefer to keep the reaper as far away as possible. "I'm disposable and you know it."

"...fuck."

"Rian Murphy. Put the weapon down and surrender. You're surrounded."

In true belated fashion, the cavalry had arrived, but for the moment they were merely circling. Waiting. Without moving his head, Levi caught the eye of a colleague hiding behind a rack of tank tops about ten yards away. But it seemed that Murphy had spotted the agent too, because before he could react, the pressure on his ribcage disappeared. There was no relief for Levi though. Not even a second later he felt it again. Only this time the cold steel crushed his ear.

"... play the game, FBI or I *swear* I'll take you down with me."

Despite the gravity of the situation, and the drumming of his heart as it tried to escape from his chest, Levi was curious. Murphy could have left at any time. Hell, he didn't even *need* to be there in the first place. He could have slipped out before any of them even picked his likeness out of the crowd. A man like that did not elude capture for so long without developing a few tricks of his own.

Like a way to —

Son of a bitch.

"Okay! *Okay.* Stand down. This is Malach. I repeat. *Stand down.*" Full realization hit Levi with the energy of a derailed freight train at full speed. The *entire* operation was a farce. There was not a *single* thing about this day that the FBI or their Interpol counterparts were in control of... and if Levi had been allowed to entertain the idea, he would have admitted the sting Murphy just pulled off was genius.

If he had been allowed to.

"*You* called the tip line, didn't you?"

"Move. Into the change room."

Levi moved as directed, acutely aware that the further he got from backup, the slimmer his chances of survival were. If there were any to begin with. It only took a few steps before the only objects in his line of sight were the racks of discarded clothing that nobody wanted... and it didn't take a genius to know that he was, effectively cornered.

How had things gone so bad, so fast? Twenty fucking seconds.

"You know they're gonna be in here soon, right?"

"Yeah, but we won't be here."

Rian shoved him forward, causing him to stumble through the door into one of the fitting rooms. He felt rather than saw that Rian followed, squeezing himself into the cubicle behind him. The door slammed closed before Levi could even muster a thought about objecting, and one look at the gun Murphy aimed at his chest dispelled any faint trace of hope that the agent would escape with his life intact.

"See that's the beauty of these old buildings... there's always a way out."

He watched in sullen silence when Rian nudged at the mirror with his free hand, raising his eyebrows in surprise when the glass swung backwards to reveal a hidden passage within the confines of the wall.

"Let's go. I want some distance between me and your *friends* before they start getting clever."

For a few precious seconds Levi could only stare between the opening in the wall and the assassin that had him cornered. Something about this didn't feel right, but it wasn't the fear of dying that had Levi erring on the side of caution. "What are you doing?"

"Giving you a heads up." Rian motioned irritably with the gun. "In you go."

Levi scowled at the assassin and his stupid gun, but he did as he was ordered and passed through the opening without a fuss. Once through, he glanced up and down the passageway to assess the scene but made no other movement that might cause Rian to think he was going to run.

"Which way?"

"Left. Lucky you're thin, FBI or you might have trouble fitting through the gap ahead."

"Whatever." Levi started down the passageway, not bothering to check if Rian was following him. It was a given that he would since the assassin had gone to so much trouble to isolate Levi from his team in the first place. "Why don't you tell me what the Hell you want so you can go about your day?"

"Not so easy... you think I want to do this anymore than you do? C'mon mate, be realistic."

Some of Murphy's words were harder to decipher than others. While his accent wasn't thick, there were times when Levi found himself wanting to ask the Irishman to repeat himself. He refused though, taking the time to run the words over in his mind instead. As long as he got the gist of it, Levi figured he was fine.

"I'd give you my opinion, *mate,* but I have no fucking idea what you're talking about."

Rian's bitter laugh echoed off the passage walls behind him.

"The angels. That case you're working on."

The universe stopped moving.

Levi halted with it; his feet suddenly too heavy to take one single step forward. He floundered on the spot, lurching forward again when Rian bumped into him from behind.

The angels.

Darkness swam at the edge of Levi's vision again, and he thrust out one hand to steady himself on the dirty white wall to his right. One breath. Two. And then another. In. Out.

"I see I've got your attention."

Was he serious?

Of *course* he had Levi's attention. He had *all* of it. Levi straightened himself, pushed off the wall and turned to face the man who had just unknowingly altered his entire existence.

"What about it?"

Rian's expression was grim, though his stance was no less defensive. "It's not what you think. I've seen things, FBI. *Heard things...*"

His voice trailed off to a soft, accented whisper that Levi could barely hear. It was well hidden, but Levi caught the way Murphy's eyes darted to the corridor behind him.

Looking for his way out.

"I think you're fighting a war you *can't* win and he's *not* going to stop. C'mon, keep moving." The pistol flicked toward Levi, but despite the imminent threat, the agent refused to budge.

For a *decade* he had been waiting for something, *anything* that would give him direction, a place to start truly looking for who was responsible for Annabelle's death... and there was no chance in Hell he would take a pass on the chance to gain new information. Even if it came from a disreputable source like Murphy. He took half a step closer to Rian, only stopping when the other man raised the gun again in warning.

"Who isn't? What isn't what I think? *What do you know, Murphy?*"

The gun lowered just enough for Levi to relax again. He stepped back to give the assassin space, raising his hands to indicate Murphy was still in charge. A bleak smile hovered on Rian's lips, a mirthless line devoid of humor. Levi twisted his body away and headed deeper into the corridor without being asked. *Again.* It wasn't easy to turn his back on the wrong end of a gun. He strode ahead of Rian as though he didn't have a care in the world, however the tightness in his chest belied the confidence in his step.

I need to know.

The longer he kept Murphy away from his well-meaning colleagues, the more information he could pull out of him. In theory. Footsteps quickened behind him as the Irishman scurried to catch up, and Levi couldn't help his own satisfied smirk when Rian squeezed into step beside him.

"I only know him as Jim... He sent me to kill someone."

"The Observatory?" Levi frowned. It was the only new case he had been working on. The only new *angel* one, anyway. He grunted his disbelief and dismissed the possibility. Somehow he could not bring himself to believe that Rian Murphy was the murderer he was fruitlessly searching for all these years. Or maybe he just hoped he wasn't, which in itself, was a strange thought. "Not your style."

This time, when Rian smiled, Levi caught sight of something else.

Professional pride, maybe?

"Thanks for noticing... Yes, *her*. But no, at the same time. Let's just say someone fecked up and sent me to take care of a feisty young lady who didn't die... *twice*... and that same someone mentioned the Observatory to one of my... ahh... associates."

By now the pair had passed through several junctions in the corridor and as good as Levi's sense of direction was, he begrudgingly admitted to himself that he was completely disoriented. When they reached yet another crossroad, he stopped moving again and stuck out his hand to bar the way before Rian could protest.

"Wait a second..." Or shoot him. Or both. "So, you're telling me that—"

From somewhere far behind them, Levi heard a muffled crash, followed by the sound of shattering glass. One glance at Rian was all he needed to know that he heard it too. The assassin's gaze darted away as soon as their eyes met, flicking back and forth along the corridor as individual voices began to emerge from the darkness.

"This is where I leave you, Malach."

Levi took a hasty step backwards when Murphy suddenly pushed past, grunting as his back collided with the wall behind him. This was the first time he had seen the assassin's feathers ruffled, and he knew it was dangerous to push him further, but at the same time he couldn't help it.

Rian had dangled an answer in front of him like the proverbial carrot, and now Levi was hungry for more. He launched himself forward again and wrapped his hand around the other man's bicep. "Now wait a minute…"

"Remember, *I* came to *you*." Rian tried to shake himself free, but Levi had strengths of his own and held fast without effort. "This is bigger than both of us. *Fuck*. Let me *go*, FBI. I'll contact you again when it's safe."

Duty bound Levi to stop Murphy from escaping.

"I *can't* just *let* you leave."

It *insisted* that the assassin be detained *no matter what,* even if it cost Levi his life. If anyone had asked him that morning if he were ready to do whatever it took to bring Murphy to justice, Levi would have agreed without hesitation.

Only… that was this morning, and Levi did not know what he knew now.

… Bigger than both of us.

He's a murderer.

But he's got answers. The families need answers. I need answers.

The voices grew louder. Any minute now his team would round the corner and the opportunity for answers would be gone.

And if he didn't let the assassin go, they might be gone forever.

"God dammit." Levi bit off the curse and threw his hand up, releasing Murphy to chase his freedom through whatever escape path he had already chosen. The same hand wiped at his mouth and then up through his dark hair in quick, jerky movements that only enhanced the sudden tightness in his chest. "*Fuck.*"

He had just given away the *one* moment where it felt like Rian hadn't been in complete control. It was too late to change his mind, and he didn't know if he even wanted to. Despite his physical reaction, Levi's mind was already trying to fabricate a plausible reason for the assassin's escape.

"I know... sorry about this. Actually, that's a lie."

"Wha—"

Levi had been watching the junction for signs of life when he heard a quiet footstep behind him. A rush of air was all the warning he got. Agony erupted above his ear, and he staggered forward, shaking his head once in an attempt to clear the fog that swarmed in to accompany the pain, but it was no use. The corridor tilted as Levi's world faded to black... and by the time the cavalry arrived to save the day, Rian Murphy was nowhere in sight.

The Sneaky Beer

Levi jogged up the stairs leading to his front door several days later. The afternoon sun was fast approaching the horizon, and although he had enjoyed his usual run along the foreshore, today he hadn't lingered. Well. Not for long. He ran two laps of the lighthouse loop, half hoping to bump into Raphael on her skates again... but on the second descent through the small reserve and down the slope of the bluff, that half hope turned into an odd feeling of disappointment. Oddly, that had *nothing* to do with the fact that she was a suspect.

Not that he realized. Or would have admitted it if he did. The *only* thing Levi wanted to think about was putting one foot in front of the other. And the ice-cold beer waiting for him at home.

He let himself in, closing the door with one foot as he tossed his keys onto the stand in the entryway. It wasn't a large house by Los Angeles standards, but it had all the space he needed. The three bedrooms were more than enough to suit his needs. He took the main one, of course, a large room with a small walk-in closet at the rear of the upper floor that overlooked the valley below. The second, Levi converted to a study that contained a more in-depth analysis board of the angel case, and since he didn't encourage visitors to stay, the fold-out sofa he shoved into the third as an afterthought not long after moving in definitely made up for the lack of extra bedding if it was needed.

Fortunately for Levi—or perhaps his guests—he rarely needed it.

In truth, it was probably a little too big, but it wasn't the bedrooms that encouraged him to buy the house when it had gone up for auction after the end of the recession. And it certainly hadn't been the moldy brown bathroom tiles *or* the kitchen that lost three of its laminate orange cupboard doors somewhere along the way. No, the deck that ran across the back of the house... and the expansive view of the hills and valleys below made the decision for him. It was a taste of privacy. An illusion of space in an area so populated that sometimes Levi felt the walls closing in. Sure, it was a little out of his budget, but Levi fought hard to get it, and had moved into his new house with the echo of the auction hammer still ringing in his ears.

Right now, though, the only ringing in Levi's ears was the lingering headache from the ugly bruise Rian Murphy left on his skull when he pistol whipped him in the corridor. Levi regained consciousness in the emergency room a couple of hours later with a pounding headache... and one of his prime suspects hovering over him with a concerned look on her face and a penlight in her hand.

"His pupils are dilating fine now. With all that blood it's lucky he didn't need stitches... Yes, as soon as he wakes up properly I'll organize his papers. How long 'til radiology is ready?"

Voices so loud. Did she have to shout? "...mmmawake."

Levi blinked his eyes open, only to squeeze them shut again when the light seared his pupils.

"So you are. Welcome back. I understand you gave your team quite a scare."

"Mmm. Where am I?"

"Cedars Sinai... you landed in my ER. Lucky me."

Although he already knew it was true, Levi hadn't been able to stop the amazement from entering his tone. "...you really do work here."

"I wouldn't lie to you, Agent Malach."

... or the scorn.

"No, but I feel like you'd only tell me half the truth."

Her quiet exhale made him open his eyes again. Levi was just in time to catch the doubt cloud her eyes. "Half the truth is all you can deal with."

"Not in my book."

"They tell me you saw who did this to you."

He nodded, but the pain in his skull hurt too much for more than a gentle incline. "Yeah... Someone I've been chasing for a while now. An assassin on Interpol's most wanted list."

"Interpol...interesting. And he left you alive?"

"Apparently so." Even fresh out of a concussion, Levi kept his secrets well. "Who knows what the fu—heck his reasons were. Not me. For all I care Rian Murphy can burn in Hell."

"Rian... Murphy?"

This time he caught the way her schooled features slipped, and the way Raphael slammed them back into place. "Yeah, why... do you know the name?"

"Only what I've heard on the radio."

The conversation ended quickly not long after, with Raphael excusing herself to check on the wellbeing of her other patients. Levi, on the other hand, used the time to mull over her words, but in all honesty all he wanted to do was go home and eat a bottle of painkillers.

It took another six hours for them to release him, and by the time he made it through his front door, the fresh colors of dawn stained the hilltops beyond the valley he was too tired to admire from the floor to ceiling windows in his living room.

Four days later Levi still wasn't cleared to go back to work, but he expected to be passed in the morning when he reported to his regular doctor for a checkup.

He bypassed the entrance to his living space, angling for the kitchen to grab the locally crafted pale ale that had been calling his name for the last hour.

Bottle in hand, Levi headed for the bathroom, peeling off his sweaty running clothes along the way. His shirt disappeared first, dropping to the floor in a messy pile that he immediately tripped on when he leaned into the shower cubicle to flick on the tap. As the water heated, he kicked off his running shoes and dropped his pants, shoving the sweat scented heap against the wall. Levi already knew that his rumbling stomach would not let him linger under the spray for too long, but damn, he was going to enjoy it.

At least until he finished his beer.

Fifteen minutes later Levi stood shirtless at his kitchen counter contemplating his dinner options with an empty beer bottle in one hand. His dark hair was still glistening from the hot water, and in his eagerness to settle the hunger pangs, Levi had missed a few places with his towel. Droplets of water scattered across his broad shoulders, and the fine hairs on his chest and stomach lay flat in their damp state. The temptation to order in was all too real, but one look at the contents of his freezer canceled any of those half-formed plans... the almost countless number of leftover containers stared at him accusingly from the frozen abyss, filled him with guilt and deleted that option right out of him.

With an overly dramatic sigh, he set the empty bottle down and reached blindly for a container to let fate decide the menu, vowing then and there to start taking the monstrous number of leftovers for lunch instead.

It was a vow he had made before. And in all honesty one he'd make again.

He shoved the container into the microwave without looking at its contents and set it to defrost, moving back to the fridge to take another beer. However, when he leaned into the open door, the accented voice he *never* expected to hear *in his own home* startled him.

"Grab another one for me while you're at it."

Levi jumped out of his own skin, smacking his newly healed head against the corner of the opening.

"Son of a bitch."

With his hand plastered to the back of his head, Levi spun upwards out of the fridge, coming to his full height as he turned to confront the grinning face of Rian Murphy, who leaned a little too casually on the far side of his counter.

Where the fuck did he come from?

Rian had the audacity to look shocked... and Levi did *not* fail to notice the beer he *already* held in his left hand. A craft beer from *exactly* the same brewery as the empty one on his counter.

"What? Do your ears not work? I said I'd contact you again."

Blood boiled in Levi's veins, and he grit his teeth so hard his jaw ached. "In my *fucking house*? How the Hell did you find out where I live, Murphy?"

The Irishman snorted out a short laugh. "I found out where you live *weeks* ago, Malach. Relax. If I wanted you dead I would've taken you out already."

Unbelievable.

"I'm not as easy to kill as you might think."

Rian lifted an eyebrow but said nothing. Levi returned his contemplative stare with one that made cold-blooded killers talk, but all Murphy did was purse his lips and sip from the bottle in his hand before motioning with it to the windows on his right.

"My rifle scope from the hillside about a mile to the east says otherwise."

Checkmate. *Again.*

He couldn't breathe. All Levi could do was swallow at the insinuation that Murphy had *already* seen him through the crosshairs. *Damn.* He *never* would have seen it coming. Never would have heard the shot. And most likely, never had time to react to the sound of shattered glass before his head exploded and his brains decorated the carpet. Blood drained out of his face as his heart slowed, and a wave of dizziness tore through him. Fingers clawed into the edge of the counter and Levi pointlessly tried to hide the shock that rattled him.

Such a casual conversation about his own death. Sure. No big deal.

At least Murphy had the grace to let his imminent mortality sink in without gloating too hard.

"Your... you... *fuck.* What are you doing here?"

"I'd *like* to be enjoying another beer, but *you* seem to have forgotten your manners."

Levi blinked at him, once again speechless. Since there did not seem to be any getting rid of Murphy, Levi passed him one of his precious beers. "Right... Here."

He frowned at the bottle as the assassin took it from him. This was the last thing Levi needed. An association with a wanted criminal, one he was meant to be hunting down... not enjoying one of California's finest with. Unfortunately for Levi, this was Rian's game, and until he knew what Murphy wanted, he had no choice.

He *had* to play along.

Rian twisted the cap off and lifted the bottle to examine the label. "Craft beer eh? I'm surprised, Malach. Picked you for a mainstream kinda guy."

"When this slice of Heaven exists? Hardly." He took a long swig of his own, only to drop the bottle and reach for a weapon that wasn't there when a series of expletives cut through the air. "What the..."

Rian looked between him and the bottle, and a slow smile appeared. "Heaven might be right... damn I wish I'd hit that shelf while you were belting out that power ballad instead. Anyway..."

He set the beer down and just like that, his smile disappeared.

"I didn't risk my life to chat with you about craft beer, Malach."

Levi turned, picked up a cloth and wiped away the mess he made. Great. Not only had Murphy broken in, but he had *also* been there long enough to know Levi sang in the shower. His gaze darted back to the assassin. "I figured as much."

"How's the head?"

"*Now* you ask?"

Rian shrugged, though he looked slightly uncomfortable. "Well, I was going to lead with that, but I saw the beer and..."

"Huh... Well, it's fine." Honestly. "A slight concussion, fair bit of blood... but no stitches."

"That pretty doctor of yours did a good job then."

"Yeah, she... Wait a minute." That was *his* witness. Suspect. Or something. One Levi felt oddly protective of despite his suspicions. There was just *something* about her that he couldn't figure out. "What do you know about—"

In a heartbeat Rian's grin reappeared. "Lots of things. But she's not why I'm here."

Levi ran a weary hand through his hair and took another long pull on his beer. Any minute now Interpol was going to bust in and arrest them both for collusion, he'd end up in prison for helping a wanted fugitive and there would be *nothing* he could do about it. Even *he* would not believe his excuses.

"No offense, Murphy, but it's been a day and I'm fucking tired... get to the point."

"The *point*, Special Agent Malach, is this." Murphy placed both hands on the counter and leaned in. "For *years* I've been tracking whoever was responsible for the loss of *everything* that was important to me. For years, I've had *no* information whatsoever."

The story sounded so familiar it sent a chill down Levi's spine, but he merely rolled one shoulder and ignored the strange sensation of... whatever it was that stirred inside him.

"... what does this have to do with my case?"

"Everything. Maybe nothing. But you need to see for yourself. Here." With his free hand, Rian reached into his jacket, his fingers finding their way to the inside pocket with practiced ease. When he withdrew it, a small device was in his hand. He pressed down on the side, and the screen glowed once as the system came to life. "Give it a minute."

A few minutes later an image appeared. Levi couldn't see it clearly through Murphy's fingers, and so he motioned impatiently for the assassin to give him a better view. He was a little surprised when Rian did so without his usual sarcastic comments, but he withheld his own until he could see why one of Interpol's most wanted would risk *both* their lives to bring him information... information Levi was still in the dark about.

The image cleared.

"What. The fuck?"

Rian's smile held no traces of mirth. "You know what this is?"

"Of course I do." Levi bristled and fisted his hand against the counter. "Is this your idea of a joke Murphy?"

"Not bloody likely. This, FBI... this is the *last* thing my Ranger unit saw before it was annihilated."

So many bodies. So much blood.

But the only thing Levi could focus on were the same six words that had haunted him for over a decade.

The angels made me do it.

Prisoner Consolidation

Somewhere lost in time.

Everywhere he looked, it was dark, but that was nothing new. Most of the time it was dark. *Most* of the time the world was a place so black the deepest pits of Tiamatu blazed like Hellfire in comparison. In fact, the only light he ever saw existed when his captor came down to the depths of wherever he was to visit.

And to gloat.

The prisoner could never understand *why* the one who held him insisted on parading himself back and forth like a beast performing a mating display. But then the prisoner had lost all sense of understanding long ago.

Somewhere around the fourth millennia he lost count. Or the fourth day. Who could tell anymore?

What was I?

Who was I?

Who am I?

The only thing his tortured soul knew was pain. And the only thing he could measure was the passing of it, those precious seconds in time when the thin, razor-sharp wires that attached to him stopped draining his body of the very essence that kept him alive.

At least, he thought they were wires.

They emerged from the darkness somewhere above where he lay sprawled on the floor in his prison, the slow, sinuous gliding of a hundred tiny snakes that latched onto him and burrowed into his skin wherever they took purchase. A hundred tiny bites that mercilessly tore him to shreds and anchored in his bones, bringing his mind back to the gruesome countdown that only ended when his body dropped to the floor once again. Once connected, the snakes hauled him to his feet to begin the next step of the process. More attachments wound out of the shadows, these ones thicker and designed to hold his head in place to ensure that even if he wanted to, the prisoner could not look beyond where he was *permitted* to.

It was around the time his head was secured that the lights blinked on. Sometimes. And it was *also* around that time his captor decided to appear, taking perverse pleasure in standing at the furthest edge of the light, mocking the prisoner in his clipped, taunting voice as the wires prepared to suck the life essence out of his very soul.

Oddly, he only entered the circle of light *after* the process had begun and the prisoner was properly subdued... but once he *was* fully illuminated, there was no doubt in his mind that the one who held him enjoyed strutting around his grand prize while delivering a running update on events he did not understand.

Sometimes, he wished he could bring himself to care.

But he couldn't. Not anymore. Not when the only life he knew was this one. Held in suspension, arms and legs stretched out in a gross parody of the snow-imprints he used to carve with his body as a child. At least, he thought he did. His memories were so vague it was impossible to tell which were real and which were... *not*. He could not even see the *things* that were attached to his arms and legs and held them that way, but he sure could feel them. His captor made sure of it, always watching him with gleeful, malicious eyes until the agony kicked in and the torture truly began.

The pain... it was all he knew. But it was okay. The pain had become his friend.

Albeit a distant one.

Sure, the pain might have become a friend, but unfortunately for the prisoner it *always* brought one of its own along for the ride.

Without fail, it greeted him with a slide into despair that never ended. A slide into darkness that had *nothing* to do with the blackness that embraced him like a lover. No, that *particular* friend hung around long after the wires retracted again and he had been unceremoniously dumped back on the floor, bereft of any of the energy he initially tried to hide. Nowadays his apathy was too strong to bother. The wires would tap into *everything* he had and leave him with only enough energy to keep his heart beating for the time it took his reserves to build back up again.

The wires were clever. They could measure when he was on the brink of death, and like clockwork, the sinuous, evil appendages retracted just as his heart was about to give out and allow him that last small merciful taste of oblivion.

"Oh good, you're awake!"

He didn't respond. He couldn't. The only thing he *could* do was stare with hopeless, dead eyes at the one who had bound him since fire claimed his life.

"Nothing to say? Shame. I really wanted your opinion on something. Remember when we used to do that?"

The question was as insincere as the tone that delivered it, and the silence that followed spoke volumes about how the prisoner felt regarding what happened around him.

Nothing.

"No? Okay then... just remember, *I asked.*"

With a magnanimous wave of his hand, he stepped backward and snapped his fingers. At first, nothing happened, but after a minute, the prisoner heard a shuffling sound somewhere to his left. Like something was being dragged or pushed across the floor. Several somethings. Even if he wanted to look, the cables ensured he could not, and so he didn't bother wasting the energy until it was right in front of him.

The overhead light focused on him flared into a new level of brilliance as, in some weird simultaneous show of power, several other lights flicked on. Each new illumination pointed downward, each one shining its terrible light on an empty space that looked eerily familiar. The eager eyes of his captor bore into him, but the prisoner gave him no satisfaction.

Not until the shuffling grew louder, and from out of the darkness he saw his prison for the first time.

One by one, dark clad figures wheeled containment pods identical to his into each circle of light while others fastened it into place. One by one, the prisoner scanned each pod, and one by one his despair darkened. Every pod he could see held a captive, just like him. A trophy. But the circle of trophies was not complete.

"I decided to consolidate my... *assets.*"

During his time in the pod, the prisoner suffered endlessly. His mind had taken a vacation, his memories became flawed, and any hope he once had dwindled to nothing. But he could still count and judging by the gap left in the space opposite him, four places remained.

Four places. Four pods.

And just as the thought registered, three empty pods wheeled into place, leaving a space on a slight angle in front of his own position.

"It's a damn pity it's too soon to put the one I *really* want right in front of you..."

Despite his despondent state, the empty pods caught his attention. The prisoner was alert *just enough* to recognize it as a deliberately cruel move designed to torment him even further. In his apathetic state, his mind wandered from pod to pod again, contemplating which unfortunate souls were doomed to become his companions... but he didn't have time to do more than wonder before his jailer stepped into his line of sight once again.

"...but I think *this* one will do nicely for the time being."

His gaze jerked to the empty space when the last containment pod was rolled into place and secured by the same shadowy figures as the others. With more curiosity than he thought he was capable of; the prisoner allowed his awareness to be drawn forward to the figure suspended in the pod directly in front of him... and there was no mistaking the cry of wretched despair that erupted from him when recognition finally dawned.

Oh Stars... no.

The Case of the Disappearing Assassin

"What do you mean, he's *gone*?"

Raphael's voice was flat when she registered the ball that Kindness dropped into her lap. Against her better judgement, she returned to Envy's house when her excruciatingly polite cousin had called to inform her of an emergency... only to find Kindness sitting cross-legged on the carpet surrounded by Lego. Humming quietly to herself. Without a *trace* of the urgency that made Raphael forget about her car and make haste through the aethers instead.

"...'Ness?"

The Virtue continued pushing small pieces of plastic together, her face a mask of concentration. Raphael would have found the way her tongue poked out ever so slightly kind of adorable *if* she wasn't already fuming and fervently wishing she had listened to her instincts. She paced back and forth, waiting for Kindness to respond.

"Please... can you focus for a minute?"

"I *am* focused, Raphael." Kindness tilted her head so she could see Raphael better. A smile tugged at the edge of her lips, hesitant, as though she knew her adopted cousin was about to blow a fuse. "There. All done."

"..." She loved Kindness. Really, she did. But in times like this Raphael needed the wisdom inside her, not the childlike exterior she presented to the rest of the world. "What are you doing?"

"Making Legos." The hand-built spaceship wove through the air between them, lifting of its own accord as Kindness directed a tiny amount of power into it. "That's number seven. I have three to go. Want to help?"

In spite of herself, Raphael smiled at the faint zooming engine sounds her cousin was making as the tiny craft dipped and swayed around the room. "I see... may I ask *why*?"

"Oh..."

Her hesitation was clear, but she continued when Raphael pinched the bridge of her nose and inhaled to dispel her irritation.

"I'm sorry, Raphael."

Much like her, Kindness would not do anything without purpose... only this time it interfered with the task at hand, and Raphael did not have time for her to mosey her way to the point. "... sorry about what?"

"I can't leave any of the children in your ward out. It wouldn't be fair! You know that."

Her words came with an admonishment, pulling Raphael back from the exasperated comment that formed on her lips. She exhaled the breath and nodded, stepping back when Kindness bounced to her feet with her curly hair flicking in every direction.

"So I'm making ten! That's one each."

"I suppose you're right." Suitably chastised for her impatience, Raphael glanced at the Lego armada her cousin had made and sank down onto the rug. "If he's gone again, there's little difference a moment or two will make."

Kindness frowned and glanced down at her cousin, emphatically shaking her head, as she held out her hand for Raphael to take. "I don't think he left of his own accord this time, Raph. Come."

There goes that name again.

"But... what about your spaceships?"

Before she knew what happened, Kindness invaded her space and hauled her to her feet again. Raphael followed, bemused as the Virtue led her through a pair of sliding glass doors to the undercover patio preceding the lavish pool Envy had in her garden. It wasn't until she stood by the table that Kindness turned and wordlessly pointed to a small object lying beneath it. Raphael crouched to peer under the table, and her frown reappeared when she realized it was a phone lying face down on the terracotta tiles.

"I don't..." She groped for the phone, sliding it closer to herself before her fingers wrapped around the edges and lifted it from the tiles. Shuffling sideways, Raphael glanced curiously at Kindness before flipping it over in her hand.

The screen was cracked and lifeless.

Her brow furrowed in confusion as she tried to turn on the device. It vibrated weakly in her hand but did little else. "What am I looking at, Kindness?"

"It's *Rian's* phone. But that's not all of it."

Once again Raphael was hauled to her feet and dragged along the patio. This time Kindness pulled her through another set of doors and into the kitchen, but she faltered on the threshold, her step curiously hesitant.

"...What's going on, 'Ness?"

Kindness dropped her hand and wrung her fingers together, showing Raphael the first sign that her Virtuous front had cracked. "*This* is what makes me think that wherever Rian is, he didn't go voluntarily. Or easily."

"What was he doing here, anyway?"

Kindness didn't respond. Or couldn't. Whatever reason the human had for sniffing around was not her concern, and her cousins were well able to deal with him. What *did* concern the Archangel was the way it affected Kindness.

She waited, but before Kindness could find a way to respond, Raphael detected something unexpected.

Decay.

With their heightened senses, the pair of celestials could smell the minute traces of it. Raphael's nose crinkled. The coppery scent of blood hung in the air. It was so heavily saturated that she could almost taste the tang of it on her tongue. She turned her head to Kindness, who waved her hand, indicating Raphael should see for herself.

With a slow nod, Raphael entered the room, staring in silence at the pair of human bodies posed forever in the grisly clutches of death in Envy's kitchen. It was beyond her current skillset to see the past, but the echoes of it lingered strongly enough for Raphael to piece together what happened.

"You couldn't have *led* with this?" No stranger to death, Raphael was unperturbed by the obviously violent deaths both men had suffered. One stared sightlessly up at the lights; his neck broken so soundly his head twisted all the way around like it was attached backwards.

The other human had a pair of kitchen knives embedded in his torso, and another driven to the hilt in his neck. Blood pooled around his body, a sticky, pungent mess that would *definitely* stain Envy's white floor.

Raphael spun in a slow circle. "How long?"

Kindness poked the broken body daintily with her toes. "I went to the farmer's market this morning. Got home about two hours ago." Her pink sock nudged the corpse again, and she wrinkled her nose at the mess on the floor.

"I called *you* as soon as I saw what happened."

"Does Envy know?"

Her cousin sighed. "She hasn't been home for days, Raphael. You know that she likes to keep busy. And who knows what she's been up to. I mean..." She hesitated, then nudged the corpse again betraying her growing frustration.

"...she has obviously annoyed somebody enough to send an assassin after her and look where we are. The assassin has a conscience, so they sent someone else."

There it was. A hint of the wisdom Raphael was waiting for. "Is that what you think happened?"

"I think so?" Kindness walked from one end of the kitchen to the other and back again, following the same steps Raphael trod only moments before. Her expression was troubled, yet thoughtful. "Raphael... I think you should call the FBI human. The cute one that thinks you're suspicious."

"No. We need to clean this up ourselves, Kindness. I— he's *not* cute." It was the archangel's turn to hesitate. The FBI agent tailed her now and then, even after his little visit to her ER, but so far Raphael had nothing to hide from his overzealous mind. Her eyes flicked to the window, and her uncertainty crept into her expression.

It *did* strike her as odd. What were the chances that his escapades with the assassin and the fallout from her cousins were related? And if they were not, how did *her* involvement with his other case relate? Did it at all?

It was all too convoluted, with no clear pattern emerging from the darkness to guide her way.

Father. We need you.

Sure, Raphael could alter his memories. Make the bodies disappear. Change things to her advantage. Make him dance naked down Sunset Boulevard, if she wanted to... but all those things left a trail, and the Archangel was supposed to be hiding.

She was supposed to be pretending she was human. They all were.

Well, except Envy. Envy had departed from their path long ago. Raphael did not know what her agenda was.

"I just don't think this adds up, 'Ness. You still haven't told me why he was here."

"He's been coming more since the last incident with Envy." Kindness rolled her eyes at Raphael and groaned. Sometimes she was dense with the ways of humans, but Raphael should have known better. "Standing at the gate just... staring. Sometimes he comes in and leaves a note under the door... If I didn't know he was an assassin, I'd say he was sorry for what he did to our cousin."

Her eyes grew distant, her mind sharing with Raphael the visualization of Rian standing forlornly in a rare rain shower as though he were silently begging for Envy's forgiveness. She shook herself and closed the connection, bringing her mind back to the present.

"But he is what *he* is. Like *we* are what we are."

The hint of wisdom Kindness had given her earlier materialized and unfolded into a blooming flower that made Raphael's shoulders sag with relief. But that did not stop her from regarding the situation with mild irritation. "So, what I'm hearing is... he was lurking around, and someone got the jump on him? *Here*?"

Raphael rolled her eyes and walked out of the kitchen, leaving the dead bodies lying on the floor behind her before the irritation snowballed into something else. "Moron."

Her borderline scorn wasn't because she harbored negative feelings toward the assassin... but at the same time, Raphael had to wonder at the stupidity he had been showing. Envy could have *killed* him at any time. Raphael herself could have erased him from existence. Even Kindness could end his life, though she was more likely to give him one of her Lego spaceships and call him a naughty boy.

In truth, the only thing that stopped Raphael from transplanting Rian Murphy to the middle of a desert without water as a penance for his sins was the nagging feeling that he was going to be useful later.

That, and the odd sense of... familiarity she felt in the traces of his presence. Strangely, she felt the same pull with the FBI agent, only with Levi Malach it was... duller, like he was further away. Enigmas like that were too rare for Raphael to dismiss them out of hand, and so she left them both to live their lives without her interference. Or she had. After today's events, Raphael planned to observe them both a little closer whenever time permitted.

Hiding in plain sight.

Her newfound resolve gave Raphael the final push into making her decision. With determined steps, she abruptly turned and headed back outside to return Rian Murphy's phone to where she found it. But before she did, Raphael took a moment to embrace her power, and with it she erased all traces of her fingerprints from the device.

Better to be safe... after all, she was fairly certain Agent Malach already considered her a suspect.

Raphael was bound to tell the truth... but if he didn't ask, she was not obliged to tell.

It took him five rings to answer when she dialed his number.

"Special Agent Malach." His voice came clearly through the speaker. Raphael didn't need to see him to know he was exhausted.

"Agent. This is Raphael. You said to call if—" There was a loud thud at the other end of the call, as though something hit the floor, and when the agent spoke next, his voice was tight.

"What can I do for you, Dr?"

"I need you to come to 618 Canyon Drive as soon as possible. There's been an... Incident. Someone is missing."

"That's not really my jurisdiction, Miss Raphael." The voice paused before continuing, a sure sign the omission of Raphael's professional title was deliberate. *"I suggest you call the local police and file a report."*

Raphael made a face at the phone and sighed. He really was just being difficult. But she decided to throw him a bone, even though it would make her look worse in his eyes.

"Rian Murphy was here."

He started to speak but she cut him off mid-sentence and ended the call. If handing him one of Interpol's most wanted didn't get Agent Malach to come to Envy's house, nothing would.

Suspicions All 'Round

Agent Malach and his investigation team did not show up at Envy's house so much as they *descended* en masse to the address Raphael had given over the phone. Much to her amusement, she caught the sirens a full thirty seconds before the neighbor's dog did, and with nothing else to do but wait, walked calmly to the door to greet the investigator that invited himself into her life.

More or less.

"Envy wouldn't like this *one* bit." Kindness's singsong voice projected clearly to Raphael from where she had replanted herself in the same position on the floor to assemble another Lego spaceship.

"Envy isn't *here*, Kindness." Raphael absently twirled her fingers around the end of her braid, tugging on it now and then as she glanced between the hallway and the door. "...And I'm beginning to think her absence is deliberate."

Dammit.

You only do that when you feel insecure, Raphael.

Irritation flared. With one final tug on the braid, she tossed it over her shoulder and shoved her hands into her pockets instead. Raphael scowled at her own bad habit, wondering if *once again* her Father was right.

Try not to let others see.

Years had passed since He first attempted to break her of the habit. And to a certain extent, He succeeded.... but since this was the *third* time in as many months the Archangel found her fingers twirling where they shouldn't, certainty had been thrown out the window.

Lately Raphael's life consisted of her either chasing her proverbial tail or getting led around by the nose chasing crumbs she couldn't even see. Every day it was one or the other. Sometimes both... and no matter which problem reared its head, she *detested* how incompetent it made her feel.

An Archangel, incapable of seeing the pattern? Unheard of.

None of the pieces were coming together.

None of it made sense.

The worst part of it all, was that Raphael remained unconvinced the pieces even added up to point in the same direction, and *that* only served to jumble her mind even further.

Try not to let others see.

Raphael dug manicured nails into her palms, counted to three, and forced her attention on the problem at hand. The impending arrival of... one of her problems.

Cracking her neck from side to side, she leaned on the open doorway with her left ankle crossed over her right and waited. The sirens wound their way up the canyon, falling silent somewhere between the bottom of Envy's street and the gates just outside her line of sight. But it wasn't until the crunch of tires sounded on her cousin's driveway that Raphael raised her eyes and acknowledged the presence of one of the most recent banes of her existence.

Agent Malach slid gracefully out of the passenger side of the lead car with his eyes glued to her. His gaze did not waver a fraction as he drew closer, and Raphael admitted to herself that if she *had* been human, Levi Malach would have been just the *right* amount of intimidating to scare her into telling him *anything* he wanted.

Unfortunately for Agent Malach, however, Raphael was one of the most powerful creatures in existence, and the intense scowl he delivered as he stopped and loomed over her did nothing more than cause one of her eyebrows to shoot up into her hairline.

And then, before she could stop herself, Raphael's mouth decided to be petty.

"I thought you'd be faster."

"Traffic, Doctor." He was taller than her, *that* Raphael already knew... but when he straightened to his full height and looked beyond her into the foyer, the height difference became much more apparent. His stereotypical black suit jacket was unbuttoned, and since Raphael was already staring at his torso, a quick assessment told her the agent was armed. A fact that became more obvious when he placed his hands on his hips and redirected his eyes to look down at her.

"You said something about Rian Murphy. How—?"

Raphael tilted her head, pulling her attention away from the gun tucked under his jacket and giving it to him instead. "It's probably best if I don't say anything."

The sides of her mouth curled upwards into a faint smile, much like it had on the evening when she had nearly run over the top of him while riding her skates. Pushing herself off the door frame, Raphael turned and headed into the house. She called out for him to follow, her voice carrying clearly as she took the second door on the right. "You already think ... whatever you think."

"In case you haven't noticed, I'm an *investigator*—"

"Yes... but me staining your opinion with information you're going to warp is the *last* thing I need."

Levi didn't bother to hide the sigh of exasperation, or the mumbled curse that he breathed out before he responded to the second taunt the doctor had made since he walked up to the front door.

I just got here.

"I try to only see the *facts*... Raphael." Using her name for the first time without the 'Miss' attached to it sounded a little strange to Levi, but in the same way, it felt oddly *right*. And if he wanted to move past the salt barrier Raphael had erected and get her to lower those immovable defenses, he needed to make her happy.

For now.

"I gave you facts. You dismissed them." It was not Raphael's fault things were beyond his understanding. However, it *might* have been her fault for giving him information she knew he could not use... and wasn't *ever* going to be ready for, but it was the truth. And the truth mattered. Always.

"Rian Murphy tried to give me facts too. Funny how you're both so interested in *helping* all of a sudden, don't you think?" It was one of the oldest plays in the book for investigators. Suspects inserted themselves into an investigation, often becoming so helpful that nobody would think twice or give them more than a once over. Levi would be lying if he didn't admit to falling for it a time or two in the past. The best of them did.

But *two* people trying to help? Who were mysteriously connected in ways neither would elaborate on?

Yeah, there was *definitely* something they weren't telling him... and Levi was going to find out what it was if it killed him.

"I *said* I wasn't going to say anything..."

Just like that, it was all too much. Raphael had done *nothing* but be present when a body had been dumped at the Observatory... and *nothing* but try to help as best as she could to under the circumstances. And yet Agent Malach already decided that in some way, she *must* be guilty. He just hadn't decided what she'd done wrong yet.

"...why am I here?"

Her defense crumbled.

The sudden rush of... *whatever* this was overtook her between one heartbeat and the next. Raphael covered her mouth in a feeble attempt to hide the shock that rattled her so hard her mouth dropped open and her bottom lip shook. It wasn't fair for him to just...

Ugh.

Raphael was grateful her back was still facing Agent Malach. If he *ever* saw her wavering like this she wouldn't need her enemies to take her out... she would be mortified enough to *die* on the spot. So, before he caught up to her, Raphael wiped her eyes and took several deep breaths, wishing for the hundredth time that her Father sent someone else to do *whatever* she was doing there.

Watching. Observing. Not interfering. Ha. Thanks, Father.

From his position behind her, Levi immediately knew he had pushed her too far. On some unknown level he instinctively understood that Raphael could handle most things... but he wasn't stupid. Her demeanor changed, shifting from the suppressed amused irritation he was becoming used to into something else. Something that made her shoulder rise and fall and her energy to drop into a negative spike. And unfortunately, he had been the one to force it. Remorse filled him like floodwaters rushing into a dam, an overload of guilt, the likes of which he had not felt since... well, years. He mouthed a silent apology to Raphael's back, reaching forward as he closed the distance between them.

"Hey."

She must have felt the air shifting, because before he could make contact, the doctor ducked through the doorway, turning just enough to put Levi in her peripheral vision instead. Levi dropped his hand, shoving it awkwardly into his pocket while he waited for her to move again.

"…I…" He took another step, falling into place beside her, all too aware that he was looming over her like some kind of giant.

"This way, Agent." Raphael cut him off. It wasn't hard to tell there were more words on the way, but she would survive without them. Turning abruptly, she headed outside, brushing off her moment of weakness for what it was.

Momentary.

Once outside, Raphael pointed silently, directing him to the cell phone lying under the table, but before he could do more than glance down, she led him to the kitchen where the real problem waited. Part of Raphael was impressed Agent Malach held his silence while she showed him the reason for his presence, but that peace shattered the second he laid eyes on the bloody mess decorating Envy's kitchen.

"*Holy shit.*"

They were just words. A reaction to a situation he absolutely could *not* have anticipated, but with the way he mouthed them in that slow, lingering drawl, there was no hiding his surprise. In truth, Levi was still trying to get a clear view of Raphael's face after their awkward moment in the hallway, so he was *definitely* not prepared for the bloodbath he walked blindly into. It didn't take a genius to figure out that Raphael wasn't going to face him until she was ready. *Again.* And so, with a helpless shrug, he concentrated on the crime scene.

At least that would answer his questions.

"Take whatever evidence you need, Agent Malach." Raphael stepped daintily around the bodies and stood out of the way against an unbloodied wall. "My cousin is away, and I'd like this... taken care of before she returns."

"How many cousins do you have, Raphael?"

It was Levi's turn to startle Raphael. She twisted to follow his movements as he unconsciously mimicked hers from earlier. Her brown eyes widened, but this time the Archangel did not hide her confusion.

"... In total? Fourteen, why?"

"And this house belongs to... which one?"

Raphael opened her mouth to reply but was interrupted by the sound of excitement coming from the living room where Kindness remained out of sight.

"Finished another one!"

She huffed out a bemused breath. "That's nice 'Ness. I'll be there in a minute."

Agent Malach threw a questioning glance at the empty doorway, his hand automatically drifting to the concealed weapon in his jacket. But one look at the resignation on Raphael's face made him drop it to his side again, and he motioned to the doorway with his still empty hand.

"Let me guess... another *cousin*?"

"Sort of. Yes." Raphael cleared her throat and nodded at him, bound to answer. And to give him the truth. Mostly. "... She's... innocent. Finding this mess should never have been her burden."

"But you can deal with it?" The agent frowned slightly. "You're awfully calm for someone staring at a pair of bodies."

Not quite an accusation, but there was an undeniable question in Malach's tone. There was an answer he wanted from Raphael... a particular one. Unfortunately, it was one she couldn't give him.

Not in the way he wanted it, anyway.

"I'm a doctor, Agent Malach. I stopped throwing up at the stench of violence years ago." Oh, *if only* he knew how long ago it truly was. Raphael stepped backwards, angling around him as she made her way to where Kindness sat in her childlike pose on the floor once again. "Come on. You can question 'Ness while the coroner does her thing."

"A moment, Raphael..." This time, when Levi reached for Raphael's arm, he made the connection. "You never told me which cousin owns this house."

His touch was light, but to the Archangel it weighed like lead on her conscience. It was not in her nature to lie, but by everything she held dear... she had *never* been so tempted as she was in this moment.

"Yeah... I know." Raphael hesitated, knowing that Agent Malach needed the truth... but giving him that knowledge was also going to condemn *her* even further in his eyes. Her head turned, first to glance at the hand holding onto her arm, and then further, her sight traveling along his sleeve, past his shoulder to where she knew a set of amber brown eyes waited to pass judgement.

"...the one I was supposed to meet at the Observatory."

The Vanishing Agent

With the information Rian dropped in his lap, Levi was able to make connections where there were previously none. The deeper he probed into the mysterious 'Jim', the more obvious it became that the assassin's intel was right. Nobody knew a *damn* thing about him.

Not that Levi could tell anyone. No, his new informant was a card he held close to his chest, and one that he could never, ever give up. Even if it destroyed what remained of his career. It did not matter what evidence he gathered, or how many lives he saved in the process... Rian Murphy was a wanted criminal, and neither the FBI nor Interpol would cut a deal with him for something as *insignificant* as a domestic murder case.

No matter how many of them there were.

The biggest problem Levi faced now was that his informant decided to *disappear*, and therefore any new developments in his case vanished along with him. In short, Levi just couldn't catch a break, a fact made even more evident when his boss called the team to their meeting room for an unscheduled update.

Levi sighed audibly at his computer when the summons from the FBI internal server popped onto his screen. His tired gaze darted to the time display, causing him to perk up a little. If he left *now*, he would have time to head downstairs and grab his mid-afternoon coffee first.

That alone motivated Levi enough to close the file he was reading and haul himself out of his chair. He shrugged into his jacket, grabbed his reusable cup, and headed for the door. He nodded to SAC Wilson as he pulled it closed behind him, waving the empty cup in his hand to let him know he would be right back.

True to his implied word, not fifteen minutes later Levi knocked on the meeting room door. Cup in hand, with his notes tucked under one arm, he swallowed the last bite of the salted caramel slice that would give him the sugar boost he was going to need to survive the rest of the day. When nobody responded, he pushed the door open, noting with surprise he was the first to arrive, but as he slid into his usual seat, the remainder of the joint task force filed in.

"What news, Agent Malach?"

SAC Wilson got straight to the point. Levi set his coffee down and opened the file in front of him, perusing the contents to confirm his data before forming his response. "Techs have finished examining the crime scene, but we're still waiting for anything solid that might help us find Murphy."

"You haven't had any contact with him since the mall?"

"No sir. Seems he's a liar as well as an assassin. Can't say I'm too surprised." Levi was *also* lying through his teeth. But since he was confident Murphy's instructions were careful, he was also certain that nobody else knew about their secret little chat. So far there was just one since the department store fiasco, but that was *one* more than the rest of the team needed to know about.

Levi could tell Wilson didn't like his response, but with no other information to operate on, he had little choice but to move forward.

"Brown, what about the cell phone?"

Agent Brown pushed his reading glasses into his hair and peered up at Wilson. "We managed to retrieve a few messages, but it's a throwaway sir, there's no traceable data on it. But trust me, if there's *anything* on there, I'll find it."

"Good to hear. What about prints?"

Wilson's glance was lightning fast, but Levi caught it. And the message it conveyed.

See? This is what competence looks like.

"We've got prints from both bodies running through IAFIS, and CODIS is working overtime on all the DNA samples. If those two are in the system, we'll find them."

"Interpol is doing the same."

Addison spoke up, inserting herself into the conversation for the first time. All eyes swung to her, and Levi frowned at his colleagues when she shrank under the weight of their combined scrutiny. He nodded, leaning forward as he motioned for her to continue.

With a tight, yet grateful grin at him, she pushed on. "All our partner countries have agreed to run identification for us. As it stands, we don't know *who* they are, or where they're from. But since Murphy is a floater, they could be from anywhere."

Levi listened to the conversation around him shift from evidence queries to international concerns with a quiet sigh. They weren't matters he was qualified to help with, so he left it to the combined expertise of those who were. What he *could* do, however, was sip on his lukewarm coffee and lament that he had only eaten that small piece of caramel slice since the night before. Right on cue, his stomach rumbled beneath the table, but like a good agent he ignored it and shifted in his seat to get a little more comfortable.

"... about the homeowner?"

"Miss En Vee is not taking our calls."

Levi's preoccupation with ignoring his stomach ended abruptly with the odd pronunciation of Envy's name. He thought it odd, but no less odd than her *actual* name. Or the painter doctor ninja turtle that was her cousin.

Raphael. Envy. Kindness... what in the weird biblical family is going on lately?

"Her attorney informed us if we needed anything it went through him first. She's been cooperative as far as the murder investigation goes, but her passport information puts her out of the country when it happened."

"Fuck." Wilson leaned over the table and shook his head. "Can't argue with that."

"... well... there *are* ways, we all know that."

"Check it out. Nothing on the other two women?"

"They're both clean. Except for the one Malach has as a suspect."

"*Potential* suspect." Levi shrugged off their glances and refused to comment further. If someone else made a connection, so be it, but in truth, he didn't want the extra eyes peering over his shoulder. Not when Murphy's presence at the house remained circumstantial.

"Okay so we're just sitting on our asses waiting, right?"

"Yes sir."

"Let's call it a day then. We've been in here for four hours." Wilson pushed himself upright and signaled the end of the meeting with a wave of his hand. "Go home, sleep. Go dancing. Kiss your partners. Do whatever it is you do to relax. Meet back here in the morning and we'll start again with fresh eyes."

The walk back to his office was a long one, despite it being less than twenty meters from the meeting room. With every step forward, Levi felt a weight bearing down on him. Like he was wading through molasses. He had no energy left. None. Not one fragment of emotional, mental, or physical energy that he could devote to pretending that this latest turn of events did not affect him on some deep, personal level. He was tired. His body was tired... but his mind? Levi's mind was *so* worn down a lobotomy would not deliver the rest he needed.

The kind of tired that sleep won't fix.

He was even too tired to realize that his life had become a metaphor, a struggle for everything he was fighting to achieve. Two steps backward, and only one forward. It was a downhill slope he just did not want to fight any more. He couldn't... and somewhere, on his lonely, despondent walk back to the four walls that made up his workspace, the only thing on Levi's mind was that he failed.

He failed *Annabelle.*

He failed his *family.*

He failed *himself.*

And in that failing, Levi became the type of agent he *swore* he'd never be.

The one that *never* found his white whale. The one with that *one* case they never closed... and the one whose career ultimately *failed* because they could never let it go.

He trudged through the open door, fumbling with the knot on his tie with one hand, while balancing his files and cup in the other. Ten minutes. That was all he needed. Ten minutes, and then he could go home, fall into bed and just... cease to exist for a few hours. The thought gave Levi a boost, and with a low, weary moan he yanked harder on his tie to relieve the noose-like grip wrapped around his neck, only to stop dead in his tracks before the knot unfastened.

Didn't I close that door?

His eyebrows furrowed as he half turned, the tie instantly forgotten when he heard the latch fall into place behind him.

"Agent Levi Malach?"

What the Hell?

"Who's asking?"

"We've been sent to tell you the boss wants a word."

It was a testament to how wrung out Levi was that he failed to register the danger when it presented itself. Instead, he wondered what Wilson wanted that he couldn't have asked five minutes ago when they were face to face.

"We?"

Tap. Tap.

Oh.

Levi glimpsed over his shoulder in response to the tap, though he made no other outward movement. His mind whirled, racing to catch up to the warning he somehow sensed, yet remained ignorant of at the same time.

Fucking. Great.

First Murphy shoved a gun in his side, now some local gang boss had sent his thugs after him. Levi didn't need to turn his head the entire way to see the hulking presence behind him. He considered himself tall enough. And he knew his own strength... but the looming leviathan made Levi feel like he stood a whole foot shorter and was weaker than a day-old kitten struggling to escape a wet paper bag.

How did they get through security?

"I just spoke to my boss... you're going to have to be more specific."

Leviathan poked him in the back. "Our boss. Not yours."

"Sid? For all we know he might be."

British accent. Definitely lower level. Not too smart.

"True, but this piece of *nothing* doesn't need to know that."

Interesting.

"Oh. Yeah. Either way, he's coming with us, right?"

Levi listened to their back and forth with interest. "You guys know I'm standing *right* here?"

"Shut up, you mongrel piece of filth."

Levi took a step toward the man standing in front of him. With access to his office door effectively cut off, he reasoned the further he moved away from it, the less chance Sid and his mysterious friend had of getting him out of there. Unfortunately, Levi's second step fumbled when he was thrust forward by a large, open palm slapping against his spine. With a grunt, he fell, staggering into the first man on unsteady feet, who, to his disbelief, helped him regain his balance. However, Levi had no time to consider what that meant, because a second later something sharp pierced his neck.

"Shouldn't take long to take effect... Then we can leave."

Mist curled at the edges of Levi's awareness. Tendrils of thick, clouded *nothing* wound through him, coating his mind as he swayed on the spot.

"Let's just go now, I don't like being surrounded by so many—"

"Agent Malach? Levi?"

A voice penetrated the haze, coming into sharp focus with the opening of his office door. Without waiting for a response, Agent Addison entered with her head tilted downward, her eyes glued to the information on her tablet screen.

"No...Addison... get out!"

Levi tried to warn her. He tried to scream it from the depths of his lungs, but the thug who shoved him slid into position behind Addison before she had a chance to see that Levi wasn't alone.

"I think I found something. The scene at the house in the Hills... we got a fingerprint match. It's—"

"Claire..."

Once again, Levi tried.

Look at me. No, don't look at me. Just get out.

And once again, he failed. The mist swirled in his mind, dampening his voice where it needed to be a loud, shouting foghorn alerting the entire floor to the situation unfolding in his office.

Addison concentrated on her results, not the room around her, and Levi could only watch in undisguised horror as the man standing behind Addison shared an unspoken agreement with his partner. He struggled to break free, but the sudden grip on his arms was like iron, and the mist made him sluggish. *Slow.* Whatever they dosed him with was too strong, and all he could do was stare when Addison *finally* looked up at him.

It was the last thing she ever did.

"Watch. *Filth.*"

The words were sinuous. They held a degree of hatred Levi could not fathom, hissed into his ear with a malicious glee only matched by the expression on the other one's face. Levi followed the hand with drowsy eyes when it reappeared, but lost track of it again as it dipped behind Addison's back... and the next thing he saw was the sharp end of *something* erupting in a bloody mess from the center of her chest.

"Levi..."

She stared directly at him; the shock too raw for her to register the blow that had already claimed her life. Like the twisted parody of a marionette, Addison's body convulsed, impaled on the end of the blade protruding from her breastbone. Blood poured out of the wound, spreading over her stomach, and dripping down her legs while Levi just stood there, powerless to do more than roar his impotence at the horror story unfolding in front of him.

"Addison... fuck. *Someone help!*"

Except, he couldn't even do that. The mist descended, and Levi's shouts were nothing more than whispers. He thrashed in Sid's hold, wobbling from side to side in his mist driven turmoil, but achieved nothing more than a fist in the kidney for his efforts.

"*No!*"

It was almost over. Even in his current state, Levi knew that. But that did not stop him from trying to get to Addison again as a fountain of crimson blood spewed forth from her gaping mouth, coating him from head to toe.

What the fuck just happened?

Levi called out again, but nobody came. And again... but this time no words came out. Whatever they injected him with left him conscious, but incapable of doing anything but witness with dazed eyes as his world *once again* disintegrated in front of him. Addison was just a colleague, but in the same breath, she was also his partner. And sure, she irritated him to no end with her enthusiasm and her incessant questions... but she *didn't fucking deserve this*... whatever it was. She had the potential to be a damn good agent.

Hell, she already *was* a damn good agent.

But now Levi bore *her* death on his conscience too. Just like Annabelle's.

"Let me—"

Sid's partner grinned over the top of Addison's limp body at Levi and shoved her off the end of the blade, dismissing her corpse to the carpet at his feet. His eyes darted from her body to the knife, making desperate mental notes that did not make sense and refused to stay in place.

"Boss was right... that blade is *way* too smooth."

"I think we're done here."

"Fucking awesome, Sid. Think he'll let us use it again?"

If Levi thought he was tired before, now he was downright exhausted.

"What do you want from me?"

The drug in his system coursed freely through his veins, dulling his senses even as he fought to stay awake.

Why does everyone want to knock me out lately?

He didn't have the words in his vocabulary to formulate an answer to his own silent question. He didn't have *anything*, and when Sid finally *did* let go of him, Levi slid to the floor in an uncomfortable heap... splashing into the puddle of lifeblood still oozing out of the dead agent who stared at him with silent, accusing eyes. Levi reached for Addison; his eyes drawn to the one part of her body that was not tainted by blood. Clean. There. Just above her collarbone...*remember.*

"I told you."

Levi's line of sight filled with the antagonistic expression of the man responsible for drugging him. The one he now identified as Sid.

"The boss wants a word. Now..."

Piercing blue eyes filled with hateful intent set in a face that could only be described as *angry* glared at him. Levi could not understand *why*. Was it something he had done? Some case he worked on that involved this guy, or his boss, or whoever else he couldn't think of? His thoughts jumbled, piling together in one giant, confusing mess that sank into the unfathomable depths of his mind. As his thoughts sank, his consciousness followed, and Levi could feel himself fading into that easy relaxation he experienced on rare occasions when he slid into the oblivion of sleep in his nice warm bed.

"Be a good egg and fall asleep for me, yeah?"

Only this wasn't his bed. And this wasn't his house... and the warmth Levi felt seeping through his clothes had *nothing* to do with his blankets.

Levi was down. But before he was completely out he managed to get two more slurred words past his lips.

"...*fuck you.*"

Raphael and Kindness at it Again

Kindness' voice echoed through the house, drifting to the outdoor area where Raphael lay on the grass. The morning sun warmed her face, infusing her with a sliver of serenity that counteracted the chaos that her life had become.

However, with Kindness shrieking at the top of her lungs, the Archangel's peace was doomed, and Raphael fervently wished she had not agreed to keep her cousin updated. She sighed, long and deep, opening her eyes when Kindness called again. The urgency escalated with yet another summons before Raphael rolled to her feet and headed inside.

"Coming... What's got you so... *oh*. What on Earth happened?"

"I dropped a vase. But that isn't what I want you to see." Kindness disregarded the remains of Envy's Ming vase and tiptoed over the flowers sprinkled across the floor as she waved both hands at the wall behind her. "Look at the television, it's Agent Malach!"

"- once again appealing for information leading to the where-abouts of FBI Agent Levi Malach, who is believed to have been abducted from his office late yesterday afternoon. The body of his partner, Agent Claire Addison was found early this morning by a cleaning crew. Sources report that FBI security footage spotted Malach talking to two unidentified men. The FBI is apparently working with Interpol to identify them but will not comment on whether or not Agent Malach's disappearance is linked to the joint FBI Interpol task force currently on mission in our fair city."

"I need to get into his office."

"Why?"

"First Rian Murphy, now Agent Malach?" Raphael's mind was whirring at speeds faster than even she could keep up with. One disappearance was chance. But two? *Now?* There *had* to be a connection... and the common denominator seemed to be pointing right at her.

"Oh." Kindness turned back to Raphael, her expression serious. "I'm coming with you."

"This isn't your fight, 'Ness... It's okay."

"I can't help if all I'm doing is sitting here waiting for everyone to come back."

"*...fine.* But please let me do the talking. The last thing we need is a trip to the Lego store."

"My lips are sealed."

"Oh *Father*. Look at all that blood."

The body of Agent Malach's partner had been transported to the morgue hours ago, but her imprint in the bloody carpet remained. Raphael stared at the spot indicating where Agent Addison had died, and where another body, presumably Agent Malach, fell on top of her. Her initial thought was that he too, met the same violent end. Unless the reporters lied. With no evidence to the contrary, Raphael had to believe he was still alive. And if he *was* still alive, then the Archangel felt the least she could do was find him.

Even if that meant his suspicions about *her* only deepened.

"I swear I heard you say it didn't bother you anymore."

Raphael scowled at her cousin, both for the eavesdropping and the fact that she'd called Raphael out on her own contradiction. "It doesn't... but in certain circumstances—"

"Like Agent Malach disappearing?"

"...yes. Is he dead? I don't know. And unless his body shows up, I never will." Raphael was not sure how much she was willing to tell Kindness yet. About any of it. Sure, her cousin was peripherally involved, but that was how Raphael wanted it to stay. There was no reason why Kindness needed to be exposed to the darker side of humanity after so long an absence.

Not yet anyway.

"What are we looking for, Raphael?" Kindness stepped around the drying puddle of blood on the floor and moved closer to the desk to the rear of the office. She leaned over to take a closer look at what Agent Malach had left on it, and her hand had just closed over a thumb drive with a sketch of a wing on it when she heard Raphael gasp. Without thinking twice, Kindness dropped the thumb drive and turned her head just in time to see her cousin pulling at a white cloth draped over a whiteboard. "What is it?"

"Something he was working on. I'm not entirely... *oh wow.*"

Raphael could not believe what her eyes were seeing. Dozens of photographs. Dozens of case notes. Dozens of names including her own underneath a photograph of the woman she'd found barely clinging to life at the Observatory. That wasn't the only shock. No, what shocked Raphael the most was the link that so clearly bound all of these poor souls together. The same set of words that haunted Levi, and the words *she* had found *so* offensive.

No wonder he didn't like me. He thinks I did this?

It's Been a While... Brother

Raphael manifested without fanfare outside of the two-hundred-year-old house Azrael holed himself up in from time to time. Usually when he took a rare break from his duties. He was well hidden, leaving barely a trace of himself anywhere on Earth... but Raphael knew what to look for. Or, what *not* to look for. The absences were as obvious as those things that were present.

Her Father taught her well.

Infiltrate. Watch. Know. Even the ones you trust most.

And watch she did. But only for her own needs. After all, Raphael never knew when she might need her brother again. Or him, her... and it was that very thought that held the Archangel there, despite the smoldering sadness that lingered.

She wanted to run, to flee back to the dubious safety of her lighthouse, but that option was no longer present for her. Two of the humans Raphael interacted with had disappeared, and as much as she wanted to believe that it was coincidence, she knew the truth of it. It stunk, haunting the healer like the shadowy

ghosts of her past, pushing to the forefront of her mind no matter what.

And now, here she was, forced to confront so much when until now, hiding had been her only choice.

Whoever it was that kidnapped Agent Malach and Rian Murphy, had also broken into her lighthouse, and left her that note. It wasn't random. It wasn't chance.

It was the enemy their Father warned them against.

It couldn't be anything else... could it?

The realization was as shocking to Raphael as knowing such an enemy existed at all... it made her wonder what else her Father *should* have told her but didn't. She also wondered *where* he was. So far, her searching had found naught, and it seemed more and more like her Father didn't want to be found.

"Stupid." Raphael stared up at the house, feeling her anxiety rising. The last thing she wanted to do was ask Azrael for help. Or talk to him at all. Their last meeting had ended badly... something that still haunted Raphael for the reason they fell out *and* their individual reactions.

Bury it. Bury it deep.

She wasn't over it. It was the same reason Raphael held everyone at arm's length and refused to let anyone close. But she was here, and those idiot humans needed to be found. Azrael was the only one who could find them, but only if...

Raphael's shaking hand clunked the knocker down three times on the heavy wooden door. If her mind wasn't so distraught, she would have smiled at the image Azrael portrayed to the world with his old Tudor house, his stables and hedge screen that blocked the street right in the inner suburbs of Melbourne.

Whatever Raphael expected, Azrael answering the door wearing a pair of low-cut jeans and a collared shirt so crinkled it looked slept in was not it. It wasn't even on the list. In fact, her brother's whole disheveled demeanor was a surprise to the healer. Azrael was, without a doubt, the neatest of them all.

"Azrael."

Showtime.

Raphael's poker face was well in place by the time he opened the door, and there were no traces of the inner turmoil that plagued her a few moments before. However, she couldn't hide the way her voice trembled with her greeting.

"Raph" Azrael scowled at her through the crack in the door, his surprise at her presence evident in the way his eyebrows climbed into his hairline. "You're the *last* person I expected to see on my doorstep."

He turned his head, listening to someone speak to him from deeper inside the house. "It's my sister."

Raphael pretended she couldn't hear the entire conversation, deliberately tuning it out while she examined a speck of dirt under her fingernail. She *did* have manners. But they were sorely tested when Azrael glared at her again.

"Yeah, *that one*. Go exercise the horses without me, I'll come find you when I'm done."

Taking his words as a signal, she looked back up to see the door was wide open, and Azrael stood in the middle of it regarding her with an uneasy expression on his face. "I take it this isn't a social call, sister."

When Raphael silently shook her head, Azrael sighed and stood to one side, waving her in. "Let's go to my office."

"It's astounding," Azrael said after he ushered Raphael through the hallway to his main workspace. There were matching lounges beside a window running from floor to ceiling that overlooked the field outside, facing away from the city. A desk sat off to one side with a plush chair behind it, and a wall lined with bookshelves filled with books Raphael knew would be among the last remaining copies, or even the only ones ever to exist. "...That after all this time you would seek me out. Aren't you worried history will repeat itself?"

His voice was cold, and tight with tension... but Raphael said some hurtful words to the other Archangel, and he... well, Azrael had done the same to her.

One hundred and four years was a lifetime of silence. Longer for siblings charged with the same task... and longer still for twins who had always been close.

"Az..." Raphael paced back and forth, ignoring his barb even though it opened her old wounds right back up again. Her expression faltered briefly, and she scowled at him in mild irritation. "I'm not here for ...*that*... I need your help."

In response, Azrael flopped down on one of his couches, lifting his legs up onto the cushions and crossing his ankles. "Now what could you possibly need *my* help with Raphael? I clearly recall you telling me you never wanted *my kind of help* ever again."

"Do you mind?" Raphael stopped before the window, keeping her face and body calm while her mind started to replay scenes from a past she never wanted to live through again. *Ever.* "...it's not like that. I need you to find two humans."

"Ohhhh. So, it *is* like that?"

"*NO!*"

Azrael chuckled, enjoying the rise he had gotten out of her so quickly. He felt bad about it, but sometimes Raphael was far too serious. That, and he felt like she deserved it. *Just a little.* "I'm not interested in playing 'find the human' for you, Raph. You have skills. Find them yourself."

"Are we done?" He stood, and his dismissal was clear. "My friend and I have plans."

Cool. Disinterested.

How typical.

Raphael clenched her fists by her sides, spinning to face him as her frustration simmered to a raging boil.

"Your 'friend'..." Her answer was flat, but her voice cracked with a century of heartache. "Aren't *you* the lucky one?"

"Raph..." At that point, Azrael knew his taunt went too far. The flash of hurt he read on her face was as raw as the day they last saw each other... and the Archangel of Death was surprised to find sorrow where anger once held firm. "You and I both know it couldn't go any other way."

"You took him." Raphael's sorrow, however, turned back into anger and loss. Tears threatened to fall, but she clenched her jaw and held them at bay. "I *healed him*, Azrael and you *took* him anyway."

"C'mon Raphael, I am *literally* just the messenger. It was his time, you know I—"

"*Don't lie to me!* You have the power." Raphael looked upward to where all humans' thought Heaven was, seeking solace that did not exist, and never would. It took every ounce of willpower to maintain her calm, but one glance out of the window told Raphael she was failing. A storm gathered, right above Azrael's house without Raphael even thinking about touching her power. She swallowed, willing the massive cloud formation to dissipate but the burgeoning cell only grew larger.

Coming to find Azrael was a mistake. One emotional outburst and she was about to reveal herself *and* undo years of effort to remain unnoticed. Raphael headed for the windows, intending on just disappearing and taking the storm with her, but her emotional state wouldn't let her leave without throwing one more sentence out. "The only one of them I ever loved enough to *want*, Azrael, and *you took him from me*. So, I do not apologize for interrupting you and your...*friend*. At least *he* has his life."

And you, in it.

Overhead, the cumulonimbus clouds rumbled with power.

"And when it is his time, *I will reap him* too, Raphael." Azrael bit the words off with regret. It was all true. Every word she said... only it also wasn't. Azrael watched his sister struggle with her old heartache and came to a decision. He stretched his hands out to her, palms facing upright in an age-old symbolic gesture of truth among their kind. With a soft exhale, he embraced his own power, welcoming it into his being with his mind laid bare. When their eyes met, he could see the ethereal glow from *his* reflected in her unshed tears.

"I offered him a choice I've never given anyone else, Raphael. To stay and love you like he promised, or to leave and traverse the Halls to his Fate."

The silence that enveloped the siblings was so profound that Azrael swore a human could have heard a pin drop from three miles away. He didn't need to finish his explanation. One look at Raphael's face told him she understood. That she knew it had all been a lie. That Azrael had hidden the truth to protect her lonely heart.

Lightning split the sky, striking the ground outside of Azrael's window. The glass rattled in its frame hard enough to snap, but Raphael didn't see the crack that snaked from floor to ceiling... all she could see was a battlefield, a hospital tent and the lie within.

"He..." She couldn't stop the tears from falling as the implications of what Azrael just told her sank in.

He didn't love me at all.

She spent over a century alienated from her brother. Mourning a human who, ultimately, didn't choose her.

I wasn't enough.

The sky rumbled again, and the thunderclap that followed was deafening. Azrael's house shuddered, and overhead the towering, angry grey clouds burst, and a torrential rain started to fall.

Raphael's knees gave out and she collapsed, her poker face well and truly gone. Even if she wanted to, she was powerless to stop over a century of devastation and rejection from erupting in great, heaving sobs. So lost in her agony, Raphael didn't notice when Azrael placed a blanket over her shoulders, nor when he slid a full glass of whiskey into the space between her ankles. What Raphael *did* notice was his presence, as familiar as ever despite the years of silence, and when he wrapped his arms around her, she cried anew, for the time they'd lost.

"Why?" After a while she sniffed back her tears, wiping her nose inelegantly on her sleeve. Azrael had shifted them so that Raphael's head rested on his shoulder, and she was unwilling to move just yet. She felt him tense and breathe in, and to her surprise, Azrael sniffed too.

"I wanted you to think he left the land of the living lamenting that he couldn't have a life with you, Raph."

Raphael shook her head in denial, accidentally rubbing her wet face on his shirt. "Why would you do that, knowing I'd be angry with you?"

Azrael gave his twin a tight smile and hugged her tightly against his side. "Better that, than you knowing his last thoughts were of the nurse who'd treated his wounds on the battlefield."

The Archangel of Death was never surprised at what secrets he learned when he assisted human souls... but some were worse than others. No, that particular human hadn't deserved a love like his sister could offer. Or would have, before the damage had been done. The man in question had played on her emotions, manipulating her naivete into something he could use for his own gain.

"Besides..." He pushed her, causing the glass of whiskey between Raphael's ankles to slosh out onto the rug. "Even *you* can't stay mad at me forever."

"I certainly tried." Raphael sat up, hooking her slender fingers around the glass between her ankles so she didn't spill anything else. She brought it to her lips, downing the contents without hesitation. After the outburst she just had, the amber liquid wouldn't even come close to calming her frayed nerves, but it was a start.

"I'm sorry, Azrael." She wriggled away from her brother and climbed to her feet before turning to offer him a hand. To her surprise, Azrael accepted. "I know the rules... but I wanted him to stay anyway."

"He didn't deserve your devotion, Raph." Azrael plucked the glass out of her hand and crossed the room to fill it, pouring one for himself at the same time. "Will you trust me on that?"

Raphael took the offered refill, nursing the glass while she pondered her response. Eventually, she nodded. "I will. Though I am in no hurry to feel like this ever again."

"The pain fades, Raphael. You can trust me on *that*, too... and when it does, you can love another." Azrael came to terms with the human life cycle a long time ago, letting each of his lovers die at their allotted time. He loved each of them differently, but at times he too wondered if he would be better off alone rather than walking through his life with no permanent attachment.

Sometimes their immortality was a double-edged sword.

An unending life was a gift from the Universe... but was eternal loneliness a worthwhile compromise? In his own mind, Azrael found a way around it, at least for a time. His expression grew contemplative as he savored the bitterness of his gin and tonic, and he tilted his glass at Raphael.

"Don't think I won't be testing whoever it is though."

"No need, Azrael. I have no time for romance, and no desire for it." Raphael gestured to the couch, a little drained. She sank down with a grateful sigh, pushing herself back into the cushions to get more comfortable. "Besides, soon it will be too dangerous. At least for the humans I talk to."

"How so?" Azrael cocked an eyebrow at her, maneuvering himself onto the couch opposite. The tension between them had well and truly evaporated. "Has human society gotten worse since I last looked out the window?"

He cocked his head toward the glass doors; however, he could see little beyond the storm still raging overhead. Azrael chose not to comment on the deluge.

"Or is this about why you're here?"

Raphael listened to the rain for a time, thinking about his question. And why she was there. The rain soothed her, despite its origins. She closed her eyes with a quiet hum and dispelled the storm battering Azrael's chosen home.

"Partly. Yes."

When her eyes reopened, Azrael nodded for her to continue. The light in her eyes faded as she released her power and fussed with her hands in her lap.

"Things are getting worse... I fear Armageddon comes, Azrael."

Raphael watched her brother stiffen and felt a momentary pang of guilt for bringing it to his door and into his life. But she didn't give him time to speak before she delivered the worst part. There was too much at stake if she was right.

And oh, Stars, she hoped she wasn't.

"I think..." Raphael clutched her glass so hard her knuckles turned white.

"I think... Father's enemy is here."

Coming Together Again

"What..." Azrael sat back up; quite sure he hadn't heard *anything* that Raphael had said correctly. "Are you talking about, Raphael?"

"The one he warned us against." Raphael tucked her legs under her knees and pressed further back into the cushions. It really was a comfortable couch. "The one he gave us extra wards for."

Azrael rubbed a hand down the side of his face, trying to remain calm while he caught up to the page his sister was on. "*What* extra wards? Raphael. I've seen no signs of Armageddon."

"This isn't the bible, Azrael. There is no script but what Father left us... and those were vague warnings at best." Raphael sipped at her drink, much calmer after her emotional purge.

Azrael, however, needed another minute to process, and held up his hand for a pause in her jumbled explanation.

"Raph. By the stars, can you *lead* with that next time?" He abruptly stood and walked over to his desk to retrieve his laptop.

On his way back to the couch, he grabbed the two bottles of alcohol and his phone.

Before he did anything else, he sent a quick text to his friend to cancel their plans, then booted up his laptop.

On the table nearby was the tool he used for work, affectionately known in their family as the Tablet. He flicked his eyes to it and pursed his lips in thought. Somehow, he was going to have to fit whatever Raphael was about to tell him into his schedule... and hope for the best.

To her credit, Raphael managed to look embarrassed.

"Yes. I meant to but..."

He waved off her apology and topped off both of their glasses. "I feel like you're about to prove to me that I've been living under a rock... But please. Start at the beginning."

Raphael sniffed, wondering where to start *this* part of the story. In the end her decision was simple.

She started at the beginning. At the lighthouse, all those months ago.

Azrael listened to Raphael's recount of the events that transpired since she first detected the intruder in her home. Part of him seethed that someone *dared* to invade her privacy so, another part of him acknowledged a sense of pride in how she handled it, and everything else since. From the suspicious FBI agent to the assassin. From Envy to the mysterious arrival of

Kindness, last seen with their mother, departing mere days after the Babylonian Wars ended.

Raphael had been through a lot in the last year, and Azrael was there for *none* of it.

That was about to change.

"So you're *sure* it's coming?"

Armageddon. The Rapture. End of Days. The civilizations of Earth all had different names for it, but each and every one found its origins in the same place: the Lore passed down by their Father in the early days of humanity. The warning, that one day a usurper would come… and when he did, Armageddon would follow.

Raphael looked anything but unsure. In fact, the glare she shot him from beneath her eyebrows was nothing short of offended. Azrael winced.

Yes, she was sure. Shit.

"…and tell me how you think *me* finding a couple of humans you don't even like will help?"

This was the part Azrael hadn't been able to decipher during Raphael's story. Why waste the effort when there were so many more of them getting about?

Raphael shrugged helplessly. "I *don't* know. It might not. But Azrael…"

Here, Raphael paused again, unsure of how to explain *why* Levi and Rian were so important.

"… this started when they began to interfere with things. Me. Plus…" She hesitated again, and this time Azrael caught it.

"Plus?" He probed gently, knowing better than to add pressure where a mind was already battling confusion.

"I met Agent Malach when he was an infant." Raphael rubbed her leg where it had snapped, all those years ago, but she remained focused on the conversation. "Just once. And didn't cross paths with him again until earlier in the year. Rian Murphy I'm not so familiar with... but both... I just can't put my finger on it yet, Azrael. I don't care about either one specifically."

That wasn't entirely true. While she might not care about either man personally, Raphael also didn't want them to come to any harm because of her. Besides, her curiosity about them and the way they had entwined in her life outweighed any personal feelings.

"...But to find out, I need them both back."

"I still don't get—"

"You can find humans when they're near death, no matter what, right?"

Azrael paused before he responded. Usually, that was correct... but lately...

"Yes. Mostly." He nodded slowly, leaning forward to pick up his Tablet. A swipe of his finger activated the screen, and Azrael concentrated for a moment, making selections now and then while he searched for something specific.

"What do you mean, mostly?" Raphael couldn't hide her astonishment. It was Azrael's charge to shepherd humans to their next place, via the Halls, like it was hers to keep watch on the living. "Azrael?"

The living. As time went by, Raphael realized she had been failing that task for a long while. One day in their presence was enough to notice. They were destroying themselves from the inside out, and nothing seemed to be able to stop it.

They didn't even *want* to stop it.

Azrael pressed a few more buttons, rose to his feet and crossed the rug to sit on the couch beside his sister. "Look here."

He pointed at the screen, indicating several points on a map marked with an asterisk. "These are bodies that just appeared with no registration in the system Father created for me."

"That isn't many, Azrael. How does that help?"

In response, Azrael huffed out a humorless laugh. "That's just here, Raph. Look at the world map."

He pinched at the screen, wincing when the total number of marks appeared on the display. "If I show you on a monitor it'll give you a better idea... but it's *hundreds*, Raphael. Hundreds of human deaths, most in the last thousand years. Deaths that I can't account for... and I only noticed it a month ago."

"That's probably significant..." She frowned at the screen, filing the information away for later. Right now, Raphael needed Azrael to focus on the problem she'd brought to the table. "And I promise to help you with it, however I can. But—"

"Yeah good. I could use another mind." Azrael darkened the screen with a sigh, feeling much the same failure as Raphael moments before. So many souls were lost, with no way to retrieve them. "I should have come to you when I first saw it."

"We've both messed up, I think." Raphael rose to her feet and paced away from Azrael, twisting her hands in her shirt like a nervous supplicant. "And now we need to catch up... I just wish I knew what we were catching up *to*."

Azrael only half listened; his mind had moved on to exactly *how* he could help Raphael's humans. He watched her stride up and down his study. If he didn't know any better, he would have sworn she was anxious.

"Raph... if *you* can't find them, then the only way I can find them is if they're close enough to an out of system death."

"Chance?" Raphael halted in her tracks. "That's what I mean... if they're close and it's not their time... or maybe it is and I'm just reaching. *I don't know*, Azrael. And I'm *so* sick of not knowing, I just..."

"Chance is on the list. It can't account for sudden technology failure, irrational murders, that sort of thing. But to ease your mind, let me just break my own rules for a second." Azrael reactivated his screen and accessed a file only he had ever laid eyes on, and only when necessary. He muttered under his breath, naming the two humans Raphael had tasked him with finding, only to frown when he isolated their names. "Impossible."

"What is? Azrael? I don't think impossible is a word you should be saying, given where you got that thing."

"I forgot how dry your humor was, Raph." He chewed the inside of his cheek as he considered his options, wondering if he should show Raphael what he was looking at, but decided to spare her the pain of knowing the little that was there.

Even if she didn't like Murphy or Malach, knowing their time of death would upset her. Azrael knew his sister well, despite the century of silence. She was *nowhere near* as ruthless as she pretended to be, or at least she hadn't been, last time he'd seen her. "I'm *not* going to show you this. *But*, I will tell you what I'm looking —"

The Archangel of Death blinked in alarm when a date shifted under Murphy's name. Then frowned when another appeared beneath Malach's. He cursed in an ancient tongue, muttering one of the few words he remembered while flicking through his options. Nothing changed, and with another quiet curse about the impossible Azrael rebooted the entire system.

Eventually, Raphael got tired of waiting and walked over to the window to examine Azrael's garden. She smiled sadly through the glass when his current partner entered her line of sight and lay on the saturated grass to play with a brush-tailed possum. Behind her, Azrael muttered to himself again. The language unnerved Raphael in ways she couldn't describe. So many years had passed since it was last spoken, she had all but forgotten its existence.

Memories flooded in, the images of her family, her brothers, her sister... and their Mother, so wise and beautiful and generous.

A lump formed in Raphael's throat together with the memories, and she lifted her hand to trace one of her old sigils into the misted glass.

"I've never seen this before." Azrael stopped cursing. Raphael was curious, but she kept her sight on the scene beyond the window. The simple domesticity was calming. Soothing. And she begrudgingly admitted that even if she could not have it for herself, she was glad Azrael had found some happiness.

She just hoped he could help her. If he couldn't... well, maybe Murphy and Malach would show up on their own to bother her again. But she doubted it.

"I... Raphael. I think you're right." Behind her, Azrael grew more exasperated. His system check revealed no problems at all, never mind one that would cause such a serious malfunction in his list. "About them being important, or at least significant in some way. They both have *multiple* points of death, and they're all in the next five years. The first one is in – No, *wait*. What on *Earth* is this?"

Both sets of dates faded to nothing before his eyes, then faded back in again, with more dates, then question marks. And without out warning, just like the first, *they* too, faded.

The next time the dates appeared, two were closer than the others by months. To make matters worse, his Tablet didn't reveal a location. Azrael groaned in frustration and curled his fingers into his thigh. First Raphael brings news of *Armageddon*, then two seemingly random humans mess with his system.

It just wasn't his day.

"*Four days*, Raphael. In four days, both of your humans are going to die."

A heavily pregnant pause hung in the air between the two archangels. Each considered the implication of the declaration Azrael just made. On one hand, they could do nothing and let the humans die. On the other...

"This is against the rules, Raphael." Azrael broke the silence, voicing his main concern.

Raphael had turned her back to the window during the silence. Her face was a mixture of confusion and frustration, and she stared at her brother wordlessly before she could find the words to speak. Her mind jumped a century into the past, then quickly back again as the memories of *that* encounter surfaced again. She buried the emotions that came with them deep, stuffing them back into the abyss where they belonged. Now was *not* the time to be emotional.

"You worry you're contradicting the past."

"Partly. You know I'm not supposed to interfere with the natural order of things. Neither of us are. If we did, there would be nothing but trouble from all directions." Azrael knew Raphael didn't know the inner details of *his* task, but he knew she understood enough. After all, she had her own tasks and rules to follow. "The one time I did..."

"Don't." Raphael held up her hand to stop him from bringing up Samuel again. "This *isn't* like that. You said yourself their entries have multiple points of death. Isn't that enough to make *you* question *why*?"

"Of course it is. I'm not stupid." Azrael snapped back at her, his patience wearing thin. His anger was misdirected toward

Raphael. He knew it, but her appearance, coupled with what he just discovered in his Tablet about the *very same* humans she wanted information about... it was too much of a coincidence.

And Azrael didn't like coincidences any more than his sister did.

"But Raph... what if—?"

"... us going to rescue them is what triggers their deaths?" Raphael finished his sentence for him, much the same way she had when they were children.

"Exactly."

"I'm going anyway."

"Raph—"

"*No*, Azrael." Raphael shook her head so vigorously it made her dizzy. "Not this time. Or have you forgotten Father's warning?"

Now it was Azrael's turn to look confused. "Which one, precisely? He left us with many."

"*When the night burns like day, watch the skies. Be ready.*"

Raphael recited the first line of the warning she had come to think of as a Prophecy. To her satisfaction, she witnessed understanding dawn in Azrael's eyes, but once again gave him no time to comment.

"Thirty-seven years ago, the night did, in fact, burn like the day... and I was too late to see whatever fell from the sky. All I found in the impact crater was a strange medallion. Like a timepiece. At least I think that's what it is. It doesn't work in any way that I understand."

Raphael remembered that night well. And the days of wondering that followed. Had it been a sign? Was it really something her Father had foreseen? Some days she was so sure... then others, she questioned herself.

"When the Earth burns like Hellfire, watch the horizon. Be vigilant." Azrael quoted the next line himself, his voice taking on the tone of recital Raphael often heard coming from their Father. He too, remembered the night Raphael was talking about... but while she made time to investigate, he hadn't made the connection, and spent the night buried in work instead. Now, however, the Archangel wondered if he was too late to get more involved. "Are you going to tell m e *this* line has come to pass too?"

He sounded skeptical, as though he was accusing Raphael of reaching, of trying to make the words fit her own agenda.

"Only a *fool* would think humanity wasn't dooming itself with every passing year Azrael... and I know you're not a fool." Raphael pointed her finger at him, growing a little irritated at his continued skepticism. "The world has been *burning* since the industrial revolution began, and when you think about it... mankind has accelerated far too quickly."

"Alright, alright." Azrael held up his hands in surrender. For now, at least. He wanted to believe Raphael, but he also wanted to make his own enquiries. To form his own conclusions, so he could come to the table with his own knowledge.

So he could feel like he was involved.

"I will admit, they're definitely outside of the estimates we originally made for them aeons ago." He pointedly ignored the raised eyebrow Raphael threw at him, choosing to concentrate on his empty glass instead.

Raphael rolled her eyes in defeat. She knew that look. The way Azrael ignored her glances told her that he would not budge until he'd seen for himself what she just laid out for him in plain sight. She sighed, trying to exhale the frustration that was simmering inside her.

"Let me know when you get a location."

"Wait, Raph." Azrael stood up, reaching out a hand to stop her from leaving, but the other Archangel shook her head. "There isn't much time! Where are you going?"

Raphael leaned down, picked up her glass of whiskey and downed the contents. Setting the glass down on the table, she flicked her hair back and gave Azrael one last determined look. She straightened and opened her mind to the well of power inside her.

"To watch the horizon."

Torturing the Humans

Somewhere under the desert.

"Hey. Hey. FBI. *Feck it.* Wake up."

Levi groaned in the darkness, unsure if he was awake, unconscious, or even alive. At this rate he didn't want to know if it were one of the first two options. The only thing that existed in his reality since he was snatched from his own office and thrown into his current living arrangement, was misery. Whether from his rumbling stomach, his aching body or the lack of sleep, the FBI agent had not found a moment's peace.

Unless his torturers went too far and he lost consciousness, of course.

It was perhaps ironic that he awoke locked in a cage with the very man he had been hunting for the past six months, but unfortunately for the agent, he could take no solace in Rian Murphy's discomfort... because it was far too close to his own.

He groaned again, trying to form the words on the edge of his tongue. "Get lost, Ireland." They came out mumbled, without any of the fire that had initially laced his voice. Levi shifted and rolled from his side to his back, attempting to sit up.

He used his feet to push himself into a sitting position with his back to the cell wall, peering into the darkness opposite. "How long?"

Rian crept closer, but stopped once he was inside the agent's direct line of sight. He crouched on his knees by the strange metal bars that formed the wall at the front of their cell, and in the inadequate light Levi could just make out that the assassin was in no better condition than him.

Dismal.

"An hour, no more. I'd have let you sleep mate, but they'll be back soon. It's been too long already." To test his theory, Rian reached out and hooked his forefinger around one of the bars, dragging it down across one of the markings carved into it. "Ahh!"

The dim overhead light flickered, and Rian pulled his hand back as though stung.

The sensation was close enough. As far as they could tell, the markings were carved in a series of glyphs neither had seen before, but neither man was stupid. They had figured out early on that there was something strange about the electrified metal bars, and the markings running across the surface of each one. The only problem was, neither of them could figure out what it was. Or where they were. Or who had abducted both of them.

Or, why?

"Lamadu!" The voice that drifted from the darkness was weak and despondent. They had yet to see who owned the voice. So far all they knew was that it was female, and she stayed back

in the shadows as much as possible, ignoring their attempts to engage her in conversation.

"*Na, tag laptu. Sepsu anbar.*"

She didn't speak often. But on the odd occasions she *did*, Levi couldn't understand a word she said, and judging from the utter confusion on Murphy's face, he couldn't either.

"Interesting, isn't it?"

The Watcher had every right to his smug tone. Nothing ever changed, and nothing ever would. Certainly not for his latest *guests*. Not unless *he* wanted it to. Their futile attempts to get the female to speak were entertaining, and he took great satisfaction in watching them fail.

"What's that, sir?"

He cast an irritated glance over his shoulder at his second. "Why do you *insist* on being so formal when we're alone?"

Without waiting for an answer, he nodded his head at the screens displaying the camera feed from the cells nearly a mile beneath his office. "These two imbeciles haven't stopped trying to gain that girl's trust since they joined us. They persist beyond the point of ridiculous."

"Maybe we underestimated them." The Watcher's lieutenant said *we*, but she really meant *you*, though she was very careful to keep those thoughts to herself. Once upon a time, the lieutenant felt secure in her position. Arrogant, even... but lately things had been different.

Lately, things had started to change, and she was torn. Leaning forward over the Watcher's shoulder, she cast a dismissive glance at the screen. She didn't even know who they were. And she didn't care. Under normal circumstances, her boss's entertainment was of little interest to her and these two were no different. Her interests lay in gleaning whatever secrets the female held, though nothing they tried had yielded any positive result.

"I could go down there and ...persuade them to talk. Your thugs are pretty useless this time around."

An empty offer, considering she had not sullied herself with his guests since one was stupid enough to die before answering her questions.

"I'd love to send you down there to get your hands dirty my dear, but you have work to do in London." He pressed a button on his desk and a drawer slid open. Reaching inside, he pulled out a file and passed it to her without making eye contact. His eyes remained glued to the screens. "I need this done by October 24th."

He held up a hand for silence as when she objected and opened an intercom to the guards below.

"Bring me the girl. But spend a little quality time with the other two first."

The lieutenant waited until the connection ended before she opened her mouth again. "That's only two days away. Sir, even for me, that's pushing it."

The Watcher spun in his chair to face her, clasping his elongated fingers together in front of his mouth. His forefingers tapped together while he waited for the compliance that would inevitably follow.

Compliance *always* followed.

Even after all these years as his second in command, she faltered, though her own stubborn nature refused to let it show. Showing any kind of weakness was *not* an option.

Not where he could see it.

Pale blue eyes set into a devastatingly beautiful face nodded once and snapped the file shut.

"Consider it done."

"Okay, I get it." Rian moved about an arm's length away from the bars, then sat opposite Levi with his back to the wall. His eyes flicked between the FBI agent and the dark cell, though he couldn't see anything past the weak light cast by the overhead lights in the corridor.

It was torture for dummies. Keep your captives in the dark, away from all daylight so they can't track the passage of time. Rian would have thought it was brilliant if he wasn't on the receiving end of the whole idea. He threw a stray piece of paper at the bars, scowling at the phantom across the corridor. It wasn't her fault she was trapped down here, and Rian had no energy to give her... but...

"I don't know why you care, anyway. It's not like they're paying attention to *you*."

She didn't respond. She never responded. Levi didn't think she could even understand what they were saying. "Give her a break, Murphy. Gettin' mad at shadows isn't helping anyone."

"You're right."

Rian turned the scowl on him, but Levi had lived through worse. A lot worse.

"I just... why doesn't she... doesn't matter."

"Yeah... I get it." Lord, he was beyond tired. Levi couldn't remember a time in his life when he had been more exhausted. Even after Annabelle's murder he hadn't been stretched this thin.

He was so far past tired he didn't even sigh when the door at the end of the corridor creaked open a split second before the faint lights flared into brilliance. All he managed to do was shield his eyes, but not before he heard a distressed shriek and caught a flash of cloth and dark hair retreating even further into the shadows.

It was working.

"Showtime, eh?" Levi pushed upwards, using the wall as leverage again to get to his feet.

"Ah, you never know." Rian mirrored his actions. "Could be dinner time."

"True, true. They might want to mix it up a bit." Levi wasn't *entirely* sure when the idle banter between the two of them began, but he had admitted to himself a long while ago that he didn't hate it.

In fact, if the Irishman *wasn't* on Interpol's most wanted list, and Levi wasn't an FBI agent, he was sure they would have been friends.

"Tell you what, I'll flip you for it."

"Loser's shout when we get out of here."

Their cell door slid open on an unseen command and several black clad security guards entered. Four more stood outside, and through the mass bulk of their linebacker shoulders, Levi could see another half dozen or so waiting down the corridor.

"Stay awake Murphy."

It was the last thing Levi managed to say before the first fist landed and he became a human punching bag. He heard Rian cry out but couldn't do anything except protect his head by curling into a human ball. The little reprieve it offered didn't last. Two of the guards grabbed his arms and yanked them sideways, pinning him to the wall so his main attacker could really lay into him. He favored the baton, and used it repeatedly, his careful, calculated swings smashing into Levi anywhere he could reach.

Levi felt the precise moment three of his ribs cracked. Agony flared, but he was beyond reacting at that point. He barely even felt it when his right shoulder popped under the strain and his body sagged with the sudden lack of support.

The dreadful sound of the one-sided battle rang in the air, punctuated by the sick commentary from the guards in the corridor.

"My money is on the cop."

"You're a dick. The assassin took out Andy and Max."

"Ooh, that's gonna hurt."

"Speaking of dick..."

"Wanna make it interesting?"

It was madness. It was excruciating, and eventually, it was eerily silent.

On some unspoken signal, the torture ended, and the guards existed the cell, leaving a pair of barely conscious men in their wake.

Rian pulled himself to one side, out of the way of the retreating guards and rolled into Levi, who was barely holding onto consciousness. For reasons Rian couldn't understand, they always hit him harder, always damaged him that little bit more, and this time was no different.

He heard a scuffle, followed by a terrified screech and turned bloody eyes to the corridor.

He couldn't believe it.

"Wussuru."

She screamed hoarsely as they dragged her out of the cell, unsuccessfully trying to both escape and shield her eyes at the same time. Rian and Levi watched in abject horror as they saw her clearly for the first time.

She was filthy and covered in rags, her hair long and matted. Skin so dirty it was impossible to tell what tone it was underneath layers of grime that could only have come from years of imprisonment.

"Ere, love." Levi's main attacker had grabbed the girl around the waist, pinning her arms to her sides by wrapping one of his own beefy arms around her torso. He used the other to cover her mouth, silencing her screams. "The boss wants another word. Be a good girl and don't bite. Ouch.! You *little bitch…*"

Another guard pulled a gun out from the holster at his hip and pointed it at the struggling woman. The instant her eyes landed on the weapon she froze, going limp as the hold on her tightened.

"*Wussuru.*"

It came out as a whimper this time. Neither Levi nor Rian were surprised when whatever she said went unanswered as she was hoisted over one of their shoulders and carted down the corridor and into the darkness beyond.

"Ahh, there you are my dear." The Watcher was nothing but civil to his guest when the same guards dumped her on the rug at his feet barely twenty minutes later. "How are you finding your accommodations?"

He smiled at her, his grin shark-like and menacing. It was a complete contrast to the smile he gave the world… not that anyone ever lived to tell the difference. Leaning forward, he tucked two fingers under her chin, tilting the dirty face of his captive upwards and forcing her to look at him.

Terrified green eyes stared back at him, the normally faded colour standing out against the dirty grey stains on her skin. She didn't say a word. She never did, not to him. He didn't mind. He got the best of his information elsewhere, having *her* there too was just icing on the cake.

"Still not talking, eh? Pity. I would have wagered you'd break by now." He tutted, shaking his head in mock disappointment at her surprising defiance. The fact that he knew she *still* couldn't understand a word he said only made the experience that much more delicious.

For him, anyway.

The others of her kind had *not* been so tough... but then, the others had been in his *care* for a lot longer than the approximate forty years since he fished this one out of a meteor crater on the Canadian tundra. During that time, he did everything he could think of to make the displaced woman talk, but so far nothing had worked.

If she wasn't his mortal enemy, he would have admired her resilience, especially since she never, as far as he could tell, accessed the power source denied to him and his people for thousands of years. No matter what he did, or how he hurt her, The Watcher couldn't get this woman to draw on it... she was either the strongest opponent he had ever faced... or she didn't know it was there.

That didn't stop him from trying, *or* her body from healing after everything he did.

She was one of *them*, and that was enough.

"Let's try something new today, my little space traveler." He reached behind himself, his hands closing over a white wooden box carved out of a single piece of tree. He picked it up and showed it to her, his curious eyes never leaving the woman half sitting, half crouched on the floor.

He *wanted* to see her reaction, to revel in the prize he found while he wallowed in her misery. With quick fingers, he unlatched the ornate metal clasp on the lid and swung it upwards, revealing the contents.

"I believe you're acquainted with this one already."

With a predatory grin, he lifted a dagger from the velvet lining. When her eyes lit with recognition, he felt a surge of triumph rush through him. But just as quickly as her interest rose, her eyes dulled again, leaving the Watcher with a tinge of confusion.

And then her lips moved.

"*Gu.*"

"Yes. It is. Or *was*." He leaned down, bending at the hips to her eye level and raised the dagger into the small space between them. "I *should* thank you, this knife of yours has served me well... but I won't."

He waited for her to make some kind of move, watching her eyes drift from his face to the dagger and back again. But the Watcher had done his work well, and his grin turned satified when she tried to scrabble backwards instead. With lightning-fast reflexes, his hand shot out and he grabbed her by a chunk of hair, pulling her to him. He dug in, taking a full hand of her dull, matted locks as he jerked her head backwards and pierced the tender, yet filthy skin on her neck.

"I'm not done with you yet, *Sumerian*."

He moved closer still. And again, until he felt her fetid breath on his cheek. Her terrified short gasps of air fueled him in ways he would never, ever succumb to.

Not with *her*.

Unclean.

Not even if it was the last push he needed to make her compliant.

The Watcher reveled in her terror, but he wasn't done yet. For the first time in decades, he let his disguise fall, and the satisfaction he felt before paled into insignificance compared to the pure panic that erupted in her eyes. His skin rippled and distorted, altering from the flawless tan he adopted on Earth to the mottled green of his native people.

"*Anunnaki.*"

It was barely a whisper, and only the second word she ever said directly to him in all the years he held her captive. The Watcher hummed in response, low and guttural in her ear, and when he spoke next, he made sure it was a dialect she could understand.

"Let's see how fast you heal *this* time, bitch."

The razor-sharp edge of the knife slid across her skin with ease, carving into it like butter. A fountain of brilliant red blood burst out of her severed arteries, splashing over his face and chest.

That, he expected. The dagger was second to none.

The one thing he *didn't* expect however, was the look of absolute determination in her eyes, even as her heart's blood pumped out all over them both and destroyed his priceless rug.

The steel behind the horror, the fire in her fear. It unnerved him like nothing on this planet ever had, and he threw her body to the floor in a mixture of disgust and uncertainty, waving to his guards to collect her.

"Take her back downstairs. Make sure she gets food... but not until she heals. You know the drill."

"Yes, sir."

He gave a departing kick to the bleeding body on the floor, knowing the knife would not do any permanent damage. Getting so carried away had not been part of his plan, but the sight of her, and the *memory* of her wrapped in the arms of his *navigator* sent him into a furious rage he hadn't felt since... well since he'd discovered the traitor in his midst, so many years ago.

The very *thought* of that particular Sumerian always sent Alalu into a frenzy that even now, all these years later he *still* struggled to get under control.

The opportunity to make Nasaru's lady friend suffer only made his revenge that much sweeter.

There was no day or night. There was no moon, no stars, and no sun. No constellations for Luma to identify. No sunrise, no sunset.

There was only darkness. Darkness punctuated now and then by a bright light she had come to associate with pain, and a longing for an oblivion that never came. There was no way for her to gauge the passage of time, she only knew that it had been far, far too long.

Luma bounced from one disaster to the other for as long as she could remember. Dimly, she remembered a time *before,* when there had been no hurting, and the only thing that came close to upsetting her life of study was a distant war and a brother who insisted she Ascend and be ready.

So much for that.

It took longer to heal this time. Longer for her body to repair itself after the Anunnaki who held her captive sliced her throat open with her own knife, the ceremonial dagger handed to her by Tiamat before she moved on.

Anunnaki.

The green tint to their skin was the only visible difference between the Sumerians and their planetary neighbours, something their biology adapted to during the long, clouded history of their civilisation. The Anunnaki were so skilled at camouflaging their perceived flaw that even during their days as an Initiate, a true sighting was rare.

Throughout her time in this Enlil-forsaken cell, the shifting colours had haunted her dreams... and now Luma knew why.

"Hey, *mmmm,* are you okay? .... a lot of blood."

The oddly accented voice drifted across the corridor riddled with pain, but as always Luma ignored it. The only sound she made was the wet gargling noise that came from her ruined throat as her lungs struggled to breathe, but drowned on her lifeblood instead. Men, or those that looked like men had come and gone from the other cells since the day she'd been stuck in hers, and she knew these two were no different, though to their credit, and her surprise, they tried harder than most.

Soon, their captor would grow bored with them too, and their bodies would be inevitably dumped down the chute at the other end of the corridor, tossed to the depths of the Earth without a trace. Never to be seen again. With any luck they would be dead before the menace that imprisoned them gave the order, but Luma doubted it.

They rarely died first, and their screams of terror lingered in the stones long after the darkness had swallowed them.

The man kept talking even though he was damaged himself. He tried. One or both of them always tried to coax Luma into some form of response, but even if she understood what he was saying, the displaced Sumerian couldn't move, not until the wound on her neck healed itself. The guards dumped her without ceremony near the bars of her cell in full view of the prisoners opposite, and all she could do was stare at them with unblinking eyes as first she choked on her own blood, then lay there waiting for her body to knit itself back together again. It was all she seemed to do since crashing down on this Enlil-for-saken planet.

"Ni guz ankida mitutu."

I'm longing to join the dead ones.

Her voice was watery and ragged, clearly betraying the injuries that she was still healing from. Luma curled away from view as soon as she could move, retreating back into the shadows and out of his line of sight.

"No, wait." It was the other one who spoke this time, but *that* one Luma didn't want to look at all. His resemblance to someone else from her memories was too close, and her heart and soul were too crushed to see the differences, though in reality they were many.

"Nasaru! Lumasi! Gula?" She cried tears that her body could not afford to lose, mouthing their names under her breath repeatedly as her weakened, frail body continued to heal itself, praying to the Universe that this time, someone would come.

The Lighthouse

Two days.

That was all she had left to save the humans. Two days to convince Azrael to give her a location. Two days to know if by taking action, Raphael was actually dooming Agent Malach and Rian Murphy to death.

Part of her was angry, and it showed in the way the clouds rushed overhead in a frantic dance of grey and white, though there was little moisture in the air.

Aeons ago, when Raphael's affinity to the weather had been discovered, her Father urged her to control it... but for Raphael, it was an outlet for emotion she couldn't let go of under normal circumstances. Sure, there were ...accidents, and she certainly wasn't responsible for *all* the weather on Earth, but a freak storm in the desert or a snowstorm in summer? Those had Raphael's name all over them. And though it was well within the scope of her abilities, Raphael didn't *want* to control the weather. Nature did an outstanding job all by itself *without* her interference, and besides, there were the prayers to consider, and the expectation that eventually came with answering them.

It was a mistake they all made in the earliest days of human culture, back when Raphael and her siblings were young and excited about this world they were given to watch over.

And then one day, their Father informed his over-excited children in no uncertain terms they were there only to *guide* humanity, not to make their lives easier or solve their problems.

We guide, Raphael. We don't interfere. This journey is theirs to make, just as ours belongs to us and our people.

Raphael responded with her usual unsatisfied curiosity, hoping for answers where her Father usually gave none.

But who are our people? Even counting Mother, there are only nine of us, Father.

As always, her Father, the one the humans called God had smiled a little sadly at her and her siblings and then promptly changed the subject.

And so, on days like today, when her emotions were on edge and her agitation was at peak levels, the Archangel just let it go. She had bigger things to worry about than a coastal squall. First and foremost, in her mind was the interference policy, but she'd stubbornly gotten around that by telling herself that whoever this enemy was, he had come after her *first*, thereby eliminating the policy altogether.

Though Raphael would be lying if she said it didn't play in her mind... after all, she had no proof that this was their ancient enemy, just an uneasy feeling, deep inside her. Separately, all the little things, like Envy having a wound that wouldn't heal, and the message left on the note on the same counter she was leaning against, right now were just things that happened. The way humanity insisted on sliding down a curve into self-obliteration was something she had been considering... especially since they seemed to act so brainlessly against the survival of their own species. Add Azrael's 'out of system' deaths, Rian Murphy's activities and Levi Malach's odd murder case... and Raphael had a list of things that when put together, just didn't feel right.

The worst part was she was certain there was *more*, something that she was missing. Or hadn't seen yet... for about the twentieth time, the Archangel wished for another perspective.

A pull on her senses gave warning that someone had crossed through her wardings a full ten seconds before Raphael heard a knock on the large wooden front door of the lighthouse. Sighing at the interruption, she made her way through the living area to the entrance, but paused with one hand laying palm flat on the timber before she opened it. Only a second passed, but it was a second the Archangel needed to fill herself with a sliver of power, just in case.

"Raphael, are you there?"

The muffled voice that filtered through was feminine, dainty, and light despite the heavy, thick wood hiding it. Raphael sighed again, this time at least partially in despair.

The door swung open.

"Kindness? How did you find me?"

"Well, hello to you too, cousin." The shorter woman rushed through the opening, barreling into Raphael with outstretched arms that quickly enveloped the astounded Archangel in a warm hug. She stiffened, taken completely by surprise by the show of affection. It definitely wasn't something Raphael was used to. Not since she'd left her home and come to Earth.

"Hello?" Raphael awkwardly patted Kindness on the back before extracting herself and stepping backwards to let the Virtue enter. She'd have to make a few amendments to her wards, but that depended on how long Kindness was planning on staying.

Kindness grinned impishly at her adopted cousin, going back through the opening to pick up an overnight bag that she left on the doorstep. Raphael blinked at the bag, both for its physical appearance *and* its cosmetic one. It was rose pink, with even pinker pink sequins sewn into the pockets.

"I decided to come and *help*."

"That's…" Raphael really didn't know how to feel about her offer. Before she appeared on Envy's doorstep and made herself at home, Raphael had not seen Kindness for thousands of years… and even then, she didn't know her very well. Only that she and her little family were originally created to oppose her Father and everything he was passively doing for humanity. Technically, it made the Virtue Raphael's enemy… but so far the Archangel had never been able to remain angry at her for more than a few minutes. "…nice of you."

It made Raphael wary, and it made Kindness very, *very* dangerous.

Raphael pointed at the bag now slung over Kindness's shoulder. "Where did you find that monstrosity? I thought they stopped making them decades ago."

She wasn't *entirely* clueless about human fashion; it was the close personal interactions that tripped her.

Kindness's expression dropped, and Raphael almost couldn't believe it when two big tears welled up in her doe eyes.

Yes, very dangerous.

"*He* gave it to me. He said it was *vintage* and—" Kindness's head jerked backwards towards the door, causing Raphael's gaze to shift from her to the still open doorway. "Wait, where did he go?"

"Where did who go? 'Ness—"

"He was right *there*, Raph. How do you think I found you?" She shifted the bag and walked deeper into the lighthouse, her eyes scanning everything. Raphael heard her gasp in surprise, then squeal in delight about something or other. Eyeing the door, and then Kindness, Raphael was torn.

Either she had an intruder in her house, and another outside, or... Raphael realized her heart was racing way too fast, and that she wasn't overly fond of surprises. Not like this, anyway.

"No need for another storm, Raphael. It's just me."

From somewhere off to the right towards the cliffs, the owner of the voice and the giver of the hideous bag appeared, and Raphael heaved a sigh of relief.

"Azrael! You came."

"Of course I did. You didn't think I was going to let you face Armageddon on your own, did you? Where's the fun in that?" He grinned at his twin, nodding his head towards Kindness, who was busy inspecting the bits and pieces Raphael had collected over time. His grin faded a little, though his eyes remained bright. "I found that one about two hours ago. Oh, Raph."

For the second time that day Raphael found herself enveloped in a hug, though this one she gave back with a little more enthusiasm, even if it was tentative.

"I'm sorry I doubted."

Again, Raphael found herself surprised, and it mirrored in her expression. "You believe me now? Why now?"

Azrael closed the door behind him, motioning Raphael into her own lighthouse so they could talk. He pulled a backpack off his shoulders and set it down behind it, catching up to Raphael, who had reentered the living room to find Kindness. "After you left I sent Matthew home and started my own investigation."

"I thought you might."

"Father sent us *both* to live in exile on Earth, Raphael. It would be remiss of me to ignore a warning like yours. Anyway," Azrael waved his hand, dismissing their earlier conversation and his doubt. "I searched. I Googled. I walked the Earth and *listened*. Then I realized I recognized something I hadn't sensed in a long, long time so I went searching again... and I—"

"He found me!" Kindness joined the conversation, bouncing up to the siblings with her usual enthusiasm.

Azrael looked down at her like he would a favored child and smiled. "Yes. I found you. Raph, you didn't tell me Kindness had returned to help too."

His tone was just shy of accusatory, and Raphael found herself growing indignant. So far, Kindness had been helpful, yes... but not with anything that Raphael thought was part of the bigger picture.

"I didn't..."

"I *told you* Raph. I'm here to help."

It was the day for sighing, it seemed. Raphael let another one out, and this time she pinched at her own brow. "Kindness, most of what you say is twisted underneath your facade. I—"

"You don't trust me."

"*No*, I don't. Because of exactly that." Kindness's bottom lip wobbled, and Raphael's irritation flared. She reached out and poked the quivering lip.. "Twice since you walked through the door you've tried to manipulate me, 'Ness. I don't like it."

"Oh gosh, I'm so sorry Raphael." The Virtue's eyes widened, and she covered her mouth with a gasp. "Enheduanna taught us to use our natural gifts, and that my innocence was my greatest weapon."

She cringed and buried her entire face with both hands. "I didn't mean to say it. I'm sorry. I'm sorry. I *promised* her I *wouldn't* talk about her to you. I'm so stupid. I didn't mean it. I'm sorry, it—"

Her voice was muffled by her hands, but the Archangels caught the gist of what she was saying. Azrael and Raphael's faces mirrored each other's sadness when Kindness mentioned her mentor. Raphael felt her throat tighten, and the loss that accompanied living without a mother came rushing back to her a hundredfold. It was inescapable, though she had spent a lot of time denying that she was affected.

"You... you've seen our Mother?" Raphael's voice was on the edge of breaking, for the second time that week. She glanced at Azrael, noting that he too was having trouble hiding the depth of his emotion.

Kindness nodded, still sobbing behind her hands. Raphael reached over again and gently pulled them down, keeping them in her own. She couldn't miss the tinge of fear in her cousin's eyes. Ignoring her own grief to help another was something Raphael did best. *This*, she could do with ease.

"... 'Ness, please. Neither of us has seen Mother since the Babylonian Wars. Even Father was never sure where she went."

"You're in no danger here, 'Ness." Azrael threw his weight behind Raphael's. While it was true that the origins of the Virtue were questionable, both Archangels acknowledged that their mother had whisked them away to save their lives, thereby adopting them into the family and creating cousins for the children of God. When Kindness maintained her silence, it was Azrael's turn to sigh.

"I take it you're under orders?"

"She made me *promise*." Her voice was whisper quiet, and it trembled with the fear that shone in her eyes. "She asked me to not speak of her if possible because she knew..."

Tears streamed down her cheeks, though Kindness couldn't wipe them away with Raphael grasping her hands so tightly.

"I'm sorry I took her away from you."

Raphael's heart cracked. First for her Mother, who had sacrificed her life with her own family to ensure the survival of another, and second for Kindness, who lived with the burden associated with a mother leaving her children. With aeons of anguish welling in her throat, Raphael cast aside her apprehension and pulled her cousin closer, giving her back the hug she'd so freely offered earlier. She ran her hands through Kindness's hair while they both cried out their tears.

"Shh. Shh, little one." Raphael didn't look too closely at how easily caring for someone came to her when she allowed her guard to fall. It was in her nature as the Archangel of Healing... but technically she did not need to care to be able to heal... and most of the time her empathy was buried. *Deep.*

Lately though... With one final pat, Raphael released Kindness and pulled back, clasping her cousin firmly by the shoulders.

"Can you at least tell us if she's okay?"

Kindness nodded again, wiping away her tears now that her hands were free. "I'm allowed to tell you she's fine. And that she misses you all terribly."

"'Ness, how did you know to come back to Earth? I haven't figured that part out yet..." Azrael had remained silent while his sister and cousin released their emotional burdens, though he did shed a few tears of his own.

"She had a *vision* that it was time." Kindness rolled her foot around, twisting her ankle on the ground, wanting to be talking about anyone but the Archangel's Mother. "I volunteered and I'm here."

"I didn't know Mother was a seer." Azrael mused to himself as he walked a few steps away from the other two. Now that the weepy part of the conversation had passed, he wanted to see more of the place Raphael converted into her home, and so far all he had seen was the entryway and living room. And the view from the cliffs.

"Anyway," He listened while Kindness continued, smiling to himself as he picked out some of the things his sister made her own.

"I couldn't find *any* of the Archangels, so I went to Envy."

"Envy... Now there's one who avoids *me* like the proverbial plague. Remind me what has she got to do with any of this?"

Raphael remembered with a start that she hadn't mentioned Envy's link to the current circumstances when she visited Azrael's house. Just that she was moving around.

One surprise at a time.

"It was Envy who brought Rian Murphy to my attention when he tried to kill her with a strange blade." Raphael gave Kindness a nudge, urging her to make herself comfortable on one of the chairs in the living area. "... but that was *after* someone had already sent him to shoot her."

"But he couldn't kill her."

Azrael's tone was confident, but Raphael shook her head.

"From the description she gave me... I'm not sure Azrael. She was close to death when I healed her. Her own abilities aren't anywhere close to ours and her body was failing." Raphael grunted sourly. Naturally after she healed the Sin, the woman had used her cagey ways to get around the promise she made to Raphael, and Envy's disappearance only fueled the original belief that nothing had changed. She was *absolutely* untrustworthy.

"Where is this knife now?"

Raphael shrugged. "I have no idea; I never saw it."

"... that makes things hard."

"What about this entire escapade is easy, Azrael?" Raphael snorted sarcastically, finally sinking into her favorite chair. It was deep blue, and so soft she often fell asleep in it.

"You have a point."

"The knife isn't as important as how Rian Murphy, an ordinary human, got his hands on it."

"Now you're asking the real questions." Azrael looked around the room, his gaze wandering from wall to wall as if he were measuring for something. "Say, Raph, do you mind if I bring in some supplies? I like using visual aids."

"Like Special Agent Malach's office!" Kindness chimed in again, breaking her silence with her usual enthusiasm. "It was full of pictures and string and a big board of information. We almost got caught because Raphael kept getting distracted by it."

"You would too if it had *your* picture on it."

She paused for a moment, ignoring the pointed glare from Raphael. "The one at his house was almost as big. We never did find where Rian Murphy was hiding."

"What? Raphael you can find anyone." Another pause, and Azrael winked cheekily at his sister before continuing. "Usually."

"I *did* find his hiding place. One of them, at least. It was what the humans call a way point. He didn't live there."

"But you told me you didn't..." Kindness looked disappointed Raphael ventured out on her own and hadn't included her in the investigation. She folded her arms across her chest and, to Raphael's surprise, *huffed*.

Raphael rolled her eyes. "'Ness, I found it this morning."

"But Raphael you promised."

"You're here now. You're helping *now*. Kindness please don't nitpick. I'm not..." Raphael eyed her cousin, and then her brother. Both of them sitting comfortably in her home, the one she made for *solitude*, so that she could observe and be alone. Part of her wanted them to leave, but logic told Raphael that her days of isolation were over. At least for now. "... used to company. I've been alone for so long I... I'm unsure how to not be by myself anymore."

It was a strange thing for an Archangel who was one of seven to say, and once upon a time Raphael had reveled in being with her often rambunctious siblings. Unfortunately, with the passage of time, the feeling of completeness while in company had dissipated, perhaps lost forever.

The sudden intrusion to her solitude made Raphael question why she was chasing after two unimportant humans. But as soon as the thought surfaced, the answer rose clear in her mind.

Duty.

It was always duty.

That, and the sense of responsibility she felt for their lives. Being caught up in whatever was happening with *hers* was not fair on either of *them*, no matter how she felt.

"Anyway, yes."

Azrael's face clouded with confusion for a moment. Kindness's interruption, and Raphael's gentle chiding had distracted him enough that he momentarily forgot what he asked.

"Yes? Yes what?"

"Set up whatever you need. There's plenty of room." Raphael squirmed uncomfortably in her chair, not entirely convinced her response was best. For her, anyway. Her hands fidgeted in her lap, twisting around themselves as she fought to remain calm. "Ah. So... is this our base of operations?"

"Raph..." His voice was gentle. Hesitant and unsure. "We need to do this, you said so yourself. Obviously, we need a place to start. Here is as good as any."

"No, no it's fine Azrael, I promise. I just need to make some mental adjustments."

Azrael eyed his sister thoughtfully. She wasn't the same Archangel that had vanished on him over a hundred years ago. This version of his sister was withdrawn and timid. More stern. She wasn't even arguing with him about her shortened name.

It was as though the weight of her task had stripped every-thing fun from her life and replaced it with a shadow, one that wanted nothing more than to dissolve into the back-ground and stay hidden. He recognized the signs; it was like looking in the mirror and hating what you saw. Only instead of isolating himself and wearing his loneliness like a cloak as Raphael did, Azrael covered his up with a myriad of human companions that came and went as their lives cycled on. The bittersweet reality of immortality was unbalanced and unfair at best.

They were doomed to an eternity of loneliness, with brief moments of respite, should they open themselves up to it.

"So," Azrael stood up again, brushing his hands down the front of his pants. He looked impeccable, a complete contrast to how Raphael had found him several days before. "I'll be back shortly. I have some loose ends to tie up, but I'll be back before moonrise."

In response, Kindness looked out of the floor to ceiling windows, tilted her head and nodded. Raphael rolled her eyes and waved him off without speaking. Azrael could tell she was keeping silent in order to keep her doubts about him and Kindness being there under control. Not even a second later, he was gone, and the only thing that betrayed his presence was the gentle chiming of bells that marked an Archangel disappearing into the aethers.

"You should try to hide that." Kindness voiced from the cushions she had sunken into. "From memory, my creator knew the sound *and* what it meant... he was always trying to find a way to use it."

."Your creator is not my problem anymore 'Ness... but I know."

Rescuing the Humans

Four days dwindled to two... and the two became one faster than Raphael could blink. They still weren't ready, not by a long shot, but time was quite literally running out. With their hands tied, all Raphael, Azrael and Kindness could do was bounce from one clue to the next, eliminating locations as fast as they could.

A mission that did nothing but *waste* the precious hours they had, as each of the four possibilities they tried so far resulted in nothing but frayed nerves and rumbling stomachs.

Six hours. Five more locations. And not enough time to check them all. Needless to say, Raphael was losing hope where there was little to begin with. They had simply come together too late, deciding to act when the deaths of Murphy and Malach were already sealed.

"Anything?"

Kindness's voice tittered anxiously to Raphael's right, and the Archangel sighed, opening her eyes. "Nothing. There's no trace of them here. Humans? Yes. But not the ones we're looking for."

"I agree." Azrael appeared in front of them, brushing a cloud of dust off his leather jacket. He frowned, his face echoing his concern as he glanced back over his shoulder to the doorway he'd just passed through undetected. "Though we might want to revisit this place later. It took me five levels to find out what they're *really* doing in there."

Raphael nodded, though she dismissed it as a concern for now. "Later, Azrael, I promise."

Her fingers twisted in the long plait that hung over her shoulder, a sure sign of how agitated she was. "... we're running out of time."

With a scowl at her own fingers, Raphael released her hair and flicked her hand towards Kindness, turning it over to beckon her forward. "Show me the map?"

"The Orgov facility is next Raphael, don't you remember?" Kindness pulled a device out of her garishly colored backpack anyway and unlocked the screen at Raphael's request. A map of Earth appeared, complete with little red crosses over the places they had already eliminated and little blue dots over those they hadn't. "Let me just... Here."

With quick movements, Kindness changed the place they were at to a red cross with a question mark, and then turned the screen so her companions could see it.

The twins angled closer, the Virtue not bothering to hide her smile at their identical expressions. Still so alike, despite the years that kept them apart... and still so dedicated to an unfolding mission their Father had sent them on so long ago.

"I remember, but..." Her voice faded as she traced a fingertip over the screen. There had been something nagging at the back of her mind, ever since they started adding locations to their list. Some clue she was missing. "I'm... we..."

Raphael tilted her head toward her brother, anguish written all over her face. Her eyes shifted frantically between him and Kindness before dropping back to the screen again, and it was with visible effort that she spoke again.

"Dammit Azrael I can't remember. Armageddon comes, they're going to die, *and I can't remember.*"

Azrael knew the look. He had observed it countless times on humans who berated themselves for not moving fast enough, for not being there in time when a loved one died. Raphael's face was no different... but the circumstances were, and it was those that the Archangel focused on when he reached out to take a firm hold of his sister's arm. She knew better than to lose her head like this. They both did. Their parents had ensured it.

"Breathe Raph, c'mon. Close your eyes. Don't worry about the map. Let your mind go where it must. *Stop resisting the message.*"

At first, Raphael flinched from the contact, only relaxing into it when Azrael's words settled the storm inside her. Nodding her acceptance, she obeyed, feeling both shamed that their enemy was so effortlessly defeating them... and turning her into a frantic mess. One little puzzle was all it had taken for her to forget every Lesson she ever learned, and that, in itself was cause for concern.

What was going to happen when things really got tough?

Eyes closed, she let her mind drift, watching passively as it swayed from thought to thought, from image to image as it searched for what was missing in a seemingly random pattern of jumbled faces, places, and names. From Envy to Agent Malach, to the note on her counter and back to the wards around her home it wandered, never settling for more than the time it took to picture the things that had been unsettling her most since the ordeal began. The meteorite crater. The dagger. The white-board covered in polaroids and blue string. The assassin's hideout and a footprint with a faint red outline. The—

Raphael's eyes shot open again, flaring into the golden-brown brilliance that echoed her power and several pieces of their puzzle clicked into place.

Of course.

"Azrael..."

Instantly her brother was there, his concerned face hovering in front of hers. "What is it? *What did we miss?*"

"Why did we add this place?" As the power ebbed out of her, Raphael reached for the device in Kindness's hand again, dropping her fingertip onto the last place they added: an abandoned uranium mine in the Australian desert.

Kindness tilted her head to one side, while Azrael pursed his lips in thought. Raphael could see their thoughts churning, but hers raced so fast she forged forward on her own.

"Murphy flew into Los Angeles under a false name from Sydney via Seoul. That gives us nothing—"

"No, *but*." Azrael interrupted her, his voice echoing her excitement as the same puzzle took shape in his mind, too. "That mine is surrounded by desert. In that part of Australia, desert means red sand…"

Kindness gasped, her free hand fist pumping into the empty air. "And there was red sand by the chair in Agent Malach's office!"

"Not only that… Azrael when I sent my mind searching, I… I… think whoever this is, is using our own power against us. I don't even remember what I felt when I… even now it's unclear. I bet if we go there, not only will we find the humans, we'll find *my* runes in use."

"That's enough for me." Azrael bent to pick up the satchel he dropped onto the ground earlier and readied himself for transport. He waited patiently for Kindness to step forward, then reached for their hands.

"Out of sight, Azrael. I'm going to need a minute to prepare."

"I know what I'm doing Raphael, trust me. This guy might have gotten a head start, but he doesn't know who he's messing with."

"I hope you're right."

The derelict hospital buildings faded from sight, and before anyone could blink, the scorching desert sun blinded their eyes. Raphael freed her hands and shaded her face, waiting for them to adjust to the much brighter, natural light Azrael had transported them to. One glance at the sky told her it was late afternoon, though from the position of the sun Raphael knew it would still be several hours until it was fully dark.

Unfortunately, they couldn't wait that long... but Raphael only needed a minute to find what she'd missed before from a distance.

"I was right...the wardings are a little different to mine but," She frowned as her power brushed over one, hoping that her delicate touch left no evidence of her passing. "It seems alien somehow. Warped."

"Can you neutralize them?"

In response, Raphael held up one hand and pointed to a cluster of rocks in the distance. "There. I can open a point for us to slip through right there. Once we're inside I can scan again to confirm that we're in the right spot."

"On it."

Azrael moved them to the rocks Raphael was still pointing at. He said nothing, but grinned impishly at the way her eyes widened when her fingertips were quite suddenly touching the shadowed sandstone.

"What? Trudging across that," He waved a lazy hand back towards their original position. "... we risked detection. Besides, can you *feel* that sun? Immortal skin still burns, Raphael."

"I didn't say anything."

"You were thinking it."

"My—" Raphael let it drop with an exaggerated roll of her eyes. Azrael had been both careful and deliberate with their transportation. As always, his precision was impeccable, a trait he'd learned long ago... but that didn't discount him from being an irritable brother. "Give me a minute to – *ahhh*. There you are."

Raphael brushed the same fingertips across the warding she'd been searching for. She exhaled slowly as her middle finger traced slowly around the same rune she used to protect her lighthouse; an invisible marking etched into the Earth that very few creatures could detect.

The reality that whoever was inside the facility even knew it existed gnawed at her on a level she was unsure how to process.

"Interesting... it's the same, but it – *ouch*." Her hand snapped back as a shock of electricity darted from the rune and into her fingers. Raphael's arm shook, dark eyes widening in surprise, and she turned her hand to stare in unblinking trepidation at the blister forming on her fingertip. "– is made to... *Azrael*. These wards are for *us*. 'Ness, no. Don't!"

Silent until now, Kindness crept forward to inspect the area of stone that for herself. Her eyes grew distant as she tapped her own pathway to the power inside her. Only then could she truly see what Raphael had been looking at. Deep blue eyes became almost iridescent, and without hesitation the Virtue placed her entire hand over the invisible marking.

"It's okay Raphael... I know this one. *Quick!* Take my other hand, both of you. I can't..."

Neither Azrael nor Raphael had time to do more than obey her command, and both reacted before any argumentative thought could settle in. Raphael slipped her palm into Kindness's, her fingers closing around the Virtue's smaller one while Azrael wrapped his around Raphael's. His brow furrowed in further confusion when Kindness nodded at him in expectation.

"'Ness...?"

"Put us on the other side. Flip us... oh, I can't remember the words. I just know I... I...can't let go until you do or this won't work. *Hurry*. Please... it hurts."

"Uh..." Azrael nodded as he began to understand what Kindness meant. His eyes flicked to Raphael for approval, but his sister was still staring at Kindness with an unreadable expression on her face. He didn't want to think about what *that* meant. "Be ready."

There was no need for further warning, or even that one... but Azrael was nothing if not considerate... *this time*... and with one final glance between his two companions, he pulled them through the greyness between spaces and deposited them in a mirrored pose of where they had been standing milliseconds before.

Raphael was the first to let go, pulling her hand free from the contact as soon as she registered their new location. "You know you're not getting out of this without explaining how you did that, right?"

"I would gladly tell you Raphael... if I knew." Kindness nodded without looking at either Archangel, her attention still wholly on the invisible rune underneath her hand. "The energy behind it just *feels* familiar. Like I know who made it... but that's impossible. Isn't it?"

Again, Raphael and Azrael exchanged long glances, but this time their concern was visible. Eventually Raphael broke the silence.

"I would like to think so, Kindness. Your contact list before Mother rescued you and the others was... very short."

"I know. And I'll figure it out Raphael, I promise."

Raphael simply nodded in response, stepping a little further away from the others to gather her thoughts. Getting sidetracked by a mission to find out who created the wardings was impossible. All that mattered right now was finding out if this was the place they were looking for, and to that end, Raphael reached for her power.

"Raphael, wait."

Azrael's voice cut through her concentration. Raphael gritted her teeth and turned to face her brother again. "What is it? We're on a pretty tight schedule Az."

"What if..."

"I know."

There was no time left for indecision or helplessness if they wanted to save Malach and Murphy. No time left to second guess each step they took. And no time left to make mistakes.

Everything rode on this.

"I don't think there's anyone around. I can't see anyone." Kindness' was apologetic, but it broke through the silence that lay over the small, despondent trio standing in the shadow of a boulder in an otherwise bleak landscape.

"... I guess we still have that advantage." Azrael turned away from Raphael, his eyes scanning the horizon for any other signs of life. He knew from his own duties that in this part of the world, humans often lived underground, but aside from the mine about a mile away and the deafening silence coming from inside it, there was nobody around. Even with his advanced hearing, Azrael couldn't hear a lizard crawling on the hot desert sand.

"Let's go, while we still have the element of surprise... c'mon. I'll drop us as close as I can to the elevator shaft so we can...*oh no*. Raphael, it's *gone!*"

The sheer panic in Azrael's tone exacerbated Raphael's rising anxiety, and since she was already looking at her brother's face, she saw the *exact* moment true fear sank its claws into him.

"What is?"

"My power. *I can't feel it!*"

"What do you mean you can't – *Oh no! I can't feel it either.*"

"This shouldn't be possible."

"Kindness..." Raphael whipped around to her cousin and wrapped her hand around her arm. "...tell me *you* can still feel it."

"I'm sorry Raphael... I let go as soon as we landed on this side. My relationship with power is different to yours. I can't... I can't feel it like you do. And right now, there's nothing there."

Raphael pushed with her senses, opening the space in her mind where the wellspring of power usually entered, but to her utter dismay it was empty. The comforting presence that had been her companion for her entire life was *gone*, the connection severed as though it never existed at all. Her stomach churned, her face losing all color as the implications of what that meant for their mission... *and her life*... played in her mind.

"I think... oh... oh..."

Raphael interrupted herself before her explanation was complete. With a loud retching cough, she doubled over and gagged. Her body convulsed, and she took two unsteady steps away from Azrael and Kindness to fall against the rock face right before losing the contents of her stomach onto the hard packed red earth. It was fortunate for the Archangel that her last meal was the day before, when they were still hunting for the right location. She leaned on the rock with one hand on the hot surface and the other on her thigh as she continued to cough up the nothing that remained inside her.

How embarrassing.

"Sis?"

She waved Azrael away. "I'm okay..."

"You didn't even throw up after the massacre at Babylon. I don't think *okay* is the word you're looking for."

"It's *gone*. I've *never* not felt it before. Are we stuck in here, with no power?"

"Seems like it. We need to find a way out."

"No, we need to finish what we started."

"Are you sure? Raphael... as much as I want to help you, I'm feeling kind of useless right now."

Kindness strode over to Raphael and placed her palm on the small of her back. With her concern open for all to see, she started rubbing small circles on her cousin's back. After a moment, she turned her gaze to the spot on the rock where they had passed through... and then abruptly been severed from their power source. "What if... what if we can find whatever is blocking us and destroy it?"

That got Raphael's attention. She stood up straight, wiping her mouth on her sleeve as she regarded her cousin with renewed curiosity. "...like the rune blocking us from passing through. What if it's just... a network of them?"

Azrael half turned back from where he watched the mine so he could see them both. "Then we need to find one and crack it open."

"Will it be enough?"

"How should I know? You're the ward expert, not me."

In Raphael's mind, her own wardings rose into full view, and the little network she set up to protect her home whizzed through. She watched them pass by one by one, examining the connections and bringing forward the combinations she made in the process. And then, another memory surfaced, this one recent. One where she found a note on her counter and a tainted rune that had allowed a trespasser to come through.

Boo.

"Yeah... if we can make a crack..." She left the sentence hanging. All three of them instantly understood what could happen if the crack wasn't wide enough, or the Archangels still couldn't re-establish their connection.. But they had to try. Not only for the humans they were there to rescue, but for their own sake.

If the one who took the humans already knew how to block them, *what else did he know?*

Azrael shoved his hands into the pockets of his black leather jacket and took three steps forward. He turned again and jerked his head toward the mine and the buildings looming in the distance. The lack of power worried him. Being stuck inside the mine and stranded in the desert made him wish he had never heard of either human. But his sister needed him. Hell, the whole world needed him, and he refused to run and hide because they fumbled their way onto the first real stumbling block on the *exact* mission their Father sent them here for.

"Well, I guess we're walking in after all. Come on ladies, time waits for nobody."

Somewhere Under the Desert

Unbeknownst to Raphael, Azrael, and Kindness, they were being monitored. Hidden inside the mine, The Watcher was following their every move. The very second they manifested in the burning sun beyond what they *thought* was a safe distance, he had been watching.

But then again, *he was always watching.*

He had been watching for centuries. Ever since humanity took that first step, treading the path to destruction, *he* had been there.

Watching. Waiting. *Guiding.*

Now and then he would tug on a string and a King would fall. A light breeze brushing another meant the end of a dynasty. The sharp click of a pair of scissors gave another, more preferable option a platform from which to stand. Strings everywhere, leading into every continent, into every seat of power that the Watcher knew would be useful to shape the world into one of his making.

A world where *he* could flourish.

A world where *his* people could be born again.

A world where his opposition was too slow, too weak, and too *stupid* to stand in his way.

This was *his* world, and it would *not* be taken by anyone.

They were predictable to a fault. The miserable Archangel and her apathetic brother, sent to watch the skies by a Father who was too confident in their abilities, too prideful of his own cleverness to give them the first detail about *why* they were asked to live their lives in exile, away from their family. Away from their *home*.

Oh yes, he'd been *watching* when the pair arrived on Earth like lost souls getting off the bus with a worn suitcase clutched in scared hands and straw still caught in their hair. He watched them fumble, safe in the knowledge that at *any* point he could have taken them out of the equation. Knowing that at *any* point, he *could* have added them to his collection and used them for his own gain.

But he hadn't. And he wouldn't. *Not yet*. Not until he watched them struggle. Not until he watched them think that victory was within reach and his defeat was all but assured.

After all, if his victory was *too* easy, then the game he made out of it wouldn't be any fun.

So, he'd watched, and he'd waited. Pulling on the strings of humanity like a puppet-master with his marionettes. He pulled, they danced... even if they didn't know it. The Archangels and their new friend were no different. He led them on a merry dance for years now, laughing when they stumbled and tutting to himself in mock sympathy when they fell.

He pulled, and the blundering children of God danced their way to his doorstep, exactly as planned. Exactly *when* planned. If he didn't want to be found, he wouldn't have left the crumbs behind to lead them here. He wouldn't have taken the assassin or the FBI agent, or kept them alive this long. And he *certainly* wouldn't be sitting at ease in an overstuffed armchair with a glass of premium gin in his hand while he watched them sneak around the upper floors of the mine he'd been operating with the blessing of the Australian Government for *decades*.

Well... since that one Prime Minister had gone for a swim and never returned, anyway.

No, things were, in fact, running *so* smoothly that he decided it was time to shake things up a bit. He activated his communication device and keyed in the code connecting him directly to his security chief.

"Sir?"

The Watcher didn't take his eyes off the Archangel on his screen. It was almost time. "Pick your most expendable unit and assign them to the corridor outside our *guest* quarters.

"The most expendable, sir?"

Watching the arrogant confidence the Archangels arrived with rapidly dissipate when they realized their powers were *useless* inside his domain gave him more gratification than he ever could have anticipated, but for now The Watcher had other, more pressing matters to attend to. "Then put six of your best men behind *them*. We have visitors."

"What about the woman?"

He thought about the woman in the cell facing his other prisoners. The one nobody had been able to kill *or* get a *proper* reaction out of. It would be easy to move her to another facility... but since this was a game, and he was the master, The Watcher decided to try something new. Something that just might force her to play by *his* rules. "She's useless to me right now. Tell your men to drop her down the gap. I'll come back for her later."

"And the other two?"

"Let them watch their rescuers fail." He grinned maliciously at the display screen, running his eyes from the cells to the desert above. "Then throw them after the Sumerian and meet me at Orgov. We're done here."

Descending Into the Hands of Fate

The ride down into the deepest part of the mines was tense. Time was fast running out for Levi Malach and Rian Murphy, but all Raphael could do was watch as second by agonizing second the clock ticked over. It was a countdown she couldn't control. An unfolding of events that would either lead her to the successful rescue of her misplaced humans... or bury her in the despair of failure. So many times, she questioned if this was the right path. If by doing this, she was playing her hand too soon. But as quickly as the thought emerged, Raphael buried it again... because what hand did she have to play? Ever since this had all started, all she had been doing was running to keep up, and even now, with her task *so close* it was within her grasp, Raphael was at *least* half convinced that the finish line was about to move.

"Stop thinking so much."

Azrael's voice cut through Raphael's thoughts as sharply as they had earlier. She grimaced from her corner of the elevator, waving a hand at him helplessly when he offered her a reassuring smile.

"You're as worried as I am." The tightness around his eyes gave it away. To the casual observer, Azrael remained unruffled by the events unfolding around him, but Raphael knew the signs better than most. He might as well have been screaming it from the rooftops.

"True... but for different reasons."

"Isn't it supposed to be one mile deep?" Kindness had been studying the distance counter on the digital display above the door, and stepped back from the opening when their descent continued past the one-mile marker. She looked back to Raphael, who gave her a non-committal shrug in response.

"Not sure... according to the propaganda upstairs, yes. But this elevator isn't on any of the specifications."

"... the fact that it was behind a secret door *kind* of makes me think this one goes a little deeper."

Azrael snorted. "Oh really? It wasn't the fingerprint scanner that gave it away?"

"Well... that, and the bookcase. It's so cliché."

"Right? And wasn't it lucky we found that guard with his fingerprints just waiting for us to use?"

Kindness nodded her enthusiasm. "It was *very* kind of him to be sitting there so attentively asleep."

The idle banter was not *quite* enough to set Raphael's mind at ease, but she appreciated it, nonetheless. Her shoulders dropped slightly as a relieved breath cut some of the tension out of her body. It was short-lived, however, because no sooner had the breath left her lungs, than the elevator slowed to a stop. The mission they were on held more than its fair share of risks... but add their complete lack of power to the mix and it made for a very strange, very tense situation. One that was about to come to a head.

All three passengers made eye contact as the reality of their quest rose loud and large in front of them. Swallowing hard, Raphael stepped forward, placing herself between Kindness and the door when their steel cage creaked, signaling that the doors were about to open.

"... Level one. Ladies-wear, secret villain lairs and salted caramel lattes. Please keep to your left, give way to workers, and enjoy your day."

Azrael moved into position beside his sister, giving her a tight smile. "My latte better be ready. All this bouncing around is making me tired."

There was not a chance he would allow her to take the brunt of whatever waited for them on the other side of those doors. Not that he really wanted to find out. In his disconnected state, the Archangel felt more vulnerable than he *ever* had before. In all his long years, nothing could come close to the vast emptiness that echoed in his soul.

Fortunately, he didn't have long to wait, for just as Raphael opened her mouth to respond, the elevator doors slid open.

Nothing.

Save for a few wooden crates, the room before them was empty.

Kindness stuck her head out from behind Raphael, peering into the emptiness. Packing crates stuffed with straw lay scattered haphazardly around the large room. A few were sealed, but the majority appeared to be only half packed. Or unpacked. At the opposite end of the room, she could see an exit, but aside from that there was no other way out of the room besides the elevator. "I don't see any lattes."

"Me either. Maybe they're in a different section."

A bullet shot past Raphael's head and buried itself into the elevator wall behind her. She followed its path with curious eyes, tilting her head to one side when another slammed into the metal sheeting next to it.

"I think they're closed."

Cursing under his breath, Azrael yanked his sister out of the line of sight of whoever made the shot. A quick glance told him she wasn't hurt, but he could not erase the image of her bullet-ridden body that had risen in his mind. "Yeah... well too bad. We already ordered. How many?"

To her surprise, Raphael could still pick out individual foot-steps and hear beyond the normal scope of a human.

"*Too many*. I think... at least thirty, scattered throughout this floor. And something...else. Wait." Raphael looked up at the ceiling and frowned into the reinforced bedrock, confused. Something wasn't right. But without access to her power, she couldn't put her finger on what she was feeling. Or hearing.

"They're not on this level. It's a diversion. They're... about ten levels up."

Azrael peered into the crate-filled room and shook his head. "There isn't anything ten levels up. There *is* no ten levels up."

"Not on the map. But it's there. I can *feel* it, Azrael... I heard something. Footsteps. Lots of footsteps. I think it's more guards. We'll have to find a way."

Raphael waved at them for silence and closed her eyes, letting her other senses seek out the answers that her eyes could not yet see.

"Did you hear *them*?"

"I heard a... something." She opened her eyes again but had no answers for him. "There's something hidden up there."

"That has to be it then."

"That doesn't help us if we can't get out of here."

Kindness put her back to the elevator wall when the first bullet hit, but when the volley ended, she straightened, secured her backpack, and dashed forward in a running crouch toward the nearest crate. As she slid into place behind it, she made herself as small as possible.

"Two behind the end crate on the left, one on the right. The rest are... *Ouch*."

Instantly and simultaneously, Raphael and Azrael stuck their heads out from the dubious safety of the elevator. They blinked at each other and turned as one to peer at their cousin, but it was Azrael who spoke first.

"...the Hell did you do *that* for?" He chased her without a backward glance, knowing Raphael would follow. She had no choice. None of them did... if they didn't move forward, they failed. And sure enough, as he approached Kindness's hiding place, he saw his sister in his peripheral vision. He gave her a tight grin, nodding to reaffirm his support, then flicked his eyes back to Kindness searching for any signs of injury.

"Are you hit?"

To his confusion, Kindness shook her head, though she had her hand curled in around itself. "I'm okay! I got a splinter."

Azrael sighed and dropped his head forward, touching his forehead to the crate. This really was no place for Kindness. She was too... fragile. But in the same breath, Azrael couldn't fault her bravery one bit. "Kindness... stay there until we—"

In response to his sigh, Kindness huffed, her hands moving to release the clasp on her small backpack. "I'm not a child, Azrael."

"I know you're not, but—"

To their right, a scuffle erupted, cutting Azrael off before he could respond. He offered Kindness his hand in place of an apology, and pulled her into a crouch as he peered over the top of their hiding place. "You okay there 'sis?"

"Nothing to it. I think. There's one coming your way."

"Hey, that's *mine.*"

He felt, rather than saw Kindness moving away. Azrael could scarcely believe she could move that fast. He chased after her, darting around the edge of the crate just in time to witness her disappearing out of the only exit in the room. He shouted for Raphael, following Kindness into the dark corridor beyond. Thankfully, his eyes adapted rapidly to the low light, and within seconds the Archangel found Kindness wrestling with a heavy-set man just a little further down the corridor. She wasn't e ven *half* his size, but from what he could see, his cousin clearly held the upper hand.

"I *said* it's mine."

"Wow you ladies are making me look bad."

"Told you..." Kindness blew her at her hair, kicked the man groaning at her feet one last time, then grinned up at Azrael. "I came to help."

"Why'd he want your bag?"

Kindness shrugged as she hoisted the bag back into place on her back. "No idea... there's nothing in it but...Hmmm."

"What?"

"Nothing... it's just the map, a bottle of water and... that's it."

Raphael's voice drifted back down the corridor toward them. "Worry about it later. I found a staircase."

"Let's go. There's plenty more guards where those came from."

"GO!"

It wasn't a request. Raphael screamed the word again, giving Kindness a shove up the stairs when her cousin didn't move. The grenade launcher she had seen a guard hoist over his shoulder around the corner behind them would stop any forward momentum. And if they couldn't move forward, it was all over.

Mission failed.

"*Raph!* What are you doing?"

"Buying us some time. Azrael, make sure our path is clear."

She dashed back down the stairs in a blur of movement too fast for human eyes to follow. It had taken them a few running scuffles to realize that even though the link to their power was temporarily severed, their other abilities were still there. It wasn't a mythical power that gave Raphael her dexterity or speed. That was her Father, and the games he used to invent and make her play with her siblings when she was young. Day in, day out they would run and play, using wit and will to try and outmaneuver God himself on the playground he constructed just for them.

Running down a flight of stairs to steal a few weapons from the humans in pursuit was child's play in comparison. All she had to do was dodge... but Raphael moved so quickly she didn't even need to do that. She leapt off the last step, colliding with the human holding the grenade launcher as he raised it to fire up the stairs in her direction. Her open palm connected with his elbow, sending the shot wild and toward the wall halfway up the stairs instead. The grenade's velocity was so fast it slammed into the rock and vanished in a hail of tiny fragments, giving Raphael half a second of extra time to get clear of the blast range. She spun on the spot, putting the soldier between her and the explosion, dragging him down the stairs behind her as the grenade detonated in a mixture of sandstone, quartz, and steel. The soldier lost his footing when one of his comrades collided with him in the chaos. The impact propelled him forward, sending Raphael into a tumble when his weight hit her from behind. Her knees buckled, and she landed hard on her back at the foot of the stairs with his unmoving, bleeding body draped over the top of her.

All around her men bellowed in pain and confusion, their weapons ineffective against the unending rain of rock and the dust cloud that followed. It billowed out in every direction, cutting visibility down to almost nothing while casting an eerie reddish light throughout the stairwell.

"Raphael!"

Azrael's voice sounded distant, but it rang clear through the combined sound of rumbling stone and coughing men. Raphael heard running footsteps above the rest of the noise, then felt a thud before the dead soldier's weight lessened, and her brother's worried face replaced it.

"Are you okay?"

"I'm fine. I just landed... wow, all the way down here."

"C'mon. Kindness is holding the door." He hooked his hand under Raphael's arm and lifted her out of the pile she landed in with an exasperated sigh. "This isn't what I signed up for, sister."

"It's *exactly* what you signed up for."

Raphael brushed off Azrael's hand and stumbled up several stairs on her own, moving slowly to get her abused muscles working again. She was covered in cuts and bruises, and blood ran freely from a slash in her arm. Every step cataloged a new injury, but she couldn't stop. Not now. A tearing pain shot up her leg when she put weight on her knee, the shredded ligament protesting every movement.

One step. Two.

Raphael pressed her palm against the wall and breathed through the worst of it, holding still until it began to fade.

Three steps.

Gradually, her torn flesh knitted back together, and by the time Raphael hobbled past where the grenade slammed into the wall, it was almost completely gone. She took another step, but then paused to run her hand over the fragmented rock in the hole created by the blast.

"I can see light... I wonder how far this goes."

"That'll depend on how solid the rock really is."

Curiosity got the better of Raphael, despite the danger they were in. She stuck her head into the opening, twisting it up to peer into the darkness. Something made her stop, and it nagged at the corner of her mind. A faint pull, too weak to get her full attention, yet strong enough to elicit a response. With a frown, the Archangel removed her head from the opening and straightened, though her eyes remained on the broken sandstone wall.

"... This is so..."

"I can feel it too."

And then, just as suddenly as she straightened, Raphael's eyes drifted shut, her head lolling backwards as whatever was weaving down through the cracked earth breached the hole in the wall and invaded her mind.

"Mmm..."

It was like saying hello to an old friend. A lover. A feeling so welcoming, so like *home* that Raphael almost dismissed it. After all, the feeling of home had eluded her for so long it was barely recognizable for what it was. But *there!* Lingering at the edges of her mind, it called to her again... and it was a lure so *enchanting* that even if she wanted to, Raphael couldn't have resisted.

"Ohh..."

Warmth inundated Raphael. It radiated out from somewhere deep inside her soul, infusing her with a love so deep that all the petty things she had fretted about slipped into insignificance. Everything stripped away, and with it, Raphael was laid bare.

"The light comes."

She couldn't tell if it was her or Azrael who spoke. It didn't matter. All that mattered was the golden light that wove its way through the cracked bedrock. The crack that began with the detonation of a grenade far underground and didn't end until it breached the surface over a mile above their heads, right through the middle of a rune. Now that their connection had healed, Raphael could *see* it tunneling through, a sliver of brilliance in a shadowy world... and the key to their success. Her eyes reopened, glowing with a brilliant amber light that reflected back at her when she saw her brother holding back tears as the Universe welcomed them home again.

"I feel..." Azrael was breathing heavily when he finally spoke. There were no words to describe how he felt. How *complete* he was now that he could touch his powers again. All his life the power was there, and even though his time without it could be measured in hours, he had never felt so *empty*. Like part of his soul was gone.

It was as humbling as it was terrifying... and not an experience he wanted to feel *ever* again. He moved closer to his sister, reaching out a hand to offer assistance she didn't need when he heard Kindness calling to them from several floors up.

"Raph? Az? You need to hurry."

"Shit." Azrael turned his head, looking up the stairs to where their cousin guarded the entrance to the level they had thrown all their hopes into. They really did need to keep moving. He gave Raphael a nudge and headed up the stairs, taking them two at a time instead of moving in the blur his sister had barreled down them in.

"Coming."

From somewhere not far below, another sound carried up through the shadowy red light to where Raphael was still standing. She tilted her head to listen, blocking out the sound of her brother's receding footsteps as he moved up through the dusty stairwell.

"Unit twelve, report."

"Unit twelve."

"Thompson, are you there?"

"Sir, we've got a problem. Say again? Yes sir, advancing as ordered. Bourke out."

Raphael backed up the first few stairs, keeping out of sight of the soldier approaching from below. It was slow going, picking her way through the rubble backwards, but she wasn't so far ahead of the new batch of soldiers that she wanted to risk alerting them to her presence. Step by step she climbed, turning after the first few to gain more speed and expand the distance between them. But somewhere between the sixth and seventh step, when Raphael was almost at the first corner, Fate decided to intervene, and she tripped on a loose stone. Her foot slipped forward, sending the rock clattering down the stairs and into the jumbled mass of bodies lying prone on the landing.

"Dammit."

"There's someone up there."

Ugh. Of course, one of them had to slip, and *of course* it would be her, lagging behind the others that did it. But Raphael had no time to berate herself, in the short seconds it took to regain her footing; gunshots rang out as the soldiers fired wildly in her general direction. She turned and bolted up another flight of stairs, keeping her eyes on the stairwell behind her at every turn in the spiral. Her newly re-established grip on her power was tenuous at best, and every time a bullet whizzed past her head, Raphael's contact with it blurred. But she couldn't do more than hang onto it with desperation as she fled from the storm of bullets and followed Azrael up the stairs.

It was *so much easier* to fight thousands of years ago. Before humans invented projectiles for anything but hunting. Sure, the bullets couldn't *kill* her, but they *could* slow her down, and as nasty as the humans behind her were, right now time was the bigger enemy.

She ducked around another corner and kept moving, pulling hard on the faint lines of power that flowed through the opening in the wards and coursed through her body.

Just a little more.

If she could just widen the gap a little more, Raphael was certain she could make that faint trickle flow like a raging flood and break through the barriers their mysterious enemy had created. But it was no use. The scrambling clutter of so many feet on the stairs behind her kept Raphael moving, and the ticking clock in her head urged her to go faster.

Time.

I need more time.

Another round of bullets cut a swathe through the air behind her, only adding to the frustration and impotence that was building in the Archangel since Azrael had first informed her of the untimely deaths the humans were facing. Despite the bullets, the grenades and the strange wards that blocked their power, they simply hadn't found *any* shred of evidence that Rian Murphy and Levi Malach had ever been in the mine at all. Ever.

What if we're not even in the right place?

If we're not in the right place, they die today. If I fail them... I fail Father and I fail myself.

The sense of looming defeat before they even started was as overwhelming as it was infuriating. And not to mention humiliating. How could their Father have thought they were ready for something like this... *whatever* it was? If it was even the reason He'd sent her and Azrael into exile in the first place. How could He have been so callous, sending them both into the world alone, ignorant of the task He appointed them? And how could Raphael ever face Him again, knowing that these thoughts were manifesting in her mind?

"...*arrrh!*" Raphael had no answers, for there were none to be found. All that she could do was push forward, find her brother and Kindness, and see what secrets this level held. If fortune was on her side, they would find Levi and Rian... and if not, she'd spend the rest of her life looking for answers.

And then getting revenge.

With her resolution set firmly in mind, Raphael pushed back at the trickle of power that was inside her, following it back to the crack in the wall two floors below. Her little game of push and pull had not done much to widen the gap, but it *had* widened a little, and with a deep breath to steady herself, the Archangel pulled again.

As it seeped through, Raphael twisted her hand into a claw and lifted her arm behind her head. Her palm grew hot as it suffused with the power she was about to unleash... and with a furious shriek, Raphael threw her hand forward, hurling her ball of concentrated power into the rock face that hovered above the staircase. The earth shook, rumbling like a moody fault-line, and from deep within the bedrock Raphael heard first one crack, and then another, and yet another still. More red dust billowed in the air, leaking out of newly formed cracks that widened, splitting downward like lightning bolts, spreading with untold speed as the first of her attackers rose into view.

Another crack, this time above her own head, and Raphael bolted, running up the final staircases as fast as her legs could carry her. One flight. Two. And all the while behind her, the screams of the dying gave up their pursuit.

The Art of Being Human

In the abyss, there was only pain.

It held him close, keeping his mind awake when he would rather let go and drift away into the blissful relief that sleep offered.

Sleep. A momentary pause in the agony that meant he was awake. There was no warmth of a lover's embrace in the suffering that his existence had become. No, pain held onto him like the bastard it was, denying him that which he really wanted.

The end. Or *an* end.

Sleep came in small doses these days. Or hours. Or years. Who even knew anymore? The *only* thing Levi could rely on besides the pain, was the ever-dwindling stream of sarcasm that drifted to him from the mouth of Rian Murphy. He knew the assassin was only trying to keep him alive, to keep him conscious so he didn't slip away and leave him to fend for himself, alone in the three-by-three-meter cell that was the epicenter of their lives.

"Hey. FBI... drink this."

Something cool trickled into Levi's mouth, bringing him back from the edge of sleep. He coughed, then immediately regretted the ragged, wet hack as his broken ribs pierced a little deeper into his lung. If infection didn't kill him, he would drown in his own blood soon enough. He was convinced that the only reason he wasn't *already* dead was that Murphy had him propped up at an angle that somehow stopped his lungs from filling up with blood.

"Why...?" Not for the first time, Levi asked his unwilling cell mate why he was bothering to keep him alive, and not for the first time, Levi watched through swollen eyes as Rian shrugged his question away. He reached for the cup that Rian was holding, but let his hand fall back down again when the assassin refused to let go.

"We're on rations mate... don't need you wasting what little those bastards give us."

"Just keep it, Murphy. Save yourself."

"Don't get all noble on me..." Rian set the cup aside with a sigh. Sure, he thought about letting the agent die. After all, Levi *was* part of the joint task force formed to take him down... but despite his professional life, Rian Murphy was not a murderer, and if he let Agent Malach die, he might as well be holding the knife that slit his throat.

No, he wasn't about to be responsible for the agent's death. Not under these circumstances, anyway. This wasn't a fair fight. This wasn't a battlefield, and this *definitely* wasn't the way he wanted to win the little wargame that had sprung up between them before their capture.

It was a small comfort, and a technicality his beloved mother would smack him over the head for, but to Rian, technicalities were often the only comfort he could take. *Especially* with the life he led. So, to that end, he had vowed to keep Malach alive for as long as he could, and while he couldn't exactly get the agent resting comfortably, he *could* put his medic training into practice, and treat Levi like he would treat anyone wounded in the field.

"... you know I'm only keeping you alive 'cos you haven't answered my questions yet. Stubborn ass."

"I knew it. Selfish bastard."

"Now's a good time if you're in a sharing mood."

Levi's face twisted in agony as he pushed himself up into a better sitting position, but it didn't matter where he leaned or what angle he put himself at, every movement sent another wave of intense pain shooting through his body. Even his toes hurt. And if he could have rolled his eyes at the assassin's tenacity, he would have. He had no real answers for why he continued to be so stubbornly silent about what he found and what he already knew, but part of him wondered if it wasn't what happened to Addison *right in front of his fucking eyes* that held his tongue. She hadn't known what Levi did, but whether he liked it or not, she was still part of it. And that peripheral involvement got her killed. He told Rian that much, at least.

"You first."

"Oh, for fuck's sake, Levi." In all the long weeks they were held captive, that was the first time Rian used Levi's first name. Gone were the faint edges of sarcasm that usually accompanied his words. All they held now was frustration laced with suffering. And God, was he *beyond* understanding. He dropped a weak palm into the dirt and summoned energy he did not have to force his companion out of his infuriating stubbornness. "We're both gonna *die* down here... what's the *fucking* point in keeping your silence?"

"You... picked an inconvenient time to make a good point. Fuck." Levi let his head fall back against the stone, ignoring the thud that created a dull echo in his mind.

Murphy was right, as much as he hated to admit it. His silence, his suspicions, and *his secrets*, who was going to find out? And if they did... Levi knew he would be dead and forgotten, rotting away in his cell. Nothing mattered. Not even telling Murphy... but Levi found his lips moving anyway, even though all hope of survival was gone.

"I lied to you."

"What?"

"I don't... think the Interpol case is why we're here."

"No shit." Rian leaned forward, his eyes dark and determined in the dim light despite the pain it caused him to move. "... you think it's the angels."

"There's no... such thing." Out of nowhere, Levi thought of the enigmatic doctor, Raphael, and the trouble she caused him since rolling into his life. His lips curled into a faint, aching smile. He no longer considered her a suspect, and his only regret there was that he'd never get the chance to tell her himself that she was off the hook he hung her from in his ignorance. From the doctor, his mind traveled back through the rest of his case, pausing now and then when a victim's face flared anew in his mind. On it traveled, flying back through time to where it all began. For him, anyway.

The big picture.

Fuck.

Several things began to click into place for Levi... and the loudest was the obvious clue he had been given at the Observatory.

How could I have missed that?

She *was* involved... but maybe just not in the way he originally thought. Something must have shown in his expression in the darkness, because as the thought crossed his mind, Rian shifted, somehow becoming even more focused than ever before.

"... the first body I found was my fiancé. The last one was at the Observatory. There are ten years and twenty-six bodies between them, and I don't have a fucking clue who did it."

Rian's expression was suitably awed, but Levi felt no satisfaction as he watched the Irishman processed the information he'd been given. After a moment, Rian swore under his breath and settled to the floor beside him.

"But you think it's got something to do with why we're here?"

"What else *can* it be? Your photo..."

"... yeah. My photo. My unit. It's the only bloody thing that links us."

Levi coughed again, this time covering his mouth with his dirty palm. The sight of blood was never pretty. Even less so when it was coming out of his own lungs, and when he spoke again, his voice was edged with a rasp that hadn't been present just moments before. "Tell me."

Another painful memory surfaced, but this time it was Rian that hesitated. This time it was *Rian* that was being asked to voice a secret that hadn't been told and would never see the light of day even if he screamed it at the top of his lungs. He bowed his head, sending a quick prayer of apology to his old unit. Telling this story meant he failed to get his vengeance. Telling this story meant it was over... and Rian didn't need a brighter light to know his own dark eyes reflected the hopeless misery he saw in Malach's.

He opened his mouth to share the information Levi had traded for and confess the darkest parts of his life, but before he could speak, the tomb-like silence surrounding them shattered.

From the far end of the corridor, they heard the distinct sound made by the mechanical door sliding open. They exchanged exhausted glances that said louder than any words could that both believed that this would be the last time. Levi knew *he* couldn't survive another beating, and even if Rian *could*, the one after *that* would claim his life, too.

Dying didn't trouble Levi anymore. He welcomed the sweet embrace of death. What upset him about it was the fact that nobody would *ever* know what happened to him. He would become one of his own statistics. A missing person among so many thousands of others. A body that was never found because *nobody knew where to look*. A case that was never solved because it would never be opened to begin with. Murphy would end up the same... except the authorities would probably just assume the assassin went to ground. Maybe they would think Murphy killed *him*. Or he they joined forces. Whatever theory it was, Levi no longer had the energy to care.

He listened as the tread of too many footsteps to count grew nearer, watching with dead eyes as well over a score of heavily armed men came to a marching halt right in front of them.

Nobody was more surprised than Levi to see the majority of them shift their attention to the woman hiding in the shadows, and from deep within the darkness, he came an all-too familiar scream. But before he could summon the energy to wonder what happened, the *entire* corridor erupted into chaos.

Ever since her throat was cut and she'd been left to drown without dying, Luma had been a listless bag of bones that did little but breathe the damp, stale air circulating throughout the rocky prison cell that dominated her entire life. She did nothing but lay there, alternating between staring at the stone ceiling and, during the hours when she felt brave, watching the men across the corridor.

Not that they could see *her*. She kept to the edge of the darkness, just out of sight, rarely showing herself even when what passed for food was thrown within reach.

Today was no different. Except for the odd, worrying sensation that *something* was going to happen, Luma was as apathetic as ever about what was happening around her.

So many days. So many years. So much time... none of it meant anything to her anymore. The meditative state she spent so much time in when she'd first crashed here was lost to her ages ago. At some point, Luma lost the ability to find her way into the peaceful state that initially offered her so much comfort in the darkness... and now all that remained, was the shell of what she used to be. And within that shell, Luma wasn't even a spark in the inferno of potential that her life *should* have become upon her Ascension.

No fanfare, no celebration. No guidance. No rites or ceremonies. No brother to help her. Just a journey into the unknown with a dead mentor she would *never* get to understand, and a home wiped from existence.

The yearning for home welled up inside Luma as she lay there on the cold stone floor. Her matted brown hair cushioned her head, creating a sponge-like surface for her to rest on. If she could, Luma would have gladly cut it all off. It weighed heavily on her head and did nothing but cause added discomfort to her already miserable life. But, short of pulling it out by the roots, there was nothing she could do about it. Even then, pulling it out was only a short-term solution since her hair never stopped growing, so Luma left it. At least she had somewhere soft to lay her head as she lay there with her eyes closed and *listened*.

It was about all she had left.

She could hear the soft words spoken by the nearby men, hear the ragged breathing coming from the more injured of the two. Over time, she witnessed how their relationship transformed from mistrust to the odd bond of tentative friendship created by their mutual incarceration. It warmed her heart to some degree, but Luma knew that in time, it would mean nothing. Enemy or friend, *they* would die regardless and then, at some point *she* would have new faces to ignore. She moved on from their conversation, directing her thoughts to the corridor and the doorway that offered no escape. Nothing moved in the immediate area, and just as Luma was about to pull her mind back, her ears detected something else.

Her eyes shot open as the sound of running feet reached her ears, and from somewhere deep within wherever she was, Luma felt an explosion vibrate through the rock she lay prone on.

The light comes.

She didn't understand what the words meant, but those were secondary to the way the earth rumbled around her. In a past long distant, Luma clearly remembered feeling the same way when her own planet began to break up underneath her feet. Dread engulfed her, wrapping itself around her like a tentacle, anchoring her in place when she wanted to leap to her feet and scream her frustration into the void.

Not again! Please... not again!

And then, she felt *it*.

From somewhere far above her head, Luma felt the presence of something she hadn't felt since that day long ago when Nasaru had wrapped her in his arms and forced her Ascension.

An-Ki!

It wound down through the rock, a tiny trickle, a sliver of light in a world that had none, burrowing its way down, down, *down* into the bottom of the earth to a destination unknown. She reached for it, crying out for deliverance with outstretched arms, begging for the Universe to put an end to her grief.

But An-Ki didn't see her. It didn't sense *her*. For Luma didn't know *how* to make the connection herself and couldn't do more than *feel* what was so close, yet so horrifically out of reach.

Like trying to catch a rainbow with broken fingers.

"No... come back."

A pair of blazing lights ran back and forth in her mind's eye, with a third, slightly dimmer one mirroring their movements. Despite the rumbling, Luma stared at the ceiling in confusion as whoever An-Ki *had* chosen moved ever closer to her position.

"Grab her."

Rough hands hoisted Luma to her feet, instantly breaking her concentration. Another pair of hands shone a torch in her face, blinding her to everything but the bright light that burnt her eyes. She screamed, struggling to break free so she could shield her eyes, but it was to no avail. Her captors held her so tightly she could barely move.

"Do it. Then come back here. We're going to – *shit. Move!*"

Luma could barely see past the glare in her eyes, but she knew fear when it manifested, and the man who spoke was riddled with it. With no small amount of effort, she turned her head and squinted through the bodies, but except for some kind of commotion in the entryway, her unreliable heightened senses couldn't tell what was happening.

"Got it."

All she could focus on was her own predicament. Her head bounced sideways as the men holding her arms dragged her forward, but not before Luma caught the widened eyes of the men huddled at the rear of their cell. They were watching as one, their horrified bewilderment clear as she was dragged past their doorway and beyond... and it was *then* that Luma realized what was about to happen.

The chute.

"Na! Na!"

She didn't know how far the drop was, but Luma already knew that if a fall from space at terminal velocity didn't kill her, then this one didn't stand a chance.

But then, she figured her captor already knew that.

"I think she knows, Sid."

"How'd you figure that then?"

"Eh, she's been here longer than most. It's in the eyes. *She knows.*"

"Oh well. Doesn't change a damn thing."

"Ey love." One of the men hoisted her higher, then leaned over to look her in the eyes. The other stepped back to give the other the space he needed. No point in getting his own hands dirty when his companion was eager enough.

"No hard feelings eh? Bossman said he'll come back for you later."

Luma found strength where she thought there was none. She dug her heels into the floor so hard it jarred her knees, stopping all forward momentum before the man holding her could throw her through the gaping hole in the wall. To her horror—and her complete surprise—he reached into his jacket and pulled a knife out of a specially made sling he was wearing beneath his clothes. In the heavily shadowed light, she could barely see more than the glint of steel, but it wasn't that which held her attention.

He waved the knife at her, jabbing the sharp point into her side when she refused to comply. "In you go then. Good girl."

His tone was conversational, but edged with an iron determination that no amount of logic could dissuade.

"Gu!"

"Quit fucking around Dave. Throw her in or we'll miss the evac rendezvous."

Without warning, Luma darted forward, stamped her foot down and reached upwards, taking hold of the knife hilt with both hands. Or at least, she tried to. All she managed to do was wrap her small hands around his much larger ones, but that, coupled with her foot coming down hard on his was enough to unbalance him. With her one advantage almost over, Luma dropped her weight, lifting her feet off the floor to pull *his* arm downwards, and when he swayed, she twisted herself and *pushed*, driving the knife deep into his stomach.

Dave's mouth dropped open in an 'O' of surprise and he stumbled forward into Luma, who frantically tried to duck out from underneath him. She clawed at him with one hand, tugging on the arm he held in a vice-like grip while attempting to edge herself away from looming hole and the unknown drop that awaited her.

But it was far, *far* too late for that. Dave's momentum, coupled with Luma's slight weight still creating an unbalance sent them *both* toppling headfirst over the ledge.

Sid walked over to the opening of the chute with his radio in hand. He opened a channel to his superior, watching in detached fascination as the two bodies tumbled out of sight.

"... The girl is in the air."

Fighting Through

Raphael stumbled out of the door to the stairwell and collided with Kindness. The fight was pure chaos, a running battle of speed instead of skill that lasted until Raphael finally relented and brought the ceiling down on their pursuers, blocking their path. She held off for as long as possible, using the re-established bond with her power as a last resort... but she was beginning to think it should have been their game plan all along.

"There's no doubt they knew we were coming." Azrael was still breathing hard after his mad dash up the stairs. Raphael could see his chest heaving from where he stood behind a workstation of sorts. Apparently, he had plenty of time to investigate though, despite his lack of breath, because he was busy stuffing several detachable hard drives into his satchel.

It was a good idea, even with the urgency that still loomed before them, and Raphael merely nodded when he tapped on the bag, indicating the work they'd no doubt have cut out for them later. Her eyes flicked to 'Ness, who grinned almost impishly back at her cousin as she shrugged her own bag back into place. The petty thought that while she'd been running for her life, they were almost idly choosing electronics fluttered through her mind, but Raphael was far too gracious to voice it. For now.

"They *had* to have. We were *so* careful. I –"

The sound of somebody clapping caught their attention. For about the tenth time that day, Raphael turned, noting that her brother and cousin were also turning, which was strange, considering they were all facing different directions to begin with.

"Good show so far. Bravo!"

From somewhere above her head, Raphael heard the distinctly tinny sound of a voice coming through a speaker. She moved deeper into the room, turning again as her mind drove through the level she'd emerged on, seeking the owner of the voice that taunted them. But aside from a large cluster of bodies about a hundred meters to her right, there was nothing that stood out. Except now she knew which direction to head in.

"Show yourself."

"All in good time, my dear."

The trio moved closer to each other, each keeping their eyes on a third of the room as their backs met in the center. Whoever was speaking seemed to think this was some kind of joke, because all three of them could clearly hear the laughter in his tone.

"What do you want?"

"Nothing. For now."

"Why did you take the hu... those men?"

*"Oh, come now Raphael. I can call you Raphael, can't I? Anyway, as I was saying... let's not be modest. **I know what you are.** I know what you **all** are."*

"I don't know what you're talking about... I'm just a –"

"What? A doctor? A grief counselor? The Cousin? I thought we agreed to not be modest."

"I didn't agree to anything."

*"So you didn't... my mistake. Regardless, I'll do you a favor, little Archangel. If you can get to the humans you value so much **before** it's too late, I'll let you take them. But I'm bored, therefore this conversation is over, so –."*

"No, it *isn't*. We'll find you." Raphael's harsh tone desperately interrupted the metallic, disembodied voice that wouldn't stop taunting them. The fact that he mentioned a time limit told her that he was up to something... and that their presence tipped his hand, and in doing so, brought forward the deaths that Azrael predicted when she first appeared on his doorstep.

Cause and effect, in all its glory.

The voice, however, continued over the top of Raphael's words as though she hadn't spoken at all.

*"...I'll leave you in the hands of my most **trusted** lieutenant. Do try to keep up next time, children. I **really** was hoping for more of a challenge."*

The tinny sound cut out, fading from existence faster than Raphael or Azrael could blink. At the same time, Azrael raised his hand and pointed to the second of three doorways that led deeper into this unmapped area of the mine. "This one."

"Not so fast."

"What now?" Raphael groaned under her breath, and her face twisted into an expression of despair. "What could he *possibly –*"

Kindness peered into one of the open doorways, confused. "Envy?"

"Thought you'd have figured it out by now, Raphael. But you just *don't get it*, do you?"

From the darkness inside the first doorway, the slender figure of Envy appeared. Her hair was lighter than it was the last time Raphael had seen her, and her eyes were a different color, but there was no mistake. It was her cousin who emerged to block their way.

"What are you doing here Envy?"

"What are *you* doing here, Kindness?"

Kindness sniffed and folded her arms across her chest. "I came to help."

"Who? Who *exactly* did you come to help?"

"...You. Raphael. Azrael. Everyone." Kindness shrugged, keeping her expression as calm as possible. "It's my mission."

"Some mission. You betrayed me. You betrayed *us*."

"I did no such thing!"

"We don't have time for this." Azrael waved his hand and lifted Envy into the air, binding her in his power so she couldn't move. So far, he had been content to play along with the game, to blindly accept everything that was thrown at them... allowing events to play out naturally, *as they should*. But with the appearance of yet *another* obstacle, the Archangel of Death had reached his limits. He stalked toward Envy, away from his sister and cousin with one hand outstretched. The determination on his face spoke volumes about how close Azrael truly was to the end of his tether.

"We're taking the humans."

"Go, Azrael. There's no time left! I will deal with Envy."

"Kindness we're not leaving you with her."

"I'll catch up with you in a minute." Kindness tied her hair into a ponytail, tossed it over her shoulder and steadied her feet. Nobody could mistake the steely expression on her face, or the way she eyed her cousin Envy with a resolve neither Raphael nor Azrael had ever seen before. "Put her down. She won't hurt *me...*"

When neither Archangel moved, Kindness raised her hands and *shooed* them away.

"I said go."

"She's right Azrael." Raphael touched her hand on her brother's shoulder, drawing his attention to her. She glanced to Kindness and smiled, giving her cousin the authority she needed. And the support. "This is between them. We're needed elsewhere."

"I don't like it. But you're right. Divide and conquer." He dropped the lines of power securing Envy and let her drop to the floor without cushioning her fall. For a second it appeared he was going to move even closer to her, but with one exasperated glance from Kindness, Azrael retreated to the exit and chased after his sister.

"Show her who's boss, 'Ness."

"I've got this."

Envy brushed herself off and threw a disdainful glare at the now empty doorway before turning back to her cousin. "Oh, you *do*? *Tell me*, Kindness... how *exactly* have you got this?"

"Oh no, you're not getting to me that easily. Not anymore."

"Trust me, my dear... I already have." The Sin reached up to rub her fingers thoughtfully across her chin while she examined Kindness. As angry as she was that Kindness had turned up with those do-gooder Archangels, this was still a situation that could be turned to her advantage. "How's my house?"

"Good. I cleaned up all the blood."

"The *what*?"

"The blood your minions left behind when they came for Rian Murphy. Or was it *you* they came for?" Kindness smiled at Envy's confusion. "He's a nice boy... you should have listened to him when he came to apologize. At least that's what I think he wanted."

"I never sent anyone for Rian Murphy. I'll take care of that dick myself."

"Oh? Interesting." Her eyes narrowed, but Kindness would not let anything distract her. Not even how blind Envy was.

"Anyway, Envy... don't you think you've dallied here long enough?"

Envy gave her a scornful glare and retreated a step. "I'm *exactly* where I need to be."

"Wrong! You're *supposed* to be with me." Kindness felt Wrath's lessons boiling to fruition as she advanced another step for each one Envy made in reverse. "You're *supposed* to finish your training so we can both –"

"There you go with the traitor talk again!"

One step forward, one step back.

"I'm not the traitor, *you are.*"

"You lie. You *abandoned* me. *You* abandoned all of us."

Envy tried to dodge Kindness, but her inexorable march forward continued, only ending when her shoulders scraped against the rough sandstone walls. She raised her hands, but Kindness brushed them aside to jab a rigid finger into her chest.

"You don't even know what you're talking about! The others are all safe. They're all where they're supposed to be... it's just you, Envy. And because it's *just* you, *I can't be where I need to be either.*"

"... the fuck are you talking about?"

"We're the *last*, you and I. The last to be United. The last of the Sins and Virtues to be released from the bonds of our creation. The last to be accepted by An-Ki."

"More lies. Propaganda drilled into you by those fools and their father! An-Ki." Envy spat the word and wrinkled her nose at Kindness. "You've really lost your mind."

"It's you who is the fool, Envy." Belatedly Kindness realized she had taken hold of Envy's jacket in a tight fist, and with an uncharacteristic grunt, the Virtue shoved her cousin back and let her go. All the long years of study. Watching her family bond and learn, while she had nothing but an empty space beside her. For as much as Kindness needed Envy, it was the same in return. And with her absence, Kindness hadn't been able to take the steps she needed to be accepted by the Universe and into its service.

Unlike the others, most of whom had long since departed their Sanctuary and taken up the duties that Fate assigned them to. Kindness watched them depart, one by one with a growing despair in her heart, and a sadness that echoed throughout her entire being. Without Envy, she could not Unite, and if she could not Unite, then the Universe could not accept her. She tried. Oh, Heavens, she tried, and her family had done what they could to help, giving of themselves so that she could learn about each of them and thereby become more than she'd been created to be. Pride, Lust, Greed. Kindness knew them all. She knew Humility and Chastity and Patience. War. Temperance. All of them.

All but Envy.

"It is *you* who missed out on what Enheduanna offered us. It is *you* who didn't get the knowledge of our Family, including *mine*."

"What the fuck do I care about what you know?"

"Because what *I* know, Envy… will be *your* downfall." Kindness didn't taunt or mock. She stated it as fact. The wealth of knowledge she gathered from their Family was bound only by the limitations they were created for, and once Enheduanna had found the Path around the ties that held them back, the rest of the Sins and Virtues thrived.

All but Kindness.

"Bullshit." Envy launched herself at Kindness, wrapping her arms around her cousin's middle as she tackled her to the floor.

"Traitor! Just do what you came here to do and *get the fuck* out of my life."

Envy's snark was the last straw. Kindness had been beaten, abused, and manipulated. Under orders from her creator, her life was forfeit if she ever came back to Earth, and yet here she was regardless. Still pleading. Still trying to get her Opposite to see reason and rejoin her so they could *both* step into Fate and be truly free.

It was more than anyone should have to deal with. Without warning the Virtue snapped. Her eyes flared into brilliance, the gold light behind them shining brighter than any star in the night sky. She *yanked* on her power, screaming with indescribable agony as it filled her… and then *immediately* fought against her and tried to escape the confines of her limited control. An-Ki tore shreds off her soul, incinerating her from the inside out, but Kindness refused to let go. Instead, she hurled a wave of light at her Opposite. Envy flew backwards into the same wall she had leaned against only moments ago. Still lost in her wrath, Kindness moved forward, pulling on more of her power until it blazed from her fingertips. *Never* in her entire life had she held so much raw power. The Universe was as comforting as it was ruthless, and it terrified her to the core. Her whole body vibrated with it as she hurled anything that wasn't tied down at Envy, her shrieks of rage echoing off the stone walls.

"I. Did. *Not.* Betray. You."

With every bitter word another piece of furniture landed on top of the Sin where she lay stunned on the floor. Kindness moved closer, her breath coming in short bursts as she struggled with power that fought so hard to be free. Little by little, she eased it back until, as abruptly as she'd pulled it into her, Kindness severed her connection and dropped to her knees beside Envy's head.

"*You* betrayed *me*, Envy. Without me, you are Incomplete. Without you, *I* am Incomplete." Her voice was a whisper in the dust-filled room, but to Kindness it roared louder than a waterfall. And no less dangerous, considering what just happened.

"I tried. We *all* tried. I studied so darn hard to be Complete without you but..." Kindness sat there despondent, leaving the remainder of her sentence hanging silently in the air until, at last, she climbed to her feet and took a single step back from her Opposite... and the one that ruined her life.

"The Universe tested me and found me wanting...and I will *never* forgive you for that."

The Games We Played

Without a backward glance, Raphael jogged through the doorway and left Kindness to deal with Envy. It troubled the Archangel to be separated from her cousin at such a critical time, but she trusted that Kindness was right. Envy wouldn't hurt her... not much, anyway.

"I don't like it." Azrael interrupted her thoughts as he caught up to her.

Raphael's steps faltered, but she pushed forward with grim determination, angling in the direction she *hoped* was right. "You think I do?"

His response was long coming. Troubled and uncertain. "I don't know. I didn't think she..."

"I know, Azrael. Me either."

A crash ruptured the air behind them, followed by an ear-splitting shriek. The Archangels turned as one to peer back down the corridor, too stunned to do more than listen.

"I've never even seen her angry..." Azrael's uncertainty about Kindness had vanished, replaced by a subtle note of pride. He huffed out a quiet chuckle and accepted that Kindness was more than *either* of them had bargained for. "I'm glad she's on our side."

"Come." Raphael touched her brother's arm, tugging his sleeve to get him moving again. She *needed* him to go. It was equally as hard for her to leave Kindness behind. Over the past few days, she had grown fond of her cousin, despite her initial reluctance to spend *any* time with her at all.

But Raphael also understood what Kindness offered when she decided to fight Envy alone.

"We don't have *time*. Our cousin is giving us what she can, Azrael... we cannot waste her gift."

This was her sacrifice, her *help*.

Almost no time remained before Azrael's invisible counter ran out. Every second that passed was another second too late, but Raphael retraced her steps and clasped her palms together, linking her fingers as she raised her hands in front of her chest. She bowed her head to the empty passageway leading to their cousin, and the fight she joined on their behalf.

"Be safe, Cousin."

The simple gesture of reverence was all she could spare before the sense of urgency returned to smother her awareness.

"Come, Raph." This time Azrael beckoned Raphael to move, and so she did, falling into place beside him at a junction that resembled most of the others.

"I fear we dallied too long in that other room."

The clash between the Sin and the Virtue dissipated into nothing as they hurried toward the cluster of humans Raphael sensed ahead of them. But the resulting silence was once again splintered by a heart-wrenching wail brimming with such despair that Raphael doubled over, clutching at her own chest as the despondent cry tore at her heart. It sped up, hammering away in her chest, and she sucked in several deep breaths, attempting to dispel the wave of absolute terror that surged into her from the darkness ahead.

To her side, Azrael staggered sideways, shaking his head to dispel the effects of the scream.

"What the Hell was that?"

"I don't think it's a *what*... I think it's a *who*."

It blasted through them again, ringing in the air like a distress beacon flaring into the night. Azrael shot forward, chasing the sound. It called to him, winding through his soul with an echo of misery he would never forget. He darted ahead of his sister and turned another corner, hoping to spot the source, and ease its pain, but the wail abruptly cut off, leaving him in such complete silence cold fingers of dread crept down his spine.

"No!"

Was it too late?

He ran through another archway and slid into the next room with reckless abandon. There was no time left to play it safe, but Azrael skidded to a halt and scanned the room while he waited for Raphael to catch up. To his right another two workstations and a coat rack holding an odd assortment of utility belts lined the wall.

It was the left side of the room that caught and held his attention.

A steel grid hung on the wall, decorated with hooks designed to store weapons... and every hook was full. It was a torturer's wildest dream manifested in perverse, neat rows all within arm's reach for easy access depravity. Several guns dotted through the collection, but they paled to insignificance next to the screws, needle-thin knives, hammers, sharpened stakes, scoops and whatever else the twisted owner of the rack could think of. Many items were blood-stained. Azrael's nostrils flared at the faint coppery scent, but he rumbled in outright disgust when a piece of bright, fresh gore dropped from a spiked baton to splat into a puddle of crimson blood on the floor.

"*Why* must they..."

Even after all his years on Earth none of it made sense to him. The corruption that some humans succumbed to knew no bounds... and although Azrael had seen it all countless times, there was something about *this* place and *this* time that played heavily on his mind. If they could just *save* Murphy and Malach from the living Hell they had been cast into, then maybe *he* could continue with *his* task without disliking what he saw in his own reflection.

How can we just stand by when men do this? Why must we be content to watch? What guidance do we offer from the shadows?

Time stood still, but in reality Azrael analyzed the horrific scene in seconds. He gave the torture rack a wide berth, vowing to exact revenge on behalf of the victims that perished lost and alone in the God-forsaken place. One look at Raphael's pinched features told him that his sister felt the same.

"Raphael…"

"I'm fine." She wrapped her fingers around the edge of a heavy metal door beside the torture wall, her knuckles white with tension. "Did you see anyone?"

"Not yet."

The door itself was ajar, left open and forgotten in the haste to beat the Archangels to the prisoners, and after a quick glance through the gap, Azrael identified the cluster of humans that they tracked through the complex.

"How many do you count?"

He nodded at the opening, then stood off to one side while Raphael copied his actions, then pressed her body flush against the opposite side.

"Twenty armed men and… *oh.*"

"What?"

For the first time since Raphael materialized on his doorstep, Azrael saw hope flare to life in her eyes. "We were right… It's them."

"Thank Father." Relief blossomed inside him too, but Azrael refused to let it take hold. He cast his mind ahead to the group in the corridor, idly wondering which of them screamed so loudly only moments ago. Murphy or Malach? No, the scream sounded female, and felt… different. But so far he hadn't detected any human mind that could—

Wait.

"Raph! There's someone else... *and I don't think she's human!*"

"If that's the case then we'll deal with her after."

"We might have no choice. Speaking of..." He jerked his head toward the door. "I'm open to suggestions."

Raphael narrowed her eyes in thought. Twenty humans were not too much of a threat to her and Azrael. Even alone it would be easy enough... but they hadn't come this far only to lose her wayward pair of humans to a stray bullet or the vindictive slash of a knife.

"Just so you know... three minutes."

Tick tock.

She scowled, and threw it at her brother with a deep, frustrated sigh. *Three minutes.* That was what it boiled down to. Three minutes to save two lives she had no idea of the importance of. Three minutes to get past and defeat twenty armed men without a single one of them getting to Malach and Murphy first.

Three minutes.

No pressure.

The soldiers knew Raphael and Azrael were there. That much was clear. Several of them stood guard, watching the doorway and each time she peered around the door frame, two had crept that little bit closer. In seconds they would burst through the door, but Raphael didn't plan on still being there when they arrived.

"Azrael... do you remember the running game?"

"Of course. Camael used to win all the time... but why are you asking ab – *ah.*" Azrael stole a glance at the guards, lingering a little longer than the last time. "Right. Yes, I see. High or low?"

"I'll go up. I was always faster than you were."

"I wouldn't say *always.*"

Raphael snorted her response, recalling the *one* time Azrael ran faster than her during this particular game. "I had two broken toes and I'd just been through The Test."

"I *still* beat you."

"You know what the best part about this is?"

Raphael stood up straighter, bounced from one foot to the other and kicked out the knee she had injured earlier. In the back of her mind, her power lingered, ready and waiting for her call. Ready to put an end to the nightmare that plagued their days and tormented their souls. She smiled at her brother, a slow grin that widened as she opened the conduit inside her and flooded her being with raw power. It dipped and soared, singing wordless tunes in perfect harmony with the Universe and everything within.

A bootheel touched the floor, light as a feather yet louder than a freight train.

The pungent smell of cheap aftershave.

A breath, slow and steady not three feet away.

Raphael swung into the doorway, meeting the surprised eyes of the first soldier as he burst into the room. With her feet set, the Archangel raised her palm and *shoved* her hand into his solar plexus. His chest caved beneath her hand, collapsing with a sickening crunch under the force of her blow. He sailed back into his partner and Raphael grunted in satisfaction when they landed together in a tangled heap on the floor.

Without missing a beat, Azrael joined her and steadied himself for what came next. His eyes locked on the guards ahead of them, cataloguing their positions. This had been one of their favorite games to play as children... but never in a million years did Azrael think it would be useful in combat.

Until now.

The very thought awed him. Their Father had *known*. He had shown them how to *win* by teaching them how to *play*.

Eyes ahead, Azrael.

Feet on the floor.

Find the target.

Don't miss.

The memories flooded his mind as clearly as if they'd been created the day before. Their Father's voice, encouraging them in a tone that promised a celebration for everyone, no matter who won. Azrael smiled with the memory, dipping his head in acceptance of the Lesson even as he turned a curious eye back to Raphael with their Father's voice lingering in his mind.

"What's that?"

In response, his sister delivered a swift kick to the uninjured man crumpled in front of her. She exhaled, blowing a stray strand of hair out of her eyes, and dropped into a running crouch.

"We can cheat."

She was a blur. A glowing blur of soft amber against the faded red stone walls of the underground mine. The beacon of light her Father trained her to be. *This.* This was what Raphael been sent to Earth for. To watch and protect, to guide and follow.

One foot. Two. One in front of the other. Keep going. Dodge that bullet. And that one. Shit. No time!

Less than three minutes left before her humans were lost forever, but for Raphael time had slowed until it almost stood still. Gone was the urgency that plagued her for days. Gone was the uncertainty that simmered beneath the surface. And *gone* was the ever-present belief that she just *wasn't* enough.

This, she could do.

This, by comparison, was easy.

With her well of power secure, Raphael *sprinted* down the corridor, using both power and speed to propel herself forward. A bullet nicked her arm, speeding in the opposite direction, but the Archangel didn't slow. She leapt sideways, her feet springing from the sloping wall of the corridor as she angled upwards, altering direction almost as often as her feet touched the surface.

Just like their Father taught them.

Another bullet grazed past, punching through her shoulder, shredding tendons, and exiting her back without losing momentum. Raphael missed a step as the impact knocked her off balance, and changed course again as the soldiers first registered her presence, then raised their weapons to stop her.

Or try to.

Behind her, Raphael heard Azrael move, taking the agreed low path along the floor. She didn't look back, but from the sudden shouts of alarm, the Archangel knew he was moving in a pattern as swift and unpredictable as hers. With their enemy's focus now split, it became easier for her to move freely, and as she drew closer to the cluster of armed men, Raphael changed direction one more time.

"Shoot her!"

"– the fuck is she doing?"

"Oh shit! The other one! He's too fast. He's coming! I –"

The shouts continued, becoming more and more desperate as first one, and then another was cut off by Azrael's approach. Gunfire erupted, shooting bright sparks into the confusion, and tainting the air with gunpowder and smoke. From her position on the ceiling, Raphael spotted a struggle between two heavy-set men and a much smaller figure, but one glance at the mass of dark hair was enough to know that whoever that unfortunate person was, they weren't the reason for her presence.

And then the scream punctured the air again. A torn, wretched sound that pulled at her harder than it had before. Her eyes skimmed back to the dark hair and the struggling figure being hauled away, and it was *then* that Raphael discovered who the scream belonged to. Terrified green eyes locked with hers across the distance between them. Awareness wrenched at her soul when she looked into the woman's eyes, but she couldn't stop.

Not yet. Not until her task was complete.

I'm sorry.

Stifling a cry of despair for her inadequate apology, Raphael ran on, sprinting over the heads of the bewildered men below her. She *had* to stay focused. Raphael forced her sight to a clear space on the floor in front of an open cell. Beyond it, the corridor was almost empty.

There!

That *had* to be it. There was no other reason for the soldiers to gather so closely, if not for the inhabitants of the cells. The only signs of life beyond those metal bars were the pair of soldiers and the struggling woman held between them.

Six more.

Five.

Three.

When Raphael was level with the last of the humans, she sprang forward, pushing with a hint of power to give herself a boost. With the added momentum, she soared clear of the cluster and into the empty space behind them. Her body twisted as she descended, somersaulting in a graceful downward arc that looked out of place amongst the rough movements of the soldiers sent to stop her.

Tick tock.

A Heavenly Light

I must be dead already.

Levi could not believe his eyes.

There, right in front of him the impossible unfolded.

This is a strange afterlife.

Everything remained the same. The lighting in the corridor. The labored breathing of the assassin beside him. The dirt beneath his fingertips. The ever-present cold that seeped out of the rocks around him and chilled his bones. The slow flow of his own blood as it oozed into his lungs. The stench of his own body covered in blood and filth and the sickly-sweet smell of infection. The score of men standing outside his cell.

Everything remained the same.

Well... everything *except* the lithe figure that burst out of the shadows and aced a superhero landing behind them. He *had* to be dead, because *nobody* brushed off a two-hundred-and-fifty-pound man like he weighed little more than an annoying speck of dust. And if he *wasn't* dead, then his eyes had *definitely* malfunctioned, because it was *impossible* for a person to glow like a firefly. Levi understood bioluminescence... but

the soft warm light that somehow emanated from every part of
...her... was as ridiculous as it was mesmerizing. It bathed the
corridor with an ethereal radiance, bouncing from the walls and
back again to highlight her every move. Light danced against
shadows, casting the illusion that a great pair of wings sprouted
from her back. Even the long, dark braid that hung loosely over
her shoulder shone pure like the morning sun.

Braid?

A memory tickled his mind. Levi frowned, squinting his
bloodshot eyes as he struggled in vain to sharpen the image. He
blinked at the light, counting each pass of his eyelids one by one,
but his poor deceased brain could not process what was clearly
there... but also fucking impossible.

Definitely dead.

"Look at that..." From somewhere to his right, Rian's
worn-out voice filtered through into Levi's obviously deranged
mind. "... isn't that your doctor friend?"

Strange, that Rian was there. Or perhaps not. Maybe Rian
was dead too, and this was some kind of odd lingering moment
before their souls parted ways forever.

God, even when he was dead, Levi was tired.

And weirdly, he didn't feel any better. In fact, he didn't feel
any different at all.

His chest huffed painfully as a weak chuckle burst from
blood-filled lungs. One hand twitched on his thigh, but Levi
couldn't summon the energy to point. As far as deaths went,
this didn't seem so bad. At least he got to watch his asshole

guards get their asses kicked by a tiny woman before he went to Hell. Maybe soon the pain would stop too, and then he would *really* be able to sleep.

"Did you see that landing – *wait*... you can see her too?"

"Course I can. She's right there."

"... *how?*"

There was nothing else Levi could say, and *no way* he could deny what he was seeing now. Even as his sight began to darken, Levi's dying mind still tried to find some logical explanation for the glowing apparitions in the hallway. A shared illusion was possible, but unlikely, even in this situation... and if it wasn't an illusion, and that really *was* who it looked like... then Levi was further out of his depth than he *ever* thought possible.

Darkness crept closer, blanketing his eyes like a creeping fog. Levi blinked again, giving his head a tiny, painful shake as he fought to stay alert, but weeks of being beaten and abused finally caught up with him, and as he slipped into the black void that had been beckoning for him to sink into its cold embrace, the last thing he saw was *her* face hovering over him.

Firefly... so pretty.

"Raphael! Side left."

Azrael made quick work of the man poised to strike his sister from behind, cutting his thick legs out from underneath him with a swift, firm kick to the back of his knees. He spun, putting his back to Raphael to face what remained of the soldiers sent to bar their way. Two held their guns low, too afraid to shoot in such close quarters but the third suffered no such qualms, and had his muzzle raised and trained on the Archangels.

When will they learn?

He was tired on so many levels. Physically, he could endure for as long as it was necessary, though eventually he would lose stamina. Azrael could already feel it seeping into his body. For days they had been on non-stop high alert, chasing down Raphael's humans without rest. Sure, as Archangels they had access to an almost unlimited power source and could multitask with ease... but there *were* limits, and Azrael was quickly coming to his.

"I've had *enough* of this."

With his sight fixated primarily on the man with the audacity to point a gun at him, Azrael reacted. He raised his hand, dismissing the trio with a flick of his wrist. At first, nothing happened, but Azrael waited, his whole-body tense with impatience. The irritated set to his mouth altered to a grin as tendrils of pale gold flew forth from his fingertips and wrapped around them like a loose spool of thread that drew tight when the Archangel tilted his head to one side and pursed his lips together in thought.

"Enjoy the sunshine, assholes."

They disappeared with a muffled pop, but not before Azrael's dismissive flick turned into a joyful wave. He lowered his hand, sighing deeply into the sudden, profound silence blanketed the underground corridor.

Silent, except for the fading scream that echoed throughout the stone... and the labored, wet breath of a dying man and the unsteady, fading heartbeat of his companion.

"I'm not going to ask where you sent them." Raphael cut through the silence; her soft voice edged with hardened steel. Empathy for humanity was one thing. But empathy for those that got in her way and tried to kill her? Try as she might, Raphael could find none. Besides, if she spent time wondering about those specifics, she would miss the point of her entire mission... which was indeed the cell she landed in front of.

"Rian Murphy... Levi M—"

Two steps were all it took for her to reach the bars. Beyond them lie the end of her quest, and the reason for the disruption to her quiet solace. There was no hesitation from the Archangel. She reached for the door and wrapped her hand around the metal handle as one of the shadowy figures coughed weakly for her to stop.

"*No!* Wait!"

Too late, Raphael realized the danger. An electrical current charged up her arm, setting fire to her skin and she was hurled away from the bars by an unseen force. It threw her across the corridor, crashing her into the wall in a painful clatter of bones that collapsed to the floor in a stunned heap.

"Raph!"

"I'm okay... what the Hell was that?"

"The bars. They're... electrified or something."

"No kidding..." Raphael climbed to her knees and hauled herself to her feet to retrace her steps. Through the bars she saw the disheveled, grimy face of Rian Murphy staring back at her.

"We can't touch them."

Talking hurt, but the alternative was worse. The alternative meant this might not be real after all, and he would soon slip away for his appointment with Death. Rian sifted through his thoughts, struggling past each one to find the word he was looking for.

"*Sepsu an-something*... That's what *she* said the first time. She..."

He rolled his eyes to the left, where the strange woman had been taken.

"... hmmm..." Raphael rubbed the back of her head. Blood coated her palm, seeping through her braid at an alarming rate, but she turned her mind to their newest problem.

Powerful... something. Where had he heard those words? *That language?* Questions hovered on the tip of her tongue, but like with everything else that day, there was just no time.

Later.

She brushed Azrael away when he saw the blood and frowned at the bars. The wound had already stopped bleeding, but the headache would linger. Powerful, yes. Infallible... no. Raphael sent a tendril of power to wind around the bars, her dark eyes fixed on the reaction of the metal. With one bloody finger she traced a pattern into the air, filtering the flow of her power through it. Her mind probed gently as more ten-drils enveloped the bars and demanded their secrets.

"The girl..." Levi's weak voice broke her concentration.

"Shit. I think they killed her."

"*No*... can hear... screaming."

"Raphael! Azrael! Are you down here? Oh, there you are!"

Azrael spun to greet his cousin. "Kindness! What happened to –?"

"I'll tell you later. We need to leave! The mine is going to collapse!"

"We're almost done. Raph?"

"Nearly got it...*there!*." Without hesitation, Raphael tightened her hands on the bars again, and this time, when her fingers made contact, the *only* thing that moved was the door when it obediently clattered sideways on its runners. She rushed into the room, reaching out to envelop them with her powers before her knees hit the dirty floor.

Please be alive.

"Agent Malach... can you hear me?"

"Firefly... so pretty."

"He's..." Raphael didn't need power to see that Agent Malach's condition was serious. Too serious, even for her liking. She pressed two fingers against his neck out of habit, but it was with her mind the Archangel assessed how critical his injuries were. "I need to get him out of here. You too, Rian Murphy."

"Take him... I can walk."

She shook her head without explaining. "Not the way we're going. You're –"

From the eerie depths of the mine beyond the cell, Raphael heard another sound. She raised her head, turning to peer into the darkness it drifted from.

"Who..."

"There's a lass. *She's still alive.*" Despite the agony it caused, Rian twisted to face her. He touched her arm to draw her awareness. Her eyes flicked from Levi to him and back again. "I don't know who you are but... *please...* We can't leave her here with those fuckers."

The woman. The same presence Azrael sensed earlier. The same figure she had seen struggling in the hallway. Raphael nodded. It was the right thing to do, she knew it was... but nevertheless she was torn. Levi Malach needed her attention *now...* however, something inside Raphael instinctively knew that saving the mysterious screamer was just as important. She looked between the darkness and Agent Malach, her anguish clear for all to see.

"I'll take them Raphael." Azrael's cut through her rising anxiety, instantly soothing away any concerns she had about losing Agent Malach. If the Archangel of Death didn't want him to die... then Levi would live. But still...

"His pain is too great, Azrael."

"Believe it or not, I *do* know a few things. Meet us at home. Go."

She nodded again and rose to her feet, but not before sending a gentle wave of healing to the assassin and the FBI agent they had fought so hard to save. Just enough to keep death at bay. Just enough until she could finish what she had barely started. In truth, it would make more sense for Azrael to find the female... but as he already pointed out, Raphael was faster and therefore more likely to save her from whatever danger she was in.

With one last glance at her new patients to reassure herself, the Archangel took a step backwards. Then she abruptly turned, bolted out of the cell, and sprinted down the corridor.

It didn't take a genius to follow the trail left by the soldiers. Or to guess what had happened to the unfortunate woman when her eyes fell on the wide opening. One direction, one choice.

Raphael skidded to a halt, then lost her footing when her shoe slipped on something wet below the ledge. Her keen eyes picked out the reddish tint in the dirt a split second before the tangy scent of copper assaulted her nostrils, but she didn't stop to investigate. Instead, Raphael vaulted onto the ledge, using her power for balance while she conjured a glowing ball to light her way through the tunnel ahead.

Only... it wasn't a tunnel that emerged from the darkness, it was a void.

A wide, fathomless void that even her light could not penetrate the edges of.

How did she cross through here?

Raphael pushed her glowing orb further out, using all her heightened senses in the hope of detecting *anything* that might tell her where the girl had been taken.

And then, she heard it.

From far, far below, a faint scream echoed, and Raphael's heart sank into despair. So far down already... and dropping further by the second. She redirected her senses, angling them down, down, *down* into the void as she rose to her full height on the ledge separating her from the corridor beyond. *Nothing* stared back at her as she readied herself. An empty, *sinister* chasm of death that hungered for more.

But it wasn't feeding today.

"It's a race then."

The glowing orb of light leapt into the void in a wide arc, plummeting through the darkness faster than it should have been possible. It lit the way past smooth stone walls that no light had *ever* shined upon, illuminating wide-eyed cavern dwelling creatures that had never, ever seen sunlight. Veins of precious metal and ore passed in the blink of an eye, their crystalline beauty unseen in the desperate race to close the distance on the lingering screams below. With every passing meter the orb picked up speed, accelerating past the remains of human settlements long forgotten in the mists of time, falling with the single-minded purpose of the one who controlled it. And *there...*

right there, at the very edge of the pale gold light, the unbeliev-able manifested into reality. Descending behind the orb with her ethereal wings spread wide, a miracle occurred.

For the first time in aeons, an Archangel soared the skies.

END

Afterword

Thank you for joining me on this adventure! If you enjoyed my story, please consider leaving a review on Amazon or Goodreads, tag me in your social posts and share the experience with your friends.

Raphael, Luma and their friends will return in *Out Of The Shadows*, releasing late 2024!

Be among the first to dive back into the Universe, pre-order your copy HERE!

To stay updated, check out my website at www.mannaclarke.com and follow the path to my socials!

Much love,
Manna

Glossary

Names, words, and terms used so far in the Armageddon's Blade series.

For a more comprehensive guide please visit www.mann aclarke.com.

Names

Alalu – (The deposed king of Nibiru who escaped to Earth and discovered gold; died on Mars) An Anunnaki ship captain searching for wartime victory.

Apsu – (Primorial progenitor of the solar system.) The sun.

Enlil – (Lord of Airspace) The reigning King of Sumer. In the Sumerian creation myth, Enlil separates An (heaven) from Ki (earth), thus making the world habitable for humans.

Gula – (Lady who the dead brings back to life) One of the Ascended Masters on Sumer.

Kumarbi – (A Hurrian God holding senior rank in the Hurrian pantheon, son of Alalu.) An Anunnaki scientist).

Luma – (Taken from the Sumerian deities *Lamma* and *Lahamu*. Lamma is a protective deity also known as Lamassu, or Lama. Lahamu is a child of Tiamat and brother to Lahmu.) An Initiate of The Way on Sumer, a planet in the Draco system.

Lumasi – (Part of *Lamma*. Also known as Shedu, the male counterpart of Lamma, and Lahmu. Lahmu were a protective deity and are also the child of Tiamat.) Lumasi is the brother of Luma.

Nasaru – (Guard) Anunnaki interstellar navigator.

Neperdu – (Happy/bright) An Initiate of The Way and friend to Luma.

Tiamat – (Primordial Goddess of the sea and the symbol of the chaos of primordial creation.) An Ascended Sumerian. Mother to Luma and Lumasi.

Words

Anbar – heavenly metal

An-Ki – (Heaven and Earth. First born son of An on Nibiru. Universe.) The living power of the Universe.

Ankida – joining (heaven=earth joining)

Anunnaki – (A group of deities from the ancient Sumerian, Akkadian, Assyrian and Babylonian cultures) A warmongering race from the planet Anunn in the Sumerian solar system.

Arammu – love

Bab-ili – Gateway of the Gods; Babylon, Marduk's City.

Beliti – lady

Emuq – power

Enir – brightness

Etutu – darkness

Gu – mine

Guz – long

Ina – the

Irnini – sweet smelling lady

Isimud – (A Mesopotamian God. The divine attendant of ENKI. Depicted with two faces.) The most elite spy network of Sumer.

Kuan – heavens (opening the heavens)

Kussum – seat

Lamadu – learn

Mitutu – dead ones

Mudutu – knowledge

Mul – (Celestial body who shine in the heights. Star) Spoken like a curse of frustration.

Na – no

Naga – my

Nanna – (The moon God/Goddess) A term used to in relation to the Sumerian moons.

Nisiqtu – precious

Nuru/Immaru – light

Redum – soldier

Salamu – safe

Samsum/Utu – sun

Sepsu – powerful

Shi – life

Shumsu – name

Sinnis – Female

Sumerian – A race of humans that existed billions of years ago in the area of space known as Draco.

Tag laptu – touch

Wussuru – release

Terms or phrases

Ana harrani sa alaktasa la tarat. – Road whose course does not turn back.

Eli baltuti ima"idu mituti. – Dead will be more numerous than the living.

Ina lu itti sina pana. – The man with two faces.

Na adannu na su'ati. – no time for that.

Asar basu ni – where be I?

See you in the sequels...

Out Of The Shadows
&
The Sacrifice Of Truth